—but not to keep.

But Not To Keep

Also by Roger Kahn:

THE PASSIONATE PEOPLE
THE BATTLE FOR MORNINGSIDE HEIGHTS
THE BOYS OF SUMMER
HOW THE WEATHER WAS
A SEASON IN THE SUN

But Not To Keep

Roger Kahn

PLAYBOY PRESS
PAPERBACKS

For Wendy, my wife;
For Buz Wyeth, my friend;
And for Alissa,
who never gets written about

PART ONE

In the deserts of the heart
Let the healing fountain start ...

W. H. Auden,
"In Memory of Yeats"

CHAPTER ONE

The Beaches at Pokanoket

I

They walked along at midday, clearly father and son, making their way down sand cliffs toward the sea. They hurried silently in skidding strides, heels scooping dark brown traces in the sand, until they stood above a narrow, pebbly beach. The sky blazed, as a Mediterranean sky in August, and curiously, the blinding blue imparted a sense of unease. Seminal perfection, David Priest thought. He shuddered and reached to touch his son's left hand. On such a day, on such a day as this, did Yahweh summon Abraham to murder Isaac.

Where the two had stopped, cliff and sand gave way to a clay outcropping that was caked and salty, and even under sun-blaze, faintly moist. During spring, a snowless spring that had been dreary with rain through all New England, water runoffs rutted a narrow slit at the center of the outcropping. To an imaginative eye, the slit was cradled in an elongated oval. Some summer residents of Pokanoket Island called the clay outcropping "The Mons."

The man spoke first. "Those waves have had five thousand miles to work up vengeance." David Priest looked into the sun, smiling, as though vengefulness were a quality that gratified him. "They've had plenty of time to plot what they'll do to people who get in their way."

David Priest was tall and loose-muscled. Looking at the corners of his eyes, you could see squint lines. Above his full brown mustache, touches of puffiness suggested the middle thirties. But no flab showed at David's waist and his legs were long and supple and straight.

The boy nodded. "Those waves are dumpers, Dad." Joel looked lean, like his father, and his face formed a gentle unwrinkled triangle. "Regular, though. You can time them." Joel considered the ocean studiously, in the manner of a child trying to catch up with the world all at once. His hair was the color of untrodden sand. The breaking of waves had great importance to him.

"Hello! Hello, seafarers," Trudy Schuman shouted from a beach that widened off to the right. Windjammer Beach, the place was called. "Come over to us. We have cranberry juice with vodka."

"Seafarers? She means sandfarers, Dad," Joel Priest said. "We haven't even got wet." The boy's full, delicate lips curled toward a smile.

From his balanced footing on The Mons, David waved to Trudy Schuman. Trudy rose. She wore a two-piece red bathing suit and as she stood you saw a full-bodied woman, heavy-busted, strong-thighed but not sloppy.

Her life was ordered. Winters, Gertrude Beckmesser Schuman, M.D., presided over a charged and intense psychiatric practice, from a white, brick tower on East End Avenue in Manhattan. Summers she metamorphosed into Trudy Schuman, prowler of the beaches of Pokanoket Island, who sang siren songs, sometimes a half tone flat.

"Maybe after swimming," David called.

"The cranberry juice and vodka will be gone."

"No, Trudy. We want to try the waves. Finish the juice and save the vodka for me."

Three men sat on the sands beneath Trudy's thighs. She had a Levantine look—dark, slanted eyes, a voluptuous mouth and long dark hair. The hair spun over one shoulder, stark black against the red bathing suit and her breasts. She drew men to her; capons mostly, David thought, and he remembered other days of heat when he had listened to the capons laboring toward elegance on other contested beaches, glazed with sun.

"Have you read Serrano on Jung and Hesse?"

"Of course, but I would rather have read Hesse on Jung—or even on Hesse."

"Do you know about the Carlist-Marxist movement in Spain? I marvel at a curious thing, to find a Communist who seeks a king."

"Don Carlo Marx." (Applause.)

"And Meestair Nixon. Yes, your Meestair Nixon. How can anyone be surprised? Why, in Brazil, to have a letter delivered promptly, it is expected that you give the postal clerk a bribe."

"But Mister Nixon would take the bribe and still deliver the letter late."

"After first steaming it open." (Laughter.)

Wordplay and disembodied ideas each floating, and both, the wordplay and the ideas, wanting passion, in the hot sun on the idle summer beach.

David remembered another bit of play with Trudy Schuman two weeks earlier. "I have a diaphragm," Trudy told him. "I've taken the pill. I even had an IUD inserted."

"And?"

"My husband charms you?"

"Yes."

"He's a limp old man who can't maintain tumescence."

Roused, David kissed her neck. Trudy moaned loudly. David drew back. He did not like aggression masked as submissiveness. No, David Priest did not like that particular love joust at all.

At the left of The Mons, the sands of Pokanoket broadened into a graceful crescent, backed by slope and thicket. To reach the center of this crescent, known as New Eden Beach, you did best to follow a patchy trail that wound from a two-lane blacktop through a mile of burs and brush. A billy-clubbed, blue guard protected the easy path from highway down toward Windjammer. The rigors of the walk discouraged all but the young and the vigorous, so New Eden Beach society developed a natural exclusivity. Windjammer Beach was restricted to the wealthy and their friends and children. New Eden belonged to boys and girls of summer.

Now at New Eden Beach, young people tanned themselves and teased and swarmed. WASPs from Harvard with tan, downy chests, and girls from Bryn Mawr, who spoke the tight-lipped tongue of Pennsylvania Oxonian; scholars talking with their hands of Shakespeare's seven blank last years and cocktail waitresses who, sleepy-eyed, said "Shakespeare?"; weavers from Greenwich Village and potters from Alfred College and dropouts from Berkeley and from Bard; Sligo redheads and Norse blondes and stocky Jews, hairy as monkeys; blank versifiers and riders of snarling motorbikes all swarmed and sunned and threw rubber balls and plastic disks and rolled into clay pits that turned them gray as elephants until they dared the surf, which buffeted them clean again and pale and naked. They were all naked; no one wore clothes. New Eden Beach adjoined Windjammer so closely that less than a shout separated the two; more than a glance perhaps, less than a look.

Once Trudy Schuman had announced to her capon entourage, "If they're going to present their naked young bodies to us, why don't we present our naked middle-aged bodies to them?" Some of the capons forced smiles, but to the wealthy men and women who had developed Windjammer Beach, New Eden was an obscenity that grins could not obscure. The nudity was always distracting, but never worse than when a boy and girl strutted beside the sea and walked in front of Windjammer Beach, laughing and swinging arms in a windmill mockery of innocence. "Really," Trudy said, "they act as though they had invented buttocks."

Standing on The Mons, the gray border between the wealthy and the naked, David Priest said to his son, "Ready to lose a race?" It was an old challenge between them. David was swift on land, and sure and graceful.

"To where?" Joel said.

"To the water."

The surf slammed hard against the sands and waves crashed against each other, spinning froth and launching treacherous, unpredictable currents.

David and Joel started running together, touching fingertips for balance as they hurried down the bank. "Ah!" Joel cried out. His toe had caught a rim of clay, making him stumble. David's hand moved to Joel's wrist, supporting the boy, guiding him, and Joel kept his footing. Then the father sprinted ahead across ten yards of sand and dove into a breaker. Undertow clutched him. He stood against the sea. Pebbles beat on his shins.

Joel ran, a spoked wheel of arms and legs, the fair hair flapping on his neck. David waited in low surf and considered the sea. White water sprayed fifty yards off and spilled into dangerous surging troughs. As the father paused, the boy rushed past him. Joel's flailing run carried him into the water, where suddenly he assumed poise and sureness. Springing, he plunged over a hard rolling wave, which slapped his feet, flipping him over. He surfaced grinning. A larger wave bore down.

Joel bobbed, waiting, and dove under the curl of water. He came up shiny, with matted hair, shouting his joy.

David Priest proceeded slowly. He felt less confident in water than on land. "I'll be with you as soon as I figure these flicking waves."

"Lower," Joel shouted. "Dive lower next time. Otherwise you'll get wiped out."

How old was Joel now? Thirteen, soon to be fourteen. Mostly a boy awakening to a new day every day. But sometimes, surprisingly, a man. Sometimes, shockingly, a baby. Still, the best thing, oh yes, the best thing that had become of David was his son.

"All right," the father called. "I'm coming for you." He swam to meet the boy with choppy strokes.

David lay on his back, looking at the land. The figures on the beach receded as tiny, insubstantial memories. To the west, past Windjammer Beach, the cliffs held high for miles; sandy clay, a hairy topping of trees. The green against the sky. Odd. Green wasn't supposed to go with blue, but how the distant shiny oak leaves matched the sky. The beach looked pale and narrow. Smooth between sea and land, the seed of Adam played, and now the seed began to play a mime. Two figures from New Eden Beach walked on the sand in front of Trudy Schuman and the others. A bustle of movement. One seated capon rose. The capon-man was bald. A belly spilled before him. He wore red boxer shorts. His legs were spindly. The naked strolling figures glided. The girl was blond.

The portly capon-man moved in front of the couple and put his hands on his hips. The boy and girl stopped gliding. The portly man spoke to the boy, who shook his head. The man beat his hands before him. He seemed to be shouting. The girl talked now, her movements slow and languorous. Her hair was long and straight.

A second capon-man joined the discussion. He wore

a white hat and a yellow shirt. He pointed toward the water and toward New Eden Beach. Property rights, he must be saying. The drab Colonial theme, where Pennsylvania Quakers and dour descendants of Cotton Mather joined in a common greed they called morality.

The three great Constitutional guarantees.

Life: As certain as a skidding roadster.

Liberty: A magazine gone broke.

Property: As fixed and constant as Ben Franklin's greed.

The girl grew animated. The boy stood motionless. Both capon-men from Windjammer Beach made angry, spastic gestures. She threw back her head. She touched the boy's arm and they turned toward the water. Mean high-water line. Anyone was free to walk where the sea began. The boy and the girl shook their heads and seemed to be talking softly to each other. Then the girl spun her smooth tan body and faced the older people. She placed a hand at a bicep. Her fist shot forward. Fuck you, September Morn told the rich capon-men.

David smiled and would have laughed, but the buffeting ocean reminded him that the calm place where he floated was uncertain. He did not want to swim beyond, into white water, and getting back to shore would require work and timing and wind. What was the beach-capons' response to the nude who said "Fuck you"? He tried to imagine the speech. "This is private property. You're trespassing. Been in my family since my grandfather's time." Legalisms.

"How'd he get it?" That from the naked boy.

"Fought for it, that's how he got it."

"Well, I'll fight *you* for it."

And all the while, the languorous naked girl. Had she been smiling?

"Watch it," Joel's cracking, almost manly voice sounded too late. White water came spilling over David's face, stinging his eyes. Water filled his ears and the wave spun him. He tensed his body, the way he would on land to take or give a football block. The ocean ignored him, gripped him, let him surface. "Hell," David said. He disliked being rolled before his son. He made for shore, checking the waves behind him and marking his progress. Land was no more than twenty yards away. Undertow sucked him and something crashed into his neck. He saw dark blue, then white. The white, the top of the water, was where he had to get to. He was slammed sideways. He tried to curl into a ball. He heard a hissing noise amid the roaring. Brown leaped at him. Christ, he was on the bottom. What made the roaring noise inside a wave? The ocean flattened him and he was spinning. Pebbles scraped his knees and raked his belly. He looked for sunlight and saw black spots. Not joking now. Out of control. He dragged along the bottom and tried to shout. Absurd. So close to shore. Such shallow water. No way to breathe. *No way to fucking breathe!*

A strong grip steadied David. Blindly he clambered to his feet. He shook the water from his head and saw Joel's face, half grinning, half concerned.

"Whoosh," David said.

"Are you all right?"

"Yes. Winded. Fine."

"It was funny at first," Joel said. "You were lying there, like we were in a bay, looking at something. And this one breaker smacked on top of you. And then, in closer, you got caught. Two waves were breaking against each other. They made a V."

"I was the point?"

"Kind of. When I saw you were in trouble I grabbed you."

"I wasn't really in trouble. Just winded."

"Come on, Dad. I'm a stronger swimmer than you."

"Only when I'm hung over."

"Come on, Dad."

"Whoosh."

Joel wore a brief black bathing suit with an emblem on one hipbone. He put a hand on the hipbone and looked beyond his father. "Junior Lifesaver," the emblem said. "Hey," Joel said, suddenly childlike. "Can we go over to the bay and sail a Sunfish?"

"Maybe later. Now I want to sit on the sand and take some sun." David closed his eyes. Salt smarted on his face. He felt a chill. Trudy Schuman stood in front of him. "Trudy," he said, "you're blocking out my sun."

"How's the water?" Had she seen him somersaulted in the silt?

"It makes you work."

Trudy nodded mechanically. She would not have seen or recognized that variety of violence. "Come to our beach." Her thick thighs looked immaculate. "Today we have Elwin Lewine from *The New Yorker,* and Eleazar Horowitz. He sells things, but you would like him. And someone from Yale who is completing a biography of Pushkin. He tells me Pushkin was part Negro, which may account for the ardent nature."

The people collector, Callie called Trudy Schuman. "But aren't all psychiatrists people collectors?" David said. "That's their job."

"Not like that one," Callie said, with casual contempt. Callie, as free as Joel, as blond as day.

"I've promised Joel that I'd take him boating," David said to Trudy.

The doctor nodded at the boy without interest.

"How's Gus?" David said, needling. Gus Schuman, twelve years older than Trudy, was stone bald and thirty pounds overweight. He and his wife vacationed separately.

"Looking for diamonds," Trudy said. "Gus loves to look for diamonds on bodices. So. I will see you anyway at Gabe Cassidy's tonight, but for now, come and share our beach and bring the boy."

David shook his head. Sea noise rang inside his brain. On New Eden Beach, a girl paraded caked with clay. Her breasts, her hips, her pubic hair, were gray. She smiled at David. Pretty elephant.

"So?" Trudy said.

"No, thanks," David said. "I'd rather be with Joel." Together, father and son climbed the ridge of sand and, while the sea clamored behind them, made their way lightly up the clay outcropping called The Mons.

II

At his rented white summer cottage in the early evening, David was dressing in a gold-buttoned navy-blue blazer and trim gray slacks. Lately, as he dressed for Pokanoket parties, he felt he was preparing for a hunt. Tonight's prey was prearranged. Callie. Caroline Maitland Devon, as blond as day. He stood in front of a mirror, inserting gold links shaped like dumbbells into the cuffs of a pale-yellow shirt. Callie. There seemed a sound of springtime to the name.

"A drink to steady your hands?" Joyce, his wife, was relentlessly submissive.

"Thanks." He finished with the jewelry and took the Scotch.

"What time will you be home?"

"When the bar closes."

"I don't mind you going to parties. I know you're restless." Joyce Steindler Priest was drinking Bombay on the rocks. The gin relaxed her, but she was a stocky woman and gin also made her gain weight. "It would be nice, though, if we could spend an evening reading together, like old times."

David nodded and parried. "It would be nice if it still were the old times." Joyce had bobbed dark hair and a squarish face with features that were broadening. It was hard for David to remember how she had looked sixteen years before. "But I don't know what I want to read now," David said, "or what I want to write, or even just what I want to do." His wife made him feel old, and uncertain and guilty.

"David," Joyce said. "I love you. Joel loves you. If you lose us, there'll be nobody else. Nobody else will love you."

Callie Devon. Passion surged from Callie, outright and direct. Not love, not yet. Just lust.

"Go away for a while," Joyce said. "Go to Paris like Hemingway. Go to London like Shaw. Live wild for a time. Joel and I will wait."

The cottage bedroom was small. David dropped onto a maple settee. "I don't have to live wild," he said. "I don't like turmoil. I don't seek turmoil. Turmoil seems to seek me." Joyce sat next to him. He glanced at her face, to see traces of the handsome, tennis-playing gamine that had been. She sighed. He caught Bombay gin on her breath. Hell, perhaps she caught good Scotch on his.

"It's the dead baby," Joyce said. "I mean, coming between us. It's the dead baby, isn't it?"

"Anne? Her hair was red and I can see her mouth open when she cried."

"I never saw her cry."

"I know. Goddamned obstetrician. It was a damn beautiful delicate mouth." David sipped more Scotch and looked at a pseudo Winslow Homer seascape, nailed to a gypsum wall. "I don't think it's the dead baby. I don't have any right to that. It was your tragedy. You carried her. You had to go through labor."

"And I can't swim," Joyce said, "and I'm not good at big parties. Is that it? Are those it?"

"Please, Joyce. Don't ask me to explain myself and us."

"But, David." Joyce's voice ascended in tight terror. "It's slipping away. This crazy impotence. Won't you try a sex clinic? There's this woman at Mount Sinai. Or psychoanalysis?"

"Not good for writers. You got to let the brew foment." His own words sounded like half-assed Hemingway and Hemingway was half-assed with women to begin with, so the imitation was quarter-assed Hemingway. But what else was there to say? Joyce had let herself become fat. Was that something to say? To call a fat person fat. Her body clumped and sagged. Could he explain? Your body clumps and sags. Leaving aside everything else, as if he could leave everything aside, forgetting, as if he could forget, that Joyce's self-neglect came as a slap at the marriage and at himself; disregarding, as if he could disregard, that the baby Anne, his daughter, took death blows from Joyce's body within Joyce's loins; if he could ignore such things or would ignore such things, he still did not like to look at clumps and sags, or touch them.

"That feller would put his pecker into a woodpile," someone had been saying once.

"And why would he risk them splinters, Mister Bones?"

"Because maybe under the woodpile there was a snake that he could fuck."

A portrait of the artist as a hard-on.

This crazy impotence, Joyce said. It wasn't crazy. He was not a blind erection. She put him off, that was all, and what was there to say?—I'm not impotent, my darling. It's only you who put me off? So there was nothing to say, but one sentence of quarter-assed Hemingway. "I got to let the brew foment," David repeated.

"And destroy your insides?" Joyce said.

David stood up and said very softly, "Remember. 'The intellect of man is forced to choose perfection of the life or of the work' "

"But work? What work?" Joyce's dark eyes moistened. "You aren't working and you aren't Yeats."

"And I'm not going to try to be."

"But if you find yourself, you can be fine, dear. Very fine."

"I have to go."

"David."

"Yes?"

"I can do anything for you but be beautiful."

III

Cold salty air restored him. He was going to be late. Behind him, Joyce would be drinking more Bombay gin. Joel would be gluing a gray model of the nuclear aircraft carrier *Peacemaker*. Volumes of Marcuse, Mann, Cheever, Fowles and Walker Percy would gather mold from summer dampness beside moist attractions by Emily Dickinson, Mary Gordon, and Joan Didion. David hurried his red TR-6 along Upper Road, a narrow twisting blacktop. He was proud of the way he spun the car through turns and stayed in lane.

Pokanoket Island, fourteen miles long, killed its modest share along Upper Road and Middle Road and Lower Road. Each summer's bounty of drinking parties would cost a life or two and half a dozen marriages. Big houses presided on Upper Road behind stout dangerous fence posts. The houses down the slope were smaller. Upper Road, Middle Road, Lower Road defined a three-class society for sedate summer Marxists. The worst violence was vehicular and, later, psychic. Red August foreshadowing shades of Black September.

Gabriel Cassidy, anti-Communist left, gave gaudy summer parties. He was a lawyer with some literary trade, which he discussed, and some dealings in Greece, about which he said little, and he was brother-in-law to Willie Silverberg, an alcoholic tough-guy novelist who had buckled during the red-baiting days of J. Parnell Thomas. Like two other authors of pseudo-leftist bestsellers, Willie Silverberg had sent his closest friend to jail. The Triumph wheeled onto the driveway, scattering gravel. David Priest sprang out and hurried toward a rolling lawn where thirty people drank under multicolored paper lanterns.

David knew his host slightly. His invitation had come from Sol (Clipper) Zellbach, another lawyer, conservative as Cassidy but famous for one sentence in a brief attacking censorship. "There is nothing so dangerous as a Puritan convinced that he is in the right."

"Hello, Clip." Zellbach had brown crinkly hair. High cheekbones gave him a Tartar look. "Who's on your arm?"

Caroline Devon nodded. She had a long, fair face and bright sloe eyes. Even under the pale light of paper lanterns her skin glowed and the dark eyes twinkled. A grown-up tomboy's face, fresh and eager. Whether the eyes twinkled laughter or mockery was the question.

"You're late," Caroline Devon said, "and I'm the only one that's allowed to be late." Her face was smooth and young. Only an angular jaw suggested aggression.

"Storms at home," David said.

Caroline nodded. "Not my home." Now the eyes truly were mocking.

"There's the customary action on this scene," Clipper Zellbach said, "and Trudy Schuman's been asking for you, David."

"I thought, Callie, you and I . . ."

"You're half an hour late, David," Caroline said, "and I wasn't sure you were coming at all."

The lawyer smiled and Callie Devon stepped closer to him. His arm circled her waist. It was not a large arm; rather the waist was astonishingly thin. David considered, without seeing, Callie's extraordinary buttocks and her powerful, smooth thighs. "I got a little tied up with my son," he said.

Zellbach and Callie nodded and waited and David

walked toward the bar, where Gabe Cassidy, a powerful, thick-necked man, was monitoring a young red-
bearded bartender.

"Dave Priest," David said, extending a hand.

"Of course," Cassidy said, smiling, slightly buck-
toothed. "You were a City Hall reporter for the old
Mirror, and an uncommonly good one."

"The *Journal,*" David said.

"No matter," Gabe Cassidy said. "Do you know
Jeremy Johnson, here? Scotch and rocks good enough?"

Jeremy Johnson ran a network talk show that had
buried two opposing discless jockeys.

"Sure. I know your stuff," Jeremy Johnson said. His
face was square and wide-mouthed, grown-up and un-
finished. Before she died, Dorothy Parker said Jeremy
Johnson was made of plastic. "I'm out here visiting
Gabe for two days," Johnson said. "I'd stay away from
New York longer, but my mugger can't afford it."

"No pension plans for those guys," David said. But
Jeremy Johnson was spinning away to try another wide-
mouthed joke on someone else.

The lawn slanted downward from the bar, and in
the dim light it took David a minute to find Callie and
Zellbach. They were standing very close and talking
very quietly. "Give me the cast here, will you, Clipper?"
David said. He did not care about the cast of this particular summer party; he was using conversation to
put off intimacy between the lady and the lawyer.

"Well, there's Jeremy Johnson and Rick Sensabaugh." Zellbach managed to look patronizing. He
talked in an unhurried way. He had time to yield. It
was still early. "Did you ever see Rick fight?"

The look of certain women at certain times caught
David Priest like a blow in the solar plexus. Did the
sudden blow he felt now color his expression?

Rick Sensabaugh hit. He had been a splendid fighter,
superb at body punching, and then a hook to the middle

and a right to the face and a hook to the jaw dropped Sammy Malacon of Caguas, Puerto Rico. The punches killed him in the Madison Square Garden ring and Sammy Malacon died twitching and after that Rick couldn't fight anymore. Except at parties.

Certain women. Callie Devon. The face of a Quaker nun. Sweet lady, in thy sack is my salvation.

"Finally," Clip Zellbach was saying, "Elwin Lewine, who writes the endless *New Yorker* series on small-town America. He's got *New Yorker* snideness without the *New Yorker* style of the good old boys, Jack Kahn, Joe Liebling, or John Lardner." Zellbach smiled at what he was about to say. "Mocking small-town America in *The New Yorker* is postgraduate college humor."

"Can I talk to Callie for a minute?" David said.

"I'll freshen her drink," Zellbach said.

Certain women at certain times made David breathless. "Well," he said. "Well." He put both hands on her waist and breathed deeply and said, "I can circle your waist and my hands aren't big."

"I haven't made any babies," Caroline said. She smiled impersonally and looked past David's shoulder.

"What is this, Callie?" he said.

"What is what?"

"I thought we had a date."

"We did and you were late and missed the date."

"You couldn't wait?"

"Parties like this frighten me, if you must know. Prize fighters and crazy television people and God knows what or who rolling in the bushes. And I was alone and nervous and I didn't want to be rolled in the bushes. Clip was nice to me. So we're together, Clip and I."

"A kiss for solace." David leaned toward the sloe-eyed face and caught the perfume and nuzzled Caroline's neck and smelled her skin and kissed her gently. She stood stiff. She might have been a tree.

"Callie."

"Not here. Not when I'm with somebody else. But, you know. Maybe more than kisses next time."

"But now." David's whisper growled.

"One Stolichnaya on the rocks." Clipper Zellbach announced his return too loudly.

David shrugged. "See you guys," he said. He turned and found himself facing Jeremy Johnson, the comic.

"You hear they auctioned off Hitler's old car?" Johnson said. "It's got four forward speeds. First, second, third and Poland."

"That's all right," David said. But Johnson was gone.

Gabe Cassidy's house, which was nine years old, had been built to resemble the home of nineteenth-century captains. The shingles—they had been preweathered by a company called Insta-Vintage Shingles—were weathered gray and high up two chimneys rose behind a widow's walk bounded by Insta-Vintage rails. You approached the house by climbing four steps onto a large porch. The front door opened into a center hall, which spread into a foyer leading to a flight of stairs. Two large rooms, each fashioned into octagons, opened from the foyer, and as muscled Gabe Cassidy presided on the lawn, fluttery, birdlike Hildy Cassidy hopped within. Hildy, the sister of Willie Silverberg, the tough-guy novelist, was a fair-haired petite lady, with small sharp features and so many wrinkles in her neck that someone had remarked, "A fly walking across Hildy's neck would break a leg." She seemed preoccupied, busy, uncertain.

"You are . . . ?" she said, at the doorway to the living room.

"David Priest."

"A writer."

"Sort of."

"But no big book," Hildy said. "No big book yet. You're lucky for that, you know. My brother Willie writes big books and every time he starts another book he thinks it has to be big too, and that's why he's a semi-alcoholic."

"I do mostly journalism," David said.

"But you want to do a big book."

"Yes," David said, very slowly. "Yes. I want to do a big book, or just a good book." He looked for compassion in Hildy's tentative blue eyes.

"Oh, my dear," Hildy said. The blue eyes hardened. "A book is only a book is only a book," Hildy Cassidy said.

In front of a fireplace where an artificial Prest-Pine log burned blue and red, Elwin Lewine, the *New Yorker* man, was discussing a review he had written for the Sunday *Times*. "It's by one of this new ripple of Irish writers," Lewine said. "He's half Catholic and wholly dreadful." Lewine's flat-nosed face reminded David of a hippopotamus. "I've played bridge with the writer and so I end the piece by saying that what we need from writers like him is more euchre and less Eucharist."

Trudy Schuman laughed deep in her throat.

"What was the book called?" David said.

"Oh, I forget," Lewine said. "I usually have total recall. In this case, it's total recoil."

"Like a panicked snake," David said. He stepped forward, unaware that he was clenching his fists.

"If a book is only a book," Hildy Cassidy said in her fluttering voice, "then a review is only . . ." She blinked three times as her voice fluttered toward silence.

"I'm going to tell you now," Elwin Lewine said, "so this doesn't go any further: I boxed at Colgate."

"Not quite Robert Cohn," David said.

"Stop this," Trudy Schuman said.

David considered Lewine. The man was thick-bodied, probably sluggish, but you could never be sure. God-dammit, his own point was pure, even angelic. Something called the *Edinburgh Quarterly* wounded Keats. A generation of reviewers ignored Schubert. You always rooted for the artist over the reviewer, provided only that the artist did his honest best. Bardic best. Symphonic best. Bad best. Best, any best, deserved decency. It was frightening to stand naked out there, naked and vulnerable and stained by hope. David had known Clem Aylward, a slight, wiry writer from the Southwest who ghosted a half-dozen books. Reviewers took some seriously. Clem Aylward did not. He respected his bank account and his retreat on Marathon Key. Then he wrote a cowboy novel. A Serious Cowboy Novel. *The New Yorker* commented anonymously, "Mr. Aylward knows everything about what a cowboy eats, when a cowboy sleeps and how a cowboy thinks. Unfortunately, he knows nothing about composing novels." End. Fin. Aylward, tougher than most cowboys, abandoned writing for publishing. He now presided over the Century Press, where he helped shape two dozen novels a year, including several compositions of excellence.

With critics and artists, you always rooted for the artists. That was David Priest's point. It was angelic, almost simplistic, except to critics. Except that David having missed his date with Callie Devon, actually his point may have been something else. His point may have been to kick someone, something. His point may have been to pick a fight.

"If you want to shit on books," David said to Elwin Lewine, "do the rest of us have to watch you spread your cheeks?"

Lewine put down his drink deliberately and stroked his knuckles and stepped forward. Suddenly, David was spinning, trotting across the room, with such suddenness that there was time only to gasp.

"Davey, Davey. What were you gonna do? Be like me? Lose in one round to a fucking amateur?" Rick

Sensabaugh had put his fighter's bulk behind a shove that sent David spinning.

"What a snide bastard," David said.

"Sure," Sensabaugh said. "So why are you bothering with guys like that?"

"What's going on?" Gabe Cassidy appeared, the host commander.

"Nothing's going on," Sensabaugh said. "'Something almost went on but it didn't go on, so relax, Gabe. See what the girls at the foot of the bed will have."

Cassidy looked drunk. "Another martini, Mr. Priest?"

"Please, but it's Scotch."

"You got to take this bullshit lighter," Sensabaugh said. He had a fattening Irish face, scar tissue at the brows, and a boyish look, except that his left eye sometimes darted to a corner of the eyeball, then flickered back, something he explained by imitating a punchdrunk boxer's voice and saying, "Uh, I on'y had, uh, forty fights."

"C'mon," Rick Sensabaugh said. "When you're with Ricky Sensabaugh, every night is New Year's Eve. Right, Davey?"

"Right."

"And there're good chickies here. C'mon."

Drifting, David thought. Damn drifting. Except it might be something more, something like the wave that overwhelmed him in the afternoon and spun him, rolled him, and in the pain had granted him a purpose. To best the wave, to roll against the bottom, to survive. And now a party to see a girl, whose look was poetry. Weave, weave the sunlight in your hair. As golden as other people's poetry. He summoned his own blurring lines, written in solitude to Callie a month before.

> *What is it that becomes of people like us,*
> *Carrying unspent love within our loins?*
> *What is it that becomes of people like us,*

Of our loins
Of our unspent love?

At eleven-fifteen, Elwin Lewine, the hippopotamus, returned to his theme of the new ripple of Irish writers. "I liked the old Micks better than the new Michaels," he said. Lewine had been drinking for three hours. He looked wobbly.

"Oh, that's good, Ellie," Trudy Schuman said.

"With Jews, it used to be Sam, and now it's Barry," Hildy Cassidy said.

"I'm a Mick man," Lewine said. "Mouse, Mantle, but not these rosy rosarians, counting every other bead."

"That's enough of that fucking talk," Rick Sensabaugh said.

"It's bullshit, Rick," David said, meaning to calm the old fighter. "You know. We were talking. Bullshit."

"Bullshit is right," Sensabaugh screamed, and moved at pudgy Elwin Lewine.

The fighter looked wild. Lewine took half a step back and danced forward. He faked a high left and drove his right fist into the pit of Sensabaugh's stomach. The fighter made a groaning cry and fell retching to a brown and white woven rug before the fireplace. He lay on the rug spinning and wheezing. Lewine dropped to both knees and continued to pummel Sensabaugh.

"Stop, my God, stop," Hildy Cassidy cried. She straddled Lewine, skinny legs stretching her gold skirt taut. "Stop. Stop." Hildy put an index finger into each of Lewine's ears and pressed. Getting his breath back, Sensabaugh clutched Lewine's wrists. The two men shoved and grunted. Hildy kept her fingers in Lewine's ears. "Stop it, Elwin. Stop it. Please!"

Trudy Schuman retreated toward a white bookcase, empty but for five pieces of painted pottery. She put her hands to her wide hips and looked stricken. David

Priest considered. Nobody was really hurting anyone on the brown and white rug, and what the hell. It wasn't his party. It wasn't his fight.

Gabe Cassidy burst into the living room, a strong man who might have pulled the two apart. The host commander wobbled. "What's this?" he said.

Clip Zellbach and Caroline Devon stood against a large curved window, which, by day, showed the Cassidys' tennis court. Zellbach puffed an empty pipe and gazed. Sensabaugh and Lewine made half rolls on the floor, still grunting. Fighters as lovers, David thought.

Zellbach shook his head faintly, clinically. "The way doctors observe the human body," he had said, "lawyers observe human behavior. You try not to be judgmental—until you get to court."

Callie Devon, hands at her face, looked pale and very beautiful. She wore a velvet harlequin blouse, mostly red and black, that hung loosely over slim shoulders and showed a suggestion of her bust. Beneath, David saw pale-green Pucci pants that clung to Callie's belly and strong thighs. It was extraordinary, David thought, the small-busted girl's body above and the grown, strong woman below. The face, so finely sculpted, opposed her hands. They were large as his own, strong milkmaid's hands and restless. Now Caroline's hands lay still and slack. Milkmaid's hands in English meadows long ago. As the wrestlers writhed, Lewine's red jacket rolling across Sensabaugh's plaid sports shirt, David lusted for Callie.

"Enough. Goddammit. Enough." David was surprised at the strength of his own voice. He threw himself on the fighters, shouldering Hildy Cassidy backward. "Cut it out." David shoved a hand against Elwin Lewine's flat face and pressed the heel of his hand against the chin. "Now get out of here, Rick," he said. "Come on. Fight's over. Stand up."

The combatants were spent. David gave Lewine a

second shove and stood up. Behind him, Hildy Cassidy was holding her wrist and whimpering. Gabe strode over and stood beside his wife. "It's all right. It's all right," he said. Then to David, "What the hell did you do?"

Rick Sensabaugh was crying. David knelt over him. Sensabaugh had been cut on the nose. The plaid shirt was ripped. "Lose to a fuckin' amateur. Davey, Davey, what the hell's getting to be the fuckin' matter with me?"

"He wanted to fight more than you did," David said.

"Lose to a fuckin' amateur in front of all those people," Sensabaugh said. He sobbed.

"We'll get you washed up," David said. "There's blood on your nose."

"Hey, Davey," Sensabaugh said. "I'm fighting Gavilan at the Garden. He throws a bolo and he really hurt me. Like the side of my face would come off. I didn't cry then."

"You're upset. That's why you're crying now."

"Son of a bitch. He didn't have any business spouting off about us Irish. He didn't, did he?"

"Just writer talk."

"I coulda taken him. I didn't want to hurt him. I get scared to use my fists. I coulda taken him. I shoulda got the Gavilan decision. Judges were afraid the goddamn spics would riot."

"Just wash up, Ricky."

The fighter stood. The rip in his shirt ran from nipple to waist. "A kike and a Mick, huh, Davey?" Sensabaugh said. "We gotta stick together."

"Sure," David Priest said, swallowing. "Kike" was the word, above all others, that made *him* want to fight.

"Your blazer is filthy," Caroline Devon said. She took David's left arm firmly and brushed the close-knit cloth. He felt the milkmaid's hand strong on his wrist and noticed still down braceleting her forearm, and he'd broken up the fight and the lawyer had the girl.

WRITER AVERTS RIOT; ATTORNEY GETS LAID. DID JUSTICE TRIUMPH? (PART 29.)

The answer always came out the same. Justice was put to rout. How could you hold anybody's interest with twenty-nine consecutive bland endings? Justice was put to rout and the lawyers got laid. "Do you always stay out of fights?" David said angrily to Clipper Zellbach.

Zellbach's mouth curled into what did not quite become a smile. "When it counted," he said, "I was a Navy pilot. Flew fifty missions off a carrier. You knew that."

"Let me take your jacket, David," Caroline said. "Maybe we can borrow a clothes brush from Gabe."

Hildy, still whimpering, was saying, "My wrist. My wrist."

"All right," Gabe Cassidy said. "It hurts, but at least it hasn't been amputated. Just take it easy and stop slobbering." He seemed embarrassed that his wife was making pain cries, but not distressed until he saw that David was observing him. Then he kissed Hildy's left cheek in a spasm of conspicuous tenderness.

Trudy Schuman held Hildy's wrist for a moment. She shook her head. "Such animal aggression," she said. "Such wasted aggression."

"Well?" Gabe said.

"Probable green-stick fracture," Dr. Schuman said. "You'd better have some pictures taken and get her to an orthopedist."

The clothes brush lay upstairs in Cassidy's bedroom. It was a rectangular room, with a single maple bed against the wall.

ANOTHER LOVING ISLAND COUPLE SLEEPS
SEPARATELY. ONE SUMMER OF SEX. (PART 42.)

A soft gray watercolor seascape hung above the bed, next to a wedding photograph of Gabe and Hildy. Did they recognize themselves in the picture or did they see two strangers? David wondered.

"Now," Callie said. "Let's see about getting you neat. Take off your sports coat." She found the brush and dropped into a green lounge chair, and sitting very straight, knees together, whisked dust from David's jacket. "Doesn't it frighten you to walk into the middle of a fight," she said, "or to get into a fight yourself?"

"Yes, but I like to fight. The sensation, I mean. I like being afraid of something and going forward."

Callie shook her head.

"I think it has to do with being Jewish," David said.

"What doesn't?" Callie said.

"Circumcision."

She smiled and continued to brush his jacket.

"I mean," David said, "it's like all those Jews of Europe going to their graves like . . . You know the line from Hamlet."

"I don't know the line from Hamlet."

"Go to their graves like beds. I want to think that if I'd been there, and the *Sturmdrängen* came, I would have taken a few with me. But I was too far away and too young, so now I keep getting into fights that started out to happen to somebody else."

"I don't know lines from Hamlet because I grew up in a house where there weren't any books."

"A pretty house, I'll bet. A farmhouse."

Caroline pressed her lips and nodded. "A stone farmhouse in Deerfield County, Pennsylvania, and I had a father who was so gentle he couldn't endure the harshness of things. When a calf was born, his eyes would fill with tears. One calf was born with brain damage. A crazy calf who bucked like a colt. That was my father's favorite. He fed it and looked after it until it died."

"Poetry. Were there poems in the farmhouse?"

"My father liked one poet. Robert Frost."

"He never saw the harshness in Frost's poetry?"

Busy with her hands, the girl seemed not to hear. "What sort of name is Priest?" Callie looked up. "I mean, Pokanoket is insane, but I can't imagine meeting a Catholic called Rabbi."

"My grandfather wanted to be American. He changed the family name. Cohen is Hebrew for Priest."

Callie stood. The jacket was brushed clean. She began to poke about the room.

"God," David said. "Your buttocks."

"My best part," Caroline said. "Once I had a low-grade infection and every day for two months I had to get a shot and each day the doctor put a Band-Aid on a cheek, so he'd remember to give me the next injection in the other one. And I didn't mind, although I'm private about my buttocks. My father spanked me once when I was twelve. I cried for a whole night, out of humiliation."

"There's a small secure lock on Cassidy's door," David said. "We have half an hour."

"It was an honest farm, really," Caroline said. "My father called it Hickory Ridge. Eighty rolling acres, clear of rocks, and thirty miles from Philadelphia."

"The glacier didn't get down that far, to dump rocks."

"And there was my mother, who liked figures, book-keeping, and my grandmother, who had a fortune and lived twenty miles away, and my bitch sister, who read *Love Comics* for literature and said from the time she was ten, 'Run with a rich crowd and you'll marry a rich feller.' "

"And no Shakespeare."

"No Shakespeare."

David reached out and embraced Caroline and they kissed, tongues touching, and either to tease or out of passion, she thrust her loins at his and he felt or thought he felt a mat of hair against his crotch and then, as the kiss waned and he wondered how to stop without rejecting her, Caroline withdrew. "Let's see what's on the desk," she said.

"It's not our room."

Caroline strutted toward Gabe Cassidy's desk and picked up a note. "Oh," she said. "Oh. I'm so embarrassed."

"Let me see it," David said. He read. *How lovely was the night, and all you did. You should be a musician and play . . . woodwinds. Trudy.*

"Not a very original note," David said, the old breathlessness charging back. "There's a famous joke about a trumpet player and a dowager—"

"Come, dear," Caroline interrupted. "They'll be noticing downstairs."

"They think it's broken," Clipper Zellbach said. He had lighted his pipe. He had not moved from the window.

"What's broken?" David said.

"Hildy's wrist. Gabe's taken her over to the medical center to wake someone up and get x-rays."

"The party's over," Caroline said. She brushed David's cheek with the chill suggestion of a kiss and looped an arm in Zellbach's and started toward the door.

"Say," Jeremy Johnson, the wide-mouthed comic, said to David. "You know why the Israelis gave the Suez Canal back to the Egyptians? No boardwalk."

"Not fucking funny," David said.

The room was almost empty. Plastic glasses stood everywhere—on the glass-topped table before the flowered sofa, and on two end tables, and on the wooden arms of chairs—and wherever there were plastic glasses, you could see rings left by other plastic glasses. Someone had drowned a cigarette in gin and tonic. Yellow oozed from the butt. David turned and there was Trudy Schuman.

"So?" she said.

"You alone?"

"You know my flirtations. I had something with Gabe. Hildy is a casualty. So not now."

"Something with Gabe? Here?"

"You're such a child. He doesn't sleep with Hildy."

"I know he doesn't sleep with Hildy and I don't feel like a child. I feel like an idiot for shoving her so hard when I stopped the fight. I guess that shove broke her wrist."

"So?" Trudy said. "You need some solace for your guilt?"

Trudy drove a massive green station wagon and David followed, keeping the red Triumph close to the right. That was a trick he had learned from Rick Sensabaugh. "No matter how much I drink, I'm always safe to drive," Sensabaugh said. "I go slow and keep far to the right." He'd been convincing until one night on the Henry Hudson Parkway he had sheared off a light pole with the front end of his Cadillac. But even the light pole, Sensabaugh pointed out, was on the right.

A picket fence bounded the lawn in front of Trudy Schuman's house. The house itself was white, with blue shutters and a large square living room. As David trailed, she walked upstairs and looked at the four children, from twelve to two, sleeping in bunk beds.

"This little one," Trudy said, as they stood over a sleeping girl whose head lay pillowed on her long blond hair. "This is the only girl and the only one my husband loves."

"I don't know," David said. "I don't know how you love one more than the others."

"Oh," Trudy said. "You are young. Fathers and

daughters. Don't you know? There is a saying from China: A man can stand everything in a divorce except losing his daughter. He cannot stand that. A lost daughter is a needle in the father's heart."

"So he stays married to you for the daughter?"

"And for convenience, and for economics. I wouldn't be an inexpensive divorce."

"But how expensive is an empty life?" David did not know if he was talking to Trudy or to himself.

"I wondered about music," Trudy said. She wore a dark skirt and a bright peasant blouse. "I wondered if you would like to hear a Beethoven adagio. The piano isn't good, but it plays."

Trudy poured drinks and sat down to perform the adagio in F from the *Waldstein* Sonata. *"L'Aurore,* 'The Dawn,' is what the French call the *Waldstein,"* David said, looking at Trudy's music. It was the Breitkopf edition. "This sonata stands at the center of Beethoven's creative life. Like the *Eroica."*

"You play?"

"I listen. For the *Waldstein* he marshals his forces. The Haydn days are done. The beginning of the sonata really is a dawn. You can't put music into words, but it's like haze lifting and the morning coming, all that morning and all that noonday. All that great incredible fucking burst that's Beethoven."

"I only play the slow movement," Trudy said.

The *Waldstein* adagio opens with the birthing of a melody, through dissonant moments in the bass. A suggestion of the melody appears, descending gently, always gently, in semitones. Beethoven has been severe and his severity is not fled, but it will wait for another time, another work. The melody, simple as tears, floats from the piano and surrounds the world. Thus at the hands of Arrau or of Schnabel. Trudy Schuman had been drinking.

"I wonder," David said, as Trudy's adagio stuttered

downward. "Maybe just a little radio. Don't want to wake the kids." Her assault upon the music made him wince.

Trudy stopped playing and took a long sip of a clear, strong fruit liqueur. She smiled at David and walked out of the living room. She reappeared in a gold robe, belted at the waist. "Well?" she said.

"Well, what?"

"Well, are you going to wear your captain's clothes all night?"

David removed the gold-buttoned blue blazer, which Caroline Devon had brushed clean. The radio was playing "Night Train." The song struck an urgent, repetitive, coarse beat. Porn music, David thought. Cliché porn, corn porn. Trudy still smiled and began to do a dance. She put her left foot forward and tapped. The golden robe slipped open to her thigh. She extended her right foot. Trudy Schuman spread her arms, clicking her fingers and gyrating her hips. But not in time to the music. "Night Train" sounded its beat. Da-da-da-da, da-da-da-da. *Dat.* Da. A Baltimore-strip-joint song. Trudy Schuman, of the olive eyes and sensual features, was dancing a Levantine dance.

God, David thought, this woman is a hybrid. At the piano, she confused herself with Myra Hess. Dancing, she confused herself with Blaze Starr. But the thighs were smooth and they had been waxed clean of hair and as David sat in shirtsleeves, holding his Scotch, he stared very hard at the pale-gold robe, looking for the outline of the pubic triangle.

Trudy Schuman was fluttering now, her hands were fluttering, and her eyes were closed, and she was making little ballet runs back and forth. "Night Train" stopped. The radio played "You Do Something to Me" ("that nobody else can do").

Trudy stood still and dropped her arms. She opened her eyes and said, "Well?"

"Well, what?"

"Are you going to keep the rest of your clothes on all night?"

"What a pleasant invitation to the dance."

"Come," Trudy said, and took his hand, and David followed her up the stairs, placing a free hand on the robe, above a large, drooping buttock. Goddamn, he thought. Callie Devon's buttocks are tight. He remembered a feeling in Brooklyn, long before. The theater had been dark and John Garfield bore his fire to Abe Pollonsky's movie *Body and Soul* and Lilli Palmer, with the Viennese face under fair hair, and the mouth, the mouth suggesting something he had never felt. He ached with a grown-up passion, and in a giggling teenaged way, he and Shelley Goldberg swapped dates and he put his arm around Shelley's date, a pretty, dark-haired girl called Frances. And Frances's shouders were too big and even then, when he was eighteen, he guessed she was going to be a clubwoman, reading precisely what certain book reviewers ordered her to read and attending fashionable concert series, as though deaf. And his girl, Marya. Well, she was with Shelley. He and Shelley went to the men's room afterward and each urinated for a long time.

"Stones?" Shelley said.

"Uh-huh."

"Well, I could see you were making out good and so was I," Shelley said.

"She's got a body," David said.

"I was making out better," Shelley said. "But what does it mean, Davey, making out with the wrong girl in the wrong place?"

"Keep pissing, Shell," David said, trying to sound wiser than he felt. But he could not answer the question then. Nor could he now.

A queen-size fourposter ruled Trudy Schuman's bedroom. She sat in front of a small three-way mirror above a night table and began to brush her hair. She let her robe fall open. She shrugged and the robe dropped to her waist. Her breasts were full and flat, with large nipples. Two or three long black hairs grew from each brown band. No waxing there. "The mirrors," David said, "give you six breasts."

"Get undressed."

David stripped, carefully folding his gray slacks on a green wing chair. He knew his build was trim. He stood naked before Trudy Schuman, lightly holding in his stomach.

"You're hairy," Trudy said.

"Trait of the race."

"So hairy," Trudy said. "When I've seen you on the beach, I'd never have thought you'd have so hairy a tummy."

"And you?"

Trudy stood up. The golden robe fell away. Her belly bulged. The pubic hair was thick and carefully shaped. David placed a palm on her pubic hair.

"So," Trudy said. "So? You need some solace, but you aren't hard."

"A lot of whiskey."

Trudy walked to the bed and bent, buttocks together, and drew down a yellow flowered bedspread, showing cool blue sheets. She mounted the bed and rolled over and said, "Turn out the light."

"I don't like it completely dark."

She lit a reading light. It was white with an etched umber design of twisting vines, a candlestick wired to become a bed lamp. David turned out the overhead light and eased himself on top of Trudy Schuman. Her hand went quickly, surely, to his penis. "So," she said. "So now you're getting firm. Ah," she said. "It feels good to hold you there."

There was none of the aggressive passion of the moment when he had kissed her neck and drawn a cry.

She thrust his penis into her and even as his hips worked, part of his brain remained an unmoved observer. He was lying with a lady, gone too much to fat, who would use him as she might use a candle.

"You are pleasing me," Trudy Schuman said, and smiled.

David thrust. "Oh," Trudy cried. "Go deeper, deeper. Oh. Oh, my God. Come. Please come."

Her orgasm came rolling, deep, with groans. "Why?" she said. "Why?"

"Trudy. No questions yet, Trudy. I haven't come."

"But why do you want me instead of going home?"

"I don't know, Trudy. I haven't come."

"But you did want me, and very much. I've known that for a long time."

Caroline, David thought. Callie, bouncing on some drab cot with a lawyer.

"Before we make more love," Trudy said, "you must say just why it is you want me."

"Damn," David said. "Things are."

"Why, David? Or I'll sit up and read a book."

"Because," David Priest said slowly, "I would rather sleep with you than sleep with my wife."

"Ah," Trudy cried, and stretched her arms and placed her hands upon his buttocks and bounced and rolled until he came softly, biting his lower lip.

IV

Pale sunlight, dimmed by yellow curtains, raked his eyes. His tongue felt bloated. He shifted in bed and a shudder ran down his left side. Crazy little room. All the furniture. Heavy stuffed pieces. An ornate French painting. Heavy naked ladies beside a river. The frame was gilt. Crazy to pack so much into the bedroom of a summer cottage. He'd never do that himself, and Joyce—why did he have to think of Joyce?—would take what she found and put in nothing of her own. He had to think of Joyce because Trudy Schuman was snoring just the way Joyce snored when she slept on her back.

He sat up. It is a strange and vaguely unsettling thing to awaken in someone else's bedroom, to open your eyes when morning fear runs strong, and to see nothing, nothing at all, that suggests your home or safety. Trudy slept on her back. Her mouth was open. David looked at the large, flat breasts and the open mouth. He liked his women lean, with firm bodies, and one of the problems with Joyce, maybe *the* problem with Joyce, was how she had let her body go. So he had gone from one gone body to another gone body. He was awake.

Trudy snorted and rolled her head. She made a gargling sound and resumed loud snoring. David gathered his clothing. His slacks looked neat, but the blue blazer had got entangled with Trudy's golden Isadora robe. The jacket was a wreck of creases. He looked at Trudy's face. The nose was broader than he had thought. Grossness. David dressed carefully, and after putting on the wrinkled jacket, walked out into light, salty mist. He sat on the wet grass, shaking his head and slipping on oxblood loafers.

Five minutes after the Triumph started, it began losing power. At every little rise in the blacktop, the sports car slowed and David had to downshift. He stopped and raced the engine. The car roared healthily. Then, at the next rise, it all but died. The morning was brightening. From the rise he saw through mist soft, rolling lawns. Beyond, pale sunlight speckled the sea. "Fucking car," David said.

He rolled—there was no power now—down toward a fork in the road and coasted onto a triangle of sand. He cut the engine and sat on the hood of the sleek red useless Triumph, drawing his knees up and waiting for another car.

It would not matter very much, except for Joel, in which direction he hitched a ride. David recalled the Polish Jew who survived Auschwitz, where all his family had died. Someone asked the Polish Jew about relocating.

"I want to go to New Zealand," the survivor said.

"But New Zealand is so *far.*"

"From where?"

Pokanoket Island was not Poland and Joyce Steindler Priest was hardly Hitler, and just before a potato truck driver offered him a lift, David Priest began to laugh at himself.

It was past eight o'clock when he reached his beach house. Joel was striding through the door in an orange surf suit that reached halfway to the knees.

"Hi, Dad. Where's the car?"

"It broke. That's why I'm so late."

The boy nodded. "Broke bad?"

"Just bad enough so it won't go."

"I never liked it that much," Joel said. "Let's get a new one. Blue."

Always the sea with the boy, David thought, even to colors. "Where are you headed?" he said.

"For a swim off Hampshire Hollow."

"But you don't go alone into rough surf. Two people have to swim in rough surf."

Joel shook his head. The sandy hair flopped. "Look. I've been going into rough surf by myself a lot this summer. That's why I'm so good."

David's face twisted. He looked at Joel, tanned and fair, restless to bound into a reckless day.

"Christ, kid," David said. "No, kid. Christ." He clasped Joel to his wrinkled blazer. "Now isn't that ridiculous, me calling you Christ, because if you're Christ, you know what that makes me? That makes me God. And that's just crazy because God, you know,

I mean people like you and me who're Jews, we learned at Auschwitz God does not exist."

Babbling, David thought. I'm babbling at my son. Except I mean it. Home talk. Work talk. Party dialogue. Too many worlds, and each world not a world at all, but a mockery world, and all the sum of all the mockery worlds add up to misty mornings. I'm too hung to see. Or taste. Fuck the metaphor. I am Lazarus. I shall tell you all. I am too blind to taste the misty mornings. My mind, my fucking mind, makes party dialogue.

David grasped Joel's shoulders and held the boy at arm's length. "Look. I should be around more. I should be with you more. I'm sorry."

"Dad," Joel said. "Dad? What's the matter?"

My own father, David thought, who walked in lurches and fell in love with doom, went off each morning and came home each night. The house was always the same, whatever poisoned his hours in between. My own father *wanted* to be a father.

"Can you forgive me, Joel? Can you forgive me?" Clutching the slim, frightened boy, David slumped to the ground. He knelt, gray slacks on sandy dirt, and shook his head and tried to talk and could not. Joel sprang back and David fell, his face against the ground. He tasted sand.

"Are you all right?"

"Yeah, fine." David spat sand from his tongue. He stood and turned to hide his face and brushed dirt from his slacks and said, "Can you forgive the terrible, selfish father that I've been?"

"You're not terrible," Joel said. "You're not selfish."

David started toward the small white house and said, not turning, "Come on. I'll make us both some breakfast."

"I can take care of that," Joel said. "When you're not around and Mom's asleep, I scramble my own eggs."

David walked into the house, the boy safely behind

him. Tears started from his eyes. Now what the fuck would that achieve? He looked into the bedroom. Joyce was sleeping with her mouth open. David felt surprised to see how much she resembled Trudy Schuman, or how much Trudy Schuman resembled her.

CHAPTER TWO

Songs of a Wayfarer

I

David Priest woke slowly, resisting the day. He thought, A life defines itself in sandy-mouthed awakenings. It was September. Summer was past and the beaches at Pokanoket were empty, save for the gulls who walked at four o'clock. They would plant trident footprints before the waves, unconcerned about the transience of their tracks. The room was hot and new and strange as David awoke, feeling sandy-mouthed and empty and transient.

He turned on a big brass bed and stretched and yawned and looked through a doorway at a painting someone else had hung. It was a butte and it was also a man with a mustache, except that sometimes it looked like a butte with a mustache. The colors were black and brown and mauve. David called the painting "Hangover in Search of a Head." Humor was one way to contend with loneliness.

WRITER JESTS, THEN CHUCKLES.
CHAIRS FAIL TO RESPOND.

Being alone was another way to contend with loneliness.

WRITER JESTS, THEN CHUCKLES.
LAUGHTER FILLS EMPTY ROOM.

But where were the listeners? There was nobody to listen to the laughter in the empty room.

The chairs and the bed and the painting had been acquired by someone David had not met. The woman was a casting director called Rosetta Stein who had gone off to work in London, where, David supposed, she interviewed crisp English beauties. Tuck your tummy in, Miss Christie. You have a pretty figure when you remember to suck in your tum. David tried to fancy Julie Christie and Rosetta Stein naked in his bedroom, but the fancy was spoiled by a remark that he remembered. "Rosetta Stein looks like David Susskind with tits."

He had rented Rosetta Stein's apartment on West Fifty-seventh Street, in an ancient thick-walled building, because it came with furnishings, sheets and towels, stereo, even books. He was impatient with nest building. He wanted an instant place of his own. Rosetta Stein's furniture. His apartment. He had broken with Joyce. He had left his wife. It had only been two weeks. He missed her snoring.

"I'm leaving you, Joyce."

"You've left before."

"No. This time I'm serious. We aren't doing each other any good. Or Joel. This bickering."

"You don't have to make a speech. You don't have to tell me about Joel."

"I'll pack some things. What I have to say is—"

"You don't have to say anything." Joyce blinked. Were her eyes wet?

"I'll help you pack." Her eyes were dry.

"It's a matter of conscience," David said.

"I know," his wife had said. She sounded bored, resigned, impatient for her solitude.

The last scene, last scene of all between them, was playing flat. Where was the music? She should be singing "Addio, senza rancor." "Do you have your antihistamines?" Joyce said. "You know goldenrod pollen makes you sneeze."

Conscience, David thought on the big brass bed. I invoked conscience.

WRITER CONCEALS ERECTION:
PLEADS CONSCIENCE.

Why hadn't Joyce kept herself trim, like Julie Christie?

Was it conscience that had moved him here, or cock?

He was charging himself with ambiguity. (He was not his own best friend.)

Nolo contendere. (Who the hell wanted to be his own best friend?) His sentence was to sleep with guilt. (With guilt and Julie Christie *at the same time?*)

"Oh, shit," David said. He was awake.

Solomon (Clipper) Zellbach practiced law in a steel-sheathed glass building that rose among other steel-sheathed glass buildings on Park Avenue. Glass boxes looking out on other glassed-in boxes, Frank Lloyd Wright had said. David and Joyce once hunted for a Wright disciple to build them a home and they had found the disciple, but not the money, $86,000 plus extras. What difference now, David thought, entering a revolving door.

Zellbach's waiting room was paneled in oak. The receptionist, Ms. Jensen, sat behind a sliding window. David lit a cigarette. He had not smoked for six years. Eleven nights ago, he had tried a Salem at a party. Now he was smoking two packs a day. Ms. Jensen did not wear spectacles the way secretaries did in old movies. Her face was square and bony. David imagined putting spectacles on Ms. Jensen's nose. *Voilà!* What a reverse. Eyeglasses made Ms. Jensen beautiful. Did anyone think of sex as much as he?

After twenty minutes, Zellbach appeared, not apologetic, trim in a tight-fitting brown tweed suit, and smiling a fixed, arch smile. For an instant, the teeth reminded David of a Tyrannosaurus. "Come in," Zellbach said, warmly. "Have you seen the layout?"

Zellbach led David into a conference room, walled with books, into a kitchen area and then into a corner office with windows facing south and west. Zellbach's desk stood in the middle of the room. "I like it in the middle," he said. "I like the spaciousness. I often feel more comfortable in the office here than at home. In a way, I suppose, the office is my home."

"I want a divorce," David said.

"I suspected you wanted a divorce."

"I want it neat. I don't want a mess in the papers. I don't want to hurt Joyce and I certainly don't want to hurt Joel."

"The divorce will hurt them both."

"I mean as little as possible."

"And you'll be hurt yourself."

Far to the west, David saw the Hudson River. The September day was clear. He could see far past the river border of the city. "I'll be all right. I don't have any reason to worry."

"Well, your wife has already engaged Gabe Cassidy and I've been in this sort of thing with Gabe before. So I have a reason to worry. Gabe is tough."

"He almost got divorced himself."

"But he didn't. He decided to stay with Hildy. He voted for marriage. You're voting against it. That creates an emotional element. It will make Gabe tougher."

"He doesn't frighten me."

"He frightens me. I see the scenario ahead. You're tall. You wear a mustache. You're intellectual. You're semiradical. Suppose we find ourselves before a devout Catholic judge, who's short, clean-shaven, bigoted and dumb. Gabe Cassidy will try to play the divorce trial so that it isn't decided on its merits. And your case isn't that meritorious anyway. Gabe will put you on trial. Your life, your beliefs—*you*—will be the issue judged by a hostile court."

"And?"

"And, my friend, that judge will shove a red-hot poker up your ass."

Lawyers, doctors, auto mechanics. They not only knew the answers. They knew the questions. You walked in to ask about a chirping noise or an old hernia or a divorce and suddenly you were led childlike into a discussion of valve guides, sarcoma in connective tissue, or star chamber proceedings. David lashed out. "Hell, Clip. You're only married after a fashion yourself."

"That's not relevant," Zellbach said. The Tyrannosaurus teeth clenched. "Even impertinent. You're the one in trouble, not I. Now what is your income going to be this year?"

"About fifty-five thousand. I'm ghostwriting a book for an actor. Rickie Conklin. The one with the six marriages."

"How's that going?"

"Fair. The material is good. He keeps getting cuckolded. We have pictures of his third wife, Miss Utah, going down on a doctor in the doctor's office. But Rickie Conklin doesn't want the lively material in the book. When I press him, he tells me Miss Utah is the mother of his daughter. He doesn't want the lady to be a cocksucker before the world. And I tell him he hooked the publisher by promising to talk about cocksucking in Hollywood. And he gets sullen and starts drinking, and after three martinis, he pulls out the picture of Miss Utah and the doctor and he says, 'How'd you like to have her going down on you?' I'm almost finished with the book. It won't be any good."

"Well, that's another problem," Zellbach said, "but you've done your best. You aren't liable, unless the contract contains a furnish-fellatio-photo clause." Zellbach smiled at his own joke. "To represent you in this divorce," he said, "I'll need a retainer of two thousand dollars. If I can't placate Cassidy and we have to go to court, the retainer will be four thousand. I'm giving you a break. I usually charge someone in your bracket five thousand up front."

"I don't mind paying," David said. But I *do* mind paying, he thought. There were these times when some lunatic muse seized his tongue and made him say precisely what he did not mean.

"Nice talking." To someone from the electric company who had demanded a $150 deposit.

"Your help means a lot to me." To a magazine editor who had rewritten one of David's graceful essays into banality.

"I love you." To a girl he did not find attractive who suddenly announced, "If you think I'm going to bed with you, you're wrong."

"The money doesn't matter to me," David repeated. "I want the best representation I can get." Well, that was better. He meant half of what he said. He wished Zellbach had not used the image of a short judge armed with a glowing poker.

"It's hard to tell about professionals," Zellbach said. "They don't rate us in *Consumer Reports*. But as your counsel and your friend and with absolute neutrality, I assure you that you do have the best representation you can get. Now. Let me continue. Who else is there?"

Ms. Jensen rang. Zellbach said something about convertible debentures. "I'll be down to the Street at eight forty-five tomorrow morning." David lit another cigarette. Zellbach hung up.

"There isn't anyone else," David said.

"I've practiced law for a long time. In ninety-nine cases out of a hundred, a man does not simply wake up and say, 'My marriage isn't everything it should be.'

Ninety-nine times out of a hundred, when he says that, he is waking up beside somebody else."

"There still isn't anybody. I like your friend Caroline Devon. But nothing's happened with her."

Zellbach's mouth turned downward. "What hasn't happened is unimportant for our purposes. What has happened?"

"You may not believe this, Clip, but I don't like detailing my sexual history. I'm not much for verbal gangbanging in locker rooms."

"This isn't a locker room. Adultery is not only grounds for divorce. It is also a crime. To defend you against any eventuality, including a bellicose judge, I want to anticipate every eventuality. David, this is not a social situation. You have to drop your guard with me the way you have to drop your pants for a proctologist. You better trust that the doctor isn't gay; you better trust that I'm not looking for gossip. If you can't trust me, you'd do better with other counsel. Now, please, can't you tell me what's going on?"

"Dalliances are going on," David said. "Liz Wesley, a picture researcher for *Time*. Single. Bonnie Jordon. Publicity woman. Divorced. Marilyn Freed. Heiress. Legally separated. Nothing serious is going on. A night's release."

"All right," Zellbach said. He was making notes with a silver fountain pen. "The ethics of the bar require me to ask if there is any possibility of reconciliation."

"None."

"Think hard. I won't ask you again."

"None."

"Then we want to reach agreement, Gabe Cassidy and I. I'll try to keep the negotiations confidential. The idea which I'll try to sell Gabe is not to violate the privacy of the marriage. The court will simply certify what we work out. Under New York State law, then, after you've lived apart for a year, you're automatically divorced."

"I want the grounds to be incompatibility," David said. "That's honest."

"Joyce has something else in mind."

"What's that?"

"She claims she has evidence of adultery."

David stood up and walked to the window and looked at the Hudson River. "Which one?"

"Trudy Schuman."

David turned and smirked—contempt mixing with anger—and moved back to the chair. "I'd have imagined it was some gabby teeny-bopper." He shook his head. "Trudy?"

"It isn't a good idea," Zellbach said, "to leave *any* lady in heat. And it's a simply rotten idea to leave in heat a lady who has only to pick up a telephone to spend the next afternoon drinking vodka with your wife."

"Is that what happened?" David said. "Did Trudy Schuman tell Joyce?"

"Apparently," Zellbach said. "Gabe Cassidy has me outgunned. We want privacy and silence. I think I can get that. For their part, they want money."

"How much?"

"I'd say alimony and support could run you eighteen thousand a year, plus percentages if your income jumps. I ask you again. Is there any possibility of reconciliation?"

"I have no alternative. There isn't any choice I see except divorcing Joyce." That sounded tentative. Was he asking Zellbach to argue? " 'Bad marriages kill people,' " David announced. "Tolstoy said that." The ashtray on Zellbach's desk was shaped like a fielder's glove. David lit a cigarette, although one still smoked in the glove. "Damn," he said. "God damn."

"In reading Tolstoy," Zellbach said, "my impression was that he said something else. He said that all marriages kill people. Is there still no possibility of reconciliation?"

"Just give me a pen to make out a check for the retainer." Writing, David mumbled, "One stupid night."

Zellbach seemed not to hear. He leaned backward. "Liz Wesley? Is that the Liz Wesley who lives on East Sixty-third?"

"Ash blond. A vibrator called Prelude III in the night table. She likes to use the vibrator while she's fucking."

David looked at a bookcase full of red leather volumes called Significant Appellate Division Decisions. "This place is a bit of a locker room at that," he said, glaring at his counselor and friend.

The Tyrannosaurus teeth were not Tyrannosaurus teeth to Clipper Zellbach. Or crocodile teeth. Or carnivore's teeth. They were simply *his* teeth, thirty-two cuspids, incisors, molars. Four capped. One saved by an innovative root-canal procedure that the dentist, an insufferably jovial man named Louie Lewisohn, called The Panama. Each Panama Root Canal cost $1,150, which may have explained Dr. Lewisohn's ebullience.

The method of controlling interviews with law clients —klaxons of terror amid spasms of compassion; courtly friendliness mixed with cold command—were not manipulations to Clipper Zellbach, not playing a game he had to win. They were techniques to get on with a job efficiently, as much for the client as for himself, he would say if asked. He was asked seldom.

The four-thousand-dollar retainer he had mentioned to David Priest, for no more than forty hours of work, did not appear excessive to Clipper Zellbach. It was less than the cost of four Panama Root Canals. Besides, he was good and he could be brilliant and he remembered how hard it had been to go from City College of New York as Solly to Harvard Law School, where he called himself Solomon and tried to display controlled wisdom.

He wanted the others at Harvard to know how intelligent he was, and he did not want to appear as an ostentatious Bronx Jew. He had played basketball for City College. At Harvard, he taught himself to sail along the Charles River.

His nickname.

He was tacking in a fourteen-footer in sight of Soldiers Field and the wind stuttered and the mainsail luffed and a beautifully trimmed twenty-two-foot Day Sailor beat past his borrowed Comet. In the other cockpit a classmate, Hartley Barclay, wore a black-and-green rugby shirt. Hartley W. (for Winthrop, as in Massachusetts Winthrop) Barclay laughed and shouted, "That's not the Yankee Clipper luffing over there. It's the Bronx Clipper."

The nickname spread.

He could not elude it, so he tried to fashion the nickname into something compatible with Harvard and sailing and the Charles. "Call me Clip," the Bronx Clipper said, and slowly (one had to be patient with such things) the word Bronx fell away. It wanted euphony. Slowly (he was patient) Solly Zellbach of City College metamorphosed into the Clipper from Harvard Law. He was an efficient and expedient young man.

How difficult it had been, so much control so early, and he could summon brilliance, although in most divorce cases he did not need to. The law of divorce was routine. The tactics were patterned. The judges were disinterested, uninteresting men and women. No Holmes, no Mr. Justice Cardozo, ruled which party had custody of what child on Easter Sunday or who was awarded the copper kettle and the three pewter salt cellars from Harriet's Happiness House, the Niagara Falls Finest Gift Shoppe.

Particularly when his client was a woman, the first demand was that he be consoling. Sol Zellbach, the Bronx Clipper, did not like that.

Having to be consoling.

Servility.

There had been enough servility and servitude. His father, Kalman Zellbach, worked as a waiter for thirty-one years.

The call for brilliance, rare but always possible, justified four thousand dollars for forty hours of divorce work, the lawyer believed. For four thousand dollars, a mere four thousand dollars, Clip Zellbach had saved one man's control of a publishing business. The man's wife threatened to charge and prove homosexuality, unless she was awarded half the company. Zellbach answered opposing counsel with a psycholegal memorandum. The publisher would admit homosexuality. It was not unique in the literary field. He would cite Christopher Marlowe and Wilde. Several contemporary authors, gay, lesbian, straight, would testify to the publisher's character and good works. Then Zellbach would charge that the publisher's wife had "maliciously and sadistically disrupted normal connubial relations, scarring a formerly healthy libido beyond healing." The publisher would want damages for his bent sexual drive. Collecting was questionable. However, in open court it would be asserted that the wife was a lousy lay.

The woman dropped her claim to the publishing business and accepted a moderate cash settlement. Clip Zellbach knew the woman, whose name was Phyllis. He had slept with her. She had been exciting and she was proud of her sensuality. It would be cruel to deny her passions in court. She had not been a lousy lay at all. But business was business.

He did not read much now, but he remembered what he had read at Harvard Law and at City College and before. (During his analysis, the doctor suggested that he focus on literary law.) The doctor had a porcelain-white face and there were too many lines of vein on her calves, but long black hair made a lovely frame for the porcelain face.

"I'm not here for advice on my law practice," he said. "I'm trying to reconcile the past and the present." And then he was repeating The Story. His father waited on tables at a dairy restaurant, taking more tables for his station, always walking faster, and his mother saved and hoarded so that there was money for her child to go to Harvard Law and more than that to buy small apartment buildings his mother said were fit only to rent to "Colored." The Story ended: "Which is how my father retired from waiting and became a slumlord."

"Which is how," the doctor said, "The Story always ends."

"If it bores *you*," Zellbach said, "can you imagine how unspeakably it bores me? It's debasing, of course, but finally it is my paradigm of tedium. That *is* why I've come. The Story bores me. The law bores me only slightly less. I'm in therapy to find a cure for boredom."

"Is there anything that does not bore you?"

"Sexual intercourse with new partners."

The doctor with the porcelain face was named Gertrude Beckmesser Schuman.

"Only with new partners?" Dr. Trudy Schuman asked.

He sat up straight in the tan imitation-leather chair that faced the doctor's desk. "Would *you* fuck me? Now."

"I have another patient," Dr. Trudy Schuman said.

"Not for twenty-five minutes."

After they became bedmates, Dr. Schuman continued to be his therapist. She said they respected each other as practical, professional and expedient people.

Following Dr. Schuman's suggestion, he moved his practice toward literature, but there were not enough writers who wanted legal counsel and had the income to pay for it, so he represented publishers as well, beginning with a small house in Greenwich Village but moving up, adding clients so that he had to work harder, always faster, like his father.

Clip did not think that representing writers and pub-lishers placed him in conflict of interest, any more than there was a conflict in representing a wife in one divorce and a husband in another. He said that when Trudy Schuman asked him during treatment. That evening she told him again that he was an expedient man. In level tones he said, "You are an expedient pussy." She wanted to smile. She winced.

The law practice grew steadily as grass, dully as grass, and Zellbach branched beyond it and offered an-other service. He pooled funds and invested in stocks, commodities, natural gas leases and real estate trusts, often with tax advantages. He managed the investments without a fee, other than ten percent of the profits. Many of the speculations materialized, and Zellbach was able to maintain his wife, Geri, at Chappaqua, Pokanoket (summer), Fort Lauderdale (winter) and at a rental property in Bermuda (in between), which left him free to roam New York. He called the city his asphalt turf.

The affair with Dr. Gertrude Schuman waned. She was no longer a new partner. He accumulated money beyond the fantasies of his father. Some therapists might have pointed out a parallel. His father used his trade to acquire property. Clip used his profession to acquire property, profits, the beginnings of wealth. Dr. Trudy Schuman did not think that it mattered to make the point, since Clip would reject it, and after that he would hurt her. She had read Mendel, Clayson, et al., on pa-tient-dominated psychotherapy, and she had herself re-entered therapy with Dr. David Mendel.

Analysis had barely penetrated Clip. Law continued to be a useful bore. Politics appeared trivial. He was approaching fifty. Accumulating money interested him, but held no challenge. What sustained him was what had always sustained him.

Sexual intercourse with new partners.

"Satyriasis," Dr. Trudy Schuman told him at last. "An aspect of your expediency."

He deflected her with a quotation.

> *". . . his delights*
> *Were dolphin-like, they showed his back above*
> *The element they lived in."*

They exchanged looks, but his was gentler. He had won.

He did not think of himself as Dr. Trudy Schuman thought of him. He was not expedient. His father, Kalman Zellbach, was the expedient one. Clip believed he had surpassed his father. If he had read Camus, he would have regarded himself as an existential man.

II

Walking back to the apartment, David Priest tried to focus on the precise moment when he had decided to marry Joyce Steindler.

He had now decided to unmarry her.

Unity was important in all things. Hadn't Aristotle articulated that as *Homonoia*?

Disunity dominates. Hadn't Tolstoy said that as he lay in the railroad station called Astapovo, encountering death?

The only consistency, perhaps, was the Cyrillic alphabet. But had anyone said consistency exists?

Nobody, perhaps.

Perhaps nobody.

They had lived in Brooklyn. The year was 1959. Rock songs erupted from transistor radios and they discovered they both preferred other music. "Tenderly" and "Autumn Leaves" and Brahms was his and Tchaikovsky was hers, Tchaikovsky and Balzac belonged to Joyce. They were dividing up history. It would be later before they reached a property settlement.

How pleasant it was riding bicycles under the sycamores that grew along Ocean Parkway. He had never proposed to her, never thought marriage. They were content with cycling, or tennis, or talking books or playing at sex, and in those days there was a saying and David listened to sayings. In those days.

He was well read on love and women, and somewhat frightened and wholly ignorant. He listened to sayings.

Nobody is happy. A few people are lucky enough to be content.

He listened and he accepted. In those days. The sexual riddle came with masturbation. It was a thought afterward: Is this what moved Hector toward Andromache, Napoleon toward Josephine? Is this tickle, relieved in a john, what fired flames of poetry?

> *And all the best of dark and light*
> *Shines in the aspect of her eyes.*

Girls with feather cuts streamed around him. He was not on Ocean Parkway. He was walking up Madison Avenue, and he did not believe in sayings anymore. Certain feather-cut girls around him knew *Père Goriot* and Byron. They would be stirred by the first movement of Brahms's Piano Trio in B Major. Was that a reason to marry them?

Possibly. A possibly excellent reason. Three excellent reasons, possibly. He did not believe in sayings anymore, but in patterns. He was a marrier. It was better, since he was going to marry someone, to begin the marriage with one lyric poem, one allegro con brio and one novel in common. (It was important, also, that she possess firm, prominent buttocks.)

Joyce Steindler had wanted him, she had wanted to marry him, and being wanted made him feel content. He did not reject her; it was decent not to reject someone who wanted you. Contentment and decency were about to cost him twenty thousand dollars a year. If he were truly noble, he'd be on the hook for fifty thousand dollars.

> *First she licked him*
> *Then she tricked him*
> *She outslicked him.*
> *He cried victim.*

Joel.

He had forgotten. The twenty thousand dollars would sustain Joel. David was a victim and Joyce was a victim and Joel was a victim, but only Joel was innocent.

On the day when his decision to divorce reached irrevocability, he had forgotten his son.

David turned at Fifty-seventh Street and started uphill toward the west. Hurrying now, he saw his father, dead eighteen years. He saw the mild face and heard the stern, deep voice. "A decision, right or wrong, is better than indecision. Any decision you reach makes you feel better once you reach it." His father had not been divorced.

A couple approached David Priest. The boy was bearded. The girl had stringy hair and flat, heavy breasts. They seemed surprised to hear a tall, prosperous-looking man, who appeared to be thirty-five years old, speak aloud as he walked by himself.

"Bullshit, Dad," the man said.

The phone was ringing in the empty apartment. Living with Joyce, he had shunned telephones. Now he sprang across the bedroom and into the living room and brushed back his hair, before reaching toward the receiver.

"Hullo." The other voice sounded boyish and tentative.

"Who's this?"

"Callie Devon."

"Caroline. Where are you?"

"On Mom's farm, but I'm going to New York. I have to break up a romance and I have some friends on East Sixty-third and I can stay with them."

She needs companionship, David thought. Requirement for an end of an affair. "I admire you for returning to the scene to break it up. I always run."

Her voice was surer now, the timbre darkening toward contralto. "I hate loose ends. David, how are you?"

My companionship, David thought. Why else the call? "I've been breaking up a romance myself. Breaking up a broken romance."

"They're always broken, aren't they, before you say the words?"

"I've just talked to a lawyer about my divorce."

"You aren't feeling mighty, then."

She could hold her poise. That was a nice thing in a woman, like courage in a man. "It was Clip Zellbach and he was fairly helpful. But I'm not feeling mighty. Not at all."

The faraway contralto said, "You have to remember to be patient with yourself."

It was easier to show pain to a woman than a man. Women should be the doctor class everywhere, not just in Russia. *Be patient with yourself.* The platitude from the pretty woman calling cheered him more than Zellbach's hard-bought concern. "Who is the romance?" David said.

"You'll find out anyway. The romance *was* with your lawyer."

"I keep finding out that there are only six or seven people in the Western world."

They would meet at Auberge Paris, a two-star restaurant on Fifty-fourth Street, which M. Guy had decorated with a mural of the Tuileries, with sports car models and with pictures of Grand Prix drivers. Hard, weathered men smiled down from yellow walls.

M. Guy said, "Ah, Mr. Priest," and tilted his chin and grinned. "That tall brunette last week."

David waited.

"Very nice, as we would expect from you."

"She was nicer in the restaurant than when we were alone," David said.

"Ah." The grin widened. "But that, of course, is not my business."

Auberge Paris had become another part of the locker room. The verbal gang bang clamored. He had let M. Guy tempt him to the dirty dance, and now the jejune Frenchman smirked. Well, David deserved it for suggesting that the tall brunette, whose name was Helen, had not been a performer in bed. In the taxicab she had moaned and squirmed and pressed his hand against her pubic tuft. Then, at the top of five flights, Helen turned brusque—was there ever so icy an inversion of hysteria? —and slammed the door to her apartment. Not even thanks for dinner, not even a *look* at her bed. "What you got in there?" David bellowed angrily. "Quiet," demanded a baritone response. He had been warming her up for someone else. Favor for a stranger. Oh, hell, why not? Stranger might sometime do the same for him. But he shouted through the metal door, "Fuck off."

Laughter.

Helen corrected loudly. "No. Fuck on."

Laughter. Shrill but not at all hysterical.

If only he could accept more graciously the luck of the draw with women. He had once in Brooklyn. He had accepted his mother. There had been no choice then, really.

He had accepted women twice in Brooklyn. He had accepted his wife. For five years anyway. No longer, but as long as possible.

Had the two, mother and wife, worn out his grace and his ability to accept? Couldn't have. He didn't feel that old.

If only he could live without having to draw, without bouncing from woman to woman. He was a monogamist. That came from deep. But he had not yet found anyone with enough magic to share his monogamy.

If only he did not have to justify himself to M. Guy.

"Tonight's woman is even more attractive," David said.

"Ah," M. Guy said. "Then you must have a corner table."

Caroline did not appear until eight-forty. David drank Scotch whisky slowly, thinking of what was ahead. She would be receptive now. She had called him. Sheldon Ormont, the gynecologist, talked about women constantly, and what better topic, the way women supported him. Even Marx would have blinked. David thought of the bodies on the table. Fifty-five patients, draped and spread, fifty-five every day. Freud would have blanched. "The worst bitch gets docile when you've got her in the stirrups," Sheldon Ormont said. "No, they're not concerned that you'll excite them. At least, mine aren't. They're afraid they're going to be hurt." At the end of a romance, Sheldon Ormont said, all women were emotionally naked. "It's like the stirrups then, the way they're unprotected. Some put on twenty pounds. Some drink. A lot just fuck and fuck. I don't know why"—he could hear Sheldon's medical tenor, an assertive manner masked in a high-pitched voice—"but busting a romance is different for a woman. It's worse than busting a romance for a man. We may

get cold nuts for a while. But they're left lying open."
David considered his drink. This would be a functional
time to see Caroline, if Sheldon Ormont, M.D., fifty-five
patients a day, knew what the hell he was talking about.

"Hullo." Caroline's voice was tentative again, but
she looked radiant. Her black silk dress reached the
floor. Turquoise glowed from a choker.

"Beautiful," David said. "Turquoise against black.
You against turquoise and black."

"Oh. Thank you. A martini with ice, vodka and an
olive."

"Wait till I kiss you hello." He brushed a tanned
cheek. They were standing. When they sat, Caroline
clutched his hand beneath the tablecloth.

"Was it horrible with Clip?" David said.

"He flew me to Bermuda three weeks ago and I borrowed some money from Mother and I tried to pay him
back tonight. He wouldn't accept anything."

"He had his weekend." David caught her eyes and
laughed. "From what he's charging me, he can afford it.
Let him pay. Or rather, be my guest, through him."

"He's going to take back my air fare, whether he
wants to or not."

The martini came, with another Scotch. "It's only
splitting," David said, lifting a glass.

"It isn't pleasant," Caroline said fiercely. She looked
at him, calming now, the sloe eyes steady, soft and still
intense with aftermaths of anger. "How was it with Clip
for you, David?"

"As you say, it isn't pleasant. I mean, my wife and
I—" What was he doing? She doesn't want to hear
about your *wife*. "My wife . . . I won't violate her privacy, but we share certain residues of affection."

"Then build on them."

This was different from times on Ocean Parkway.
This girl was lonely and upset, but defiant. Maybe we'll
make it tonight and maybe tomorrow and maybe you're

pleasant as hell, but I don't really need you. He squeezed her hand. "We can't build on them. It's too late."

She waited.

They were power politics, these beginnings. Caroline telephoned. After that he ruled. Now Caroline expressed independence. Power shifted. Caroline sat silent; she had gained command.

He could maneuver.

Oh, hell. He wanted to tell her.

"Joyce and I can't build because the bad feelings are stronger than the old affection. She drinks a little and that used to annoy me mildly. She fakes a little. If I comment on writing, she repeats what I say as though it were her own idea. *That* used to annoy me mildly. The small annoyances build on each other and feed each other and multiply each other until the relationship becomes one large annoyance. Besides, she's sloppy."

"That's a very nice protection of privacy." Caroline sat holding her glass and smiling.

She recognized the power shift. She had anticipated it. Women develop anticipation as a way of equalizing men's physical strength. People call such cultivation intuition.

"I meant I wasn't going to discuss her behavior in bed," David said.

"Well, that's only one area of privacy. Everybody goes to bed."

Anticipation and teasing. Together they gave women power beyond physical strength. Synergism, David thought. Metternich knew that. He must have studied the Viennese women before his Congress. Joy. Anticipating Freud.

As with Caroline's voice, boyishness touched her face. It was too long for classic beauty. The nose was thin and straight. The mouth, showing a moistener but not red lipstick, looked narrow. The chin thrust out in aggressive angularity. But the eyes burned darkly and when Caroline smiled, her lips widened toward voluptuousness. It would be extraordinary to force that Cotton Mather mouth into a halo of ecstasy.

"Did you go to bed in Bermuda?" David said.

"Of course I went to bed in Bermuda." Caroline held her head back. She was gazing at her glass. "We took showers together and Clip got ice from the refrigerator and tried to put the ice inside me and I screamed." It would be rousing to hear her composure vanish into squeals.

"But it was funny, David. It was all funny. It's all too funny. Can I have another drink? Please?" Shelley Ormont the gynecologist did know what he was talking about. (She was letting go; she could not seem to help herself.) "Let yourself sort of decompress," David said, "and take the next martini on the rocks."

They ate young lamb under a white wine sauce and Caroline Devon said she loved the food and pressed her left hip close to David. "Decent?" he said.

"What?"

"Was Zellbach decent about breaking?"

"I was afraid he might not be, so I insisted on meeting in a public place. I picked a pub called Chad's. Yes, he was decent. Until the end. Then he got unpleasant. He made a fist. I told him not to think he could go beating people up. I told him I was leaving to be with you."

"Did you say anything that prompted him to make a fist?" David sipped Chablis. A waiter leaned toward them. "It's all right," David said. "Waiters hear everything."

"I get angry. Not really. I get sharp. Clip kept telling me places we could go together. Theater. A coast in Spain. I said I wanted to see all of Europe. It would take time. He mentioned his wife. Or I did. He said his wife wasn't any of my business. He said I was acting like a hooker, bargaining for a better deal. He repeated that and then I said a silly thing. 'Fuck you, buster.' He made the fist."

"And you mentioned me?"

"You are my shining knight, but your name didn't save me. Suddenly, one of the girls I'm staying with walked into Chad's. She's really attractive. Clip looked at her. His eyes jumped up on stalks. He relaxed and unmade his fist and I ducked out."

"What was the other girl's name?" David said.

"Liz Wesley. Do you know her? She works for *Time.*"

"Ummm," David said. He had finished his lamb. I've talked about my wife, he thought. Don't start about other girls. Talk *to* her. Talk *at* her. "There's cold ruthlessness in Clip."

"I know. And belligerence. He said lawyers had to live by arguing. Even when he was tender I had a sense that love to him was war."

In Brooklyn, David thought. Mother and I warred at love. Not a lawyer, either of us. We talked at each other.

"I'll be frank," Caroline said. "It *was* upsetting. The relationship with Clip was upsetting, and sometimes exciting. Breaking the relationship was upsetting and even frightening. I didn't find much gentleness in Clip. Do you?"

This divorce, the threatening anger from Joyce, is love at war.

"But I don't look for it, in the way you would," David said, "and should. Today was mostly business. A divorce like mine is more psychology and luck than law. Clip made that clear. I've made mistakes dealing with Joyce. A lawyer can't correct them ex post facto. The best way to deal with a woman in divorce is to make her as happy as possible and let her feel that she's rejecting you. I've messed that up. She feels rejected. I don't fake things well."

"That's a *good* thing, not faking things at all."

"I can't really answer about gentleness in Clip, because we didn't talk about what's important, which is Joel."

"Who?"

"My son. He's almost fourteen and really a most remarkable boy."

"I didn't know you had a son."

"He can play the piano a bit. Bach's Two-Part Inventions. He rides the surf. He ice skates like a Hyperborean wind. I've been drinking. He's a beautiful boy, full of hope and fair and young, like you. My writing isn't what it's going to be. I saw a poem once by Ben Jonson."

"Boswell's shadow?"

"No. Ben. And he'd had a firstborn son, also called Ben, who died and he had done this poem: 'For his epitaph write, Here doth lie/Ben Jonson, his best piece of poetry.' "

"Pretty," Caroline said.

"Pretty? All the rage and disappointment, the bent dreams in those lines. It's more than pretty." In an old New England cemetery once he had walked with Joyce among the headstones of children. Jonathan Caleb, two years, six months. Rebecca Bartlett, one year, three days. Trampling softly on the graves. Josiah Bowen, five months, two days, taken up by the Lord on February 7, 1803. "I'd be upset," Joyce said, "except the children would be dead by now anyway." Foreshadowing, from the winter of 1803.

"I don't understand about *your* writing," Caroline said, "why it isn't what it's going to be."

"I'm facile," David said. "That always traps me. It's easy to turn out journalism or even to write a junky book. I've been working with the actor Rickie Conklin, who was always marrying beautiful women and always getting cuckolded. Notes toward a definition of self-destruction. A hell of a theme. But the actor didn't want to talk about self-destruction or think about self-destruction, and as soon as I showed up, out would come the martinis and he'd start making speeches about Christianity."

"I'm not a Christian myself," Caroline said. "My father was a deist, like Jefferson, he said. Mother made me go to church, but did you know at certain liberal Congregational churches you don't have to accept the divinity of Christ? Did you know that?"

No, David did not know that. But he did know—you had only to read *Ulysses*—about consubstantiality and the heresy of Arius and the edict of St. Ambrose and the great Christian schism, long and jagged as the schism between Jesus and God.

The Christians argued about the two eternally.

Their flesh, if it was flesh—was it the same?

Had Jesus existed in other form before the Incarnation?

Was Jesus part man, or a divine in a fleshly shell? (Corporeal punishment.)

If both Jesus and God were God, could either One be greater?

The Christians argued about such things in English and German and Latin. They grew angry and sometimes executed one another. *Bello Catolico*.

David believed in neither. Not Jesus. Not God. But he understood. He had a theory. The New England cemetery. Graves of children. Ben Jonson's piece of poetry. Christ the son. They were the same story sung over and over.

For Lycidas is dead, dead ere his prime

Strange his own offering should be a daughter. Strange and terrible. The boy Joel. They have such promise. Football games, music, tennis. World born again.

Renaissance painters sold Christianity as a mother story. Mama and child. Mama madonna. Italian dressing for gallery windows. The Christian story was about *father* and child. And the child was full of promise and the father failed the son.

. . . dead ere his prime

Joel.
They have such promise.
Must not fail.
Fun?
Caroline's voice was calling him back. "Fun. I mean, hearing all those Hollywood stories must have amused you."

"Rickie Conklin speaks in lines from a bad movie. 'I'm not ashamed to say I trust The Man Upstairs. I happen to think God is a pretty nice guy.' Or in quick, silly jabs. 'If more women out here had open hearts instead of open legs, this would be a damn sight better place.' That from Rickie Conklin, who'd fuck a statue if it had pubic hair. Does that offend you?"

Caroline met his eyes merrily. "Only if the statue were male."

"Well, I've let myself get trapped into books like *Rickie* and a standard of living rises and you get typed and you keep doing what you have been doing. It's a double waste. First, the book I'm finishing on Conklin won't be much good. Second, there's the book I might have been writing all this time. That might have been all right, but it doesn't exist."

Forget power play. Let her see him. He liked her, when he took the time to listen to her and to look. "You must feel you walked into a windmill," David said.

"It's all right," Caroline said. "I want to hear."

"I've read maybe too much," David said, "and I read

better than I write. Now do I dare to go all out? Do I want to lay everything all out there, and to hell with readers and to hell with critics and most of all to hell with whether it sells? Maybe I dare. Maybe I don't. Then I read some of my own serious sentences and I think of Hardy or Dostoyevsky and say what the hell am I doing in their racket? Or Shakespeare, arrogant, spaniel-eyed son of a bitch, throwing two dozen images around when five would do, but the images are so glorious, you want to cry. When I write a book with Rickie Conklin, I'm cheating. I'm not competing with the real writers because I can always say the book was as good as any ghosted Rickie Conklin book could be. I don't expose myself. I may not fake well, but I'm willing to cheat."

"Or you're afraid not to cheat," Caroline said. She placed a hand on his thigh and pressed her fingers into him. Her hands were powerful. She looked up, as though expecting to be kissed.

"Writing a real book," David said, staring at an empty brandy snifter, "is a fanatic act. Who will read it? Who'll care? You sit alone in a room, armed with fanaticism— that your view of something, aspects of self-destruction, is new and powerful and pure as flame. You have to have a fanatical drive to impose your view on others. But is it that—fanaticism, or is it nihilism? Writing a real book." He laughed coldly to himself and winced at the mocking sound. "Adolf Hitler wrote a real book."

"Why can't you be happy with journalism?" Caroline continued to press his thigh.

"Because I am touched with fanaticism. Because when I was fourteen and I read a Keats sonnet, I wanted to do that. I wanted to make that sound." David sighed and shrugged and leaned toward Caroline's ear. "Because," he said, "a real book lives. Because," he said, "I don't want to die."

As they were leaving, M. Guy detained him near the

bar. "Nice," he said, "but how can I put it? The brunette from last week was a bit more womanly."

"Thanks for the corner table," David said.

Caroline strode about the apartment and David watched her stride and felt intense delight. Through the long black dress he could make out a line of bikini underpants. Was that sexy or was it obvious? Was the sexiness of underpants consubstantial with flesh?

"The walls," Caroline said. "Did you pick the color of peach?"

"It was here."

"That painting," Caroline said. She indicated the black and brown and mauve butte with a mustache. "It should go."

"Anything else?"

"Where's the kitchen?"

David rose from an ivory French provincial sofa that crouched against the wall beneath the painting. He walked toward a white cabinet and opened two doors. A small electric stove and a square refrigerator squatted beside each other.

"Where's the kitchen?" Caroline said again.

"I don't cook."

Caroline knelt, hoisting the long black skirt to her knees. She opened the refrigerator, exposing six bottles of club soda, a jar of Ritter's tomato juice and a jar of Elam's natural peanut butter, with defatted wheat germ oil added.

"When I was first married," David said, "my mother-in-law came to look at the one-room apartment we had. She poked into all the closets and my wife wanted me to throw her out. Her own mother. That's what comes of poking about."

"Well, if you expect me to stay here, David"—Caroline's eyes shot out playful flecks—"I have to know where I am."

"Diagonally across the street from Carnegie Hall," David said.

Caroline was smiling to herself.

"Do you want to stay here, Callie?" David said.

"Yes."

"Do you want to go to bed with me?"

"Yes."

"Then you have to ask me."

She blinked in surprise and held her smile. Power. Had he overplayed? At length, she laughed a little singing laugh. "Will you go to bed with me, David?"

"Yes, I will, Caroline."

They stood in the middle of the square living room. He put his hands on her shoulders and pointed her toward the bedroom. "We'll make the beast with two backs," David said.

"What?"

"Nothing. Something from the spaniel-eyed son of a bitch. Let me undress you."

The long gown zipped down the back. Caroline let it fall to her feet. She shrugged out of her half slip and stood in a black bra and black underpants. A line of brown down from the underpants to the navel.

"I thought black underwear went out with the fifties," David said.

Caroline giggled. "When I went to college, my clothes were so country that my roommate said she thought I'd be wearing an undershirt instead of a bra."

"No. That's a bra, all right. And a nice bra."

He moved forward. They stood beside the brass bed. He unhooked the brassiere and lifted it and began to kiss her nipples. She shuddered and he could feel her shudder.

"Shouldn't we lie down?" David said.

"I believe that's customary."

He stripped off his own clothes. She lay on her stom-

ach, still wearing black underpants. The reading lamp
was bright. White fuzz showed at the small of her back.

"I want to write something real," David said. "Something good." He sat naked on the bed. "I want to very
much. In fact, I would want to for you."

"You don't know me," Caroline said. Her head was
cradled on her arms. Her back was straight and very
long.

"I do," he said. "Writers see things more sharply.
Dante wrote for a woman he had glanced at, never met."

"I try to be more practical than that."

"Practically," David said, "what do you do?"

"I paint. I work with watercolors. Sometimes gorges
and moraines. Usually houses and fields and harvest
skies."

"That's practical," David said.

"It is for Andrew Wyeth."

"Well, maybe you and I can help each other," David
said.

"Is that a proposal?"

The long waist. The mix of boyishness and woman.
The muted manner, volatile with sex. Or did he only
imagine that, the sexuality? How lonely he was here.
How fucking lonely. "Yes, I suppose it is. I want you,
Caroline, and I want you to promise to marry me." An
instant engagement.

Writers see things more sharply. He had said that.
Now, damn it, act. "We think alike. I know we do."
Taking a chance? He was betting a maiden in the Bel-
mont Stakes. But risk. You've got to fucking risk. On
writer's sight. On life. "The sex will be marvelous. Nothing is more important than marvelous sex. We'll mix
your country with my city." (A writer's ultra-sight.
He'd chanced it now. But who had said he was a
writer?) "Christ. Promise to marry me before I take
you."

"Or I take you."

"I'll write some decent things."

"I understand," Caroline said, "that writers have a weakness as lovers."

"No," David said. "Oh no. I'm very hard."

He slipped his left hand onto her buttock. Her pelvis bounced. "Writers," Caroline said, "sit on the side of the bed talking about sex until everything sexual dries up."

He turned her roughly and pulled off her underpants. The pubic hair, thin on the mound, grew thick between her legs. "Yes, David," she cried, as he entered her. "Drive into me. Kiss my breasts, David. Marry me, David. Fuck me hard."

He rode waves, billowing beneath him. They leaped and broke, waves that were bright and foam-flecked, like Caroline's drawn lips. They rocked him from side to side and bore him up and drove him downward, making him cry out. His back arched. He saw the grimace of her mouth. "Oh my God," he said in fright. He rode the waves.

A sudden calm. Riding the hips, hair against hair, part of him fluttered away. All my manhood is throbbing, he thought, and the part that flew free cawed laughter.

Her wince of ecstasy. Sweat beading her upper lip. Her tossing head. He trembled. The disembodied part of him observed. It had risen high above the bed, fluttering with the wings of a tern. It hovered and spoke, in a voice that was his, but higher and harsher: "Copulating rabbits. Animals fuck."

Her eyes were closed. Her face went rigid. A wave crashed into his loins. He moaned. He heard again the cawing laughter.

"Aiiee." Caroline was shrieking in her spasm. "Aiiee. Aaaugh." Then softer, "Ooow."

She lay under him sobbing. "Husband," Caroline said in tears.

"My honey," David said, dry-eyed. He shook. He
sex existed. "My honey," he said, and touched her cunt
could not stop shaking. He had not known such violent
and heard her shout again.

It startled him, both the man who shook with passion
and the winged passionless observer, how much her love
cry sounded like a scream of pain.

III

He had not enjoyed his mother, nor she him. Dorothy
Priest, a lean, slim-hipped woman with dark, angry
eyes, taught psychology at Brooklyn College and maintained a small practice at premium rates. She specialized
in marriage counseling. Dorothy Priest liked to control
situations, and the rambling clapboard house in Flatbush where David grew up was more her home than her
husband's.

Outside, maples and sycamores spread among drive-
ways on a block of other clapboard houses owned by
accountants and lawyers and a junior high school prin-
cipal. Children played city games in the street. Sometimes they knelt on the crown of the road and rolled
marbles toward a cigar box at the curb. They had cut
arched openings in the cigar box and the idea was to
slip a marble through an opening. Or they put a penny
on a crack in the sidewalk, stepped back three paces
and bounced a tennis ball at the coin. With the right
throw, the penny flipped, head to tail. They chalked
a triangle on the asphalt, drew in home plate and two
bases. Someone pitched underhand and the batter hit
the ball with an open palm.

Other games grew raucous. They played touch football and David's friend Shelley Goldberg threw arching
forward passes with great precision. David was swift
and sure-handed, and he and Shelley spent hours devis-
ing pass patterns.

"Go out," Shelley said. "Go out four steps and turn around and make a lot of noise and stamp your foot. The other guy will come up and cover you. Then go out longer and I'll hit you in the hands."

"I got a better one," David said. "I go out on the right for three steps and I cut. I hit a car fender, there'll always be a car fender, and I holler for the ball. You pump and then I spin and I go deep and take the ball over my right shoulder."

"That's something," Shelley said, "if we can swing it."

"We can swing it," David said. "We need to give that play a name."

"It's your idea," Shelley said. "We'll call it the shit play." He was a heavy-shouldered boy with porky jowls.

"I don't know about that," David said, "but we can compromise. We'll call it the S play in the huddle."

The S play always worked. David would spring and cut, sneakers squeaking on the asphalt. He felt easy with the strength of his legs. Slam a palm against a fender and shout, "Here go, Shell." The pattern seemed final. Defenders hurried to where they thought the play would end. Then David fled between them, sometimes shouting in exultation as he gathered Shelley's pass in his sure hands.

When David was thirteen, they organized a game against a team from another neighborhood. Athletic Jews confronting a rugged mix of Irish and Italian boys. The blocking went hard. Shouts rang through the street. Near the end, losing by a touchdown, Shelley called for the S play. David cut. Somebody bumped him. He hit the fender and spun, bawling, "Here go." Now he would have to run between two bigger defenders.

He sprinted and faked to his left, fooling one man. He ran around the other and looked up. He had broken his pattern. The ball hung in the air, far to his right.

David cut again and caught the ball and scored the tying touchdown. It was the best catch he would ever make in football. Whoops sounded. A police car appeared. "Break it up, boys," said a sergeant.

"Big game," David said, panting. "We only need about two minutes more."

"I said break it up. There's a doctor on this block. The noise is getting her upset."

David wore an old green shirt. The top of one sneaker was torn. "There's no doctor on this street," he said. "There's a psychologist. She's my mother. She wouldn't want to bust up our game."

"Don't smart-ass me," the policeman said. "There's a Dr. Priest. She called. Break it up now, smart ass, or I run you in."

"I guess we have to change the name of your play now," Shelley Goldberg said afterward, as they sat on the sidewalk. "SA, for smart ass."

"That's funny, Shel. Really funny. I'm not a smart ass."

"I didn't mean you were," Goldberg said. "I meant the smart ass was your mother."

David's father, a stocky, thick-chested man, with a tan, bushy mustache, practiced labor law and grew tomatoes in the backyard and agonized about a condition called cardiac neurosis. Legions of physicians, Dorothy's friends, assured Arthur Priest that there was nothing functionally wrong with his heart, but Arthur, who was given to silences and watching baseball games and considering the implausible glory of Thomas Hardy's novels, continued privately to agonize.

David could not understand his mother's dislike for him, and he tried to explore it with his father. They were working in the yard behind the clapboard house, planting dark-leaved pachysandra.

"Well," his father said, "your mother is a strong, even commanding woman. You hardly ever see her cry."

"I've never seen Mom cry," David said.

"I have," Arthur said. He was weeding on his knees, wearing baggy blue slacks and a blue-gray sweater. "Everybody cries. You know that, don't you?"

"You don't cry," David said.

"Everybody cries," Arthur said, straightening. "'Without the meed of some melodious tear.' Do you recognize the line? John Milton in 'Lycidas.'"

"What's meed?"

"A recompense. A prize."

"How do you get to know all that?" David said.

"You read," Arthur said. "You read and read. *Lacrimae rerum.*"

"Latin," David said. "The tears of things."

The father's gray eyes brightened. "Tears can be pain," he said, "or simple sniveling or utmost sorrow. Sometimes tears are a ceremony of love."

"A ceremony of tears," David said, in a shaky voice.

"That's close enough," his father said.

The garden, forty feet by twenty feet, was bounded by a wood fence painted white. At the border, Arthur had planted lilacs that would not bloom.

"But it's difficult for your mother to release. Function of being a psychologist, or becoming a psychologist, is a function of inability to release. Do you understand what I'm talking about?"

"Not exactly."

"No matter. Maybe there'll be time." Arthur Priest's hand moved under his sweater, toward the left side of his chest. "Your mother is a wonderful hostess—you've seen the parties—and a brilliant woman, not unable to release, since pain makes anybody cry, but unwilling to release. Uncomfortable. Do you know what I'm talking about now?"

"No, sir."

"And you don't know what happens when a woman has a baby. But first they shave the pubic hair. That's supposed to prevent infection, but it's mostly ritual, I suspect. You're shaving now. You use water and lather to soften your beard, such as it is. Your mother was shaved by a nurse who was too busy to use water and lather. She simply took a razor and shaved. When they let me back into the room, your mother was crying."

"Mom crying?"

"Then a woman gets an enema. The nurse was busy, and Leo Levine, our friend, our party guest, gave her the enema."

David blinked and lifted a pachysandra from a carton marked sphagnum and planted it into a troweled hole.

"You were seventeen hours proceeding from uterus to light. Your mother insists that Jonah, emerging from the whale, is a symbolic childbirth. But the whale didn't scream. I was down the hall. I heard your mother." Arthur Priest massaged his chest. "God knows whether I should be telling you this here and now, but later you may remember echoes."

David felt a clutch of love.

"Daddy?"

"Yes?"

"Am I making the trowel holes deep enough?"

"Fine." Arthur Priest bent back to hands and knees. "I heard her after fifteen hours," the father said, finally. "She was crying, screaming, begging to make the hurting stop. It's a matter of pride with your mother not to call other professionals by title, but now she was crying to Leo, our friend Leo, 'Doctor, doctor, help me, please.' Then she made the most horrible howl I've ever heard."

"That's how babies get born?" David blinked at the ground.

Arthur Priest took his hand from his chest. He stood up and walked toward his son and punched David gently on the upper arm. "That's how you got born. That's why you don't have brothers or sisters." The father smiled faintly. "That's why we're kings alone." His eyes looked sad. "You understand. King Arthur and King David. How does our garden grow? But wait a bit. I'll get the Buick. There's a nursery out in Queens with a new fertilizer that supposedly could turn Sinai into Eden. Maybe we can make the lilacs flower yet."

David was sixteen and beginning to idolize his father. He loved the ranging mind, the calm acceptance of the world, the careful, complex answers to David's questions.

Love is a riddle, he thought, and a kind of silence and an answered question.

He wanted to ask more about Mother, but they had talked as deeply as they would that Saturday.

On Tuesday Arthur Priest submitted to a physical examination. As Dr. Leo Levine said afterward, "I turned away from the table and I heard a funny sound, and when I turned back, your father was dead."

"You said cardiac neurosis wasn't serious," Dorothy said in a hard, merciless voice. Accuse. There was no one to accuse. Accuse the doctor.

"We don't know about such things with complete certainty."

Death was the complete certainty. Death had just made last Saturday forever. His father was dead. Dead as Jude, David thought, and just as unfortunate with women. (Arthur Priest might not have agreed.)

Dorothy Priest immediately began rituals of sanctification. Her voice, normally a soft, assured contralto, changed when friends telephoned. "Yes," she would say in a tentative boyish soprano. "How the gods must have loved Arthur!"

"No," she would say. "I won't marry again. How could I find anyone ever to replace Arthur? He was a saint."

Overhearing, David winced. The martyr's tone, he thought. Sad but too courageous to be devastated. She is playing a role for friends, for the world, for herself. Outsiders believe it. Mother is a splendid actress. I see it best.

Mater martyr.

She stops smiling on cue and looks sorrowful. Cue the tragic widow. Got the glycerin tears? Okay. Now say Arthur.

Mama mummer.

"Mom," he said one night as they dined at the long antique pine table, covered with an ivory cloth. "Couldn't you be a little more cheerful with your friends?"

"What do you mean?" Dorothy Priest had a long, thin face. The chin thrust out in aggressive angularity. But her black hair, showing streaks of gray, glistened softly.

"You know. I mean, be sort of happier?"

"No. I don't know what you mean." Her black eyes simmered.

"Well, I miss Dad too, but we're still alive."

Dorothy made a small cry and placed a long hand to her face. "Oh," she cried again in the boyish voice. "Oh. To hear that from my own son and his." She sat upright. The dining room was dimly lighted. She shook her head and as she spoke, she was once more contralto. "I shouldn't be surprised. You've always been a self-centered child, even from the beginning."

What he had been was a child, simply that and nothing more and nothing less. Alternately, Dorothy insisted on making him something more or something less. She taught him lines from Shelley:

> Oh, lift me as a bird, a leaf, a cloud!
> I fall upon the thorns of life! I bleed!

At four, David was instructed to mount a wooden chair and say Shelley's poetry. Dorothy presided, listening to her son, surveying the reactions of guests. David recognized early that he was in part a doll, to be wound and displayed at certain intervals. See the doll move. Hear it speak. This is my doll. Envy me my Percy Bysshe doll. Isn't my doll better than yours?

He was also a knifing intrusion. As he had torn her body being born, so his existence cut the pattern of her life. Classes Monday, Wednesday and Friday. Patients on Tuesday and Thursday. Ten hours of sleep a night. The diffuse demands of David's childhood irritated his mother.

"There's nothing to do."

"If you had real imagination, you'd be occupied."

"I can't cut this liver."

"You're seven. A seven-year-old child should cut his own food. Why, when I was seven . . ."

Her songs of herself grew into epics. Why, when she was seven she cleaned the stables of Augeus, conquered Troy, founded Rome, threw Lucifer out of heaven, and then sat down to breakfast. Childhood in older days was more challenging.

"Can I have fifty cents? For a movie? Shelley Goldberg's mother says it's all right to go to a neighborhood movie by yourself when you're twelve."

"That's a difference between Mrs. Goldberg and myself. I think in higher terms than all right. You have collateral reading due. You haven't been living within your allowance. I'd like you to finish *The Last Days of Pompeii.*"

"It's boring."

"Only to a boring mind, a bore. You aren't that. You can be ahead of the pack and I want you to be ahead of the pack, but you won't stay there wasting Saturday afternoons at the movies."

"Do I get the fifty cents?"

"After you read, we'll see."

"We'll see" meant no. It always meant no. He disliked artifice. Disliking artifice and, perhaps, his mother, he finished *The Last Days of Pompeii*.

After Arthur died, Dorothy reserved four nights a week for dinners with David. A succession of housekeepers served the meals—Dorothy Priest would not cook—on white Rosenthal china banded with gold. Impressionists hung on one wall of the dining room. A square, smoky mirror hung on another. From his chair, David could see the backyard, where he had worked with his father.

"I would hope you would go into psychology," Dorothy said, over lamb chops that a maid called Ethel had undercooked.

"I sort of want to write."

"Write?"

"You know. Like Thomas Wolfe or Hemingway."

"Yes. I know Thomas Wolfe and Hemingway. Oh, my dear. You aren't shy about the company you intend to keep."

"I don't mean I'll be that good. I want to try."

"I lecture on the psychology of literature and, David, those men were geniuses. I love you very much, as you know, and you are ahead of the pack, but I've never deluded myself for an instant that you might be a genius."

"Poetry," David said, looking beyond his mother toward the empty yard. "I'd like to write that."

"But, my dear, my dear, where is the spark? And how will you make a living? I don't have a business to leave you."

"I'll be all right. I got ninety-five in English all last year."

"You cannot be a poet or a novelist," Dorothy said. She was wearing a dark-red dress with a V neck. "With your talents, and I don't deny you have some, you could become a journalist. But do you know what journalism is? A field for people who can't decide what they want to do."

"I've decided I'm going to try to write," David said.

"You'll tear yourself apart," Dorothy said. "You'll try to reach goals that are beyond you and you won't approach them and you'll destroy yourself, or at least your chance to be content."

"I know how to be happy," David said.

"Nobody is happy," Dorothy said. "A few people are lucky enough to be content." She looked at him with noncommittal kindness. "We all imagine objectives. Do you think I dreamed of sitting in my office and facing glaring couples hour upon hour?"

"I wondered what you did in that office," David said.

"Today I told an accountant that he was hostile toward his son, a hyperkinetic. I mean a very high-strung child. That hostility motivated the accountant's wife, who neglects to shave her legs, to have an affair with a married carpenter, whom she has made into a father image. The affair punishes both her husband and her actual father, a puritan, who rejected his daughter by dying. She is now rejecting the husband and the father and the father's puritanism. Perhaps I can straighten things out. I can show these people a path. But they need the will and the strength and the intelligence to follow directions.

"It's honorable work, David; still the people are dreary. Most of my patients and most of my patients' problems are drab. I am bound to help them, but do you think that's what I wanted, helping drab people? Or do you think I had grander dreams?"

"Grander dreams," David said.

"I wanted to write psychological biographies," Dorothy said. "Lord Byron was waiting. But you were born. Things happened. I had to compromise."

"I was trying to explain about myself," David said. "I *am* going to try to write."

"You make me wish I had a business to leave you," Dorothy said, "even despising business as I do."

When she died, five years later, after a fall on cement steps in front of the clapboard house, Dorothy Priest left her entire estate, $165,000 and the house, to her sister, Sylvia, the wife of a surgeon who lived in Cleveland and with whom Dorothy had not gotten along.

David's grief was dry-eyed. He had shared moments with his mother and father. Common memories had made an earthly trinity.

His father died.

His mother died.

When he died himself it would be as if those moments had not existed. Indeed they would not, unless he made them live. He ached to write. He began to think about fathering a child.

IV

David moved into a three-room ground-floor apartment near the old house. Plumbing pipes in the living room were hidden by a false plywood cabinet stained birch. He had graduated from Columbia and found work as a reporter at the New York *Journal-American*. The fascist *Journal-American*, he came to say. Young reporters enjoyed pejorative descriptions of the newspapers that employed them. The *Herald Tribune* was the Yale Alumni News. The New York *Post* was the Downtown Daily Worker. The *New York Times* was the Insurance Company on Forty-third Street. And the *Journal* was the fascist *Journal-American*.

He had become a journalist, fulfilling Dorothy's prediction, and he wanted to be more than a journalist, also fulfilling Dorothy's prediction. After a year of general assignments, David won the City Hall beat. He liked the reigning mayor of New York, an elegant, ice-eyed Irishman named Richard Dumferling Lyons; or perhaps he liked the idea that the mayor of New York City called him by name. He relished the company of press room men, who patronized him for his youth and admired him for his ability to write forcefully.

"Kid," said wattled Morris Dressner of the *New York Times,* "why are you scowling at the fucking machine?"

"Thinking," David said, staring at his Smith-Corona. "Want to get it right."

"Think all you want, kid," Morris Dressner said, "and you're pretty damn good. But remember this. However right you get things, it ain't the *Iliad.*"

"I just want to get it right."

"Right or wrong, it still ends up lining a garbage pail," Morris Dressner said.

"But if he gets it right," said bland, bald Bert Gimbel of the *Post,* "that garbage pail may be standing in the kitchen of a professor of English."

"You're right," Morris Dressner said. "I forgot our friend is a college man. He aspires to reach the highest type of garbage pail."

"Pulitzer pail," David said. "Shut up, so I can finish."

The transience of the stories he wrote did indeed bother him, but he enjoyed the work and he was pleased to see his name in the paper. Besides serious writing— what his *mother* would have called Serious Writing— was a challenge. Put off. A dream deferred. He would face that later, when he was more practiced. Langston Hughes, the poet, spent years as a journalist.

"You ought to get out of this, kid," wattled Morris Dressner said. "Try to be a real writer, like that guy J. P. Marquand. He makes a bundle."

"I'll dedicate my first novel to you, Morris," David said. "I'll call it 'Up from Garbage.' "

"Fuck you," said Morris Dressner of the *New York Times*.

"Wit," bland Bert Gimbel said. "I'll bet you didn't hear wit like Dressner's at the university."

Joyce Rhoda Steindler appeared one day in the sweltering, littered city room of the *Journal-American*. She was delivering a story on a student movement at the Brooklyn College campus. A group demanded that black candidates for admission have an automatic five-point bonus added to their high school average. In the story, Joyce explained:

> The adjustment, advocates pointed out, would afford meaningful equality to a group that historically has been deprived and, more than that, cruelly deculturized.

An assistant city editor assaulted the story. "It's too long," he said, "and you use too many adverbs and goddamn adjectives, and besides, this movement is bullshit. Special bonuses for blacks! Did the Irish get that, or the Jews? You want to be a stringer all your life, or you want to learn how to be a reporter? Put the adjectives in the can. Point out that the demand is unprecedented and mostly bullshit. Use simpler English. Maybe we can make some space."

Joyce sat at the desk next to David's, blinking at tears. She had a pug nose. Her face was somewhat too square, under dark bobbed hair, but her mouth was full as a peony and her eyes, green-gray like the eyes of David's father, looked soft and bright.

"Forget it," David said.

"Beg pardon?"

"The fascists who run this place don't want to hear about Negroes, unless the Negroes are named Louis Armstrong or Jackie Robinson, or Rastus. As in all the Rastus jokes."

"I don't really say the campus thing is a good movement or a bad movement," Joyce insisted. "I just report it, without comment. Isn't that what you're supposed to do?"

"Just reporting something gives it a kind of endorsement," David said. "Not that this is a great newspaper, but for everything we print, there are ten items that we skip."

"I can see the press releases in the wastebaskets," Joyce said.

"Then can you see the point? It isn't first a question of whether you have a good movement or a bad movement. First, do you have an important movement? Newsworthy. By printing your story, this not-so-great newspaper says yes, the movement is newsworthy. Okay, that's one. Two, you have a hell of an issue here. You can argue that persecuted blacks should get relief. You can argue that the sanctity of education should be preserved."

"Attacking the adjectives," Joyce said. Her eyes were dry now. "Homer was an adjectival writer. He didn't just write 'Hector.' He wrote 'brazen-helmeted Hector.' "

"Forget it," David repeated. "The classics aren't relevant. However right you get it for the New York *Journal-American,* your story ain't the *Iliad.*"

Joyce grinned. Her teeth were prominent. David thought of the teeth against his neck. "Usually," he said, "the girls I go out with don't know how Homer wrote. Their friends may, but I never seem to go out with the friends. You sound like somebody else's girl. I'd like to go out with you. Somebody else's friend."

"I'm Homer's friend," Joyce Steindler said.

They met that Saturday at two for bicycling to Coney Island and maybe swimming and surely a ride on the Cyclone, wildest of roller coasters, and surely, doubly surely, they would sit in the front car. Joyce lived in a small flat near Ocean Parkway.

"Mr. Priest," said the mother, whose name was Sonia. "It's a great pleasure to meet you. After I graduated from Samuel J. Tilden High School, I thought of becoming a journalist myself. But Sol, my husband, wanted children and a woman after all has obligations to a man." Sonia Steindler who wore a flowered housecoat, was a short, stumpy, pastel woman. "My husband, Sol, would love to meet you, but he's working."

"On the weekend?"

"He has a very special kind of job."

"Oh, Mother," Joyce said. "Daddy's a wonderful man, but how can you say his job is special? He's a waiter at a Childs restaurant."

"Non-singing?" David said.

"Non-singing," Joyce said.

"But he works only a walk from Carnegie Hall," the mother said. "That's the most cultural Child's restaurant there is."

The flat consisted of a foyer, a square living room lumped with overstuffed pieces and two small bedrooms beyond. Joyce had to share a bedroom with two younger brothers, who were wrestling behind a door. David heard shouts. The door sprang open. "He twisted my ear," yelled Larry Steindler.

"He bit my leg," Stevie Steindler shouted.

High flush burned on their faces. Their shoulders hunched. Were they asthmatic?

"Boys," cried Sonia Steindler. "We have a visitor." Her accent seemed oddly British. Visa-tour. Brooklyn Cantabridgian. "Say hello to Mr. Priest."

"No," Larry said. "Steve picked his nose."

"He picked his nose too," Steve said, "and wiped the snot on my shirt."

"Boys, boys," Sonia said. "I was a great reader, Mr.

Priest. William Shakespeare. The Complete Works. Thomas Babington Macaulay."

"Snot-shirt. Snot-shirt."

"Let's get out of here." Joyce tugged David's wrist.

They rode bicycles past benches where withered men and women sat curled on their canes. Joyce wore plaid Bermuda shorts and a patterned blouse. "With the trees and the mall," she said, "I think of Ocean Parkway as the Champs Élysées of Brooklyn." She cycled briskly.

David rode two lengths behind Joyce so that he could watch her buttocks as she pedaled. They were flat but full. Her legs were long, thick at the ankle, and straight. He wondered about her breasts and pedaled hard and passed her and looked back. Nobs showed under the embroidered blouse. Small nobs. Doorways.

After a while, when they had settled into cycling side by side, Joyce said, "Do you like music?"

"Songs," David said. "The shore was kissed. The evening mist. A silly thing about blue rain falling down on my window pane."

"I mean *music*," Joyce said. The peony mouth puckered. "Tchaikovsky."

"I like Brahms a lot. My father played Brahms for me. Chamber music. The clarinet quintet and Opus Eight and the B flat trio. My mother said Brahms was diffuse; he opens the heavens and then marches directly into chaos. My father said that Brahms was yearning, but he only said that to me. I never heard him disagree with my mother."

"I'd love to meet your father," Joyce said.

"No you wouldn't. First, like him, you'd have to die."

She slowed her pedaling and made a gentle, toothy smile. "I'm sorry."

"So am I."

Benches beside them. Wraiths curled on canes. Withered remnants. Gabardine salesmen. But alive.

Not my father.

Brahms. Even the beard gone. But still the scores. Brahms's yearning still. Part of him is alive.

Not my father.

My father's yearning.

Vanished.

Except.

Myself.

"We ought to swim." They had reached the end of Ocean Parkway and come to Brighton Beach. Brick houses squatted in rows along streets named Neptune and Surf.

"I can't swim well," Joyce said.

"It's not a contest," David said. "I'm not Weismuller myself."

"I would have made a good heroine for *An American Tragedy*."

Vulnerability. Everyman's undoing. David was vulnerable to pleasing girls who made with ease an easy literary allusion. Later his vulnerability pattern widened and changed its shape.

Callipygian buttocks.

Wasp waist.

Waist of a wasp.

Ash-blond tuft. Rare. Rare even under a wasp waist. Rarer than a strong and arching elm.

"I like that, Joyce, the way you make literary allusions naturally."

"Oh, I must remind you of somebody. Your mother."

"But my mother swam beautifully," David said. "She was tall and when we visited friends with a pool, she'd dive and let her long hair drift behind her. She seemed to kick without effort. She was good at the appearances of things. People sat and watched her hair streaming in the water, her black-bright hair streaming long."

"I'd like to have met her too."

"You would not have. She devoured innocents like an alligator."

"That's right," Joyce said. "She's as dead as my father. Oh, but you're so young."

Someone had folded mother's streaming black-bright hair beneath her in the coffin. Beneath the occipital skull. Crack there half an inch wide. But the bruise burst forward near the left eye. Oddity of blood flow after death.

"Forget it," David said. "You've read *The Stranger?*" They promised subtle makeup to cover all. No bruise would show. No visible swelling. She will appear, sir, most beautiful and tranquil. David ordered the coffin closed. The embalming cosmetician looked bereaved.

Mother died today. Or maybe yesterday; I can't be sure.

"What is," David said, "is, and it doesn't matter why."

"I'm majoring in psychology," Joyce said, "and existentialism seems superficial."

"Acts," David said. "We live by acts. The Book of Acts. Hamlet enters, flourishes, exits. Acts One through Five. Did Harry Truman's motive matter to the poet Saito, who was incinerated at a writing table on a cloudy day in Nagasaki?"

Joyce shrugged.

"I've played this argument before. With my mother. I'm not arguing so much as chomping. Mother also *argued* in an alligator way. She could devour objectors whole."

Joyce reddened. "Your mother was Professor Priest," she said in surprise. "Professor Priest was a marvelous teacher. I studied the psychology of lit with her."

"I lived it," David said. "It was fifteen years before I found the courage to make a dissent. I played with alliteration. I said my mother was the Alligator Arguer. My secret motto was Fuck Freud. If that bothers you, change the mental spelling. Phuck Phreud. Come on; let's rent bathing suits and go for a wade."

Joyce chose a knit red suit and they trudged across hot sand on a blazing, crystal, public beach. Close to the water, they sprawled, bellies down. David placed his right hand on Joyce's neck.

"I'm not a cat."

"I like to touch."

"Let's talk."

"I'm twenty-three and a very successful journalist and I work like a son of a bitch and I don't have any money."

"Why do you curse?"

"I can't tell you in twenty-five words or less. Besides, you don't want to know."

"I do want to know."

"It's complicated and it could be boring. Fucking boring."

"Then bore me." Joyce laughed. "I didn't say screw me; I said bore me."

He laughed at her laughter. She was opening up. "I curse out of a confusion of motives," David said. "To make you nervous. A girl in a bathing suit on a first date makes me nervous. Seeing, say, eighty-seven percent of your body now discomforts me. I don't like being discomforted. Using rough English is a fucking equalizer. I mean, I don't like being nervous alone.

"My father never cursed. Impossibly dignified but never stuffy. The father of my memory. Mother disdained cursing; she said profanity was a mixture of aggression and failure of vocabulary. That's pat," David said. "Pat and patent, but partly true. I distrust Freud, but I don't proscribe him. In the end you marry someone who looks like your mother, which is significant, or you marry someone who does not look like your mother, which is significant.

"Maybe cursing is a dialogue with my dead parents. Maybe it's the pain cry of a twenty-three-year-old orphan. But I don't really know, and analysts don't really know. They have key words. Priests have cassocks and doctors wear white and analysts use key words. The analysts charge for words, like writers. They should be socialized."

The hot sand ground deliciously under his belly. "The great phrase," he said, "the ineluctable meaning . . ." Joyce looked rapt. David paused as if reaching for a polemic. "The great phrase is bullshit," he said.

"Profanity doesn't make *me* nervous," Joyce said.

David shook his head, surprised at his own intensity.

"It's just curious," Joyce said, "for someone who works well with words to curse so much. And that's not Freudian or bullshit and you don't have to prove your virility by cursing in front of me."

"Points," David said. "Two points."

"What's that?"

"Basketball. Your boobs."

Joyce twisted gracefully and sat up, but she reddened. Her breasts were flattish. She knew; they knew their brows, hips, their breasts, their clits. Could make you want to be a doctor. Undressing them all. Not the clothes alone, but the pretensions.

"I started to ask before," Joyce said, somewhat primly, "why don't we talk about what *you* want to do?"

"I'm doing what I want to do." His mother, the Alligator Arguer, had called journalism a field for people who couldn't decide what to do. But she was no journalist. Couldn't write well enough, in truth. Why bicker with her still? Enough death. Enough memory. Enough Mama.

"I'm doing what I want for the time being," David said. "Then I'll move on. That's the way, isn't it, even

if you never travel. I want to be a father. I ache to have
a child. But not yet; it isn't time. The City Hall stuff I
write—"

"Is good . . ."

"Thanks, but it's postgraduate stuff. Joyce, don't get
upset, but that deskman who reprimanded you made
sense. Do watch adverbs and adjectives. Use specific
descriptive words. To a writer, a brown sweater stained
with green ink is better than a clean sweater. Strong
nouns and active verbs. Forget 'to be.' 'Let be be the
finale of seem.' "

Joyce smiled a gleam of teeth. "Wallace Stevens."

"Terrific," David said. "And watch the Freud. Mother said that at forty-five he went chaste, saying he had
no more time for copulation." He thought, the great
man became a Jewish monk. The envied penis drooped.
A languid flower, appended to Freud-in-Bloom.

"Liszt entered a monastery before he was forty-five,"
Joyce said.

"But first he fucked the aristocracy of Europe."
David thought, the pianist had it all laid out. Good man,
bad seed. Else why would his daughter have welcomed
Adolf Hitler to Bayreuth?

A tanned, handsome couple lay on a blanket five
feet away. Their radio made a clamorous sound. "Bill
Haley and The Comets sing 'Rock Around the Clock,' "
an announcer shouted.

"I'm going into the water," David said. He reached
toward Joyce's back and patted her buttock. "You stay.
You don't have to prove femininity by being one with
this gentle, dirty sea."

He swam far out. She stood against mild waves. It
thrilled him to break beyond the tentative bathers,
crouching, tense, although the sea was mild. At length a
lifeguard whistled. Damn. Joyce was a pleasing young
lady. He wanted to swim so far that he impressed her.
So far even that he felt fear.

Flapping near shore, she seemed embarrassed. Her look brightened as he rode in on a grainy wave. "I'm just not good at this," Joyce said. "Not good at all. But I'll get you at tennis."

"I hit the ball pretty hard," David said.

"I have a drop shot."

"Why are we talking tennis in the ocean? Let's lie on the beach."

As they lay down, she stroked the dark hair on his forearm. Raising himself, David kissed her. He rolled away and sat up. "I want to be fair," he said. "The idea of marriage frightens me."

"Not as much as it frightens me," Joyce said.

"No. I've seen a bad one. My mother lording over my father. He couldn't deal with her in any way except acceptance. So nothing became of my dad. He didn't become."

"My father simply runs away. He's read Gibbon. The whole *Decline and Fall*. And he waits on tables." Bad for a man, David thought. Servility. Playing a woman's role. Even Hercules went soprano when Omphale webbed his love. Or kissed his cock.

Jocye drew her legs up and folded her arms around her knees.

"Pretty," David said. "You look pretty that way."

"Dad is just a nice guy," Joyce said, looking toward the ocean. "If my mother were supportive to him, he could become more than he is, but she can't be supportive. She should have married money."

"My mother *made* money and couldn't be supportive. She had dinner parties in Flatbush and she called them salons and remarked on my dad's necktie being not quite right. He escaped from her protesting. I buried him in a Sulka foulard. That was quite right. My mother conceded that. But then, according to my mother, whatever I wrote wasn't good enough. She had lost her husband, the target. She needed a replica target. There I was, young but with an excellent taste in neckties. So—

"Whatever I read wasn't advanced enough.

"Whatever I dreamed was too ambitious."

"What you're saying," Joyce said, "is that we had the same mother."

"What I'm saying is that my mother, your esteemed Professor Priest, was a glittering bitch."

Joyce put a strong small hand on David's shoulder. "You don't want to live against that. Sulka has changed the patterns in its foulards. You need a nice girl."

"Except I don't want to be married."

"And I don't either."

The tanned rock-music couple swaggered up the sand and turned Bill Haley's volume to its maximum.

"I mean," David said, "I don't even want to be engaged."

"Right," Joyce said, decisively. "Let's just say we're engaged to be engaged."

A keening male soprano shrieked on radio:

> Say, little lady.
> We'll make hay, little lady.
> Any way, little lady.

David was speechless with shock. Then he said, "I guess."

They bicycled back to his apartment and bought shell steaks and tomatoes and frozen shrimp cocktail, and Joyce asked David to sit in the living room and play the Bruno Walter recording of Brahms's Fourth. He took down a volume of Frost and skimmed through "Birches."

Mechanical, sometimes. Music and poetry. When the beauty was not felt, one was being obscene. He was trying out an obscene, formal prelude using Brahms and Frost as aphrodisiacs.

I'd like to get away from earth awhile.

It was odd that he had never noticed that line before. A marvelous line, overlooked in David's obscene preludes. A portrait of the artist lost in foreplay.

He had read "Birches" first the same year he was trapped in Music Appreciation for the Gifted with a teacher named Miss Schmidtman. Miss Schmidtman, high-cheekboned, pretty once, but hard-faced by then. She insisted that *the way* to *mem-oh-rize* was to rely on verses.

Robert Schumann, the Melody Man.
Robert Schumann, the Melody Man.
Every note he wrote
Was a golden note.
Robert Schumann, the Melody Man.

What a course! Enough to give a gifted student distaste for music and verse all at once.

Bruno Walter's mellow allegro sang in David's apartment. *Allegro non troppo.* Bruno Walter never was quick. Miss Schmidtman's lyrics to *that* symphony returned and assaulted David.

This is the Fourth
Of old J.B.

Too much. The music and the doggerel.

This is a fifth
Of new J.B.

He wanted to make his mind move more slowly. He looked into the long, narrow kitchen and saw Joyce at the stove. Had she been tuned to Frost? Was she touched by old J.B.? Either the booze or Brahms would do now for his purpose. Poor Brahms. Fell in love with Schumann's wife. La belle dame of a madman hath him in thrall. That was the yearning. Forever after, his taste ran toward chambermaids and whores.

Joyce overcooked the steaks. Then she overapologized for the overcooking. "The stove's a little messy," Joyce said.

"The hell with messy stoves. Fuck 'em."

"I like to cook. I hate cleaning things."

"The steak was fine," David said. "We'll leave the dishes and play more music. I think I'd like to have a little Scotch."

They sat on the coral sofa and sipped drinks. At eighteen, David had read a Dutch manual on seduction. Jewesses were supposed to be among the most passionate of women. The pages came alive when David was eighteen. Erect. It was particularly important to approach Jewesses delicately, avoiding suggestions of vulgarity.

"Unlike a man, a woman has many erogenous zones." Look up erogenous. *Producing libidinal gratification when stimulated.* Look up libidinal. *Pertaining to psychic energies derived from primitive biologic urges.* What the hell was that? They must be talking about fucking.

A woman's zones, the manual instructed, are stimulated sequentially. First the cheeks. The cheeks are gently to be kissed. Proceed then to the mouth. Kiss without pressing firmly. Firm pressure may frighten a young girl. Murmur. The sound of a masculine voice among kisses is erogenous to many women. Murmur.

> *Murmur a little sadly how love fled*
> *And paced upon the mountains overhead*
> *And his face among a crowd of stars*

David's manual was called *Sexual Arousal in Young Women*, by Dr. Rienst van Wooten, M.D. What manual, David thought, had Yeats perused? The cunt of a slatternly housemaid. Manual training. Finger fucking came first. Then fornication out of doors.

Prooceed from lips to ears, kissing the lower lip, sucking it inward. Gently close the mouth over the young woman's ear lobes, first on one side, then the other. Now lightly tilt her chin, remembering that too-firm pressure, at this stage, is threatening. Kiss the throat, licking as softly as though it were a very apple of Eden. At this point, under no circumstances bite.

The ardent woman will cry out. This can alarm young men. The sound may be a moan, as with pain, or a wheezing as with asthma. This is a pleasure function. She may laugh. Such laughter should not be confused with merriment. It is a symptomatic reaction of the ardent woman's neuropathic system to arousal.

Touch the breasts, with extreme lightness. Touch. Do not poke. Roll the nipple gently between thumb and forefinger. Her cries may become louder. The laughter may descend to giggling. In the neurologic system of the healthy female, a tenderly stimulated nipple produces intense excitation, including erection of the clitoris.

Clitoris. Look up clitoris. (And while you're at it, look up her sister too.) *A small organ at the ventral part of the vulva, homologous to the penis in the male.* Vulva. That's the whole works. Look up homologous. *Having the same relative position, proportion and structure.* The clitoris is the female cock.

That's right, he thought. Who was it who had said in high school that putting pepper on the clitoris drove a woman wild? Shelley Goldberg said it. Old schoolboys' tale. "But how do you work the pepper mill under a panty girdle?" David had said to Shelley.

Extinguish lights, advised Dr. van Wooten. Many

women, however ardent, are possessed by timidity at having their sexual parts observed in clear light. *Another reason to be a doctor*. Except some patients would be sick. Some would be old. Some would be both. True doctor fantasy: Examine only attractive young women. Halt, lame monopedes and victims of trichomoniasis need not apply.

Help her undress. Continue to murmur. You will now be erect. Kiss her breasts as gently as you kiss her cheeks. "Rude ram to batter such an ivory wall." That was not Rienst van Wooten, M.D. That was the poet of swordplay who wrote *Othello*.

She may writhe, as though in pain. These are pelvic thrusts, a pleasure function of the normal woman in arousal.

Enter her gently. Her own hand, delicately placed upon your member, can serve as guide. Once within, thrust slowly and regularly. If she complains of pain, move higher on her body. This brings your rigid member and her clitoris into direct contact. Do not at this time stroke the clitoris further; many young women find such contact unendurably intense. Softly utter encouraging words. It is more difficult for women than men to realize orgasm.

Rude ram.

Mannered ram.

Goddamn you, van Wooten. I don't even have a hard-on.

"What are you thinking?" Joyce said, on the coral sofa, fastening a hand on David's knee.

"Brahms," David said. "I was considering Johannes Brahms. What it must be like to walk about with all that music inside your head."

He leaned toward Joyce. He put his right arm behind her and slipped his left hand under the peasant blouse and found a nipple. He was skipping steps. Van Wooten would disapprove. Shakespeare and Brahms might both applaud. David was getting hard. Joyce gasped. The Dutch doc could go stick his cock in a dike.

"The record," Joyce said. "Hadn't you better take the needle off Brahms?"

He walked to the old fruitwood Capehart phonograph he had salvaged from the Flatbush house before the movers from Cleveland struck. When he returned to the coral sofa, Joyce was sitting very straight, smiling faintly.

"Where's the big smile?" David said.

"That's for special occasions."

"Isn't this special?"

Joyce nodded and smiled wide. He pulled her head close so he could feel her teeth against his neck and again he slipped his hand inside her blouse, rubbing a nipple in a small, orbicular motion.

She suddenly moaned so loudly that David drew back. The smile was gone. Her lips were drawn against her teeth. How does that catch you, van Wooten? David thought. Shortcuts, and I get a moan like that.

"My old psych teacher," Joyce panted, "told me that this was bad for young people. Getting this excited."

"Which old psychology teacher?"

"Your mother."

He had beaten van Wooten. Not his mother.

"Oh, fuck," David said.

"Don't curse."

"Can't we leave my mother out of this?"

"She said hard petting causes males to get a pain in the, uh, groin."

"That's a half truth, a limited truth."

Damn.

Mother. He was losing his erection. "Males don't have to end up with a pain in the, uh, groin."

"And there's a female thing, your mother said. Too much petting gives girls a condition called engagement pelvis."

They were sitting apart holding hands. "Look, Joyce, I've read a lot of books on love and I've never heard of that."

"Too much blood flow to a woman's groin messes things up. I mean, after a while her groin starts to ache."

Would Mother never cease tantalizing him? "You've had that?" David said.

"With somebody once. He's moved to California."

"Well, empirically," David said, "I can think of a way to handle our groin problems." He gazed across the wall at an abstract Chinese print of sailing ships buffeting a pale beige sea. He felt amused and confident.

"How?" she said.

"By fucking."

He led her into the bedroom, which had been papered blue and gold. "No paintings," he said, "because it's tricky hanging paintings over wallpaper."

"The lights," she said. "Shakespeare calls light the enemy of love."

"I like light. I like to look at things. Your body."

"But I don't like to be looked at," Joyce said. "I'm not a thing."

He flipped the switch.

"You get into bed and wait," Joyce said. "Do you have something? You know. A Trojan?"

"No. I have a Ramses. They cost twenty-five cents more for three, but they're thinner and safer."

"I never heard of them."

"Would you hurry, please, and get undressed."

"But there's no hurry. We're alone. I can get home as late as two. Just lie there and relax while I get ready."

He remembered the moan. She called for a robe from the bathroom. He fetched her one and poured himself another Scotch and slipped back into bed, sipping and waiting. This could be something. He had heard that some women actually bellowed in passion.

She entered, dropped the robe and eased into bed beside him. He kissed her neck and said, "Would you guide me?"

"Where?"

"Inside you."

"Touch me first."

She rolled and groaned beneath his stroking.

"Now," David said, and forced her thighs wide open and drove into her, listening, listening for the bellow.

"Ooow. Oooh. Ow. Oooow!"

"Ride the pleasure," David commanded.

"Ow. Don't. Nice girls don't fuck. Please take it out. Oh, God. It hurts. It hurts, Barry. You're hurting me."

"I'm David. Barry's gone to California. What's the matter?" Where was Dr. Rienst van Wooten?

"It hurts. My groin hurts. Take it out."

"Try to relax."

"I can't. Stop hurting me. Ow, uh, ooooow! Stop."

He withdrew, breathless, She turned and clutched a pillow to her face.

"I'm sorry, Joyce. I thought you were excited."

"I was excited and I am excited. But you're so big and there's something I should have told you. I haven't ever done this before."

"I thought with all the psychology and the rest. Oh, shit. I didn't mean to fuck a virgin."

"Well, now you have," Joyce said. She lay on her stomach, silent.

"I don't mean to hurt anybody," David said.

She still lay silent.

"Look, honey," David said. "We'll get married. It will be easier."

She rolled over and drew his neck against her mouth. "I am excited and you haven't hurt me too much. I was scared. Please stroke the outside, the way you did before. We can live here. I'll make the apartment pretty for you, David. I'll hang the right pictures on your wallpaper. July. Would you like to be married in July? I'm through with college then. We can get married in July."

You naïve bastard, van Wooten, David thought. You treacherous gynecological cunt. With all your trivialities, you forgot to mention the atomic bomb.

Van Wooten was somewhere else, dead, and he had hurt Joyce. He, David Priest. Not van Wooten.

Now if he married her, he could make certain that she would not be hurt again.

What the hell, she seemed damned nice.

What the hell, maybe they could help each other.

What the hell, what the hell, it was only marriage.

V

Joyce did not want her mother present at the wedding. "If she's there, it will become *her* wedding. You don't want to marry my mother, do you, David?" Joyce's gray-green eyes glittered with amusement.

"I didn't even want to marry my own mother," David said.

"So we'll have the two ladies there just in spirit."

"And I'll try to find a best man who exorcises."

"A small wedding, then," Joyce said.

"No TV coverage, except for Walter Cronkite. He seems more like a friend than a reporter."

"Or like the doctor, before he sends the bill. Inform the networks. Miss Joyce Steindler is not available for interviews this year."

"How about a nude spread in *Playboy?*"

"For that I could be available, provided the photographer is a good friend."

"I'll call Cronkite," David said. "He's interested in such things." They laughed and talked intently. "When my friend Shelley Goldberg got married to Nancy Fox,"

David said, "Mr. Fox underwrote a huge ceremony at the Three Cantors Caterers. I had to be best man. Shelley was still in med school and he was broke and as we walked in he said, 'Just what I always dreamed of. Getting married in a rented tux and Thom McAn shoes.' "

"That's what comes of exaggerated expectations," Joyce said. "I want our wedding to be the nonevent of the season."

David smiled. "I remember Nancy and Shelley, big as Shelley is, looking lost among guests. The guests didn't notice them. The guests were too busy eating their way through Mount Ararat, sculpted in chopped liver."

"Who got to nibble at the ark?"

He smiled, but said, "Look, Joyce. I'm serious about agnosticism. It's a positive belief. Exalting man, or humanity, instead of God, who doesn't exist."

"Who may not exist."

"We can only be sure of the tangible. We know that Mount Ararat exists because when we reach out and touch Mount Ararat the chopped liver of an ark smears our hands. But God?"

"My mother's rabbi says God is fulfillment."

"That, if it means anything at all, means that your mother's rabbi is slick."

"If you don't want a rabbi, a judge is all right. The big thing is that I have you."

Someone at City Hall suggested a Brooklyn magistrate named Irwin Rosenthal. He was said to be more literate and sensitive than many of his colleagues. David covered City Hall on his wedding day, July 15. Magistrate Rosenthal, assigned to Brooklyn night court, would marry them at an eight o'clock recess.

They drove to the courthouse in a light-blue Ford that they had bought together for eight hundred dollars. Remembering Shelley Goldberg's Thom McAn comment, David had splurged on a forty-dollar pair of Italian shoes. Magistrate Rosenthal, a gaunt, tall man with grayish skin, did not appear notably literate or sensitive as he shuffled from his chambers. He may have been worn down by petty thieves and braying lawyers. He may have been drinking. "Bailiff," Rosenthal said, hoarsely, "show them a cell. Have you young people shared a cell before? You're going to share one for the rest of your lives."

They walked down a flaked cream corridor and into an eight-by-ten cubicle that had been painted pale green. The magistrate slid shut a steel-barred door. An automatic lock clacked. "Can we get out?" David said. "Your sentence hasn't begun, Judge."

"Not yet," Rosenthal said. He began talking about himself. "I'm just a magistrate, not much at Borough Hall politics. Friends in the press, nice enough, but mostly young like you. Can't do anything for me. Fellow I used to sit with got ahead. His friend was John Oakes, the *chief* editorial writer for the *Times*. That fellow moved ahead, you can be sure."

"Can we get out of this cell?" David said.

"You know my fee for marriages?"

"An Upmann cigar." David reached into the breast pocket of his jacket and withdrew the cigar, which was sheathed in plastic. Anal? Penile? Negro penile? Whatever, he handed the one-dollar talisman through the bars.

"Release them," Rosenthal told the bailiff. The magistrate began to cough.

Joyce wore a translucent yellow dress over a pale-yellow slip and looked, David said, pretty and plump as a peasant bride. David wore a charcoal suit over a white button-down shirt. They followed the shuffling magistrate back toward his chambers. The bailiff helped Rosenthal into a robe. The magistrate placed the Upmann cigar next to the gavel on his desk. He cleared his throat twice and began to speak.

"There has been so much killing in our time. Asian slaughters; African blood baths. And to what purpose? None. To no purpose at all. We live in times like Shakespeare's times. We know the meaning of his phrase 'casual slaughter.'

"Particularly we who are Jewish understand."

"Join hands, please."

"David," Magistrate Rosenthal said, "Joyce, Europe has seen the extermination of millions like yourself because a madman decided that to be Jewish was a crime.

"Purpose? Again we ask, What purpose? We ask it as the victims would ask. For what purpose were we murdered? And our answer must once more be, None. We died for no purpose at all."

Rosenthal was standing straighter now, his shoulders back. "So much for hate. What of the other crime? Indifference. Where were the fabled leaders, Roosevelt, Churchill, while the madman Hitler burnt the flower of Europe's fields? Preoccupied. Drinking brandy. Dealing for votes.

"Joyce, David, you come to me, and not to a rabbi, because you are not conventionally religious. But remember, however you may regard yourselves, the rest of the world regards you as Jews. And ever shall!"

"I do remember," David said.

"I now want to ask a very great thing of you." Rosenthal's voice was suddenly strong. "Let this marriage mark an end to hate. Let this marriage symbolize an end to indifference. Let this marriage be the beginning of a golden future time. A time of love."

Joyce's arm trembled against David. The magistrate moved through formalities. After David and Joyce exchanged gold bands, he said, "Mr. and Mrs. Priest, I've performed scores of marriages. None has ended in divorce. Don't you be the first to let me down."

"Oh, no," Joyce said.

"That's a promise," David said. He felt oddly moved. The judge nodded, smiled faintly and went out to face a docket of petty thieves and raucous drunks and child-beaters. Before stepping through the doorway to his own court, Magistrate Rosenthal hunched his back again, as if in fright.

"Not exactly a nonevent," David said, hugging Joyce.

"He was wonderful," Joyce said.

David had made a mistake, he thought. He had resisted the need for a larger ceremony. There is a reason for ceremony at marriages, there is a reason to celebrate weddings, a reason for onlookers to bear witness.

Commitment. The most scholastic Catholic mass was a public proclamation of faith, before witnesses, a swarm of kneeling chanters, many myopic, but witnesses still.

Commitment. Perhaps if Joyce had been more conventionally pretty, David would have wanted a large ceremony to show off his bride and conquest.

Perhaps if he had paused.

He had *not* paused.

What the hell, what the hell, David snarled within himself.

It was only a quickie service in night court.

By October, Joyce was pregnant. They had not discussed a child, but once in a while they made love without a condom.

"I guess once in a while is enough," Joyce said.

"What's that?"

"I've missed a period and I'm late with another."

Damn, David thought. They were sitting on the coral sofa, listening to Heifetz play the Bach A Minor Concerto. The small apartment still looked as it had. A smattering of furniture, the sofa, chairs and prints—somehow, in sum, not quite enough. They were sitting in a temporary room.

"I know a doctor," David said. "Leo Levine. Friend of the family." They had regular payments to make on the blue Ford and they entertained, which cost them according to a formula they called David's Law. For every bottle of Gallo table Chianti a guest brought ($1.99), *you* had to buy a bottle of Scotch ($6.75).

Joyce had begun substitute teaching at P.S. 343 in a Brooklyn ghetto, and the work was hard and paid badly. It was, she said, the only job worth doing that she could find. Because the work was demanding, she had not yet begun redecorating the apartment. But she would soon. She really would. The place didn't need much anyway, she said.

"A lot of girls are late with their periods," David said. "It isn't sure unless it's confirmed by a doctor."

"I've never been late," Joyce said. "My body's a walking calendar. Besides, yesterday at school I threw up."

Dammit, a baby. In fruitful intercourse, there should be some sign. The great D major chord from the Brahms Requiem. A wanted child. As sperm and egg unite, tenors should choir:

> *The souls of the righteous*
> *are in the hand of God,*
> *and there shall be no torment touch them.*

Let a chorus proclaim that humanity will be enriched by one, David thought.

A seed is planted.

The uterus has become a fruitful husk.

Let tenors choir. Sound organ pedal notes.

Crescendo!

That was the imagining. As it was, the strongest sign

of the seed begun was that a schoolteacher excused herself to vomit.

David wanted fatherhood. That was not the question. But did he want a baby? The place looked bare. Heifetz's fiddle sounded oily. During this particular twilight David did not want to consider diapers, bottles, pediatricians. All his life had been a preparation for fatherhood. But dammit, a *baby*. A fucking baby. It was the wrong time, the wrong music, the wrong room.

"I won't be a mess," Joyce said. "There's a pill to stop the nausea. Bonamine, I think it's called. When I go to the doctor, I'll ask for it."

He remembered his father and his father's bent dreams, Dad telling him about his mother. He must have loved her. Ah, but did he like her? A link. His dad disliked his mom, who disliked her son.

He thought of Dad discussing Tess Durbeyfield and Franck's Symphony in D Minor and the pitcher called John Whitlow Wyatt. "Why, Whit could throw at the point of a batter's chin, and take the hair off closer than an electric razor." David smiled. Those talks were the deepest family tenderness he had known.

The baby would grow into someone to talk to. The baby would seal his pact with Joyce. In the garden once, his father said, "For a responsible man, the birth of a child makes divorce unthinkable." Why think that now? Had he been considering a divorce from Joyce? From Joyce the Good? Not till this moment. But she was not only Joyce the Good. She was Joyce the Willful. She was pregnant because she had wanted to become pregnant.

"Aren't you excited?" Joyce said.

"Overwhelmed," David said. "I need time to think." Parthenogenesis, David thought. "Let's hear how Heifetz zips through this allegro."

His times with Joyce blended into flatness. There was nothing specifically wrong with their marriage;

there was nothing specifically right. They were young and successful, starting out, but where was the adventure? David wondered. Soon or late, he would look for that inside some other woman.

The child. Maybe the child would bring adventure. Absurd. He knew better than that. Before the child became someone to talk to, it would have to learn to talk.

Angst, sharp as a Prussian foil, touched David's solar plexus. With his doubts, should they go ahead and have the child? If he had doubts, perhaps Joyce doubted too, beneath her persistent good cheer.

The lady near him on the couch, wearing a poorly cut teal dress, under which she was becoming rather too plump, was pregnant with a child, which he, which they, might not be ready to receive.

I'm sorry. We're crowded enough here as it is. You'll have to try another manger.

He thought to act. He thought to propose abortion. But then the mocking thing within him made a warble in a minor key.

What the hell.

What the hell.

It's only a baby.

"I hear you can play tennis through the fifth month," Joyce said. Heifetz hurried through Bach's allegro too quickly for the music to exult.

After Dr. Leo Levine made the diagnosis, he sent Joyce home with several booklets, a bottle of vitamin pills and a caveat against needless drugs. "Morning sickness is natural, so it's safe, if unpleasant," he said. "Pills to stop vomiting may not be so safe."

"He measured me," Joyce told David.

"With a ruler?"

"No. With a kind of calipers, checking my pelvic bones."

"Embarrassing?"

"Terribly, except, of course, you're curious. And scared. You're a thing to them, really, patient number thirty-six F, for female, and I tried to think of that. That it was impersonal. But it wasn't impersonal and he kept calling me 'my dear.' They make you slide down this table and put your feet in stirrups and I kept my knees together. I didn't want him to see my bottom. But he made me spread my knees and he put some instrument into my parts, and then he put his hand into my bottom."

"Into it?"

"It smarted and I yelped. He said I had a nice bottom and I should be relaxed about his examination."

"Let's not dwell on that. It's how Levine makes a living. In a sense, you are a thing, patient thirty-six F, for female. A reproducing thing. A thing of cervical dilations and Chadwick's sign."

"What's that."

"I was reading a textbook. In the fifth month of pregnancy, the vagina assumes a purplish hue."

"David. Don't be clinical."

"According to *Aspects of Pregnancy,* by McSwiggan, Marvin, et al., it happens to the vagina of every woman who has a baby. Queen Elizabeth. Jacqueline Kennedy. Lana Turner. Let's go to a movie."

"I'd like something else. I'm awfully happy to be pregnant. Could we have a party to celebrate?"

David and Joyce were at a transitional social stage, feeling strains of boredom with old friends, but uncertain about reaching toward new ones. Some of David's schoolmates had found work in the garment business. A few were medical students or interns. One of Joyce's close college friends had gone to Stanford for graduate study in Persian history. The other had married hurriedly and fused with other brides, in a development on central Long Island, where people made pretend lives in real cages.

Joyce bought fresh prints and a round glass cocktail table and invited thirty guests for Halloween. She ordered platters of turkey and ham and David ordered bottles of Dewar's Scotch and Dant bourbon, and Smirnoff vodka and Gilbey's gin, which he set out carefully on the new glass table beside a new Dansk ice bucket. Joyce placed pastel candles about the living room. The party would begin at eight-fifteen. At nine-thirty, David was to call for order. Then, without great chords from Brahms, he would remark in an understated way that Joyce was expecting.

A mad private newspaper headline appeared in David's head.

PRIESTS ANNOUNCE PROPAGATION; REACTION MIXED. FECUNDATION OF BROOKLYN BRIDE DRAWS PASTEL-GREEN ENVY; GOLDEN CHEER TRIUMPHS, 16–14, ON SPIRITED RALLY. COUPLE GRACIOUS IN VICTORY, BUT DECLINE INTIMATE INTERVIEWS. SUCCESS ATTRIBUTED TO JOINT EFFORT. RAMS AND MONTREAL CANADIENS ALSO VICTORS.

He lit the pastel candles at eight o'clock and poured himself a Scotch.

"I'd like a small martini on the rocks," Joyce said.

If everybody had his private newspaper, David thought, the press would be truly free, but tedious. Headlines would announce news in order of personal importance.

GEORGE CLAXTON SUFFERS TOOTHACHE!
GOES TO WORK ANYWAY!!
GWEN W. MEEKER COMPLETES TERM PAPER!
NO SPELLING ERRORS!!

General news would follow in smaller type:

Earthquake Destroys Moscow; Echo
Quake Sinks Malibu in Pacific Ocean.

"Should you?" David asked.

"Dr. Levine said moderate drinking wouldn't hurt."

SCOTCH EASES CLAXTON PAIN; HE MEETS MISS
MEEKER AT SCHEDULED TRYST NEAR BARNARD;
LATE FOR DINNER IN CENTRAL LONG ISLAND
TRACT HOUSE.

Was there a George Claxton, a Gwen W. Meeker?
Why not invite her to the party?

The guests arrived in clusters. Three medical students. Four teachers from P.S. 343. The garment
brigade. Two of Joyce's cousins, who were studying
pharmacy.

"The rule," David announced, "is that I make the
first drink for everyone. After that you're on your own."

Joyce's cousin Robin Schwartz, a tall, thick-lipped
man with protuberant teeth, approached David. "Is
there much money in this writing?" Robin said.

"You don't go into it for money."

"Maybe. But we're all in business. Joyce got to get
clothes. You ought to think of pharmacology. You
know what you can make with a drugstore on Long
Island, say Valley Stream?"

"How much?"

"An easy seventy-five thousand, once you get established, and it isn't hard to learn."

Shelley Goldberg had grown into a somewhat smaller
Babe Ruth. He had the same broad face, the same thick
nose, the same rhinoceros torso. Shelley was starting
an internship in obstetrics. "Any chance you getting
assigned to Israel?" Shelley said.

"Israel who?" David said.

"Look," Shelley said. "You're writing well and Israel's a better story than City Hall, even for the fascist
Journal-American."

David was growing impatient with the old needling.

"When I call them fascist, it's okay," he said. "When an intern does, I think, check out the American Medical Association. Fascists are closer to where you live."

"I'm working from within," Shelley said, laughing at David and himself.

Larry Shaw, redheaded and wiry, had played junior varsity high school basketball with David. Given a chance to shoot, he invariably preferred passing. Selfless, or tentative? No one knew. "Say," Larry said. "Seeing your by-line, I can tell you're doing okay at the paper. And Joyce. She's not a sylph, but they mostly all get fat, eventually."

"She'll lose weight," David said. "Right now she's expecting." He had meant to understate the announcement, not throw it away.

"Say," Larry Shaw said. "Great. I'm working for my uncle."

ANNOUNCEMENT OF PRIEST PROPAGATION
BORES SHAW

"In the slippers business," Larry said. "You know, I tried med school for a year down in Guatemala, but I couldn't hack it. I mean, they had one cadaver for the whole freshman class. I finished NYU with a 3.8 average, but I couldn't get in anywhere except Guatemala. And they say anti-Semitism is dead. Hell, I'm happy in business. I'll bet you didn't think slippers could be interesting, but they are. All kinds of leathers. Styles. You know, maybe I could have gone to dental school, but this is better. It's not dull and it's not like medicine, where being a Jew means you have to be twice as smart."

Being a writer, David thought, means you have to be twice as smart, regardless of color, sex or Adolf Hitler. He stood near the table on which the bottles rested. Joyce approached. She wore her yellow wedding dress. "Hey, Dave," she said.

"My first name isn't Hey."

"Well, Dave, they aren't mixing. Just standing around in clumps. Ya know?"

"Have you had a second martini?"

"Small one. Very small. Hey, Dave, they're not mixing and you're not mixing either."

"You're the hostess," David said. "Mix them."

"I've never given a big party before. I don't know how."

"You say, 'Mr. Claxton, this is Miss Meeker. I want you both to meet Rachel Tannenbaum.'"

"Rachel's at Stanford studying Iran."

"I know."

"What you're saying is, you want me to be the hostess *and* the host."

"What I'm saying is what I've said. The woman runs the parties. My mother ran the parties. You introduce people, Joyce. I make the drinks and tell some stories. That's how it is."

"But I'm nervous. I need another small martini."

"There's a baby inside you who doesn't need another small martini."

"Hey, Dave. Don't tell me what to do. Now mix me one."

Three apprentice doctors and their wives stood near the Capehart phonograph, listening to Shelley Goldberg. "When we do a hysterectomy at Downstate and we take out the right ovary, we call that the North American. Left ovary, South American. Both ovaries, All American. A little dialogue over all that blood helps keep you loose."

"I couldn't stand surgery," said Howie Simpson. "I just want a nice quiet eighty-thousand-dollar practice in internal medicine."

"You make more than that in a good year in slippers," Larry Shaw said.

"Whoo," Shelley said. "Let's forget medicine and

tomorrow we can all go to the track. David's a member of the fascist press. He can get passes."

"I don't make a lot of money," David said, "and my wife is expecting, so Aqueduct will have to run without me." Another announcement like a discard. A child thrown out amid the hoofbeats of maiden six-year-old claimers.

"Joyce is pregnant?" Shelley said. "I'll have to have a talk with her; and *you'll* have to go easy with her now, Dave."

"You ever been an expectant father, Shelley?"

"No, but I treat pregnant women, and the first rule is that you go easy. Funny things happen. They hear about the pain, and they worry about Down's Syndrome—Mongolism—and they sublimate and the anxiety comes out in funny ways. Not the pickles-and-ice-cream crap. Suddenly they cry a lot." Shelley put a large hand on David's shoulder. "Or they drink."

"She's nervous about this party, Shel. Anyway, she has a doctor."

"Well, there're some good doctors and some bad. Myself, I never practice at parties," Shelley said. "Just understand, which a lot of doctors don't, that pregnancy is more than a physical strain. It's some sort of psychic experience. If you keep them happy, you get a better baby."

Joyce appeared, leading Marion Bocca, a dark-haired woman with angry eyes and a strong, broad nose. "Marion runs the teachers' union at school," Joyce said. She spoke slowly. She was holding another martini.

"God. Goddammit, go easy with that stuff," David said.

Shelley Goldberg turned away.

"Joyce tells me that you write well," Marion Bocca said. "That you've composed some poetry."

"Nothing I let out of the room," David said.

"You have to be careful with talent in this society,"

Marion said. "It's easy to make money and become a clown. Capitalism gives artists coupons for composing junk."

"And communism persecutes Shostakovich," David said.

"That's Soviet communism," Marion said, "an aberration."

"It's always difficult mixing art and commerce," David said, "although Yeats maintained that in sixth-century Byzantium, the finest mosaics brought the artists the most money."

"What you're saying," Joyce interrupted, "is . . . uh."

"Sort of," David said, tightly. He took the glass out of Joyce's hand.

"I'm sorry," Joyce said afterward. "I guess I drank a little too much. The baby and the new life and everything. I guess I had a few too many toonis." She sat up in bed. She wore red and white striped pajamas. "I'm sorry if I embarrassed you. So many people."

"You didn't embarrass me. You worried me for the baby." One lie. One truth.

"Sooo many people. A few too many tiny toonis." Joyce dropped onto the pillow. A private smile lit her face. She fell asleep and made soft, comfortable snores.

David turned out the light and lay on his back. Who were these people whom he had entertained? Who was this woman carrying his child?

A house full of strangers. Well, Shelley Goldberg was a friend. But most of the real people were missing.

The real people. His father and mother. A real person in the woman's belly, waiting to be born.

Far off, a siren sounded. Somebody dying, but no one who called out, "David Priest."

Christ, he was lonely. Could you miss a baby not yet born?

Of course the party had been peopled by strangers.

How many friends can you keep in balance at one time? Three. Perhaps four. But the crowd swarming the apartment had been the *wrong* strangers. Too placid, too shallow. The only idea that lingered was Shelley Goldberg's ominous metaphysic of pregnancy. Where were the petit philosophers, the grand poseurs, the roiling writers and their ranging characters?

Where were guests who were worthy?

His dead mother's voice knifed into him. He had brought Shelley Goldberg home to meet her. "No," Dorothy Priest said later, as goddess to young god. "He's no one for you, David."

The Jewish Priests.

A chosen family.

A higher folk.

Like Germans.

He heard his mother talking about Walt Whitman, as though she and Whitman were intimates. His mother patronized J. Alfred Prufrock. His mother urged David, when he was twelve, to write compositions in the style of Joyce's *Dubliners*. Dorothy Priest's tongue assaulted him on his marriage bed and David writhed toward sleep.

VI

The doctor said David had better get Joyce registered at Flatbush Community Hospital. "Not that the pattern of the labor is classic," Leo Levine said, "but you're a novice at timing. You may be missing some mild pains. Anyway, first-timers are better off with the girl under professional care. Get Joyce to the hospital immediately." It was March. Rain spattered black crusts of city snow.

A black attendant glowered in a corridor of the hospital. "We want to find her a comfortable lying-in room," David said.

"You wait here," the attendant said. "She goes to an *examining* room first. We treat everyone the same." The black man stared, without expression.

Defiant, David thought. Militant. What a place to find Kenyatta. Presiding over women entering labor.

"Joyce," David said. He touched her hair and said good luck and watched her follow the attendant through swinging doors. He lit a cigarette and stared after the doors, feeling useless and annoyed at being useless. Still, he waited where Kenyatta, the attendant, commanded.

Three minutes later Kenyatta returned and handed David a paper bag.

"What's this?"

"Her clothes, baby. They don't give birth with clothes on. The way they make some of these girdles, that could *really* hurt. The waiting room is over there."

"Is Dr. Levine here?"

"Not yet."

"But I called him," David said.

"Doctor will be here soon."

Kenyatta, hell. The black attendant was skinny and swish.

"Don't worry, baby," the attendant said. "The interns are examining her now. They're sharp. Three of them. Real sharp Jewish kids. Get yourself a cup of coffee, baby. Be cool."

Presiding over women entering labor, David thought. The holy agony of childbirth: three Jewish kids and Martin Luther Queen.

"I'd go in for coffee with you myself," the attendant said, "but I've got to take care of the next one. They work us, baby. Watch out for her clothes now. That maternity dress is the prettiest apple green."

"Yes," David said.

"I'd like that color myself, but they make us wear this silly washed-out white. Be around, baby. Be cool. Wilson Webster's my name."

The nurse in the picture on the waiting room wall pressed a finger to her lips and said, "Shhh," but the stocky, black-haired man who was crying into his fingers did not notice the framed poster. A man David's age, wearing a green plaid blazer, strode back and forth. "Harold," an older woman said to the green man, "I don't like this hemorrhaging."

"Dr. Sopkin says it's under control."

"Harold! A girl could die! Hemorrhaging! From there!!"

"Hello," David said to the weeping man. "I'm Dave Priest." The man drew his fingers away from his eyes. "I'm Mr. Pagano." Mr. Pagano blew his nose into a yellow handkerchief.

David wanted to run; he did not want to be with wailing strangers. He wondered about Joyce, stripped naked in a cubicle behind the double doors, poked by a herd of interns with fingers like horns.

"What's upsetting you?" he asked Mr. Pagano.

"The doctors don't tell you nothing. My Marie, she's in there suffering. They don't care."

"They have good drugs," David said. "Demerol. Scopolamine. The pain is not supposed to bother the women too much."

"It's the doctors the pain don't bother," Mr. Pagano said. "My Marie was hollering like hell when I brought her in, and they give her something, and I could still hear her hollering like hell." Mr. Pagano cringed and resumed sobbing into the yellow handkerchief.

David had cried when he was eleven and an orthopedist set his broken left arm. Radius and ulna both cracked when he was clipped playing football. He had sat on a table, left arm bent like a bow, and the doctor chattered nervously. "Don't kick me now. Don't kick." The man twisted the arm and fire darts shot down from David's elbow. He cried that day, but he was eleven years old, and he had not cried since and he did not intend to cry again. Mr. Pagano was bawling and the woman who talked about hemorrhaging sat sniffling. This is a public bathroom, David thought. Who would have expected, from all the movie scenes about maternity, the buffoons waiting with cigars, that there would be such weeping in this room?

David felt that his reserve, his *belief* in reserve, was under challenge. He would make a dry-eyed ceremony to celebrate the birth of his child.

A tall, square-jawed physician appeared and Mr. Pagano jumped up. "Not yet," the doctor said, "but soon." He turned to the man in the green jacket. "We've got the bleeding checked."

"Doctor," the green man said tightly. "If there's a choice. I mean Madeline or the baby. I mean. I want Madeline." Quite suddenly, the green man sobbed.

"There's nothing to be upset about," the doctor said. "If something unusual were to develop, we'd get the baby out at once with a Caesarean and they'd both be fine."

"Dr. Sopkin," said the older woman, "am I to understand that you're delivering this man's baby too?" She pointed to Mr. Pagano, who was standing.

"Yes. But there are several of us. We work as a medical team."

"My Madeline," the woman shouted. "My Madeline bleeding from her womb and you're worrying about somebody else. Doctor, tell me. Is money really that important?"

"We worry about all our patients," Dr. Sopkin said. His jaw set and he wheeled and left in a military exit. The woman's long face grew gaunt. She clutched the green man and began to blubber.

"Some bitch," Mr. Pagano said.

David rose from a red Plastex sofa and walked in tight circles, carrying the paper bag in which Wilson

Webster had handed him Joyce's apple-green maternity dress.

"Dave?" Leo Levine stood at the doorway. He was a short man, with a thick nose and Ubangi lips. He combed his crinkly gray-and-black hair straight back. "Come into the hallway and we can talk."

"How is it going?" David said in the corridor.

"Primigravida," Levine said. "That's first-time mother. It's often slow. We need the cervix to dilate enough for the head to be expressed. Her cervix isn't dilated more than two fingers yet."

"Meaning?"

"You might as well go home. I'll call you when her pace picks up."

"You're staying?" David asked.

"There's no need. Beatrice. My wife. She's having a small dinner party. The residents will monitor Joyce."

"Is Joyce comfortable?"

"Not very," Dr. Levine said. "She's having more than usual pain. But they get over it. They bellow a little, but as soon as they see the baby, the healthy ones forget the pain."

"Everybody bellows," David said. "The relatives bellow in the waiting room."

Levine pointed vaguely toward the nurse saying "Shhh," in the picture. "We call that place where she's hung the wailing wall."

"But very bad pain, and being out of control," David said, "can leave psychic scars. I wish you'd stay a little longer."

"Thanks for the psychological diagnosis," Levine said. "My wife is waiting."

"It's *my* wife in there," David said.

"I'm going to give you something to calm you," Levine said. "These green-and-black pills. One every four hours. Beatrice is waiting. I'll be in touch." The stocky, crinkly-haired man wheeled and withdrew. It was the same medical-military withdrawal David had seen practiced by square-jawed Dr. Sopkin. They studied that in medical school, David thought. Disengagement 401. Prerequisite: Regarding the Patient as Enemy 400.

He telephoned Sonia Steindler. Although it was almost the dinner hour, she wasn't dressed. "Still, I'll be there as soon as I can to see my darling."

"The doctor says there isn't any hurry," David said. "Then maybe I'll come tomorrow," Sonia said. David wandered into the waiting room. Mr. Pagano still cried into the yellow handkerchief. Square-jawed Sopkin, the physician, strode in wearing a green gown. "Another boy, Augie," he said, smiling, to Mr. Pagano. "Haven't weighed him yet, but he looks about nine pounds. He's fine and so is Marie."

Augie Pagano tried to embrace Dr. Sopkin, who dodged. "You see," Augie Pagano told David, "God is good and everything works out good because of God."

"Dr. Sopkin," said the gaunt-faced woman, "how is my Madeline?"

"We're going to do a section," Dr. Sopkin said. "She'll be fine and so will the baby."

"A section?" the woman cried. "Oh, my God, she'll be scarred."

"We can cut transversely," Dr. Sopkin said. "Then when the pubic hair grows back, nothing will show."

"A section," the woman said and whimpered.

The maternity waiting room repelled, almost sickened David.

The imperious nurse in the picture commanding silence was WASP. The real nurses were black and bored.

Here Jewish businessmen-doctors entered as Wagnerian gods. The trumpets of Tannhäuser proclaimed each gynecologist.

Here the topics of the day were clipped pubic hair and stretched vaginas and bleeding wombs.

Here everybody wept (except himself).

Despite the WASP nurse pleading for silence in front of doctors, the people wailed and talked of blood and cunt. All the people wailed (except himself).

David got up and walked outside into the evening. The rain had dwindled to mist. Warmer now. Under city soot, cusps of snow were melting. Torrents of spring in Brooklyn. Filthy water rushing toward a sewer.

"Hey, baby." Wilson Webster was smoking in the rain. "You can go home."

"There's nothing there to go to," David said.

"Except maybe Scotch, baby. She'll be long. I heard the doctors talking. You won't be a papa till the morning."

"Well, if she has to wait, I guess I can wait too."

"At the wailing wall in there?" Wilson Webster said. "I'm on a break. We could get a drink over at Doheny's. It's only natural for you to drink under this pressure."

It would be nice to take a drink now. Five drinks. Ten.

CHILD STRUGGLES DOWN BIRTH CANAL.
THE MOTHER YELPS; FATHER DRINKS.
'TIS NATURE'S WAY, BLACK QUEEN AVERS.

"Congratulations, Mr. Priest. You are a father."

"Shwell. Shcall me Prop."

"It's safe to have a drink with me," Webster said. "I mean, it isn't like I was saying we had to *go to school* together."

Drunkenness repelled David; Joyce had drunk enough for both of them through the pregnancy. But he was able to laugh at Wilson Webster's humor.

David turned to explain that he needed privacy to think, but the black nurse read rejection in his eyes.

Wilson Webster flipped away his cigarette. "Some other time, man. Some other baby, baby."

Sore-necked, dull-eyed, ash-tongued, David sat under the cold WASP nurse at dawn. Dr. Leo Levine entered the waiting room, wearing a green surgical cap. He led the square-jawed Dr. Sopkin. "It's over. You have a daughter."

"Her name is Anne," David said.

"It was more difficult than some," Levine said, "and I want you to shake the hand of Dr. Herman Sopkin. He saved your daughter's life."

"Her name is Anne," David said. "If it had been a boy, we were going to call it Arthur for my father. This way we keep the same first letter."

"In the intestines of a neonate," Leo Levine said, "there is a substance called meconium. It's a greenish mass of dead cells and mucus. Your baby was born under rather severe pressure, causing it to express meconium through the anus. In the birth process, the baby breathed. When it was born, its air passages were clogged with meconium. Dr. Sopkin just happened to be nearby and he grabbed a respirator and used it to apply suction. That cleaned out the baby; that's why it's alive now."

David shook Herman Sopkin's hand. "Her name is Anne," he said.

"Would you like to see the baby and Joyce?" Levine said. He led David out of the waiting room, where a man of thirty in a blue suit now sat, blinking tears. They proceeded to a nursery, where eight newborn children lay in cribs.

Levine tapped on the glass and directed a nurse toward an incubator in a corner. The nurse was Filipino. The Filipino nurse lifted Anne Priest from the incubator and bore her to the window. Anne's hair was red. Anne Priest, twenty-eight minutes old, opened her mouth. Through the glass David heard her cry.

Araagh.

A redhead, David thought. He remembered a lacing of reddish hair in the mustache his father wore.

Araagh. Anne Priest turned very red.

"May I hold her?"

"Tomorrow."

"Why the incubator?"

Araagh.

"She had a hard passage."

Araagh.

"She'll be more comfortable in the incubator for a day or two."

Araagh.

An intern stood over Joyce in a recovery room. "Just a minute," Leo Levine said to David. He drew a curtain round the bed and David heard him say to Joyce, "Now draw up your knees and spread them wide apart.

"What happens sometimes, Barry," Leo Levine said beyond the curtain, "is that in hard labor they pop a hemorrhoid. See that one there."

"A beauty," raved Barry the intern.

"Now replace it digitally," Levine said.

Joyce screamed in pain.

"Not quite," Levine said. "Like this."

Joyce screamed louder. Then, in a soft voice, she said, "Please don't hurt me anymore. Please don't hurt me."

"You're fine, young lady," Levine said. "I'll open the curtain. Don't make such a fuss."

"I'm sorry, doctor," Joyce said.

David had never seen eyes like Joyce's. They were pocketed by flesh, red with weeping, bright with terror. "It's fine, honey," David said. "You're fine."

"Did you see her?"

"A redhead. Beautiful and sexy."

"I'm sorry, doctor," Joyce said to Levine. "I'm sorry I screamed so much. I wanted to be a good girl."

"You don't have to be ashamed to scream in front of your doctor," Levine said.

"I'll call your mother now, Joyce," David said.

"I'm sorry I acted like a baby," Joyce said, vaguely.

To go to sleep David thought of a black boulder. The boulder stood against a wide black sky. He did not understand how he could see the outlines of black against a black backdrop. The rock became a mountain of coal. He heard a sound.

Araagh.

The coal caught fire, blazing inextinguishable red.

His daughter's hair.

Araagh. "Hello, Araagh," he said, and fell asleep.

The phone would not stop ringing. David twisted on the bed. He looked at a clock. Six-twenty. Couldn't people wait with congratulations?

"David?" It was Leo Levine. "Your baby has had a convulsion."

"Lots of babies have convulsions. I need sleep."

"No. This is serious."

David sat up. "Critical?"

"Yes, I'm afraid it is critical."

"All right," David said. "I'm going straight down to the hospital. Don't bother Joyce. I'll talk to her myself."

"No," Dr. Levine said. "I've had experience with these things. I'll speak to her very gently."

"Leo, she's my wife. I know how to talk to her."

"No, David," the doctor said, and hung up.

When David found Joyce in room 414A, she was eating breakfast. "Did you hear?" she said in a tiny voice. "Did Dr. Levine tell you?"

"How is Anne?"

"Very sick. Dr. Levine is getting a pediatric specialist, Dr. Ausubel."

"What's the matter?"

"Dr. Levine isn't sure." Joyce shook her head and sipped orange juice. "David, he thinks it might be brain damage."

"We'll have her tutored," David said. "There are all kinds of things we can do for Anne, if she needs them. We can afford it. I can write more articles for magazines."

"He thinks she may be blind, David."

My redheaded daughter, David thought.

"And possibly spastic as well."

"Joyce, I don't know how to say this."

"You don't have to say anything. I don't want her to live if she has no chance to be happy."

David hugged Joyce. He could mouth two words. "Guts. Brave."

"No, I'm not brave. Something was the matter with me. I was scared. I couldn't get the baby out fast enough. It was no good. It was my fault."

"It's nobody's fault," David said, "and I've heard about this pediatrician, Ausubel. Excellent. I'm going to look around for him. Be right back."

He had never heard of a physician named Ausubel, but David found Reuben Ausubel, M.D., standing beside Leo Levine at a nurses' station. Ausubel had dark crew-cut hair and steel-rimmed spectacles. The light hit the glasses in such a way that David could not see Ausubel's eyes.

"My wife and I have been talking," David said to the glint of spectacles. "We've agreed on something. We don't want a vegetable." The sentence sounded malformed. In his mind, other sentences rang eloquently. But those sentences would not come out. They would not be born.

"Whoa," Ausubel said. "You're getting ahead of yourself."

"Dr. Ausubel thinks he may be able to help your daughter," Dr. Levine said.

David blinked. He thought, remember Lear. "She lives; if it be so, it is a chance which does redeem all sorrows that ever I have felt."

"Really?" David said.

"Precise findings with neonates are difficult," Ausubel said, "but I believe there is a bit, perhaps, of brain damage."

A bit, perhaps, of damage. David thought of young girls: the Maypole dancers' bodies swayed to music. The body dances; the brain throbs. Alive.

"Occasioned, probably, by an insufficient oxygen supply, in turn caused by the meconium blockage of the respiratory passages. We are now concerned with extent of damage rather than cause." The glinting glasses said, "Practically, what's done is done."

All the music. All the pipes and timbrels. "We don't want a vegetable," David repeated.

"Our ethical canons," Leo Levine said, "require that we do everything we can to save your daughter. You understand our position, David?"

"We've had good results with calcium treatment," Ausubel said. "It nourishes, so to speak, nerve tissue. Dr. Levine and I both know our ethics, but a certain calcium dosage seems to work in a desirable way. It appears to save only what nature intends to be saved. So that if there is massive brain damage—the vegetable state you mention—the treatment will not help your daughter."

"She won't live, David," Dr. Levine said.

"But if the damage is not severe," Ausubel said, "she may be fine. Look after your wife. I'll be working on the baby."

"Her name is Anne," David said.

Toward three in the afternoon, the telephone in Joyce's room rang. "We seem to be getting results," Ausubel said. "I just thought your wife would want to know."

David turned to Joyce and said, "Now don't get high, but the pediatrician seems cheerful."

Joyce's face twisted, like the face of a child older than Anne who was about to cry. "If anything bad happens, tell the doctors, I want Anne's body given to science."

"Sure," David said. "Sure." He began to think of doctors dissecting the corpse of his redheaded daughter. The wide blue eyes. The skull, the infant skull, would be laid open. The bone would be red with blood and gray with unsullied pieces of a damaged brain.

Think of something else. Think of a ball game. Carl Furillo's throw.

He could not think of Carl Furillo's throw.

Think of a press conference. Think of a stream near Mill River, Massachusetts, when the ice is breaking and the water froths and the maples along the bank burst toward leaf.

Think of showing New England spring for the first time to a child.

Green leaves. Red hair.

Think of the farthest, coldest, whitest star.

Don't think of anything at all.

At five o'clock Dr. Ausubel called and said that things were going even better. David told Joyce that the pediatrician's cheer was doubly a good sign. "They prefer to give you the darker side, so that when there's improvement, they become miracle men. That's then reflected in the fee."

"I don't know how you can talk about money now," Joyce said.

"I do because doctors do," David said. "There's a

saying around medical schools. Bill 'em when their eyes are wet."

"You haven't cried," Joyce said.

"I don't cry," David said. "I simply don't."

Ausubel telephoned next at seven-thirty. David announced recklessly, "City desk."

"Is this room 414?"

"It's 414A."

"David Priest?"

"Yes. Is she out of the woods?"

"Your baby, sir," said Ausubel, "is dead."

A sense of relief and a horror at that sense shook David's spine. The waiting was done. Joyce looked at him, and he saw in her eyes that she knew. She gazed at a print of strawberries on a wall and he could not embrace her, although he knew he should, and he said, "One dies on a doctor's examining table and one dies in a hospital incubator. What's happening to my family? What the FUCK is happening?"

"Please," Joyce said. "Don't use that word. Not now."

Leo Levine walked into room 414A with his head down and his thick lips drawn against his teeth. "May I sit on the bed, Mrs. Priest?" He looked immaculate in blue-gray Harris tweed.

"You can still call her Joyce," David said. "We aren't angry at you."

Levine sat and clasped his hands. "Mrs. Priest, I want you to know that I am probably guilty of errors in judgment."

Joyce made a rueful cry.

"There were signs from the beginning," Levine said. "Your waters didn't burst. I had to burst them for you. Do you remember when I did that, going into your vagin-uh?"

Joyce blushed. She shook her head.

"Your cervix was unusual. When I went into your

vagin-uh, I felt a band of cervical tissue that would not dilate. Certain doctors read that as a warning."

"You didn't?" David said.

"Perhaps not well enough." Levine sat, hands folded, the medical penitent. "What I want you to know, Mrs. Priest, is that certain physicians with the same signs would have performed a Caesarean. I didn't. That's a mistake I'm going to have to live with for the rest of my life."

To David's ear, it did not play. Levine's delivery was too sure, his grief too orderly. "Just get out of room 414A, Leo," David said.

"It isn't easy speaking to a bereaved mother," Levine said. "You aren't making it easier." He sighed and shook his head. "Certain doctors might have taken more extreme measures immediately after the meconium episode. That could have meant slightly more risk to you, Mrs. Priest. In my professional judgment, we were going to pull this baby through. The evidence proves otherwise. I am eternally sorry."

A stage speech, David thought. The sigh, the mourning look, had been rehearsed before and played for others, couples and singles, about the leukemic, the cancerous, the decapitated. Possibly this scene had played before in this same room. "Get the hell out of here, Leo," David said.

"David," Joyce said. "This isn't easy for the doctor. Don't be unpleasant."

The bastard was dumping guilt, David thought. Mea culpa. Mea maxima culpa. Forgive me, Father, Mother, left without child. For I have sinned.

Leo Levine, M.D., had come to express contrition, after which he would be better able to sleep.

But fault existed, David believed. There was no such thing as no-fault death. And hearing out this man who had cared for her womb and breasts and heart and embryo, Joyce would finally rage against herself. It was not the fault of her doctor, but her body. Her body had killed her child.

"I want you to respect me for admitting honest mistakes," Levine said. "Our system is based on free choice of physician. You're a healthy woman, Mrs. Priest, and you'll be pregnant soon again. I want you to feel free to select another physician, if you choose."

"Oh, no, doctor," Joyce said.

David put his hands on his hips and tapped a foot and said, "Anything else?"

Levine rose, with a suggestion of weariness, and kissed Joyce on the brow. "I'm sorry, doctor," Joyce told him.

The doctor walked from the room almost lightly. It was, David reminded himself, about time for the start of one of Bea Levine's small, heady dinner parties.

On the way out of Flatbush Community Hospital, David saw the thick face of Mr. Augie Pagano, aglow with energy. "Hey, how'dya do?" Mr. Pagano said. "I got a football player. Chris, we call him. He's got a neck like a linebacker already."

Outdoors, beside the hospital awning, Wilson Webster smoked. The rain was mist. "I got the shaft," David said. "Or my baby did. She died. And then the doctor went and dumped his guilt on my wife."

"You're just a statistic," Wilson Webster said. "So is the kid."

"Like hell. And I wonder what damn psychic damage that Levine has done to Joyce."

"That's what you live for, baby. To find out things like that." Webster blew smoke. "You know, in Kenya, baby, the women birth them in the alleys. There's statistics in Kenya too. Ten thousand newborns die each year because while mothers sleep, the rats get at them."

David started to walk home. In summer he would take Joyce to Scotland and walk the clean high moors.

Two children threw a rubber ball under a street lamp, ignoring the mist. David felt his own face moisten. Rain.

He thought of Mr. Pagano slobbering in the wretched waiting room. He licked his upper lip. He tasted salt. David realized then that he was crying. He was crying in the street and his own tears, which came so hard, were all that he could offer to make ceremony for Anne, who had had red hair.

Something spoke in tones as dry as bone.

What the hell, a lot of babies die.

What the hell, you two are young; you can have more.

What the hell, what the hell, it was a *little* death, and all that you can cry is a tiny mistfall of tears.

PART TWO

A Kind of Fathering

Here's to the happiest years of my life
Spent in the arms of another man's wife
My mother

Old Cantabrigian Toast

CHAPTER ONE

Caroline and David

I

All at once, Caroline Maitland Devon discovered Bonwit Teller, Bergdorf Goodman, Lord and Taylor, the Pucci boutique at Saks and the rows of sly specialty shops on the East Side of Manhattan whose show windows have and do and always will lure ladies off the streets in chaste seduction. Nothing is violated but the purse.

Caroline burst into the Fifty-seventh Street apartment she now shared with David Priest and stood against a dark-paneled oak door and said, "The colors—the fuchsias, the cerises, all the colors bursting from the fabric. But not in a gaudy way, David. Somehow they aren't gaudy. My goodness, I'm talking too much, aren't I?" She wore a familiar light-tan suit that lacked elegance.

Excitement and the cold of an orange autumn day colored Caroline's cheeks. Her hands fluttered from waist to thigh. Her sloe eyes shone. The enthusiasm and the high color made her seem naked and boyish.

David sat before a black typewriter, set on his gray-veined marble table. The typewriter was a hulk upon the marble. He was a hulk beside the typewriter. "I don't know if you're talking too much. I wasn't listening. I was looking." Boyish? Not with thighs like that. He sat up straight.

"I want to buy some dresses," Caroline said. "Real New York dresses. We can get them on a charge account and it won't hurt our budget. We only have to pay one-twelfth a month. I tried on a Pucci bikini that almost shows my nipples but doesn't quite. Don't worry, David. It doesn't quite."

Her flush deepened and she hurried to David and hugged him. "I sound like a gold digger," she said. "What have you been doing?"

David stood and placed his hands at Caroline's waist and lifted her so that their faces met. "Fortunately for you, mining gold."

He kissed her and let her down and she looked at the page in his typewriter. It was marked "The Fucking End."

"I finished the Rickie Conklin Saga," David said.

"With a fuck?" Caroline said.

"Sort of. After six wives, three mistresses and four blond cheerleaders from Pepperdine College, Rickie Conklin achieves orgasm."

"How?" Callie said.

"He has a wet dream."

Caroline laughed and said, "Come on. How do you end it? You can tell about certain books by reading just the first and last paragraphs. Those are the parts the author rewrites most."

"All right," David said. "This last paragraph was written one time only: 'Even Einstein died with something more to learn.'"

"That isn't bad, really," Caroline said. "Or is it?"

"I don't know anymore, or care anymore. It's just a Hollywood one-liner. Rickie did say it, so it has a certain relative truth. It is not a fiction, but an utterance, which is more than you can say for the Sermon on the Mount."

She was right about first and last paragraphs, though in a layman's limited way. However repeatedly you rewrote the last paragraph had better flow out of what went before.

"Go, bid the soldiers shoot." Undistinguished by itself.

"Go, bid the soldiers shoot." (A dead march. Exeunt, bearing off the dead bodies.) Including the body of the murdered Prince of Denmark. Stirring beyond description, beyond tears.

On the other hand, a catchy line—a quick, grabby, pushy, clever Hollywood line—could at once be made absurd. David flashed on his headline machine:

SECRET HITLER DIARIES FOUND IN PLAINS NEAR EAST PRUSSIAN FOREST; NAZI LEADER DEFENDS ANTI-COMMUNISM; CONCEDES HIS ANTI-JEWISH POLICIES MAY HAVE BEEN EXTREME. ERRORS SINCERE, FÜHRER INSISTS. HE CONCLUDES: "EVEN BISMARCK DIED WITH SOMETHING MORE TO LEARN."

Context.

To every phrase there was a context.

Perfection came when phrase and context were one.

But a phrase could be whole within itself, like a clear current, finding length and shape, within a clouded river.

Or a phrase could be an island rising.

A phrase could find meaning by itself.

A phrase could *be* meaning.

> *Life, like a dome of many-colored glass,*
> *Stains the white radiance of Eternity.*

You could restate Shelley's phrase only in poorer English.

Shelley's image and his gnomic were not separable.

Perfection of another kind.

The meaning is the meaning.

Where had he heard *that* phrase before, and if he knew so fucking much about writing, why was he ghosting the memoirs of a twerp?

"You do care," Caroline said, "and I care too. No matter who you collaborate with, it's still your work."

"Honey, honey, honey," David said, lifting Caroline again. "Do you know the definition of a twerp? Someone who sniffs the seats of girls' bicycles."

Caroline made her face look displeased. "Gross."

"A wimp is worse. A wimp farts in the bathtub and bites the bubbles."

"Put me down, please," Caroline said.

"Well, those are other gnomics from little Rickie Conklin. They're the same to him—bathtub farting or the death of Einstein. They're meant to get approval from the crowd. So the ending isn't bad or good—until we see the crowd reaction. The book is like his life, something thrown out for approval. Not much meaning and no integrity. The Fucking End."

"Then don't waste your gift like this again."

"But the dresses, Callie, the fuchsia and cerises, and the shops, Callie, Pierre d'Alby and Jenny B. Goode."

"With my shape," Caroline said, "I look tolerably pleasing in a pair of plain tight slacks." She started toward the bedroom to change, her face no longer glowing as it had.

He was slipping manuscript pages into a box when she returned, wearing a pair of plain tight slacks. "More than tolerably pleasing," David said. He smoothed a final sheaf of papers. "I wonder if my mother would have approved of you," David said.

"A Jewish mother—a Jewish mother *from Brooklyn* —approving of a Congregationalist from Deerfield County, Pennsylvania? That goes against the Torah. I knew a Jewish mother once, through her son who read the Torah. She disapproved."

"They're not all the same," David said. "Certain

Jewish mothers are happy to get rid of their sons. It is even rumored that Golda Meir preferred running a country to fixing chicken soup." Caroline excited David and amused him and he was smiling. "I don't imagine my mother much wanted to be Jewish," David said. "She died so long ago. It's eighteen years. But I can see her rising to you as a challenge, and feeling envy. I can see you putting a possessive arm on me and staring at her with a beautifully bred look that says, 'Dear mother-in-law. Fuck off.' "

"I could handle her," Caroline said, "and probably be gentle. I'm quick at those things. The one mother I can't handle is my own. This is going to be important, David. I need your full attention."

She sat on the sofa beneath the portrait of the mustached butte and he moved beside her and took her hands. He offered a soft look. The telephone rang. A loud, shattering, unwelcome klaxon.

Joel Priest sounded lonely. "Dad, I've got this paper to do on Thomas Jefferson and I need a kind of theme, and I know you know a lot about Thomas Jefferson." The voice trailed.

"Mom knows Jefferson too."

"But she's not here."

"I'm a little busy now, Joel, and that's good, because I want time to think about Jefferson. I'll call you in an hour or so."

"I was hoping you could come over," Joel said.

"Yes, I understand. I'll call as soon as I can."

Joyce and I divorce, David thought, returning to Caroline's side, and Joel loses a father.

> . . . *your father lost a father;*
> *That father lost, lost his.* . . .

"My mother," Caroline said, "is strange and difficult. Sometimes I suspect she's a little mad."

"Your father—"

"He died on the New Year's Day that I was seventeen."

Joyce and I divorce, and Caroline finds a second father. Faulted father. Fucking father. Beats solitude for her; beats a lawyer with Tyrannosaurus teeth. Imposes solitude on Joel, who is fourteen.

"Something went out of my mother after Daddy died. Daddy's first name was Newall, and everybody called him Chuck. He was fun with me and my sister. I guess I was supposed to be a boy, but Daddy was a good sport and if I couldn't play halfback, at least I could be a cheerleader. Everybody else rooted for the touchdowns. Daddy cheered my cheerleading."

This *was* important. The game plan between men and women. First the ladies listened to you relate your life as you imagined it. They listened two or three times, to four or five imaginings. Then, in a quick reverse play, they talked about themselves. You could fake listening, murmuring, "There, there." You could interrupt them with a fuck. It was easy to fake most of them, even the beauties. Slip them a fuck and call it consolation.

There, there. I know how bad you feel.

There, there. Ain't life a bitch?

There, there. Don't you feel better now?

Errgh. Hold me! Coming! Errgich!

Or you could be straight. You could really listen, the way they really listened, the good women of Pokanoket and Manhattan. Callie Devon was setting her own. She was setting her life down and he was thinking about Joel, who looked too lean ever to play halfback.

"Some boys end up as cheerleaders too," he said.

"I was just using a silly example," Caroline said. "Daddy had socialist theories and ideas on world government that I was beginning to understand when I lost him. Then Mother started getting sick and they did some terrible operation to remove cancer from her rectum and after that she went blank-eyed and started acting funny. Since then—"

How did the father die? David thought. The doorbell chimed discreetly; sounding A and F sharp.

"You expecting anybody?"

Caroline's eyes were wide and wet. Tears naturally lubricate autobiography. "No, and I didn't order anything either."

David opened the dark-oak door. A tall, possum-faced boy said, "David Priest?"

"Yes."

"I'm sorry, Mr. Priest."

The boy extended a series of papers. As David clutched them, the boy turned and hurried down the fire stairs. "Shit," David said. "Sheet. I'm getting sued for twenty-five hundred dollars by I. Zukovsky, D.D.S."

Caroline stared at him in fright.

"It's a nuisance," David conceded, "but not alarming."

"It is alarming," Caroline said. "A process server coming round unannounced like the Gestapo."

"Ah, Callie, here's all this is. The last inning of the Divorce Game. When a marriage splits, a woman goes to a lawyer. Say there is visible money. The wretched Rickie Conklin Saga is visible money. The lawyer talks about equity and rights, but he's a lawyer. Visible money excites him. Visible money gives a lawyer a hard-on."

Caroline glowered. Her own story, and the mood for telling her story, had been broken. "Don't be vulgar, David."

"I'm being crude. Divorce is vulgar. The lawyers crouch like a fighter's seconds. The principals argue about the custody of pewter salt cellars neither likes. The judges are bored."

All right. The woman gets the pewter salt cellars. Objection.

All right. The man can have the salt cellars on alternate Tuesdays, on each Thanksgiving and every fourth Yom Kippur.

Objection.

All right. The man will provide funds for the woman to purchase backup salt cellars, for use when the originals are not available.

First lawyer: Agreed.

Second lawyer: No objection.

Clerk of the court: Write the check.

Defendant: But I meant for her to keep the salt cellars in the first place.

Judge: Too late. Case closed. Tomorrow to fresh fields and dockets new.

"I know about divorce." Caroline walked from the sofa to a frail caned chair. She pressed her knees and lips together. "My cousin Robby Maitland went through a divorce last summer. It was only the second divorce ever in our family. We walked along a beach in Cape May for three nights. He's an intern from Andover and Yale. He's thought ahead. He's going to specialize in emphysema. He says he won't be the first man to make a fortune out of the tobacco business. It took me three nights to talk Robby into giving Marilyn what she deserved. Some tablecloths and the silver."

"And then?"

"And then he tried to lay me."

"Tell me exactly."

Caroline sat up very straight. David was not sure whether it excited her to discuss sex, or whether she knew that it excited *him* to hear her talk about it.

Women weren't as volatile as men, according to Kinsey. Conditioned to turn on more slowly, and a good thing. Crossed knees were the earliest form of contraception. Sitting behind a screen, Kinsey asked questions, made coded notes and analyzed. Sex talk was less arousing to women, Dr. Kinsey said. The data was

incontrovertible and the screen protected . . . Who?
The screen protected Dr. Alfred Kinsey.

MASTURBATION HIS WAY OF LIFE, FINAL KINSEY
PAPERS REVEAL. SCIENTIST HABITUALLY PLAYED
WITH HIMSELF WHEN INTERVIEWING FEMALES.
CLAIMS TO HAVE TAKEN NOTES WITH OTHER HAND.

"Must I?" Caroline said. "I'm so embarrassed."
Her sex talk was evolving into foreplay. But it was
different from nibbling ear lobes in the ancient sex
book. This was a foreplay that the woman dominated.
David tried to smile. He could take the smallest con-
fessional fragment and make an inner movie.
"The third night on the beach, we were walking past
a lifeguard's boat turned upside down. Robby stopped
me with one hand. He's as tall as you and a little
stronger. We'd been talking intensely. They'd only been
married for three months. She had a fear of penetration,
Robby said. The intense talk seemed to rouse me and
I let him take off what I was wearing. Some dreary print
dress, and my bra, and my half slip. But I thought, not
my panties. If my cousin Robby Maitland wants to
make me, he's going to make me with my panties on.
And we lay in the sand and he got very hard and big.
The biggest I ever felt. He started to put it in, under
the rim of my panties."
"What about the moonlight? Couldn't you be caught?"
"It was a black night. Clouds and fog. When he
started to go in under my panty rim with that big thing,
I felt like Marilyn Maitland. *I* was afraid of penetra-
tion."
"What kind of panties?"
"Bikinis. Pale green. But you couldn't see the color
in the dark. When he put it in, he hurt me so much
that I began to cry. I made him stop. If he didn't, I said,
I'd rub his thing with sand. He said I was acting like

a baby and he wasn't going to put his totem pole into a crying baby."

"You couldn't rub his cock with sand if he was pinioning your arms."

"I know, and I was so afraid he'd make me do it, I kept myself crying until we got to the house Mom had rented. I *wanted* to seem like a crying baby. Otherwise, I was helpless."

"Now," David said.

"I don't want to now." She smiled and David noticed sweat beads on the down of her upper lip.

He took her from the caned chair and eased her to the ice-blue carpet. "I'm not your cousin Robby Maitland. Take off your underpants for me."

She started to giggle. Then, looking at David's eyes, she wriggled out of slacks and underwear all at once. He ripped at his fly and burst into her. "I said *now*."

Her roaring made him glad the old apartment was walled with concrete. He felt her writhe. He heard her buttocks thwack against the carpet. She was bouncing and sticky and oozing and rolling and squealing.

He came, hearing a single unearthly scream.

Afterward she lay on the carpet, still naked below a taffeta blouse. Panting, David said, "I never heard you scream like that."

"I need to have my nipples kissed. You didn't kiss them."

"It would have been too much for you. This isn't torture."

"It wouldn't have been too much for me at all."

"What do you mean?"

"David. It was you who screamed in orgasm."

Caroline curled close to him and said, "It's all right. You're so handsome. I've gotten so lucky." She drew designs on his right shoulder with one finger.

He was having trouble breathing. His thoughts jumped in staccato fragments. His *thoughts* felt out of breath.

The part of him that fluttered off and mocked him.

Could be dead.

Died in that scream.

"You don't have to be embarrassed about crying out," Caroline said.

Death could become birth.

Instead of birth becoming death.

My daughter.

"You made a beautiful love cry," Caroline said.

Fluttering thing gone.

But.

Chest fluttered as he breathed.

"The mystery," Caroline said, "of your cries and mine. A dissonant harmony."

Her love was entering him.

"It's almost unbearable," Caroline said, "when our souls touch."

Flutter in his breath now could be . . .

. . . Hope.

"Son of a bitch," David said.

"You're thinking about Joyce," Caroline said.

David rolled onto his back. Sweat matted the brown curls of his chest. "I was thinking about myself."

"But you're not a son of a bitch and she is. A bitch, rather."

"Why do you say that?"

They climbed onto the brass bed and Caroline draped herself in a sheet with deliberate modesty and sat up with both arms locked around her knees. "Because she stuck you with all those debts."

"Joyce wasn't competent with money, but she never ran up crazy debts until Gabe Cassidy, her lawyer, told her to."

"Then he's a son of a bitch."

"He is. I think he is. He'd say he was doing his job."

"That's not right."

"That's how things are."

"I'm going to call this Dr. Zukovsky and explain."

He touched her neck and kissed her lightly. "Thank you, and he'll be turned on by your charms and he'll still want his money. From Joyce. From me. From Washington, D.C. He doesn't care. He simply wants a check. Look, we ought to be talking about rings and flowery things."

"I'm just strong-jawed enough to want to know exactly what that dentist's lawsuit means."

"Sure," David said. "Quick and straight. It's a bad mark against my credit. There are others. Disputed bills. I probably can't get you charge accounts at Saks or Bonwit's. But the manuscript in the next room is twenty thousand dollars when I turn it in. So I can give you a check now for four hundred dollars to buy a dress, if that's what you want."

"I want our love not to be interfered with."

"The past impinges," David said. "Your past. My past." He left a phrase unspoken. *Joel's past.* "So take the best of the present, Callie. The wretched Rickie Conklin Saga is finished. That's a gross of twenty thousand right now. Twenty thousand dollars.

"Of course, the federal government takes a percentage to buy napalm and to investigate itself. Clip Zellbach will drain more money for negotiating the divorce. Joyce will get a chunk for prior services. Then her lawyer will slice me. Alongside that lawyer waits I. Zukovsky, D.D.S. The drab magic of divorce economics. A .twenty-thousand-dollar gross becomes four thousand dollars.

"But a glory of the present, Callie, is that we do have four thousand dollars. Four thousand dollars clear."

"It isn't fair to you," Caroline said.

"Ah, but I married her, Callie, and I divorced her, Callie, and somewhere Kipling writes: 'The sins that you do two by two/You pay for one by one.' "

He tried to pump gaiety into the words, but her jaw quivered. "I *want* you to buy a good dress," David said.

"On one condition." She forced a smile; suddenly she seemed tired.

"What's that?"

"When I come back from Saks, you let me call I. Zukovsky, D.D.S."

He dialed Joel, who picked up the prior conversation at once. It had only been an hour. "If you'd come over, Dad, I could show you some stuff on Jefferson. Did you know he built his own house? Did you know it took him forty-seven years? Did you know he died on July Fourth? Did you know when he was old, he got so poor he had to sell his library?"

"I have a few things to do, Joel. Business things. Personal things. It will just be a few weeks. Then I'll come over regularly and you can come over here and we'll . . . No, I didn't know it took him forty-seven years to finish Monticello."

"Wait. I've got more. This is going to be a good report. If you came over, I could show you pictures of Monticello being built."

"In a few weeks," David said, "we'll be together and we'll . . ."

What did you most want to do when you were fourteen years old?

David blinked and saw a speckled wall.

He could not remember being fourteen.

"We'll do a lot of, you know, *terrific* things."

"Why can't you come over for a few minutes?"

Sense of order. There was German blood on David's mother's side. First you made your divorce. Then you remade your own life. Then, remade, you started a new kind of fathering.

Sense of guilt. David knew a journalist who had left a scholarly wife and married a television actress. For more than a year, whenever the journalist's daughter visited, the actress had to go away. *He hid his wife away from his own kid.* (In that year, probably in protest, the actress became pregnant by someone else. Later she and the journalist divorced.)

Sense of terror. Joel will fix me with his pale mild eyes. Caroline will look darkly. They know me, David thought. Fixed before their eyes, like a pinned butterfly. Fixed and wriggling. Or drowned by all their love.

"What seems to be the problem with the paper?" David said.

"It's supposed to have a theme," Joel said. "I've got all these facts, but they kind of string together. They don't add up."

"What did Jefferson think about Jefferson?" David said.

"I don't know. He didn't write about himself. Mostly it's ideas."

"Except for the tombstone," David said. "Jefferson wrote his own epitaph." David recited:

"Here was Buried
Thomas Jefferson
Author of The
Declaration
of
American Independence
of the
Statute of Virginia
for
Religious Freedom
And Father of The
University of Virginia."

"Right," Joel said. "He did all those things."

David laughed. "Sure it's right, but what did Jefferson leave out?"

"Don't tell me," Joel said. "Wait. Wait. He left out that he was President of the United States."

"Doesn't that give you a theme?" David said.

"Sort of," Joel said vaguely. "You told me once a theme begins with a title."

"And you were telling me how many things your man accomplished. You can call your report: 'Thomas Jefferson: Being President Came Fourth.' "

"Good, Dad. Thanks, Dad. I'll call you, Dad. I've got to go."

"To write the theme?"

"Yes, and Mom just came home."

Curious with Jefferson. He'd had a daughter who helped him, whom he loved. Pretty, probably. Intense. Well read. Delicate sharp features. Aristocratic. Sexual. But he was prouder to have fathered a university.

What could David write? He was almost thirty-eight. He found paper and sketched an obelisk and printed:

David Priest
Ghost Writer and Scrivener
Who Made Good Phrases
Copulator with 38 Women
(Including 17 Beauties)
and Father of
Joel Micah Priest

Goddammit; he'd better live awhile.

II

"I don't know," Caroline said, "—and that is not a phrase you hear from me every minute—how much you and the Reverend Dr. Merrill Clymer will like each other. But he said he was going to try to like you, if I answered one question honestly. Was I pregnant?"

"Theoretically," David said, "if the dashboard *quarzzeit* is correct, you could be four hours and ten minutes pregnant."

He had sold the rattling Triumph, drained a savings account, cashed a life insurance policy (providing for Joyce S. Priest as irrevocable beneficiary) and purchased a gray Porsche 911. The stumpy sports car matched their mood of growling gaiety.

"Or I could become pregnant between here and Dr. Clymer's house."

David double-clutched down to third gear and kicked the car from 55 to 80. "The way to resist one temptation is to yield to another," he said. The wind whined and the car snarled and David pushed harder. At 95, Caroline made squeaky cries. Then she said, "Ticket."

"Right." He slowed the Porsche on the blacktop Jersey Turnpike. "I hate this road," he said. "Flat. Polluted. Look at those gas tanks. Too fucking many trucks. An essay in American ugliness."

"We're pointing toward a winding two-lane country road above an old canal, which—"

"I can't wait," David said.

"—is the real killer."

"Oh, no; the juggernaut superhighway will destroy us," David said grandiloquently.

"My daddy died on a winding country road. Don't drive so fast."

David had suggested that they marry in a civil ceremony presided over by a jurist who mingled Holmes's appearance and Brandeis's humanism. It might be difficult to find that judge, he conceded, and Caroline had made a trilling laugh and said that she was moving far from home, in every sense, and that the wedding was a last goodbye. It would make her farewell comfortable, and free of needing to look backward, if they were married by the Reverend Merrill Clymer, D.D., of the First Congregational Church of Wallingford Township (settled c. 1674).

"Quick," David said.."A highway death is quick."

"The word," Caroline said, "is 'mutilating.'"

It must be city people who wrote romantic singsongs about country roads, David thought. Civilians always wrote the battle hymns. If you lived in the country, where everyone drove 70, you thought of country roads in terms of skid marks. If not a father, someone you knew: a halfback or a cheerleader. If not mutilating death, then wailing pain.

"Drinking?" David said.

"Other person," Caroline said. "No more now. Please." She charged her voice with energy. "I want to tell you about Dr. Zukovsky, whom I found charming, and Dr. Clymer, whom you will find complex."

The threatening dental litigation had come to an intricate resolution. "And I didn't even need anesthesia to face him down," Caroline boasted. "Five milligrams of your Valium did fine."

All by herself, Caroline Devon had sought out I. Zukovsky, D.D.S., who practiced amid the towering rentals of Sutton Place. She glared at nurses who first purred, then snarled, and she said she would *not* come back another time. If Dr. Zukovsky did not see her after a reasonable wait, she was going to raise her voice in the crowded waiting room, on the subject of robbery by periodonture. "You know," Caroline had said, "the dentist was asked to clean someone's teeth, but he got confused and cleaned a *wallet*."

Blank music oozed from invisible speakers in the reception area and in the waiting room and in the hallway. By contrast, Dr. Zukovsky's private office was silent. Only the walls clamored.

Patients of I. Zukovsky, D.D.S., smiled through caps

and crowns in a blur of autographed photos. Caroline recognized pictures of Spiro Agnew and Sophia Loren and Elmo Zumwalt (U.S.N., ret.) and Natalie Wood and Willie Mays. "Best wishes to my real·pal, Doc Irv," Willie Mays had written.

"Miss, you have no right disrupting the office and my patients," Zukovsky said. "But I'll give you ninety seconds. Go ahead." He was a short, slight, white-haired man who carried his hands in front of his white jacket.

"You're disrupting *my* life and *my* fiancé's life, with a ridiculously unfair lawsuit."

"We charge our patients fairly and we expect our patients to play fair with us. What is your fiancé's name?"

"David Priest."

"The writer? I haven't treated him."

"It's his wife. His former wife. Her lawyer. I'm David's fiancé."

"Damn shysters," Irv Zukovsky said. "Look, we'll try to get the former Mrs. Priest to pay the bill herself."

"David says that her lawyer won't let her."

"Her lawyer won't know. Even he won't know. Understand?"

"I'm not sure."

"They know about this twenty-five-hundred-dollar bill. Now I send out a new bill for one thousand dollars. They'll think that Mr. Priest has gone ahead and paid fifteen hundred dollars. My bill will be marked 'one-thousand-dollar balance.' Maybe they'll think they've gotten all they can out of Mr. Priest. Understand now? Maybe she'll pay it. Understand what I mean?"

"You're being very nice."

"It isn't right to use a professional person." Dr. Irving Zukovsky looked hurt. "I've got to get back to my patients. Don't say too much about this, Miss. Don't be afraid to smile. Keep away from shysters. And Miss."

"Yes, doctor?"

"In case you haven't guessed, I've been divorced myself. I got shafted. Now nobody uses I. Zukovsky to shaft anybody. Come in sometime. I'd like to check your gums."

The Porsche rolled up a bridge spanning the Raritan. The countryside looked clear, but near the riverbank debris spun wearily, winding toward backyards.

"Ol' Doc Irv sounds as if he'd make a good shyster himself."

"No," Caroline said. "He's a twinkly little man and he told me that as a wedding present he'd give us both dental examinations for free."

"Terrific," David said. "I'd kiss you, except we'd plow into the back of a trailer. Then the last word we'd see on earth would be Fruehauf."

"Don't joke about auto accidents, David, and you're going seventy."

"Sorry. The Porsche is bred to hustle. There are no speed limits on the autobahns. You were going to tell about the other doctor, the Reverend Merrill Clymer."

"Well, he was considered quite the liberal in Wallingford long ago."

The trouble, Dr. Merrill Clymer told himself, was that there were no liberals or conservatives anymore. Forty years ago, labels meant something that everybody understood.

Liberals liked Roosevelt, the Spanish Loyalists, Haile Selassie, Norman Thomas, the labor movement, Paul Robeson and Jews.

Conservatives admired efficiency and cleanliness and thrift, of the sort you saw in Switzerland and Germany. They said the oceans were America's first line of defense and they said no entangling alliances and no more foreign wars. They liked Tom Girdler, Henry Ford, individual initiative, Lindbergh, Amos 'n' Andy and the joke about the mink who went to heaven and asked for a coat made of Jews.

Conservatives cared about costs.

Liberals cared about humanity.

Now all the labels were blurry, Dr. Clymer thought. Why, some leftists criticized unions and it was right-wingers who had trumpeted American soldiers into that bloody Asian war. Time had changed the politics, destroyed the politics, creating chaos. Or was that de-creation? Dr. Merrill Clymer was not sure.

Even the language had shifted. Dr. Clymer remembered when "square" implied praise. Square meal. Square guy. Square deal. Now when young parishioners drew a square in the air they were saying somebody was dumb.

How could they do that, change the meaning of words in one man's lifetime? It made Merrill Clymer angry. He was only fifty-nine and still strong enough to lift weights every morning.

The young couple coming for his blessing would arrive at eight and he wanted to put on his pearl-gray vested suit. The boy was from New York, Dr. Clymer remembered, and oh, yes, something else.

Jewish.

Well, he knew about that.

It was difficult to keep track of his suits now that Rochelle was gone. Difficult sometimes to keep track of days. The white clapboard house, with wooden Doric columns, had become too large.

The constant in his life was change.

Change was the only certainty.

(Not even love would stay.)

Except for God.

Oh, he remembered from his youth a lust for change. Clymers had farmed land in Wallingford Township since before the Revolution. Some had lived and died without venturing out of Deerfield County. He saw their names on settled gravestones. Unity and Jessica and Squire Ben. In yellow copybooks he read the records of their occupations. They acquired land. They farmed and leased it. They let mortgages and exacted tolls. His family was landed and usurious.

Breaking from materialism, Merrill Clymer looked for a theology. Catholicism repelled him. Not only by its bloody ritual but by its appointment of a priest as intermediary between man and God.

Forgive me, Father, for I have sinned. I touched her *there*.

Then did you touch yourself, my son?

Yes, Father.

Did you enjoy touching her there? How did it feel?

Yes, Father. Wet, Father.

Did you enjoy touching yourself? What did you think about then?

Yes, Father. Touching her where she was wet, Father.

Abuse is vile. Do you repent?

Yes, Father.

Truly you repent for touching yourself and touching her where she was wet?

Truly, Father.

Did you touch her *inside?* Did she make a cry?

Far inside, Father. She whimpered, Father.

As penance fifty-five Hail Marys.

Thank you, Father. Hail Father, full of grub.

This was not God Omnipotent.

It was Timothy Buckley, S.J., 280 pounds of horny virgin glutton.

Arrivederci Roma.

The Quaker meeting houses sat on ridges in Deerfield County, temples for encountering the soul, the Quakers said. But when Merrill Clymer searched, he found the meeting houses barren.

The Quakers said in solemn pride that they talked di-

rectly to God; their pride disquieted young Merrill
Clymer.

The Quakers said, "There's that of God in every man
and it is up to thee to find Him." Heads bowed and each
head crowned a servile saint. Quaker humility disquieted Merrill Clymer. Didn't they know that the ultimate in humility approached the ultimate in pride, just
as the pale horse of death and the white horse of victory were almost indistinguishable?

They followed God and neglected to war with evil.

Evil? the Quakers said. Say, rather, certain souls are
strays.

Reading theologic history, Merrill Clymer found an
irremediable weakness. Early in the nineteenth century
the Society of Friends burgeoned. (His own people,
some of them Quakers, were busy in those years extending freeholds across Deerfield County.) Borne by
black winds from the South, the miasma of slavery rose.

The irrepressible issue.

Once to ev-er-y man and nation.

The Quakers shuddered and drew back. A Quaker
could not condemn another man. He would not condemn another man. Quakers sought God in the earth
and in the sky and in the minds of slavers.

Abolitionism rose. The Quakers shuddered and withdrew.

Past Quaker silence, right prevailed.

Once to ev-er-y man and nation.

Quaker morality neglected Abolitionism.

The Society of Friends would never again be more
than a minor moral force.

"What," Merrill Clymer asked a Quaker several
weeks ago, "is your position on tobacco, if any?"

"We prefer that you not smoke, but if you feel you
have to smoke, then go ahead," the Quaker said.

The Congregational religion attracted Merrill Clymer
by default. The fellowship of congregations supported

rational Christian precepts. Within a large frame came autonomy for each congregation and within the smaller frame came yet additional autonomy for individuals. Holy. Civilized. No autos-da-fé. Still, there were rules, and there was sin. Had not God the Father yielded up his son to wash away the multitudinous sins of man?

Merrill explained to Rachel's parents, Simon and Dora Crystal, who owned Crystal's department store in Philadelphia. "Our daughter marrying outside the faith?" said Morris Crystal, a gruff, asthmatic man. "Beyond consideration. Unthinkable."

"However," Merrill Clymer began.

"However," Morris Crystal said, "if *you* should take instruction in Judaism."

Unthinkable, Merrill Clymer said in rebound. To reject Matthew, Mark, Luke, the Epistles, Christ Jesus on the cross.

Rachel, in love with Merrill and rebellion, embraced the Congregational faith and adopted the name of Rochelle.

In the days when she became Rochelle Clymer, minister's wife, Morris and Dora Crystal sat moaning and lamenting and saying Kaddish. It was as though their newly married daughter were dead.

Rochelle's rootlessness, in the ancient house with Doric pillars beneath great-rooted maples.

Her infertility.

Neither from nor toward.

"Deceased consumed at least 75 one-gram capsules of proprietary drug Seconal."

Christ damn the Jews for murdering my wife!

"For the papers, Reverend, I'll report myocardial infarct. A coronary."

Caroline guided David toward the winding two-lane road that ran above a narrow towpath, where mules once had pulled barges along the Willingboro Canal. A faded sign said "County Road 11," and the pebbled macadam bent and rose and whipped.

> *Oh, the Willingb'ro Can-al-i-ay,*
> *She creeps along her dusky way*
> *For many a mile, on many a day,*
> *Clear into Phila-del-phi-ay.*

Now only three miles of restoration remained. David held the Porsche in second gear to keep the speedometer from leaping over 40, above the ancient mule path. It had become a promenade.

The little highway climbed and David saw stone chimneys presiding over slants of field. The soil showed rich and cool and dark. Deerfield County land had weathered gently, like certain English countryside, suggesting a mellow, settled way of life.

As the road hooked right and down toward the Willingboro Canal, a corner of flagstone farmhouse reached close to the rim of macadam. David braked and swerved left. There was no reason to swerve left. The house approached the road without encroaching.

"Damn. There ought to be a sign." David steered hard to straighten the Porsche.

"Yes."

"Swerving there is pointless. It only *looks* as though you have to swerve. That swerve is like a flinch."

"Yes."

"Except what sign could there be? Do *Not* Swerve. *No* Obstacle Ahead."

"I don't know," Caroline said. She was out of breath.

"It's all right," David said. "This is the kind of car that overran the Maginot Line."

"No. It's not *your* driving or *your* car. It's something else." She shook her head. "And I am all right, or I will be in a moment."

A rotund dwarf of a flagman appeared beside a stone

hut and called for David to proceed still more slowly. The car whined across the grating of a one-lane iron bridge that crossed the old canal. On the far side the road broadened and a sign announced:

WELCOME TO WALLNFD. TWNP.
CTY. OF DEERFIELD
HISTORIC PENNA. RD.

"How much do they save on vowels?"

"That's a traditional thrift around here," Caroline said. "Ben Franklin was a printer." She had relaxed again and they were enjoying each other as they made their way to Merrill Clymer's home.

David parked the Porsche before the minister's Doric pillars and Caroline said gaily, "Pennhellenism." She fluttered a nervous smile and said, "Why are we doing this?" (It was a question, but Caroline asked no answer. She was speaking as if she were alone.)

"I should have brought my son." (David was not responding to Caroline. A man liked to display possessions at important times. And medals also. His son.)

"We're more or less agnostics," Caroline said, "come to supplicate before a tired Christian." (Don't respond, David, even if you think you understand. Our understandings are as distant as two lives.)

"Form and tradition. You have that in poetry and you have that here tonight." (David was not responding. He was substituting aphorism for conversation. Being mannerly. He had been brought up well, if harshly.)

"Why do we need a wedding in a mansion? The ceremony takes place in the heart." (And on my breasts and belly and in my loins.)

"Joel at my side suggests stability. I'm good at fathering; people pick that up." (When he stands at my side I *am* more stable. For then, at least, I'm guiltless of desertion.)

They had been staring out of separate windows. Caroline blinked and tossed her head. Branches swayed in the light that fell across her English schoolgirl's face. The mystery of light and dark. She felt David's look. She touched his knee. "I'm sorry. We haven't been together."

He stroked her hand. "Our first separation. Hip to hip in the front seat of a Porsche."

"What I should have been explaining," Caroline said, "is that Dr. Clymer has been tired since he lost his wife, Rochelle. She was a round-faced, black-haired woman, who twinkled when she smiled, except for her eyes. Her black eyes always mourned. Mrs. Clymer did things to help me. She took me to concerts at the Academy of Music. She made me take my painting seriously. Maybe too seriously. I'm not that terribly good. Dr. Clymer helped me in a different way. Oh, hell. Get out of the car, David. Let's pass muster."

Standing at the doorway in a pearl-gray suit, the Reverend Merrill Clymer, D.D., looked less tired than Caroline had described and more powerful than David had imagined. The face was broad and bony, with a wide jaw, a full-lipped mouth and tiny pale-blue eyes. The hulking body suggested games of football long ago, when leather helmets crackled in the cold. "Come in," said Merrill Clymer. He smiled at Caroline and gave David the suggestion of a glance. His eyes were gelid.

"I think, perhaps, you may be interested in certain of my things," Dr. Clymer said inside a dark, antiquary living room. His smile this time included David. Like a college boxing rival, David thought. He shows his best punch, hurts you with it, then eases into a more sporting style. But you have felt the punch and you remember it.

The minister's desk, a Queen Anne piece, was genuine. The little sculpted chair? A perfect George II.

The carved love seat? An imitation Hepplewhite, not without value.

"Oh?" David said.

"Really?" Caroline said.

"Indeed," confirmed the Reverend Merrill Clymer.

Furniture, David thought, the common icebreaker; common and politic and crude. Through these chairs, the minister was suggesting, I trace my wealth almost to the majesty of Elizabeth. Old wealth differed from new wealth in veneer. When a Las Vegas pimp got himself arrested, cohorts grasped for his Cadillac, upholstered in whorls of pink. When the head of a moneyed family perished, survivors grappled for Chippendale, behind closed doors.

Merrill Clymer's grandfather clock, by John Gautier of London, had first chimed 275 years before. "Probably a Huguenot, this Gautier," Clymer said, "fleeing the mercies of a Versailles cardinal."

"There's a French ring to the name," Caroline said.

"Perhaps the chimes play Couperin," David said.

They laughed in harmony. "Ah-hah," said Dr. Clymer. "Shall we sit among my electric potpourri?"

Ecumenism next, David thought. He is getting ready to tell me that we are all children in the sight of God.

Clymer sat in a nondescript overstuffed chair and rested his hands upon his stomach. He closed his eyes. Suddenly, his hands sprang upward and his eyes opened wide and he cried with great vehemence, "In God's name, David, how can I learn *anything* about you in an hour?"

Careful. This man was not a friend. It would be unfortunate to make him an enemy. "That I've come here indicates something by itself," David said. "You see I'm not halt, not blind, not leprous. I'll be glad to tell you anything you need to know. I'm thirty-nine years old. I have a B.A. from Columbia College and a master's degree from Columbia Journalism. I'm, uh, a professional writer." He heard his voice decline. No climax. In his mind David added a mocking conclusion. "Some of my works have been collected under the general heading of the Torah."

Merrill Clymer spoke quietly. "Good Lord, man, you are not simply asking me to make a marriage. You're asking me to *bless* a marriage. And I don't know you."

"*We* are asking," Caroline said from the imitation Hepplewhite love seat.

"This isn't just another episode, is it, Caroline?"

She shrank. David was surprised to see her shudder. Then, too quickly, "No, sir. We *both* love each other."

"Which leads me to a question that may be difficult." Clymer held stout hands before him. "Caroline, define your love."

"David is gentle and amusing and strong and purposeful and I feel good when I'm with him, and strong myself. I've never felt this dependent on somebody else, except for Daddy. I'm not always sure where I want to go, Dr. Clymer, but David is sure where he wants to go and I want to be with him."

Clymer's hands returned to his gut. The eyes narrowed and pinned David to the sculpted chair. For all David's ecumenism, he had not previously met a rural Congregational minister. The idea of appearing on approval rankled. It was like defending your driving before a backwoods judge. No, not like that. Worse. He was offering Clymer his head upon a platter. Merrill Clymer might simply turn away.

David saw a headline.

PROTESTANT PRELATE SPURNS HEAD OF WANDERING JEW. AFFIANCED WEEPS. FRESH COLD WAVE IS DUE. MONTREAL CANADIENS TAKE LEAD IN HOCKEY PLAY.

David had a shattering sense of mounting a gynecological table and being poked by the minister's hand;

white fingers, fat and gloved, jabbed and probed until they found a cunt. "I want to be open," he said to Dr. Clymer. "That is, direct. I need Caroline with me as much as I need to see another spring. My words for her are not distinctive—compassion, beauty, youth. I can't make phrases during deep emotion. Wordsworth's old problem."

If Clymer understood the reference, he ignored it. "But do you love Caroline's youth for itself, or have you come here as a borrower? I see before me a tall, stylishly attired man, who wears a mustache and says he has nothing to hide.

"Now is that mustache for style, or for concealment?

"The gentleman tells me of academic degrees. He conceals, or does not mention, that he is the divorced father of a child." Clymer's voice rose. "I am asked to bless this marriage after another marriage—your first— lost the beauty of its benediction.

"I ask myself and you, David Priest, are you using my parishioner, Caroline Devon, to forget that failure? Have you courted her to experience *her* spring, to revisit your own youth, *while draining hers?*" The Reverend Dr. Merrill Clymer paused and glowered. His hands stroked each other.

"You might as well ask *me,*" Caroline said, "if I'm using David to escape the provinces."

It does not matter how careful I am, David thought. This man already is an enemy.

"There is a truism," Clymer said, offering a conciliatory look, "that states that everybody uses everybody else. In one way or another. Except for certain saints. And Christ Jesus.

"To know you." Dr. Clymer drew the fat white hand across his mouth. He searched the ceiling, theatrically in thought. Then he said, "Why, by your trade!"

"I was a newspaperman," David said. It was a relief to talk career; the words about his writing tumbled out.

"That was good postgraduate work, but confining. Then I wrote articles for magazines on politics and television and later on artistic people. But the more artistic my subjects, the smaller my check turned out to be. So after essays on a master pianist who'd been in Jungian therapy for twenty-seven years, and on a poet who wrote erotic sonnets to his lesbian wife, I ghosted a woman's story on a safari, which bored everyone but the woman (whose husband underwrote the book), and I've just had to ghost the memoirs of the actor Rickie Conklin, which I meant as a study in self-destruction. That's all behind me."

"David's going to write his own books now, serious books," Caroline said, reaching toward Clymer with a cheerleading smile.

"There's nothing that warrants apology," Clymer said. "In fact, I admire Rickie Conklin's performing, if not all his behavior."

David blinked and heard Rickie screaming about fellatio. Rickie wore a crew cut and he was screaming so loudly that the bald spot on the crown of his head turned pink. "We need that scene," David was saying to Rickie, "not just because your wife is going down on her doctor." Rickie's third wife, a leonine actress from Orem, Utah, was terrified of penetration. "We need it because it's the first total rejection in your life." Rickie Conklin interrupted. "What the fuck do you have to say about this, pencil pusher? You'd get a girl like that and bang her asshole. The scene is out. It's my fucking life. You have nothing fucking to say, pencil pusher!"

Imagine that real Rickie Conklin performance in Clymer's glossy antiquary living room. There were too many worlds in David's brain.

"Now I'm on to something real," David said. "Just as soon as we're married, I'm going to start an exploration into black life in America." (The Utah ingenue succeeded outrageously on television. In *TV Guide*, she described her days as cool and happy. "You know, like smooth.")

ANAL INTERCOUSE EASED HER LIFE, ACTRESS AVERS. CREDITS OBSCURE WRITER'S AUDACITY. "AFTER THAT, MY PUSSY NATURALLY RELAXED," BLONDE STAR TELLS REPORTER.

"I had hoped for a Paris honeymoon," Caroline said to Merrill Clymer. "Instead I'm being offered six months in Harlem and I'm delighted."

"I want to undertake something big." David was talking to himself, to Caroline, and coincidentally to the Reverend Clymer. "Say, arbitrarily, the black-liberal issue begins with Jefferson. He freed his slaves, but only after his death. Not a satisfactory policy. The persistent question is: Can black assimilation go on as it has, sort of—forgive me, Reverend—half-assed?" Clymer puffed up in the upholstered chair, looked huge and waited.

"I reserve strong language for shocking situations," David said.

"Jefferson was a complete intellectual, but an incomplete libertarian. After his death, were his slaves assimilated or murdered? Both. Can black assimilation ever fully succeed? We don't know. The races of Europe gather, you and I, in a truce. But the black is not a European."

David leaned forward on the slight chair, a hand in the air as though preaching. "I'm going to go to Harlem as if it were another continent. I'm going to try the life up there and see if I fit it and see if it fits me. Pieces of a puzzle. Ultimately, I mean to ask, will race war tear apart the country?"

"Your conclusion?" Clymer said.

"You don't start writing with conclusions. If you're

lucky, you start with a title. I have mine. *White Man, Walk Easy.*"

"We must seem wretchedly provincial to you," Merrill Clymer said. He found David poised and fierce and strange and possibly good for Caroline, but dangerous. Christ Jesus, Jewish *essences* were different.

Merrill Clymer walked on Thaler Street in Germantown, a man of twenty-five who had won Latin awards at William Penn Charter School and played running guard for Haverford and acquired a doctorate of divinity at Union Theological Seminary, but still was a boy paying courtly call. Simon Crystal, whose features bunched around a white mustache, wheezed and rattled a newspaper as Merrill talked of the life he planned with Rachel. Country air. Blessed meek. Are we not all children of God, who is gentle?

The old man looked up from the Philadelphia *Bulletin.* "Mighty, indeed. Wise, beyond question. But gentle? I don't know what Bible you read, young man, but you cannot understand it. Baruch Spinoza understood it. He saw the slaughter there. I don't know what histories you read, but the pogroms of York and Cologne and the Inquisition do not suggest gentleness in God. I don't know what newspapers you read, but have you heard of Dachau? What are you doing about Dachau, you Christians and your gentle God?"

Merrill Clymer had come for courting, wearing a yellow rose in one lapel. He was spurned like a mutt, banished by pedigrees. Himself descended from pre-Revolutionary Clymers. Rachel, who would become Rochelle, clutched the yellow rose. She cried so hard that it made even him weep.

"I have been somewhat primitive," Merrill Clymer said, rising. "May I fix you a Scotch?"

"You may fix *two* Scotches," Caroline said.

They drank and Merrill Clymer said that rural though he had been, he had a particular feeling for the blacks. "I support much of the movement. Paul Robeson's father was a legendary preacher up near New Brunswick. I've elevated consciousness among my own parishioners and our church has what we call a Turkey Trot. Each Thanksgiving we collect as many plump turkeys as we can find and trot them over to the poor colored people in Trenton. Some of those poor colored people are charming and gifted." His voice deepened. "But do you think for an instant I would bless a union between Caroline Devon and one of *them?*"

"Meaning?" David said.

"The core of the problem in front of me is pretty much the core of the problem in your Harlem book."

"Meaning?" David said.

"Degrees of difference."

"Meaning?" David said.

"Meaning, Mr. Priest, that you are a Jew." (When they buried Rochelle, Merrill Clymer remembered, he had ordered five bouquets of yellow roses. None of the Crystals came to the funeral, and at the gravesite he had to stand alone. The yellow ocher sun played on a weed called harlequin.)

David's first sensation was relief. To deal with "Jew" spoken as a pejorative, rise and walk slowly across the room. The minister will rise in response. Keep both hands at your sides. Say, "Look, mister, I don't want any trouble." As the other man relaxes, hit him as hard as you can. Knock the base of the jaw into the brain pan, inducing stupor.

David rose and walked across the room. Clymer stood up, and hunched his thick shoulders. David kept both hands at his sides. "Look, mister," he said, "I don't want . . ." He stared into the minister's eyes. He saw fright. ". . . . to lower myself. Good evening."

Caroline stood and took David's hand. Merrill Clymer babbled. "I meant no offense. I intended to talk about differences in backgrounds that are different." He made a pleading cry. "But bridgeable!"

"I'm sorry, Dr. Clymer," Caroline said. Her strong jaw set over a wintry smile. "However, if my fiancé has no objections, I'd still like you to perform the service."

"No objections," David said, standing in the doorway, next to the grandfather clock by John Gautier, the Huguenot of London.

"Stay longer, Mr. Priest," Dr. Merrill Clymer said. "I haven't had an opportunity to ask you about your son."

Night wind stung their faces and they climbed into the gray Porsche, cold as Thule, and Caroline said, "I thought you were going to punch him when he called you a Jew."

"That wasn't his worst offense. The worst was when he profaned my boy. He actually wanted to use Joel as an *apology* for calling me a Jew."

"I'm glad you didn't swing. Dr. Clymer is a big man. He can take a punch and the word is he can give one too."

"In there I saw an interior movie," David said. "I knocked down Clymer and kneeled and I kept hitting him. I grabbed his throat." David seized the gearshift. "Jew is an incomplete comment, like man. Neither praise nor damnation. It's what a man accomplishes. It's what a Jew accomplishes. It's all the same if I'm called a Jew or I'm called a man."

Caroline took his hand and placed it under the skirt on her left thigh. "Bullshit, David," she said.

"In this interior movie," David said, "I was throttling him, truly squeezing the life from his throat. You stood over us and said, with terrible, emotionless finality, 'It's off. I can't marry a man so violent.' And I said, 'I'm just trying to make up for Auschwitz, honey.' And you didn't hear.

" 'What?' you asked.

" 'Auschwitz, honey,' I said.

"You laughed coldly. You said 'Auschwitz and honey don't go.' "

She patted his hand and moved it closer to her crotch. "Eight years old," Caroline said, as if to herself. "Rochelle was gentle to me, and Dr. Clymer in his pulpit seemed as huge as God. On a Saturday when I was eight, I slid down a rope in Daddy's barn, from the loft up top. I wrapped my legs around the rope. That's when I had my first orgasm. The next day in church, I thought Dr. Clymer was looking at me all through his sermon. All of a sudden, I began to cry."

David started the Porsche. Caroline turned into the heedless night. Within his living room window, Merrill Clymer poured another drink.

"What did Clymer mean," David said, "when he asked if this—if *I*—was just another incident?"

"Nothing. An affair. It was nothing."

"Affairs aren't nothing. Affairs are something."

"I don't like to talk about affairs," Caroline said.

"We ought to know every episode about each other."

"No, because when someone gets angry, they use things to hurt, like old affairs. Besides, you're not my doctor."

"I'd certainly like to be *your* doctor," David said, "but I wouldn't want to have to examine the other ones, the sloppy fat ones and the ones with open lesions."

"Please."

"I mean, I want to know about your life."

"It embarrasses me to talk about certain things." She took his hand again, and placed it on her crotch. "I was seventeen at boarding school and I wasn't getting any support from my mother. I wanted to paint. She said do something practical. Be a secretary. I said I wanted to be an artist. She said compromise. Be secretary to Picasso."

The engine idled and the heater warmed the car. "You remember the road near the canal and the house that made you swerve? That's where Daddy died. He was driving slowly in lane when a teen-ager in a pickup hooked the way you did, only wider, only faster, and killed my father. The boy was drinking. I know him. Steve Gowdy. He was drinking, but his father was a Deerfield County selectman, and Steve got off with a fifty-dollar fine. Dr. Clymer did a beautiful eulogy. He quoted Socrates. 'To a good man, no evil can come, either in life or after death.' But Daddy was dead.

"I had no one to turn to. My sister was engaged and she didn't like me and she isn't bright. My mother didn't cry herself. She doesn't cry. When I cried my mother turned away from me. Her eyes were blank.

"My painting teacher, Fred McFeeley. He was tall and crew cut and a good diver and married and terribly unhappy. He said he understood my feelings because he'd been unhappy so long. He worked on my watercolors day after day and I felt sorry for him and grateful and one afternoon we were alone in the studio at school and my father was dead, and I let Freddie touch my breasts. He stopped and locked the door and touched my breasts again.

"We got undressed and we made love on the floor of the studio and that was the first time. It hurt so much I yelled and he held me and then he put his hand on the back of my neck and pressed me toward his penis. It was so big I could hardly breathe. The roof of my mouth is narrow. It was so big I was frightened, but he held my neck and he moved my head and I couldn't do anything. I couldn't help myself. He came and came and it went down my throat and I thought I was going to strangle. He lay there and I threw up and whenever I throw up, I really cry.

"Somebody heard. Freddie had locked the door, but the top of the door was *glass*. We lay there on the floor, we were both naked, and I saw the assistant headmistress standing outside. Afterward, the headmistress talked to Dr. Clymer about my life, and that was that. They pretended nothing had happened. But Freddie was fired. He had a breakdown. He's not painting anymore."

"It's all right," David said. "It doesn't matter."

"It does matter. I haven't been able to go down on anybody since."

"That's all right too," David said. "I may be the last of the great straight up-and-down fuckers."

"I want to go down on you, David."

"We'll get to that."

"No!" She made a throaty cry. "Now!" She turned off the ignition and opened David's fly. Through two windows he saw the Reverend Dr. Merrill Clymer at the Queen Anne desk.

"I'm not comfortable with this, Caroline."

She put a finger against his lips and bent over his lap. Her lips made an O around his penis. He closed his eyes, blotting out Queen Anne and the Reverend Clymer, and thought, Callie didn't understand about trying to make up for Auschwitz.

As if you could.

The O moved up and down.

And to what purpose? The past was finished. Its wars were done. Its loves were told.

The restless O, steady, insistent, encircled him.

Tongue of fire.

Tongue of delight.

The maddening O.

Beyond control.

He came explosively and in deep silence and then

Caroline was hugging his waist and saying, "Oh, my new love. Oh, my good love." His eyes opened. Dr. Clymer was standing up in the living room and putting on a jacket.

"There are tissues in the glove compartment," David said.

"Was I good?"

"Marvelous."

"I liked it, David. For the first time, I liked doing that."

The Reverend Dr. Clymer stepped out of his house, paused under the Doric pillars and started toward the Porsche. "My nightly constitutional," the minister said. He had pinned a yellow rose to the lapel of his topcoat. "What have you young people been doing here so long?"

"Working on the past," David said. "Anticipating the future."

Clymer nodded vaguely and walked on.

"My Germany," David said.

"What?" Caroline said.

"In the Germany I imagine, no Jew displays a yellow star. But every anti-Semite wears a yellow rose in his lapel."

Caroline frowned. "But that's not fair to roses, is it, my love, my good, new love?"

III

The first visitation began with a catch in David's throat. Walking among the offal that littered West Seventy-ninth Street, he saw a dark brick apartment building on Riverside Drive where he had lived listlessly with Joyce for seven years.

All kinds of scenes, David thought, all kinds of crimes. He had loved Joyce enough to father Joel; after that he had not loved her often, or wanted her at all.

WRITER'S LIFE LISTLESS, BUT HIS MARRIAGE SINKS.
DOCTOR WARNS ON POST-PARTUM SEX: BETTER
EARLY THAN NEVER. WOMAN IN MUTE DISSENT,
DRINKS GIN.

David tried to put off further thought, but his mind clattered with wordplay. The deserter returns. He returns to the place he has deserted, that has become a desert place. Clattering wordplay, but wounding.

Poor abandoned woman, left to dine alone, to raise a child alone, to sleep alone.

Fucking Jewish guilt, unblinking as a star. Why must mine be Betelgeuse the Giant?

"Hello, Mr. Priest."

"Huh? Oh, hello." David nodded at Bettina Lumley, an English actress, crowned with salt-and-pepper hair, with whom, oh Christ, he had balled in the living room. Joyce could not compete with salt-and-pepper hair, or English accents, except to drink pink gin, a British cocktail when taken neat.

"Sorry about the divorce." Bettina smiled. He had not tried a second time.

"Thanks. 'Sawright."

Joyce sensed Bettina attracted him. They knew. They always knew. Sometimes they knew before you did. Civilized wives sensed out danger with jungle nostrils. That night poor civilized Joyce simply surrendered.

David wondered if Bettina's Old Vic diction would persist in heat, and Joyce, who would raise a child alone and dine alone, drank neat pink gins until she had to lie alone in bed.

"The household motto here is *Semper Fidelis*," David said.

"She snores like a bloody Cornish thunderstorm," Bettina said.

"Joyce is out for at least three hours."

Bettina worked with a long slit skirt, which alternately

covered her calves and flashed open to her pubic triangle. No salt and pepper there. Conventional WASP brown. Six nights a week, she bowed her head to Broadway crowds. The muff played to smaller audiences.

The accent did persist and presently assaulted David's ears. Bettina Lumley was the talkingest fuck David had known. "Ah, that feels splendid. Deep and splendid. I rather fear I may cry out. Someone may hear. Someone may come," Bettina said.

Fucking actress. Even now straining for puns in a monologue.

Bettina heaved. "Please don't let me be loud."

"What?"

"I said," the voice commanded, "do *not* let me be loud."

"I didn't hear you say that." Inner laughter. Bettina writhed. "It's rather difficult for me to come," Bettina said.

A middle-class Jewish girl from Brooklyn, in the form of a Soho wench. Bettina whimpered in mild orgasm. David held her with hard hands. Did London moans differ from moans in Brooklyn? Truly had he imagined that they would?

DISCOVERY OF BYRON, LAWRENCE
CONFIRMED BY LESSER WRITER:
SEX ACT CAN PLAY AS COMEDY.

Except with Caroline.

Time ran as David walked the West Side street. No more time to waste in the past; not even an instant.

Too many instants to make up with his son.

The catch persisted in his throat.

"I want to talk to you," Joyce said, "about a dentist who is not such a nice guy."

"Where's Joel? Apparently he's come across Thoreau.
I have a poem for him."

"In his room studying. Please, first the dentist. Want
a drink?"

"Not a good idea." David felt uncertain. He wanted
to differentiate a visitation from a social call.

"Oh, for God's sakes. We're not in court. I'll get you
a Scotch."

David stood above a blue crushed-velvet sofa he had
bought six years before. "May I sit down?"

It had been his apartment, seven rooms, nine stories
above the Hudson River, to wander, to defend. He
scattered old furniture through six of the rooms and
set about making the living room his own. He liked
glass and stainless steel and leather. He bought Barcelona chairs and tables of pale-green glass fixed onto
gleaming metal legs, and he covered the floor with
shiny vinyl, white squares bounded by black. A carpenter built walnut shelves around the fireplace, and
the living room was finished. He had broken with provincial Brooklyn. It was his room, his home, his view.
Curious, that he had not argued when court awarded
home, furnishings, child and view to Plaintiff Wife. Not
curious. Guilt was a most effective silencer.

Joyce reappeared with drinks. She wore a patterned
dress that hid the outlines of her figure, but showed
bulk. "David, I need an extra thousand dollars."

"Joyce, I don't have an extra thousand dollars."

"David, what are you using to furnish your new apartment?"

"It's mostly furnished. Let's get Joel."

"Not until we straighten this out. David, a dentist
named Zukovsky, whom *you* were supposed to pay,
according to an agreement *you* signed, sent process
servers suing *me*."

"He's been suing me too."

"The one thing we can't stand, after all we've been

through, is more legal trouble. Pay me, David, so I can pay the dentist. We can stand anything. I've stood a lot. Except more legal trouble."

She's had a settlement, alimony and child support, David thought. Now she wants maintenance for her teeth.

"David, it isn't right. And something else. It's bad for Joel to live in a house where process servers come."

She's overplaying the goddamn guilt game. "May I see Joel?"

Joyce stood up, a square-faced redoubt of a woman. She shook her head. Not the girl I courted, or the girl who courted me, on bicycles so very long ago.

"You're back teaching," David said. "You've got to start looking out for your own bills. I hear you're running social studies at Webster Hall."

"And working my head off, but that isn't the point, David. The point is that you are again shirking one of your responsibilities." She spoke loudly. Fort Joyce. Forte Joyce. She had not been this way. The divorce process. Lawyers had coached this into her. *Demand.* You have been wronged. *Demand.* If he makes a concession, do not pause to thank him. If he makes a concession, demand one more. Think of what you really want. Double it. Triple the doubled figure. You have now reached the asking price. *Demand.*

"I'll try to help with the dentist," David said.

"Good," Joyce said. "I'll get Joel for you."

Once you school yourself in adversary tactics, you use them by reflex. That makes divorced people as argumentative as lawyers. She's getting Joel, David thought, now that I've ransomed him.

"Dad," the boy said, walking lightly down the hall behind his mother. "Dad?" He smiled. "You're getting married?"

"Looks that way," David said.

"That's a nice blazer, Dad, and a neat red belt."

"Suede. The red matches my turtleneck." Joel wore a tattersall shirt and oxford-gray slacks. He already showed a sense of style. "I'll get you a blazer just like this," David said.

"Hug him, for Christ's sake," Joyce insisted. Father and son made a tentative embrace.

"Now just who is this kid you're going to marry?" Joyce said.

"She's not a kid."

"How old, then, is this *woman?*"

"Twenty-six."

"Come on," Joyce said. "She may be very nice, but she's a kid."

"Is she pretty?" Joel said.

"I think so."

"Have I seen her?"

"In a bikini. On Pokanoket. You probably have."

"Sounds good," Joel said.

"She looks good," David said, "except her navel is a bit large."

"Stop that," Joyce demanded. Joel played an amused look at his father. "Oh, hell," Joyce said. "Do what you want. I'll let the two of you boys be children together."

She padded off into six rooms of old furniture.

"Well," David said to Joel, as if in greeting.

"I've been busy. I would have called you more often, Dad, but I've been busy."

"Let's see," David said. "My bride-to-be is named Caroline Devon, and she's a terrific swimmer and ice skater, and she wants to start you skiing, and I really want you to meet her and I hope you can see this, really, as finding a new friend."

Joel looked small for the Barcelona chair. "A new *stepmother*, Dad," he said, solemnly. "She's going to be a stepmother. I already have plenty of friends."

He decidedly was a creature of the sun. He grew each summer, toughening as he tanned, then turned pale as the days shortened. It was different with California kids; they were *always* getting blonder and more bronze. Then at twenty-two they retired to Oregon and picked guitars.

When Joel was little, he caught croup each February. You had to steam the bedroom against the rattle of that cough and somebody, usually David, stayed up till dawn. Excess concern, but natural after the first one had stopped breathing. Red hair. A girl. Her name was Anne.

David blinked into the present. The boy in front of him, while no longer tan, was sturdy, nicely muscled and weighed at least 125 pounds. Joel had not contracted croup for ten years. His arms were beginning to look like the arms of a man. Only his face, triangular and delicately smooth, suggested fragility.

"Are you reading much besides Thoreau?"

"A terrific book called *A Separate Peace,* about prep school. I've read that twice. *Cry, the Beloved Country.* That's about these black people and a few white people and it's beautiful and very sad. We're reading some short stories by Ernest Hemingway, but I don't like the way he writes. He's kind of violent."

"So is the twentieth century."

"You mean the wars and all?"

"The wars and the peacetimes. Hemingway seemed comfortable in war."

"You can tell from his writing he liked violence," Joel said.

"Or he was used to violence anyway." ("A wife can put up with a writer for from seven to twelve years. After that she moves on.") V.S.O.P. Hemingway, after rounds of drinks and rounds of combat about the house.

"In *Cry, the Beloved Country,* there's killing," Joel said, "but it isn't as if the writer liked it."

"I wouldn't say Hemingway necessarily liked violence.

He was preoccupied by violence. You don't want to run away from the rough stuff."

"I don't," Joel said. "I'm playing hockey at John Clay, and the coach, Mr. Dunleavy, shows us how you hit a guy into the boards. You ride him and ride him and ride him. When you get to the boards, swing your elbow. Crunch."

"I played baseball. It got violent around second base, or some big goon would throw a fast ball at your face."

"You don't hurt the other guy much in hockey. You're both wearing helmets and a ton of padding. It's not a violent sport, Mr. Dunleavy says. It's a contact sport."

"We'll have to skate."

"I'm getting fast."

David smiled at the young figure, restless on the black leather chair. The Pokanoket waves. The boy's agility. "I'll skate, but don't crunch me," David said.

"Chicken, Dad?" Joel looked a challenge at his father. Boys were grown up at sports before they were grown up at anything else.

"How have you jumped from Monticello to Walden Pond?"

"Not me," Joel said. "Mrs. Talbot. We have this course for honors. Mainstreams in American Thought and Poetry."

"Well, I've brought a Thoreau poem for you," David said.

> *"I am a parcel of vain strivings tied*
> *By a chance bond together,*
> *Dangling this way and that, their links*
> *Were made so loose and wide,*
> *Methinks,*
> *For milder weather."*

"What does it mean?" Joel said.

"How does it sound?" David countered.

"Sound? It sounds good, the way you say it."

"It sounds good the way Thoreau wrote it. That's the first thing. The sound."

"Mrs. Talbot says the most important thing about a poem is to understand the poet's intention."

"Are you studying poetry by Mrs. Talbot?"

"No."

"Then how does she know the poet's intention?"

Joel sat upright in the leather chair. "I never thought of that." He made an upward glance and nodded quickly. "She's only guessing."

"There are two ways to read a poem," David said. "You can approach a poem, or you can attack it. You approach by listening to the music. You attack by analyzing.

" 'I have been half in love with easeful Death.'

" 'Sweet Thames, run softly till I end my song.'

" 'But thy eternal summer shall not fade.'

" 'How can I tell the dancer from the dance?'

"Four lines from three centuries. They all make music."

"Could I hear the Thoreau poem again?" Joel said.

"You have to respect Mrs. Talbot because she's educated. Besides, she gives the grades. But analysis comes at the end, after the music."

"The poem," Joel said.

David repeated:

> *"I am a parcel of vain strivings tied*
> *By a chance bond together*
> *Dangling this way and that, their links*
> *Were made so loose and wide,*
> *Methinks,*
> *For milder weather.*

"They read that at Thoreau's funeral. He only lived forty-five years. Tuberculosis. He wrote the poem when he was twenty. He'd been considering a bunch of flowers."

"I like the way it sounds," Joel said, *"and* I know what it means."

"What does it mean?"

"It means what it says."

"That's terrific, Joel. You're a quick study."

"And it also means that Thoreau wouldn't have had much fun playing for Mr. Dunleavy's hockey team."

Joyce wandered back into the living room and offered a soft gaze to father and son. Probably, she'd taken a few drinks. David hoped they hadn't been pink gins. He felt sorry for his old friend Joyce. Living alone. Raising a child alone. Sleeping alone. A cocktail was her undemanding friend.

"What have you boys been talking about?" Joyce said.

"Poetry, Mom, and sports."

"Don't you have an essay due?"

"On Hemingway."

"You'd better do your homework, then," David said.

"Next time can we skate?" Joel asked David.

"Next time you can skate," Joyce answered. "Come on now. Start the essay. John Clay is an expensive school. Your father and I want A's for our tuition."

Joel touched David's shoulder briefly as he left.

"A pleasant visit," David said to Joyce.

"I set it up that way. He's more upset than you know. I had to calm him."

"In pastorals father and son move together across upland meadows. For Joel and me it's living rooms and rinks."

"Would you give me the check for the dentist?" Joyce said. David stared; her eyes had become unyielding.

"I don't have a check."

"What upset him most was the process server."

"You can just tell him—"

"I'm telling you, David. I can't have process servers. The thousand dollars is your debt."

"Your teeth."

"Until you pay me what you owe the dentist, I'll simply stop the visitations."

"You can't stop them. They're between Joel and me."

Joyce folded thick arms at her bust. "I can and I will. Gabe Cassidy thinks your behavior is outrageous."

"He's a goddamn lawyer, not a goddamn judge."

"Don't raise your voice in my home."

"You're equating money and fatherhood," David said, quietly.

"Merits and issues can be resolved in court. Until then you'll stay current financially, so I can keep Joel safe from process servers, or you won't have any more visits."

"How can you set a price on my relationship to my son?"

"If you shout again, David, I'll call the police."

"Fuck," David said in a tight whisper.

She stared and started toward the telephone.

"It will take a day to jiggle accounts. Then I'll mail the check," David said. He looked around at the gleaming steel pieces he had bought. They were not his. This was not his house.

She was not his old friend Joyce.

Their past was nightmare.

Probably, David thought, this was the first time he had understood.

They were not friends.

Affection had been drowned.

They were divorced.

IV

For a moment, between sleep and wakefulness, in her old bedroom cornered high in the stone farmhouse, with Roundout Creek running down below, Caroline fancied that she was a child. She heard her father calling from the fields, "It's a golden morning every here and there."

Her mother laughed. "Every here and there?"

"That's western Pennsylvania, Lottie. The state's not all Deerfield County, don't you know?"

"You silly millhand." It was a favorite joke. Chuck Devon came out of western Pennsylvania—but from a dairy farm, not from a mill. At seventeen, he ran off to sail merchant ships. He read Jack London, Bret Harte and Mark Twain in the holds of freighters. Later he talked about a farmer-labor-sailor party. "Be quiet," Lottie said. "The Maitlands have voted Republican since 1820."

"There was no Republican party until 1854."

"That's right. We were Republicans before there was a party."

Caroline loved the blending of her parents' laughter. She enjoyed her father's mental file of random, non-marketable facts. Daddy knew *why* the Republican party was founded, and that spruce trees belonged to a genus called *Picea* and that if you stroked a pet rabbit for twenty minutes every day, and did not forget, the rabbit lost its fear within three weeks.

Farming called him back from the sea. He lived on and off eighty acres, Daddy said. If the family needed help, there was always Grandmother Maitland, who had bought Hickory Ridge Farm for them in the first place. Daddy said it never hurt a socialist to have capital behind him.

"You're bending, Chuck."

"Things bend in middle age."

"Where's the radical," Mother said, "I knew at my wedding?"

*   *   *

Wedding.
The word clamored Caroline awake.
Daddy was dead.
This afternoon she was to be married.

Charlotte Devon invited twenty-two. She neglected to ask David for a list of people he wanted to invite because that was a lot of trouble, having a crowd down from New York. With Chuck gone, she wasn't good at social things. She couldn't even run the farm. It was fortunate that Grandma Maitland had left trusts. Living alone, Charlotte Devon became concerned with tidiness, bookkeeping and regular bowel movements. This wedding would cost three hundred dollars, no more, the same as the wedding for her firstborn, Patricia Beth, who lived in Albany and didn't visit any longer, excepting every third Christmas.

Charlotte was rawboned, strong-jawed, with thick black brows and eyes that ignored others even as she greeted them. Her look was gaunt and distant. "Since Daddy was killed," Caroline said, "she's stayed within herself. I guess she's frightened." Charlotte wore an unadorned green woolen dress to the wedding.

Her guests included Walt and Becky Comfort from the Willingboro Golf Club; and Jim and Pat Kinsolving from Thursday bridge; and the Meenans, up from Paoli; and Chuck's brother, Les Devon, with Marion, who had driven clear from Pittsburgh. Splits of silver maple crackled in the fireplace and the people and the flowers and the flowered dresses made the place feel warm. Charlotte wanted to take her future son-in-law by the arm and introduce him, but it was a bother to do that, and it might annoy him, and besides, he seemed all right introducing himself.

Guests clustered in the long open-beamed living room; they stood near the hearth talking about zoning laws. Beside a window opening toward fields of corn stubble they chattered about percolation rates and septic fields. Near white-oak doors that led to the dining room, they discussed price increases in Jamaican bauxite. The conversations, similar a week before and likely to be the same a week later, lapsed at the approach of a tall, mustached New Yorker who was going to marry Caroline.

"I just don't know what to talk to you about," Becky Comfort said. Narrow eyes dominated her long face.

"Politics," David said. "Music. Sports. Fatherhood."

"Fatherhood?"

"I love to talk about my son."

"I'd rather talk sex than fatherhood," Becky Comfort said.

Was it martinis, David wondered, or frustration? "Everybody talks about sex," he said, "but nobody does anything about it."

"I'll do something about it." She had a wide beckoning mouth.

"Standing up?" David said. "Beside the fireplace? On my wedding day?" A hand fastened on his elbow. Walt Comfort, drinking sherry, had been loitering near his wife.

"Anytime you want," bald Walter Comfort said, in a low, urgent voice. "I don't make it with Becky anymore. She needs it. Anytime you want, you'd be doing me a favor."

David studied Comfort's flat, round face. The man was beseeching. David turned away. Who had said, from the summit of old age, that he was grateful mostly for two memories: springtimes and the places where he had got laid?

"Used to be cattle out there," Jim Kinsolving said. He gestured toward the western window. A dust of snow showed beneath the stubble. "Chuck was a working farmer." Kinsolving had a long fishbone scar on his right cheek.

"I used to hear that when cattle sat down it was going to rain."

"You city dudes," Pat Kinsolving said. She was snub-nosed and small and animated. "When some cows sit and some cows stand, are we going to have scattered showers?"

"That's the last time I take cattle tips from a subway motorman," David said.

"I lived in New York," Pat said, "when I was Caroline's age, working as a buyer for Gimbel's."

"She got to know a lot of Jewish people," Jim Kinsolving said. "Fine people, the Jews. Strong. Tough."

"They're just people," David said. "Strong. Weak. Tough. Tender." The ambassador from Israel had now articulated his position. Fund raising would be next.

"The toughest of them are those Israelis." Kinsolving clutched a whiskey sour and stared at David's left shoulder. The fishbone scar was turning pink. "You know what the Palestine mess is about?"

"The right of Jews to survive on their own," David said in a hard tone. The ambassador had decided to postpone fund raising.

"Some business friends tipped me. The Israelis have oil now in the Sinai. What they need next is iron. Then they're a major power, and the rest of us had better watch out."

David would have walked, but the stocky, square, scarred man like a football guard blocked his path. "The Israelis will have to invade Italy, then, Mr. Kinsolving, because that's where the closest iron mines are." The idea amused David and he pursued it.

"First, Mr. Kinsolving, the Israelis send their tanks through Lebanon. Then up through Turkey and into Yugoslavia. Are you following my geography, Mr. Kinsolving? That puts the tanks in Trieste, near the house where James Joyce lived. They make a left turn and head down the Adriatic into Venice. That's a real worry."

"What's a real worry?"

"The weight of all those tanks. Venice might sink."

"He's making fun of you," Pat Kinsolving said.

"I don't know about that," Jim Kinsolving said. "I'm trying to talk serious about Palestine. Are you making fun of me, feller?" The fishbone scar whitened.

"Don't get angry," Pat said. "We came here for his wedding."

"That's right," Jim Kinsolving said. His dulled eyes cleared briefly. "There's going to be a wedding at this party, ain't there?"

Upstairs, Caroline rose from a narrow bed in the corner bedroom above Roundout Creek, and folded a powder-blue silk robe tightly around herself and stood before a three-way mirror. She had wanted to nap, but when she closed her eyes noises and images jumped up and frightened her.

A red highway under a blinding sky.

Daddy penning sheep until one of the sheep, slavering like a wolf, attacked him.

A pebbled gray sun, paler than the moon.

A blizzard covering the highway and the animals.

The wind's shattering wail.

The sun dying.

A black sky lighted by a skull.

She had taken a Mellaril and she wanted to take another. Dr. Hackett said two would be all right, once in a while, but it was ludicrous to be married while tranquilized. Common enough, though, Caroline thought. Often the tranquilizing agent was a dream.

She dropped the blue robe and watched it fall to her feet in the mirror Fred McFeeley had given her. She kept her weight between 116 and 119. Her belly was flat. Her thighs were firm.

Once when she let her weight go to 128, she noticed

saddlebags, and Dr. Hackett explained that she might be able to gain and lose fatty pads now, but in ten years she'd be stuck with what she had. Look at the tiny saddlebags as a warning, Dr. Hackett said. She would always tend to put on weight at the thigh.

Her thighs were firm now, downed with faint blond hair that turned absolutely white in summer. She had a good, interesting, useful body, and she wished David were standing next to her before the three-way mirror. She wanted to do everything with him she had done with her other lovers. Every single thing. They would stand naked together in front of Fred McFeeley's mirror and look each other over in every panel. There would be six of them at once, and she would suck him, pleasing him, and she would watch his face in all the mirrors as he came.

She studied the brown hair growing on her loins. Horses had loins. She had a pudendum. No, that was Dr. Hackett's word. She had brown hair growing around her pussy. Low German, according to Webster. She'd have to tell David.

Pussy.

Pecker.

Peter.

Pudendum.

Words were sexy and body hair was sexy, but in the beginning you pretended differently. You made your lovers wonder. "Gross," you said.

Peter Pudendum was a hairy Latin lover.

You dressed the hair on your head and you covered the hair around your pussy, but you shaved the rest, even for the doctor. Girls said it was mechanical going to the doctor, but they always shaved their underarms before they had their breasts examined. Doctor or not, it was a man touching your breasts. It was hard to catch their eye then. They became solemn and stared about the room. She hadn't yet dared to glance at a doctor's crotch during an examination, but once Dr. Hackett had lost his breath.

That was sexy, exciting the doctor just showing your body, but it was not sexy with Dr. Hackett the other day. Taking blood and poking everywhere, even into her bottom. Hell, her A-hole. It was embarrassing, especially with the fat nurse monitoring, and she must have tightened up because his insulting fingers hurt. When she howled, Dr. Hackett looked smug and said, "Sorry, but I have to probe for growths."

If he was so smug, why couldn't he keep the nurse from getting fat?

If doctors were so assured, why hadn't they saved her father?

She shivered and covered herself with the powder-blue robe, but the pale noontime came back.

It was New Year's Day and she was seventeen and snow blew fiercely through the fields. Wind lashed old drifts and the sun shone silvery through high, scudding clouds. Beyond the dining room doors, Jim Kinsolving made ugly noises as he slept away a drunk.

"Jim has a problem," Mom said.

"I don't think he's alcoholic," Daddy said. "He gets to work every day at Extruded Aluminum."

"Pat says he had thirty-five people working for him."

"But I do think he's alcohol dependent, Lottie."

"Well, you'd better drive him home. Pat is going to be upset. It's twelve o'clock."

Dad and Mom got Jim Kinsolving to his feet. He said he was all right, but he was snorting like an overheated horse. Daddy started the yellow Chevrolet and the car rumbled down the graveled driveway, kicking up two little tails of snow.

"Inviting Jim Kinsolving on New Year's Eve is inviting a boarder," Mom said.

"Where's Pat?" Caroline said.

"She got mad at him for drinking. He was saying terrible things. That she hadn't behaved when she lived in New York; that she'd been with a lot of little Jews. So Pat drove off. Your father said he'd get Jim calmed, but instead of getting calm, Jim skipped a step. He just passed out."

Caroline was washing cut-crystal tumblers when the telephone rang.

"Is Mrs. Devon there?"

"This is Miss Devon."

"You'd better tell your mother to come quickly, Miss. There's been an accident above the towpath road."

Daddy had dumped Jim Kinsolving into the back seat. He knew the highways and how to drive on snow. But over the towpath turn, near the jutting stone house, Steve Gowdy drifted in his father's Ford pickup. The truck rose suddenly, over a mound, speeding on the wrong side of the road. There was no time to swerve. The pickup knocked the Chevrolet sideways, into the jutting house, and Daddy was thrown out of his car, which spun and spun. Daddy hit on his face and skidded fifteen yards.

He was still moving when they got there. Dr. Hackett bent over him. Someone said, "The other one's okay. Just gashed his cheek."

"Daddy," Caroline said.

He lay face down. He made a bubbling sound.

"Oh, Chuck," Lottie Devon said. "Oh, God."

The bubbling came again.

"Daddy?"

It was a gurgle.

"Chuck. Why are you making that sound?"

"Now, Lottie," said Dr. Hackett.

The sound became a grunt.

"Why is he making that funny noise?" Lottie said.

"He's stopped," Caroline said. "It's all right, Mom. He's stopped."

"Aiyee-yiiii-eeee." Lottie Devon shrieked and shrieked.

They turned Daddy over.

There wasn't any face. Just blood and bits of flesh. No face. No mouth. Only blood and pulp.

Lottie's eyes went blank. She bellowed at the pallid sun. Men rushed to console the woman, whose husband lay, faceless and mangled and dead, in the snowy road.

Caroline stood by herself, sobbing. "I wasn't finished talking to my dad."

Les and Marion Devon flanked David and assured him that they were on his side, as though the wedding were a battle. Les Devon was slight, stooped and wispish. Feverish black eyes warred with his mild appearance. Marion, a tiny, heart-faced brunette, moved with a bemused flirtatious manner.

Without having to ask, although he was curious, David learned that the Devons ran an art supply shop near Schenley Park in Pittsburgh. Leslie had wanted to become a painter, but he succeeded only in selling illustrations. "That wasn't what I wanted to do," he said, "illustrate to someone else's order. My brush strokes, but someone else's ideas."

"That's like being half a whore," Marion said.

"So I went into art supplies," Les said. "It's a business. The painting goes on as a hobby."

"Or a bit more," Marion said. "I had pneumonia last spring and Les was wonderful nursing me during the week. But Saturday and Sunday are his painting days. My fever went to 103, and he stayed in his studio, working on a triptych he calls 'Study in Violent Reds and Golds.'"

"It was finished June twenty-second," Les said. He made a small, triumphal smile and threw a commanding stare at David. "You have to work at sustaining creativity. Particularly when it isn't lucrative. People around you insist that you become lucrative and utilitarian.

"A glory of paintings is that they don't do anything. A hanging Rembrandt can't keep a room warm, or cook a hot dog. Antifunctionalism. My paintings don't sell. That's another philosophical advantage. They don't throw off moneys for home air conditioners or quadraphonic phonographs. Antimaterialism. In a quiet way, 'Study in Violent Reds and Golds' challenges the bloated values of the country."

"This is hardly the place to preach *that*," Marion said. Pride danced in her eyes as she looked at Les. She took his hand.

"The Maitlands call this farm Hickory Ridge," Les Devon said. "That embarrassed my brother. He didn't like pretense. He said he lived at Materialism Manor. You can't imagine the impact my brother made on these strangers.

"I can't even picture how he walked," David said.

"Chuck was a shuffler like Joe Louis," Devon said. "He was big and he had a way of walking with his head bowed. People figured he took things as they came. But he changed the way things came and he changed the people he came across. He was a good farmer, hardworking, respectful of the soil, and they liked him for that here. But he was just as good a socialist. When they talked, he'd bring up unemployment, fascism, Negroes. I don't know how many he won over, but he made the Deerfield gentry admit that social issues existed." Abruptly, Les Devon's eyes were pleading. "That's the beginning, isn't it, making them admit questions exist?"

"It's a beginning," David said, "but you have to go on from there."

"He couldn't. He wasn't given the chance. He made these people think. He needed more time."

"The Maitlands," Marion said, dropping her voice,

"want things the way they were. They're a rough, mercenary crowd. Or have you found out?"

"Caroline says she's broken free from her background," David said.

"You break a link," Marion said, "and another link still holds you. You break that, and there's a link beyond."

"The Maitlands are an old landed family," Devon said. "They got to Pennsylvania early and held on. Artists moved into the cities. Artists have congregated in cities since Ur. Adventurers moved west across the Appalachians. But the mercantiles stayed in Deerfield County and acquired thousands of acres and gave leaseholdings and mortgages at usurious interest. My brother found old documents that show what the Maitlands were up to in 1825."

"Sharecropping," Marion said.

"Worse," Leslie said. "They brought over people from Germany and Holland. The men worked in the fields and the women worked in the stone houses."

"There's a little sly Dutch in your bride," Marion said.

"That's right," Les said. "If the master had a whim, what was an immigrant serving woman to do?"

"The blond in Caroline's hair," Marion said, "was imported from Rotterdam."

"Only two things made this different from Virginia slavery," Les said. "The victims were whites. Then, they were victims for a limited term. Enslaved for twenty years, the prime of life. Afterwards, they were set free. Set free to starve. The history of great American fortunes is a history of exploitation. My brother and I recognized that as we moved toward socialism."

"You aren't running for office," Marion said.

"I just want David to understand the bloodlines flowing in his bride."

"She seems to have everything integrated," David said.

"She's in love, my dear," Marion said.

"Meeting you makes me hopeful she can stay integrated," Les said, "but Caroline isn't an easy one and never will be." His eyes were bright in his patient terrier face. "She'd get mind sets as a child. She did things her way, whatever anyone, even Chuck, had to say. I thought that stubborn, reckless independence somehow came from all the strains mixed in her.

"From our side, would-be artists and failed poets, making a living and never much more, farming, shop-keeping, dreaming. From the Maitlands, six days of usury and a Sunday full of prayer."

"Plus the secret Dutch gene that nobody knows anything about," Marion said.

"People slip back," Les said. "Lottie's gone back to what she was, or even less, before Chuck met her at a little gallery in Trenton. They were looking at the same Cézanne."

"Her links with the old ways stretched," Marion said. "Why, twenty-five years ago, Chuck got her into politics and she marched in a parade. The Stevenson Sweethearts. You see how she is now. She'd romance the shade of Herbert Hoover. The links stretched. They never broke."

"Caroline is wilder than her mother," Les said. "If she hadn't been wild, she wouldn't be marrying a divorced Jewish writer half a generation older than she."

"We like Callie this way," Marion said. "We liked the way Lottie used to be. But you'll always have to work with Caroline to see that she doesn't slip back."

"There's a difference between daughter and mother," Les said. He placed his right hand, small, tapering and powerful, on David's forearm. "No matter how much you love her, the girl you're marrying can't stop being wild."

Caroline glowed in a creamy wedding gown. She had felt faint upstairs and poured two jolts of Canadian whisky. Then she brushed her teeth.

The Reverend Merrill Clymer looked smaller and puffier than David remembered. He directed bride and groom toward the hearth and when they stood in place he made a noncommittal nod. Caroline smiled distantly. David inhaled through his teeth.

"*Dearly beloved,*" Reverend Clymer began.

David thought that he had wanted simplicity. He wanted a marriage that would simplify his life.

"*We are gathered together . . .*"

Caroline's body was young and smooth and innocent and sexual. But he himself. . . . Turgenev wrote of one whose tragedy was that he could not simplify himself.

"*. . . in the sight of God . . .*"

The essence of finished work was complication. But on the draft of an allegretto, Beethoven scrawled in angry pain: "Simplify! Simplify!"

"*. . . to join this couple, Caroline and David . . .*"

It was natural law for life to border chaos.

"*. . . in holy matrimony,*" Reverend Clymer said.

Across years a man earned his comforts. A young bride. But the years first imposed complexity.

He meant to strike out for simple happiness with Caroline.

She was more complicated than he dared imagine.

The minister intoned, but David ceased to hear.

He longed for childhood.

A better childhood than his own.

Putting the ring upon the finger of his bride, he missed his son.

CHAPTER TWO

White Man, Walk Easy

I

Once upon a barrelhead, David thought, staring sourly at his typewriter, someone found that writing was a business.

Shakespeare? No; the discovery predated both his tarts and torts.

Chaucer? Long before his empty purse.

Virgil? Aeschylus? David? Homer?

> *Seven cities claimed blind Homer dead,*
> *Where when alive he begged for bread.*

It must have been God who found that writing was a business.

In the beginning God created commerce and art.

And art was without form, but commerce pierced the darkness with bright coins and God saw that the storytelling business was good.

And God said let there be agents. And it was so.

And God made the publishers, and divided the editors, which were under the publishers, from the moneychangers, which were above the publishers. And it was so.

And God created great storytellers and every living creature that scrawled and typed, which English classes and sociology seminars and medical schools and law reviews brought forth abundantly.

And God blessed them and God saw everything that He had made and behold, it was publishing and very good.

And God said behold.

Then He hired an agent. "My memoirs ought to bring a seven-figure advance," God said.

Already Caroline wanted to move from the apartment furnished so curiously by Rosetta Stein. Caroline had a right to make a fresh home; Joel had a right to his own room on visitations. That meant furniture and carpets and painters and Master Charge and Visa. Economics was absurd, but it was possible to write well and, absurd to say, go bankrupt.

Alimony was making David jumpy about money, and in a coldly protective way, Clip Zellbach announced that it was time to produce a commercial book. Zellbach made inquiries and an editor suggested that David compose a nonfiction novel about a psychiatrist. The editor provided a working structure. The psychiatrist, from plebeian background—"the Bronx, perhaps?"— had built a patrician practice.

Patient One: A famous investment banker, addicted to philandering, was unhappy that neither his fortune nor his charm could win him the White House.

Patient Two: The widow of a President, a cultist sex symbol, was afraid of close relationships and penetration.

Other patients were to substantiate as the plot demanded.

The psychiatrist wanted to be a patrician, like the banker. He wanted to penetrate the President's widow. But he had been raised with conventional values and his fantasies collided with his devotion to a wife and three children and a large Colonial-style home, with tennis court, in Scarsdale. The editor felt that this suggestion of a story could be developed into a *roman à clef,* a best seller and a television series.

An agent in Beverly Hills wanted David to consider movie actresses who had passed the age of fifty. Too much was made of old athletes, the agent said; too little thought went out to beauties ripened past their prime.

One actress, pursued by the rulers of three Middle Eastern countries during the 1950s, had become so alcoholic that she was incontinent.

A dancer of great eroticism, who once comforted Errol Flynn, now supervised the herb garden in a nunnery.

A sinuous redhead had grown fat and a cool heiress had lost both her sons and a baby-faced blond still believed in her own beauty. A stroke had paralyzed the blond's left eye and her mouth leaked persistent foams of spittle. The agent wanted the book titled "The Snows of Yesteryear," after Villon's beautiful poem.

A publisher who had been pushed almost into dissolution during a wrinkle in the stock market sought a "glacial but unbiased" look at Wall Street. The man believed a good reporter would find that odds at Las Vegas craps were fairer than the odds along the Street. He wanted scenes of life and death within brokerage houses. There, the publisher said, you either were close to your first million by the time you reached the age of forty-two, or they threw you out. In the washroom of a firm called Foster, Jackson Co., a sign offered instructions for handling in-house coronaries. The pressure killed the brokers and the bond men, but first it crushed their concern for customers. The customers? They financed the business, but were expected to drop dead somewhere else.

None of the three books was wholly a bad idea. Besides, each conceivably could reap extensive royalties. But David concluded that all the books were poor projects for him, because they all began with someone else. He had better write what he wanted, David believed. He had better lay aside thoughts of commerce. He had better not let the alimony jumps plot the windings of his career. He was thirty-nine. He would be forty on March 16. He had been writing other people's ideas for too long; now he would write his own thoughts. Then his book would stand on the shelves and others would discuss it and praise it. They could even damn it. At last he would have his own book.

David heard himself saying to the Reverend Merrill Clymer that he intended to walk Harlem as another country. (How much easier it was to talk a book than write one.) He had no outline yet, only an approach.

Jefferson freed his slaves after his death. That was a metaphor for American history. Practically, America was not conceived as a country in which the majority of blacks would live free. Practically, Americans in banks and clubs and law schools and employment offices still enforced a kind of slavery. Freedom lay down the interstate highway, politicians said, as surely as heaven was suspended in the sky. But now blacks, in a practical, revolutionary way, demanded freedom while the leaders (and they themselves) still were alive. This was not what Jefferson and Franklin had conceived. Amid interludes of uneasy quiet, anger inflamed the present. The future could be integrated or the country could be torn in two.

David wanted to cast the book as an odyssey. He would wander and find a letter carrier and a barmaid and a drifter and a social worker and play their perceptions and their lives against his own. He would find invisible blacks, unknown, even unworthy, and each unseen black man, however unworthy, could stand for thousands. Most of all David wanted to find a young man who was the same age as Joel. He would try to know the black child as he knew his son.

David looked about the curious apartment and thought that he would like to have more for himself and for Caroline and for Joel. Things could turn with this impassioned, reckless venture, *White Man, Walk Easy*.

(Unless he found, across the hard seasons ahead, that he lacked the gifts and fortune to create an important and commercial book.)

It was three-fourteen. Black books were stacked beside the typewriter on the gray-veined marble table under wall shelves Rosetta Stein had painted lemon yellow. Malcom X on blacks and Langston Hughes on blacks and Eric Lincoln on blacks and a paperback novel called *To Hell with Whitey*. David stopped typing notes on the Eric Lincoln book and made a phone call. He took notes. It was three-sixteen on Tuesday, December 20. The next afternoon he was to enter a building numbered 568 East 114th Street and knock at the front apartment on the second floor. Inside he would find fragments of the Blaine family, including a boy called Theotis Blaine, who was approximately Joel's age. David thanked his contact, a Harlem social worker named Yvette Geldzahler, and returned to typing notes from Eric Lincoln.

His mind insisted on making voyages of its own. He saw scattered scenes that belonged in other stories. A white-mustached man, perhaps David himself, grew gently old. The man sat on a porch beside a patchy summer lawn and gazed through the heat at a dirt road nobody traveled. The old man closed his eyes to the sun and he was young. He ran and leaped and caught a line drive in the webbing of his baseball glove. The impact spun him in midair. Dreaming that he rolled in infield dust, the old man died.

Circumstance wrenched apart lovers who had reached their middle years. There would be no more grand passions and they had to say goodbye on the grounds of a carnival for children. Standing at opposite sides of a calliope, they called love words to each other. The calliope organ and the cries of the children blared in gaiety. The lovers could not hear one another. They tried to read lips between the moving horses of the carousel. The horses were colored blue and gold and scarlet.

Scenes kept materializing. It was as if characters he did not know clamored before him, like children, crying over and over, "Please write me."

Alice in Wonderland.

He had to follow his discipline and develop *White Man, Walk Easy*. He could not develop two or three books at a time. One book was a mindful. The time was three-twenty-three on Tuesday, December 20. Joel would be arriving shortly.

David wondered about the first meeting between Caroline and Joel. The first formal visitation, really. It should be spring (but they stood on the brink of winter). There should be stirring music. A passage from *Finlandia.* But he had given his recording of *Finlandia,* Angel S–35922, to Joyce.

The entryway should be bright with bunting. The apartment should stretch down corridors. One room, with bath and cedar closet, should belong to Joel. But there were only two and a half rooms altogether in Rosetta Stein's apartment. It was three-thirty-two. The doorbell rang.

"Hi. I'm Caroline."

"Hi. I'm Joel."

"Say, we're both wearing the same jeans."

Joel drew back and made a quick, solemn glance. "But mine are skinnier."

Caroline hugged him and Joel hugged her back.

(Quick outburst of warmth.) "Are you criticizing my thighs?" Caroline said. (Abrupt sound of caution.)

"No. But they're not as thin as mine."

"I'm sensitive about that. You can criticize my hair, my eyes, but not my thighs."

"I won't criticize them, then." Joel reddened and looked self-conscious.

"Hungry?" Caroline said. "There's cold meat loaf in what your father thinks is a kitchen."

"Joel's mother makes him *hot* snacks," David said.

"Cold meat loaf sounds fine," Joel said.

"Don't eat too much," David said. "We're going to ice skate."

"That way," Caroline said, "we won't have to sit around being friendly. We can just have fun."

The sun was chilly and metallic as they walked to Rockefeller Center. Flags flapped under the soft and huge and dimly menacing Christmas spruce that stood against the RCA Building. Clumps of people looked down on the creamy ice.

"More watchers than skaters," Joel said.

"Wait till they see my backwards crossovers," Caroline said.

"Oh?" Joel said, challenging. "I've been doing those for a long time."

"How long is a long time?" Caroline said.

"At least since I was nine."

"Now you know what a long time is," David said.

"You're from the country, aren't you?" Joel said.

"I'm a country girl."

"Try not to let the audience make you nervous," Joel said. With a show of great seriousness, he turned to lacing his skates. Joel had grown astonishingly since summer. His shoulders and forearms had thickened and the light summer hair had darkened. His manner suggested adolescence, flashing between innocence and the stammering sophistication of a prom.

David consciously held himself back. Let Caroline and Joel find each other without signals from a mustached prompter. Like psychologists, parents tended to approach children of divorce defensively. *One must cope with the child's rejective feelings by* . . . Some children felt rejected; others felt reinforced. Suddenly two parents competed for the child.

Tumultuously married, a gentleman drank.

Divorced, the gentleman chased busy, restless ladies. Remarried, he pursued his children's love.

Caroline and Joel tested one another, with whirls and zigzags, snowplow stops and hockey stops, spraying darkened city ice. Caroline turned more gracefully than Joel, but she could neither stop nor accelerate as quickly. "You do all right in your gorilla style," she said.

Joel skated with clomping steps. "King Kong."

David tried to match Caroline's gliding turns and couldn't, and tried to match Joel's clattering sprints and couldn't. His feet felt cramped and he sat on a wooden bench opposite the gilt statue of Prometheus. Caroline had sensibly ordered the day. Cutting back and forth across the ice, she and Joel were light rather than laboring. Their first meeting was like the renewal of a friendship.

They skated faster, around a lithe ice ballerina in forest green and around a plump, agile man who wore a red sweater. The man spun furiously despite his belly and heavy hips, and Caroline and Joel skated around the centerpiece, a spinning red pear.

Five o'clock. From the ice thirty feet below street level, David saw lights going out in the offices of the skyscrapers. People were hurrying to bars, to beds, to Bronxville, to all three.

He gazed at the rink. Caroline and Joel skated stride by stride. They both wore blue. They were about the same height. She said something into Joel's ear. He laughed. Then, quickly, they skated toward the bench and tramped off the ice and fastened onto David's elbows.

"Come on," Caroline said.

"Don't be afraid of the ice," Joel said.

The three made their way back onto the rink, where Caroline and Joel sandwiched David and bumped him, and he bumped them back and flailed until they all sank to the ice in a skidding, laughing fall under the disapproving gaze of an attendant who looked like a troll.

"A real fun day," Joel pronounced, in a steak house called El Choro.

"We'll have even more fun when we go to my mother's farm," Caroline said. "We can do that the next weekend we get you. We'll go riding near Fetterman's Woods or ski Chestnut Hill, if there's snow."

"That makes for a pinched visitation," David said. "I pick Joel up on Saturday and we have a long drive. I take Joel back on Sunday, and we have a long drive."

"Then change the visitation," Caroline said. "Make it run from Friday night to Monday morning. We could have two full days in the country."

"Mom won't mind," Joel said.

"I'll talk to the lawyer," David said.

"Why don't you talk to Mom?" Joel said. "What do lawyers have to do with when we can get together?"

"Or riding horseback near Fetterman's Woods?" Caroline said.

"Ideally," David said to Joel, "lawyers would have nothing to do with visitation. When the lawyers are done with their arguments, and the judges have gone to wherever judges drink martinis, and the probation officers are home arguing with and possibly battering their wives, you end up with two people, a mother and a father, living apart, trying to do their best for a child."

"Or three people," Caroline said.

"Right," David said, "but things seldom work ideally, Joel. The courts are supposed to see that the assets—what everybody has—are divided fairly. Then they go right on to divide the children."

"You're an asset," Caroline said to Joel.

"What do I have to say about visits?" Joel said.

"Legally, nothing. The court presumes it knows what's best. The court has said you visit from Saturday at ten A.M. until eight Sunday night, on the first and third weekend of every month. I've talked to people who've had experience with these things. Lawyers. Divorced people. Most agree that it's a good idea to stick to the court order until a pattern gets set up. Otherwise, there get to be arguments."

"Why do there have to be arguments?" Joel said.

"Arguments are part of divorce."

"I'd like the visits flexible," Joel said, "so we can see each other whenever we want."

"Of course," Caroline said. "We don't need courts to tell us what's best."

"But two lawyers have made an agreement that already has been ratified by the court." David sipped hard at a Scotch. "We can move for a change, but the other side may oppose us. That's the way with these damn things. If we ask something, they'll want something in return."

"Money?" Joel said.

"Whatever."

"Isn't there a judge I can talk to?" Joel said.

"If we set up a meeting," David said, "you might be the fortieth visitation case before the judge that week. You'd be lucky to get ten minutes of his time. He could be interested. He could be overworked. He could be hung over. But don't worry about that. *I'll* worry about that. I'll make a date to see Clip Zellbach next week."

Joel pressed his lips together. "I think I'm going to

study to be a lawyer," he said, "so I can make sure that someone listens to the kids."

II

As David prepared to enter the ghetto, he made coffee and considered his wardrobe. The better I dress, he thought, the more likely I am to be mugged.

Mugged alone in Harlem. He toyed with the idea. Some junkie puts a switchblade to my throat. I tell him, "Friend, you're mugging the wrong man."

The junkie says, "Gimme your bread and, man, you ain't no friend."

"But, friend!" I tell him. "I'm left liberal. Gave money to Dr. King. Cheered for Paul Robeson."

"Sheet."

"I support busing!"

Slit.

Gurgle.

The hot coffee went down smoothly, though David shuddered.

He found a frayed blue shirt and khaki work pants and an old tan raincoat with strands of horsehair stabbing through the seams. Someone had lent him the coat when he went to watch a prize fight in Chicago long ago. Floyd Patterson against Sonny Liston. The only heavyweight championship fight David had seen. It lasted less than three minutes and there was no time to get cold and the coat was too short, but the man refused to take it back.

Fright excited Patterson that night. Liston glared, with empty imprisoning eyes, and the skin on his head seemed so taut that David saw how the skull must look. Then Liston, blank eyes set in death's head, hammered Patterson to the floor. Patterson was violent, within an intelligence that made him question violence. Liston's violence was casual, inherent and whole, like the violence of a tarantula or a torpedo. Two ghettos, David thought, or two aspects of a single ghetto. He put on flapping tennis sneakers.

Caroline still seemed asleep. Wrapping himself in the old raincoat, he walked to the bed, drew back a patterned blue coverlet and kissed the crook of her neck. She made a sound of pleasure and opened her eyes and sat up and blinked and frowned. "You're dressed like a Salvation Army handout. You look awful."

"I'm dressing for protection. The idea is to look so awful that I'm not worth robbing."

Her frown became concern. "David, be careful. David, please don't get hurt." She squeezed his head toward her breasts, pressing so that a cheek brushed against a nipple. She held his neck and rubbed with little circular motions and his cheek moved on the roundness of her breast. The nipple came erect and he drew back.

> *"Tell me not, sweet, I am unkind,*
> *That from the nunnery*
> *Of thy chaste breast and quiet mind*
> *To war and arms I fly.*
> *True, a new mistress now I chase . . .*
> *And with a stronger faith embrace*
> *A sword . . ."*

"Oh, be quiet," Caroline said.

A woman with tingling nipples disdained recitations of Cavalier poetry.

"I'll be all right," David said. "I have to be going."

Pain showed in Caroline's face. She wanted him to stay. She wanted to be loved and hugged and fucked.

But it was time to begin his book.

He told a taxi driver good morning and announced, "Five sixty-eight East 114th Street."

The driver turned, showing a flat, pleasant Irish face. "What's that far east on Fourteenth Street?" he said.

"One *Hundred* Fourteenth Street."

"Oh, no," the driver said. "I don't go there."

"All right," David said. "Then you go to the nearest police station."

"Are you kidding? I don't go there either." The driver, Patrick Henahan, according to the hack license, offered David a cigarette. "Look, mac," he said. "You don't want to go up there yourself. My buddy, a nice Jewish guy, got held up by them last week. They eat you alive. They stuck a gun in his ear. A goddamned gun."

"Who's they?"

"The gigaboos."

"Do we go," David said, "or do I call a cop?"

Patrick Henahan turned and locked the back doors and swung north on Avenue of the Americas. "Suppose," David said, "you were black and you had to argue with a driver every time you wanted to take a taxi home?"

"There's black drivers," Henahan said. "Stay with your own."

"That's the wrong answer," David said. "If you were black, you couldn't find a job that threw off enough money for you to take a cab."

"I live in Queens, a place called Middle Village," Henahan said. "Transportation isn't great out there, but you know what? My wife and kids and me, we ride the bus."

"Different circumstances, Mr. Henahan," David said, but driving beside the high masonry buildings that reigned over Park Avenue, Patrick Henahan tightened into silence.

As soon as David stepped on the curb of East 114th Street near Sydenham Avenue, the driver relocked the door. He bounced across a pothole turning and speeding for downtown. David looked around. Black men standing at the corner ignored him. Three young blacks sat on a curb, passing a fat brown bag. For an instant David missed Patrick Henahan of Middle Village, Queens.

"Hey, brother," one of the curb blacks said. "You want a drink cheap?"

"Yeah. It's cold, man. We got a wine makes you feel warm. Mogen David."

"No, thanks. It's a little early for wine." David managed to smile. He was giving street drinkers conversation out of the Oak Room bar.

"Hey, brother, only four bits. Much as you want."

"What you doing 'round here, brother? You a cop?"

"No. No. I'm just visiting some people."

The blacks chattered and laughed among themselves. David started down the block. (He never answered drifters who were white.)

Cans and boxes of garbage rimmed the sidewalk. Battered cars sat in the gutter: green cars with shattered fenders, blue cars with rusting doors, and one red car, shorter than the rest, because it had neither tires nor wheels. Gray was the dominant color. The house fronts were gray and the garbage cans were gray and the sidewalk was gray. David passed a hand-drawn sign, red letters printed on gray cardboard: "Patti's Place." Was it whorehouse or saloon? The police car moving up the street was painted blue and white. Still, gray dominated. Gray. The color of old age and poverty.

Number 568 rose, four stories of gray stone, behind white steps over a ground-floor apartment. A lawn was withered into naked, clumpy earth. The iron railing that had protected the lawn bent backward, halfway to the ground. At the top of the white steps, David reached to open a door. Only then did he notice that there was no door to open.

He walked into a hall lit by a clear bulb. Empty wine bottles lay on the linoleum. He turned right, looked for a bell, found none and knocked on a plywood slab.

A voice called, "You from Miss Geldzahler's?"

"Yes."

The door opened. A trimly built woman in slacks said, "Come in." Light from the front windows cut David's vision. The sour smell of urine struck his nostrils.

"I'm Barbara Blaine, but evuh-body calls me Barbie," the woman said. Her slacks were tan and she wore a tan blouse, which lay open. There were no buttons. David saw her breasts as her arms moved. Not even Lovelace would have called these large-nippled fonts a nunnery.

"Oh, 'scuse me," Barbie Blaine said. " 'Scuse me." She put a hand to her throat, closing the top of the blouse. Still the nipples showed. "Kids and all, I been so busy, I got no time to sew."

A neatly made bed lay by the windows. Barbie Blaine followed his eyes. "Tha's my bed," she said. "Tha's where I sleep." Three low double beds stood against the chipped white walls. The low beds lacked blankets, sheets and pillows. "They's for the kids. The kids sleep in them. My bed's the good bed. You know?"

The children played against a wall. Years of tan and blue and apricot-colored paint showed in plaster craters. An old wooden television set stood beside a record player. Milady's pleasures, David thought: watching children; following game shows; listening to a plastic phonograph; copulating.

The open blouse.

She had been asking him to fuck her, perhaps for pay, here in front of the children. Hadn't she? He felt less sure in Harlem.

With her large-nippled breasts, she had at least been asking him to ask.

No matter.

It was unthinkable amid the urine reek.

Otherwise?

There was no otherwise.

"That's a nice collection of records you have," David said.

"My oldest gits 'em for me. My oldest takes care of me." At Barbara's command, children, in diapers and paper dresses, lined up to meet the visitor. Some gazed at David with large eyes. Some giggled and looked away, conquered by shyness. The children crawled and scrambled and finally stood in size places. David counted nine. The oldest was a smooth-faced whippet boy. He wore a red-and-green tam-o'-shanter.

"What's your name, son?"

"Theotis Blaine."

"You like baseball, Theotis?"

"Nope."

"Basketball?"

"Ain't got no time for that." Theotis glared at his shoes, new blue-and-buff sneakers, marked "Bauer."

"Do you have time to show me the neighborhood?"

"Why you want me to show you the neighborhood?"

"I'm writing a book."

Theotis continued to glare at his new Bauer sneakers. He wore bright plaid slacks that matched the tam-o'-shanter.

"There would be something in it for you," David said.

Theotis grinned. He was missing a lower bicuspid.

"Five dollars a day."

The boy had a long face and a broad fighter's chin. Merriment entered his eyes. "Ain't no big payday."

"I don't know about you, Theotis, but five dollars is a lot of money to me."

"You a small-timer," Theotis said, "but you got me."

"What do you mean?"

"Nobody offered me any more than a fiver so far today."

Before David could leave with Theotis, before he

could walk away from the cratered walls and the bare beds and the suffocating smell, Barbara Blaine put a hand on his forearm. She was thin, like Theotis, despite her childbearing. "Miss Geldzahler said you should get my story," she began. "I don't need no five dollars. The welfare takes care of me fine. But I need for you to listen."

The windows were closed, which is why the room smelled. The room was warm and stuffy and sharp. Barbara Blaine said she didn't like the cold. "Down Carolina where I lived, in Drummond County, the cold got so bad some mornings that there was frost on the kettles. My mother came up here and she was gettin' heat. So I come up, for the heat and the welfare.

"My mother was living on the welfare, but, you know, I thought it would be more. A little more money. I could maybe have tried to work, but all of a sudden my mother got sick and I had to look after her and my kids. Theotis and the next one, Doreen. I was seventeen years old."

"What about their father?" David said.

"His name was Claude, 'cept we all called him Buck. A big no-'count field nigger. He said he loved me but he loved the whiskey more than anybody. More than me or his own kids. Big arms and he could sing a little, but a no-'count field nigger was all he was. Got a little whiskey in him and I was a queen. A little more whiskey and I was a tramp. You know? Rough me up. Punch my face. Understand?"

"What's become of Buck?" David said.

"Field nigger. Found some other field."

In New York Barbara met a tall man named Junius, who earned a living by unloading trucks. She and Junius had a daughter whom they called Julie, and then a son named Clyde. They bought a Zenith Colorchrome TV and a General Electric Superkleen washing machine and a Wonderland matched living room set in white oak. Then Barbara's sister got sick, just the way Barbara's mother had gotten sick, and Barbara had to take in her sister's children.

That made seven, and although they were good children, the apartment was noisy. Somebody always seemed to be crying and Junius took to staying away nights. He felt restless. He needed quiet. He got headaches. Sometimes Junius stayed away until morning.

After a while men from Wonderland Furniture and the Happiness House Appliance Company began knocking on the door. They wanted payments. Soon they took back the Superkleen washing machine and one night, when Junius was watching the Yankees play Boston and Reggie Jackson was at bat, other men knocked and handed Junius papers. They repossessed the Zenith Colorchrome television right in the middle of Reggie Jackson's turn at bat. (The count was two and one.) They told Junius that he would have to go to court. Three days later, Junius disappeared. "The money and the papers and the children and the noise was too much," Barbara said. "He was a good man until he couldn't stand it no more. But if you're a woman, you keep standing it because you got to stand it. There's nobody else to stand it, if you don't."

Barbara went on welfare again. She took in another child, and then a young man who promised that he would marry her left her pregnant with the youngest girl, Melissa. Barbara didn't allow whiskey or cocaine in her home. "God knows where these kids would be without me," Barbara said. "Ain't that right? Where would they be?"

"If you could get some curtains," David said, "and open the windows . . ."

"Can't open the windows."

"A few minutes of air would freshen the house."

"Melissa gets bronichal amza," Barbara said. "You know. The amza. It's bronichal."

"Bronchial asthma?"

"Whatever you call it. You know. They can't breathe. When it's real bad, I got to run six blocks to the clinic. Theotis a good boy. He helps me carry her. In the cold. That's the reason I got to keep the windows closed."

"What's the reason you've got to keep the windows closed?"

"The cold air from the streets. It killed my mother. It killed my sister. If I open the windows, the cold air will kill Melissa too."

"What you want to see around here?" Theotis said. He had bounded down the steps, light-footed, almost elegant in the Bauer sneakers, the plaid slacks and the tam-o'-shanter.

"What is there to see right around?"

"Nothing right around. We got to move a little."

"I saw a sign for Patti's Place."

"Crazy Haitians," Theotis said. "The crazy Haitians go there and put on cockfights late at night. To fight the cocks they got to pay the pigs."

Theotis swung his arms back and forth and bobbed up and down. He was lithe, half a foot shorter than David, restless.

"Let me start out with a drink," David said. "Do you know a good place to have a drink?"

"The Black Rooster. Maybe two blocks away."

Theotis didn't know why a bar called The Black Rooster would have a red door. He didn't think about things like that. "I need fifty cents of my pay right now," Theotis said, as they stood on the sidewalk. "They won't give me no beer in The Rooster. 'Fraida pigs. You know, I told you. Cops. I can get a can at the store and keep it in a bag and bring it in and drink my drink while you drinks your drink, so that way we can have a drink together."

"I'd like that," David said.

Inside The Black Rooster, David saw a jukebox and rickety stools and a mirrored wall behind pyramids of bottles. Red and white signs crowded the mirror. They offered "two-fers" at $1.09 and "three-fers" at $1.39. None of the half-dozen blacks drinking at the bar acknowledged his approach; nor did the barmaid, a plump, round-faced woman who wore a necklace of heavy jade and silver.

David sat at a small rear table and waited. A screaming voice exploded from the jukebox.

> Yeah.
> I gotta have you.
> Cuz you my fox.
> When you got me,
> Then my whole life's in your box.
> Yeah, lady.
> Foxy lady.
> Yeah. Ooow.

Theotis Blaine appeared with his brown bag and took a seat beside David. He lifted the bag and sipped beer and beat a hand on the table to the rhythms of "You My Fox."

"You been in here before?" David said.

"On a little business," Theotis said.

"What's a three-fer?"

"Oh," Theotis grinned. Then he whispered with great authority. "When a man wants to drink a lot, like three at once, he orders a three-fer. That price they got up there is supposed to be special. Like, you know, cheaper. It's a joke."

"What's a joke?"

"The glasses are fixed up. They're what you call

magnifying glasses. A guy gets some drinks. He wants some more. He orders a two-fer and pays his dollar nine. Sheet, man, he's getting the same little drink, like a single, only the magnifying glass makes it look bigger."

It was ten minutes before the barmaid walked to the table. "Yes." Her tone was cold. The affirmative challenged.

"A three-fer of Dewar's."

"One dollar thirty-nine, like the sign says, in advance."

David gave her two dollars. "I'm not a bum."

"I didn't say you were a bum."

"I'm not a cop."

"And you're not white." The barmaid smiled blankly. She wore a fuchsia blouse. "You're black like me, but you just suffered a terrible fright. That's when you lost your color."

Someone chanted from the bar:

> *"I gotta have you.*
> *Cuz you my fox."*

"I'm a writer looking around. I was afraid you wouldn't serve me. That's why I took a seat here, in the back of the bus."

"I'll serve you, honey. This year we gonna be real fair. Serve you folks drinks. Go to school with you. Evuh-thing." She pointed at Theotis. "But I ain't serving him for four more years."

She brought a thimbleful of Scotch in a magnifying shot glass and Theotis said, "You see? You let her take you."

"Research," David said. "That's—"

"I know what research is," Theotis said. "I go to school sometimes."

"Much?"

"A little. I learns things here and there. Now, like right here *you* shouldn't tell people what you doing. Keep 'em guessing. Keep 'em loose. Maybe if they think you a cop, they go one way. Let 'em think so. Don't say too much. Then show them you not a cop. They go another way."

"Well, thank you, Theotis. You're drinking with me, but I still owe you five dollars. That beer-in-the-bag is my treat."

"There's two beers in the bag," Theotis said, his hustler's grin revealing the bicuspid gap.

The jukebox played.

> *When you got me,*
> *Then my whole life's in your box.*

Two tall men walked into The Black Rooster. They carried open cartons. One quickly walked to David. "I got records here," he said, "better than what you hear from that machine. Stereos one dollar. Quad one fifty. You like Motown, man? Gladys Knight? Diana Ross? A dollar for stereo, and one and a half for quad." He looked at David, pleading with his expression.

"Not now, thanks," David said.

The man's expression, still pleading, showed no hurt. Supplication, like rejection, had become native to him.

"Is he from a record store?" David asked.

"He his own record store," Theotis said. Theotis dropped his voice. "He gets the records off a truck, or maybe in some warehouse at night. He rips off the records, but nobody gets hurt. Them big companies like Motown and them rich singers like Gladys Knight don't need all they make. Young guy gets himself in business. Hurts nobody. I been in business myself. Like how you think I brung all them records for my ma?"

David finished the thimble of Scotch.

"I been in a lot of businesses," Theotis said. "Different ones different days. I need clothes, I get in the clothing business." He gestured at his plaid tam-o'-shanter. "You rip off people who don't need as bad as you."

"Then you come to a bar like this and sell what you've stolen?" David said.

"Yes, but you don't stay in The Black Rooster too long. I heard some old dudes make a joke that goes like this: If you stay here too long, you get to buy your television back."

"I don't understand."

"The sharp dudes know where evuh-body lives. You sit here and they figure out your house is empty. They go 'round through the window and take the television. They come back here to get rid of it. By then you cloudy. You drinkin' three-fers. You think they givin' you a break. That TV looks so good. You make an offer. Congratulations, man. You have just bought your own television set."

Theotis laughed and shook his head. "Some people baaad."

The jukebox babbled:

> *Yeah, lady.*
> *Foxy lady.*
> *Ooow.*

Relaxing at the end of his second beer-in-a-bag, Theotis said that he ran with fellers who stole from trucks and warehouses. They kept what they needed and sold the rest. "We need a lot," Theotis said. "Welfare don't give enough. Welfare gives sheet. Like what I'm wearing. My pants, my shoes, my tam, come off a truck. They didn't come from no welfare lady."

"Does your mother know you dabble in robbery?" David felt heavy beside Theotis. His words fell, sheathed in lead.

"I tell Ma the change I got comes from delivering packages. I tell her the records I bring her comes from an organization. I tell her what keeps her happy."

"Stores," David said. "Do you rob stores?"

"Couple," Theotis said. "I got reasons." He banged his palms together. "Hey, man. There's one night I got nineteen cents and I go into a delicatessen. This dude he tells me it's twenty cents for a can of beer. So I take the can and drop nineteen cents and the guy hollers and two cops are coming by. They grab me and they take me into a doorway and the big one holds me and the other one keeps beating his stick on my legs. Here." Theotis pointed to green and red plaid covering his shins. "Hurt me, bad. Hurt me, man. No reason. A fucking penny. You ever have someone beat up on your legs?"

"The man who owned the store," David said. "Was he black or white?"

"He was neither," Theotis said. "He was one of them Jew fellers."

The boy jumped up. "If the pig cops come at me again, I'll be ready to give it back to them."

"How's that?"

"We got a place. We practice fighting pigs. Come on. I'll show you."

"Some Jews are black," David said. "Some Jews are white. Some Jews have been beaten worse by state police than you can dream."

"Let's shuffle." Theotis was not interested in Gestapo stories. "You want to see things, and I want to work on my defense against the fucking pigs. Plus I need your five dollars, man. Come on."

Mount Morris Park rises out of south Harlem flatland into hills that show crags of basalt and shards of whiskey bottles. Above the highest hill, a black tower presides.

First, the curling iron skeleton of the tower served as a firewatch. Later, a hundred years ago, it guarded the last farmhouses of Haarlem.

After that it was transformed into an imaginary mountain. The park became a picnic ground and children climbing the winding iron staircase cried, "Hey. We're going up Pikes Peak."

At length, the tower became a relic. The old maple forests were gone and the wood farmhouses were gone and the picnicking children were gone and the abandoned tower grew ominous in solitude. Mount Morris Park had fallen. Attended only by an abandoned tower, it became a grassy wasteland lost among gray cement. Wasteland that had been a part of the city, long, long ago.

"Cops patrol here?" David asked, as they climbed a twisting path of chipped hexagonal stones.

"Nobody patrols here," Theotis said.

Behind them stood the formless brick buildings called Hospital for Joint Diseases and Medical Center. David knew a urologist, Nathan Coles, née Kolshansky, who practiced there. "Jewish surgeons are not welcome downtown," Nathan Coles complained. "I'd wanted to practice at Cornell. I live in diaspora. This ghetto hospital is my place of exile." Coles had been a varsity lineman at Columbia, but he was terrified now that addicts would associate him with the M.D. plates on his metallic silver Mercedes sedan. Then they might jump him and kill him for his prescription pads. His fright made Nate Coles angry and he liked to talk about other people in pain, particularly black people in pain, and most particularly he talked about black women crying out when he dilated their urethras. That is a standard palliative for non-specific bladder infection in the female; it is standard also to inject local anesthetic. He couldn't charge what the WASP surgeons charged downtown, Nate Coles claimed. He had to use his time working, not waiting for Novocaine to take hold. They grunted and sobbed, he said, but less than half the patients actually shrieked.

Climbing, David kicked a flattened beer can at a concrete bench frame. There were no wooden slats in the frame anymore, no place to sit.

He thought of sadism and Dr. Nathan Coles and he wondered why he himself was not afraid the way Dr. Nathan Coles was afraid. He had known a journalist who covered a war and moved toward shellbursts. The man said he had to see them as closely as he could. He wrote understated dispatches, taut with horror, and the war ended and the man came back to New York and committed suicide slowly by alcohol. What had he looked for in the shellbursts? What had he found? What had he seen inside the whiskey glasses? The December wind snapped at David's face.

David respected fear, but not panic. He respected drinking, but not drunkards. Suddenly, he felt concern in Mount Morris Park because there was no catch in his gut.

"What do you do here?" he asked Theotis, just to hear the sound of his own voice.

"Up there, beyond that rise, we got a little field. The fellers and me, we practice there."

"Practice what?"

"Beating the pigs, if they come bother us."

Wind blew grime. It was a cold, silent, dirty wind. They had reached the top of a rise. Below, a dozen blacks sat in a semicircle on patchy grass. A hard-muscled boy, who looked eighteen, stood in front of them. "This is my gang," Theotis said. "You know. Like a club. You gimme a couple bucks now. I got to fix it."

Theotis loped to the side of the leader and spoke intently. The leader, big and blank-eyed, cried, "Hold it!" He turned toward David. The black wore overalls and an army shirt and he rolled with power as he walked. His eyes were empty. He looked like Sonny Liston. "Crowd him," Jack Dempsey said. "Crowd Liston and you can take him good and scare him shitless."

"Yes," David said. "Good to meet you."

"Ain' enough."

"What ain't enough."

"Gimme five dollars too like Theotis here."

David kept his wallet in his hip pocket and managed to extract one bill. It was a single. "That's three dollars," David said. "Three in all. Take it or fuck off."

The black man glared but took the dollar.

"We the Purple Crusaders," he said. "I'm the leader and my name is Pharaoh. Pharaoh Gallen. Theotis says you a book writer."

David nodded.

"Just so you understand," Pharaoh Gallen said. "What we doin' here is karate practice. We don't do none of that to hurt nobody. We peaceful guys. But when the pigs comes at us, and beats up kids like Theotis, we protects ourselves. So what you gonna be seeing for your eight bucks is karate practice. But not karate to hurt no one. We peaceful, 'less somebody starts."

He turned. His interest in David was ended. "The man," Pharaoh Gallen shouted, "ain't a pig. The man done a little good for us. Let's show the man." The Purple Crusaders sprang up. "Pig drill," Pharaoh called. "Claude, you the pig. Doan use no gun. But you got a night stick. Ruben, you be the black guy. You just tryin' to get along."

Two boys walked from the group. All David's senses rose and now he heard the gritty wind rattle as it blew straight through the curling tower above Mount Morris Park.

A boy in denims held a child's baseball bat, two and a half feet long. He was playing the role of policeman.

The bat was his night stick. The other, clothed in fatigues, stood unarmed. He had shaved his head. The boys stood eight yards apart, on the patchy grass at a shoulder of the hill beneath the watchtower. Below them, other Purple Crusaders kneeled in a crescent.

"Liberation," Pharaoh Gallen said, sharply.

The boy with the bat moved forward, his right hand gripping the heavy end of the bat.

"I don't hear nothin'," Pharaoh said. "You supposed to be a white cop."

"Motherfucker," yelled the boy with the bat, pretending to be a brute policeman. "Black, nigger, motherfucker. You goan fuckin' fuck nobody no fuckin' moh."

The other shifted his weight back and forth.

The boy with the bat lunged. He thrust the knob toward his adversary's scrotum. The victim feinted left and moved right and slammed the back of his hand down on the attacking forearm.

"Aaaf," the pretend policeman cried, and dropped the bat. The victim had taken the offensive. He thrust his right hand toward the throat and then, quick as a middleweight boxer, drove his left hand upward into the sternum. If he had not held back, he might have crushed the spleen.

"Motherfucking good," Pharaoh Gallen said. The other Purple Crusaders applauded.

Now three younger boys lined up, pretending to hold guns. "Disarm the pigs," Pharaoh yelled. "Liberation!"

Five boys, including Theotis, approached the three new pretend policemen.

"Talk," Pharaoh said. "Tell 'em peace."

"Hey, man, what you got that gun for? We doan want trouble. My brother's a cop. Hey, man, be cool." The five chattered at the pretend policemen until they had closed with them. Then they sprang.

Theotis clipped a larger boy on the wrist and grabbed his arm and threw the boy over his shoulder. The boy fell, rolling. Theotis leaped after him and pressed fingers toward the throat.

They scrambled up. Now Theotis was the policeman. Now Theotis was thrown and falling and rolling. The boys jumped and lashed karate blows again and again. It was a dance, David thought, mock combat as a dance. Except the dance was practice for barehanded murder.

David sat with Theotis on a patch of icy grass. "Now we'll both get our pants dirty," David said.

Theotis was breathing rapidly.

"You showed me something," David said.

"Tell you more."

"What's that?"

"Drillin' ain't all we do. We hit some stores."

"Down around Times Square?"

"Where's that?"

"Downtown," David said. He stood up and pointed south. It was late; the dirty wind was blowing night across the sky.

"I never been downtown," Theotis said.

"I'll take you."

"It's all right 'round here, 'cept it too cold."

"I wanted to ask you," David said. "How do you take a store?"

"You take it."

"Barehanded?"

Theotis reached under the left leg of his plaid trouser and produced a thin leather case, too long to hold a pencil. He opened the case and withdrew an ice pick. "This my tool," Theotis said. "This my motherfucking store-taking tool. What you think?"

"I think you ought to spend less time with your tool and more with your school."

Theotis laughed. "You made a poem."

"I'm a writer."

"I learnt a poem in school. I learn the days I go."

"What poem?"

Theotis stood up beside David in the abandoned park.

> *"I wandered lonely as a cloud*
> *That floats on high o'er vales and hills,*
> *When all at once I saw a crowd,*
> *A host, of golden daffodils . . .*

"I forget the fucking rest," said Theotis Blaine.

III

Visitations collided with David's work, and if he had not been working on *White Man, Walk Easy,* they still would have collided with his life.

He meant the visitations to suggest security for Joel. He meant to be supportive but not dominant.

He wanted to say, "These are the books that I have loved and here is music of great beauty and here is poetry.

"And notice, if you would, the third baseman shading toward the bag. He'll give up the single to cut off the double. Two men are out. There's a touch of art to playing third!"

"I didn't know that," Joel would say, "and I bet our coach doesn't know that either."

Such stuff as traumerei.

David was making up lectures. More than that. He was playwriting. And he was acting. Personifying Shakespeare. Writing and playing two parts. Joel and himself. He was an actor, author, producer. Not Shakespeare? Well, then, a slimmer Orson Welles.

"We can never completely disregard judges in the future," Clip Zellbach said.

"Fuck judges," David said. "Fuck them once and fuck them in the future."

"Then," Zellbach said, "the judges will fuck you."

"He's my son, not theirs," David said.

"But you see him at their indulgence," Zellbach said.

They stood over drinks at the bar of "21," where Zellbach was waiting for an actress. It was pleasant to wear a vested Bill Blass suit and lean among extravagant toys after the frayed raincoat and the filthy wind of Harlem. It was January now, three weeks since David had ridden north with Patrick Henahan of Middle Village, Queens. He had called Zellbach to discuss the clash between his life and work. Or to have a drink.

"When I'm up with a special kid in Harlem, or I hear out a barmaid who used to be a nurse, or I try to get a white cop to use another word for 'perpetrator,' my schedule is uncertain. So sometimes I have to skip a visitation."

"Which is disregarding the judges of the future," Zellbach said. The attorney wore a snug tan suit, patterned in a faint rust plaid. As he stood at the bar, an elbow curled around a Scotch, he reminded David of a welterweight boxer who had been very good and also very smart. There was no scar tissue near the eyes.

"In a sense, the law is a friend," Zellbach said. "At least, it's my friend. You know my schedule of fees." Zellbach smiled with *pro forma* deference. "But you have to take the time to understand the friendly reasoning behind the law.

"When there is no divorce, the law assumes that both parents work for the welfare of the child. There must be something as extreme as documented child abuse before a court steps in. But divorce makes parents warring parties. Suddenly they're not working together for the children or for anything else. They're working against each other. So the law asks, 'Who will look after the child's welfare?' And the law answers, 'The court will look after the child.' The court then delegates rights of custody and visitation. The court becomes more than the child's friend. It asserts itself as his protector and his champion."

David ordered another round, but Zellbach put a large-knuckled hand over his Old Fashioned glass.

"The reality of divorce situations," Zellbach said, "is that they get worse slightly more frequently than they get better. If you miss a batch of visits now, you may find yourself in court next year, defending your rights to any visits at all."

"Even though I'm writing a book?"

"Especially because you're writing a book. Certain judges correlate creativity with irresponsibility."

"I appreciate your comments on our friend the law," David said, "but a move against visitation is not in Joyce's makeup."

"Very well," Zellbach said. "Let me present you with a scenario. Your book drags. You fall behind, first in alimony payments, then in support. Joyce calls to ask for money. You'd say a call for money *is* in Joyce's makeup, right?

"Caroline takes a few of the calls. She becomes impatient. While you're walking a street in Harlem, Caroline says something sharp. Your new wife does not want to feel welded to your former wife. The upshot is that Joyce is insulted. She feels alone and outnumbered two to one. Joyce calls Gabe Cassidy to complain. She adds that she doesn't want to hurt you.

"Gabe Cassidy doesn't mind hurting you. He tells Joyce she *must* get the back payments. A pattern of regular payment has to be established. He tells her not to worry about your book. He says you can always raise new money by promising another publisher that you'll write another book. He tells her he'll press you for the debt. He suggests that she press you by not cooperating on visitations."

"Is that valid? I mean, is that all right with your friend the law?"

"Technically, no. Technically, alimony-support is one issue and visitation is another. If they tried to withhold Joel, we'd fight and eventually win. But in practice, matrimonial lawyers deliberately mix the issues— custody and support, kidnap and ransom.

"There's no mystery to handling a divorce, except that it's five percent law and ninety-five percent psychology." Zellbach stared at his short Scotch and water. "You bully and you bluster and you trample children and you pretend you're practicing law. Matrimonials are a cesspool. I stay away except for friends."

He finished his drink. "All right, David. Now you can buy me another Chivas. That's a fee, David. Do you understand? Hear out the advice you're paying for.

"Do not skip a visit. In snow or rain or gloom or night. Though hell should bar the way. Do not skip a visit. If you can't make it, insist that Caroline receive your boy.

"If I know anything about psychology and I know anything about the law, do not allow a visit to be skipped."

A small, brown-haired woman with a feather cut said, "Hello, Clipper."

He's fifty, David thought. The woman looks twenty-two, four years younger than Caroline.

What can Zellbach be offering the small, brown-haired woman? A brief affair. Hammering intercourse.

"Hello, Suzanne," Zellbach said. "We have reservations at Le Chanteclair. Drink up, David, and we can all leave together."

At least he was offering her two-star French cuisine.

"Of course we can all leave together," David said. There was a Geri Zellbach, a Mrs. Solomon Zellbach, who had friends. Perhaps right now the friends of Geri Zellbach might be observing at the "21" Club bar. He is so calculating with my family, David thought, and so careless with his own.

"I'd even say we *should* leave together," David said. It would be safer for Clip to leave in a threesome.

Not everyone was conditioned to marry. Perhaps all that the brown-haired girl named Suzanne wanted were two-star French dinners, a brief affair and hammering intercourse.

He could not skip any visits.

He would have to ask Joel, next time, what the boy thought of the visitations ordered by their faceless friend, the law.

Would Suzanne squeal in orgasm?

Tuesdays and Thursdays then, each Tuesday and every Thursday, quite apart from weekend arrangements, Joel arrived from the John Clay School, bearing Laser Five ice skates, black northern boots above staunch blades of Sheffield steel. The massive skates must have looked incongruous among the shopping bags and purses, as Joel rode the Broadway bus to his father's house.

Article XII, Clause 5, of the divorce contract specified visitations on Tuesday and Thursday afternoons (quite apart from weekend arrangements). David had insisted on Article XII, Clause 5, because he wanted easy accessibility to his son. He had wanted them to see each other frequently and casually. He had wanted, in short, to continue with Joel as though there had been no divorce.

David was working hard in Harlem, developing his cast, building small arches of trust. He met black ministers and black sociologists and black auto salesmen, and he began to wonder about his premises. Good reporting does that, he knew. It shakes a man free from preconceptions.

He could not continue with Joel as though there had been no divorce.

There had been a divorce.

They could only continue differently.

The Harlem reporting made David question his title. *White Man, Walk Easy* seemed committed to alienation. He grew comfortable with certain members of his cast. He thought of calling the book *Faces in a Dusty Picture.* But that had been used.

Dusky Picture. Better, perhaps, but also, perhaps, patronizing.

Sometimes David's work spilled into Tuesday and Thursday afternoons, and then Caroline drove Joel into Brooklyn, where a rink lies beside a lake in Prospect Park. Knolls rise about the lake, and cold hills and winter trees give the city rink a lambent country sense.

"I'm sorry," David said one Thursday night, as he typed notes on a black minister named Jeremiah Tunney.

"About what?" Caroline sat curled on the ivory French provincial sofa. She was reading a British edition of *Family Happiness,* a novella in the first person in which Tolstoy plays an ardent girl who flowers.

"About imposing Joel on you so much," David said.

Reverend Tunney preached Christ's peace at the African Zion Methodist Episcopal Church and warred with couriers in a drug traffic that ran from the port of Tampico in Mexico. The minister carried a .38 caliber Colt Police Positive revolver under his cassock.

"It's all right," Caroline said, smiling to herself. "We don't live in nineteenth-century Nikolskoe. Everything's quicker. The world is immediate. Some girls rejoice over instant mashed potatoes. I'm better off than they. I have a delightful instant son."

"Do you really feel that?" David said.

The Reverend Tunney kept the pistol in a holster on the left side of his belly. That way, he explained to

David, he could draw moving the right hand diagonally up across his body. A faster draw, he said, than cowboy movie stuff.

"I don't know if I do mean that," Caroline said. She was groping out of Tolstoy's world. "It was somewhat strained the first few times. There are other things I want to do with New York City than show off my old style as a river skater. But now I really enjoy the skating. The physical release. And I'm enjoying Joel." Caroline sat up. She wore a blue jumper over a white blouse. Country clothes. "Do you know what my life was like the summer before I met you?"

"Sexually active," David said.

"Not that much, dammit," Caroline said. "I lived on the Jersey shore, where Mother has a place. My biggest responsibility was to tell her in the morning, 'The dishes are done. 'Bye, Mom. I'm going to the beach.' I'd wear a lace wrap over a not-very-daring bikini and Mom would say, 'Your navel shows. Your navel is the eye of the devil.' "

"What did that mean?"

"Probably only that Mona had been slipping vodka into her breakfast coffee. I'd say I'd be back by cocktail time, and that was it. Those were the responsibilities I faced each morning. Now I look after you and Joel and I worry about this ridiculous Rosetta Stein apartment and your divorce from somebody called Joyce. It makes the old summer seem easy."

"Not empty?"

"Oh, yes. Of course. I love you, darlin'." Callie laughed. "Empty *and* easy, if you please. But when I go skating with Joel, the best of that summer feeling comes again. No concerns in the world. ' 'Bye, Mom. I'm going to the rink.' You ought to see us skate."

"I have."

"I mean, without you there. As if you were invisible, or watching through binoculars. We skate compulsively, in drizzle, and we skate when the cold is knifing, and once we skated during a snow bizzard. We invent races. One-lap races, three-lap races, five-minute races, backwards races until the rink attendants get angry at us and point to signs that scream, 'Speed Skating Prohibited!' Then we plot races behind the attendants' backs.

"This city must seem silly to a child. Silly and cruel: 'Speed Skating Prohibited!' 'Slow Skating Encouraged!' 'No bike riding, no ball playing, no skate boarding.'"

"'Do not let your heart leap up,'" David said.

"'Kindly act adult,'" Caroline said. "'Welcome to the city park, city children. Please don't have fun.'"

David had reserved the afternoon of Tuesday, January 1, for Theotis Blaine, and Caroline had reserved the afternoon for Joel. She was finding isolation in New York, which was a benediction when she wanted to read. She had Tolstoy to catch up with, and after that the *Iliad*. You did not have to read Homer to achieve a baccalaureate in fine arts at the Philadelphia Institute of Design. It startled her suddenly to see the school as it had been: a place for making paintings and avoiding books.

She was disinterested in her runabout friends, Pam Miflin and Liz Wesley and Jen Gallison. Abruptly, she no longer ran about. Besides, she thought they would seem trivial to David. She had not ever had many women friends. She preferred men. When an affair was good, she told herself convincingly that this man, Gerald, who taught draftsmanship at the Lowell Textile Institute, was really her best friend, even though somewhere, in a middle-income apartment she had not seen, Gerald Gowdy lived with a wife and a daughter, who was four.

Callie sat on the ivory couch, the yellow-bound Tolstoy open in her lap.

Marriage was an isolating act.

As she sat, in fitted slacks and a loose turtleneck, she waited for Joel.

Her mother did not approve of David. It was difficult to tell what stirred behind Mother's stone eyes, but Callie suspected this tall, fervid idealist she married was, to Mother, simply the Jewish fella. That was mother's judgment, blank and final.

Marriage isolated Callie from Pam and Liz and Jen and Mother, and placed her in the middle of the city and within an apartment from which you could not see the sky.

Marriage ripped Callie from her Pennsylvania roots. Mother's stony disapproval hurt her and made within her a secret anger against Mother and against the community around Mother: the Reverend Clymer and the Comforts and the Kinsolvings, walking along the Willingboro Canal. It even set her against the quality of stoniness generally. Callie began to snap at noncommunicative grocery clerks and sullen taxi drivers. She had not snapped before.

Outside, within a block, you could find the studios of the Art Students League, housed within a high-windowed concrete building. She had thought that surely she would be studying at the League. She liked sketching. Once she made an ironic ink drawing called "Miss America," somewhat in the style of George Grosz.

Caroline's Miss America was obsessed with liberation. She would not shave her underarms. But Miss America's protest lacked impact. Her natural armpit growth was a childish scraggle.

Miss America opposed the national preoccupation with dieting, so her thighs and stomach rolled with fat. They would be fatter still as she responded to anxieties about a lean future and bit into a cherry-chocolate cake.

She was naked, of course, but Miss America despised

American titophilia. In a final, accidental protest, her breasts were wide and flat and undersized.

The professor said Caroline's work was too much cartoon to be a successful sketch and too much sketch to be a successful cartoon. Then he praised someone else's poster of scullers on the Schuylkill River.

Teaching was partly a matter of being predictable, and partly saying, "On the other hand."

Caroline had intended to study "Abstracting the Figure," at the Art Students League, but she wanted first to be a splendid Mrs. David Priest. A perfectly superb Mrs. David Priest.

There were libraries to catch up with and so much new music to learn. At the Philadelphia Institute of Design, it was possible also to achieve a baccalaureate without hearing a single bar of Bartók.

Being married to David was educative.

Dry word.

Smacked of John Dewey's bones.

Her loins had never gushed so richly as when she and David made love.

The marriage was educative, lonely, joyous.

It was more joyous than it was lonely.

Even so, sitting on the ivory couch, Caroline felt her breath quicken when the doorbell rang. It was as if her stepson were her date.

Joel wore a blazer and gray slacks and a striped tie and Caroline saw the suggestion of a man in his boyish face. Until he smiled. "Whoosh," Joel said, instead of hello.

"What do you mean, 'whoosh'?" Callie said. "And don't you have a kiss for your stepmother?"

"I mean Miss Searing, the drama teacher, is an idiot." Joel pecked Caroline on the cheek.

"Such passion," Caroline said. "I'm overwhelmed." Joel hugged her. "Why is Miss Searing an idiot?" Caroline said.

"We're giving a play," Joel said. *"Macbeth,* by William Shakespeare. It's set in Scotland. It's about this thane who wants to be the king."

"Why doesn't your dad think of plots like that?" Caroline said.

"Wait," Joel said. "I'd like to act Macbeth. I read the lines well, about the dagger. You know. The dagger of the mind. Even Mom says I read that well. But Miss Searing wants Becky Williams to play Macbeth." Joel frowned. "Macbeth?" he said. "A girl? Does that make sense?"

"What does that leave for you? Lady Macbeth?"

"No. Duncan. Mom says she doesn't want to interfere, but all I get to do is die."

"Offhand, I side with you," Caroline said. "I don't believe that Shakespeare wrote Macbeth as a female character."

"Besides, Becky Williams is black," Joel said, "and you know that Macbeth was not a black person."

"How do you handle Duncan?"

"Pretty well."

"But Shakespeare didn't create the king as a fourteen-year-old boy."

"But there are limits," Joel said. "Like *Othello.* Could you imagine a black boy playing Desdemona?"

Callie smiled. "You think Miss Searing is an idiot because she has exceeded Shakespeare's limits."

Joel nodded.

"Or are you really upset because your mom isn't taking your side?"

"I'm not sure."

"I know something about that sort of problem myself, Joel," Callie said.

It was a clear blue January afternoon, warm enough to thaw, mendaciously suggesting spring. Caroline drove the gray Porsche slowly, with open windows, winding along the East River Drive. "Tell me about your mother," Caroline said.

"She's not like you."

"Neither is *my* mother." To their left, a tanker three blocks long filled the East River.

"Well," Joel said, "she's kind of heavy, and she wears smocks and things like that."

"That's terrible," Callie said, careless and crisp. "A woman letting her appearance go. Your mother isn't old. There isn't any reason for her to go around like a fat old lady."

"She sort of drinks a lot too," Joel said.

"So does my mother," Callie said. She swung off the drive near the Brooklyn Bridge. Caroline remembered a poem David liked. Hart Crane called the Brooklyn Bridge a harp and altar. "Beautiful things," she said, "are usually pleasing things. That's something they taught me at school. The bridge cables are as beautiful as a harp.

"A body is beautiful too, if you take care of it, and then you're comfortable with your own body and even proud of it. Not only women, but men."

Joel listened hungrily.

"When a man lets his body go, he may hide it, if he has the right tailor. But it's more difficult for a woman." She was still talking crisply, and carelessly. "There's no excuse for a woman letting her body get sloppy. There's no excuse for a woman looking like a slob."

Joel set his jaw and watched the traffic.

At the rink, they practiced precision skating. Caroline skated figures on the inside edges of her blades and more difficult figures on the outside edges and finally a complicated turn called a Mohawk, which neither of them had mastered. Caroline led, apple-green slacks tight to her bottom, until they tired and perspired in the winter mildness, and hurried to the car, so that they would beat five o'clock traffic home.

"I may have sounded harsh on your mom," Caroline said, in the West 57th Street apartment. "I may even be harsh on my own mother."

"I don't know," Joel said. "With Mom, it's sitting around all the time. She says she has a little arthritis in one knee."

"Well, that's nothing for a growing boy, sitting around." Caroline stretched. "I feel grungy," she said. "I'd better shower. Do you mind watching the tube for a few minutes?"

"Do you have some of the paintings you made?" Joel asked.

"Oh, there's an old batch in a bureau drawer in the bedroom." Actually, Callie had sequestered four batches of her work. Three were studies of nudes. The fourth showed the seasons of Deerfield County in watercolor. Although she liked the watercolors least, they seemed most suitable now. "Where I grew up," she said. Joel dropped on the brass bed and began unrolling the paintings as Caroline left for her shower.

The bathroom certainly disrupted casual bodily functions. A fine old tub, with animal's claws for feet, was marred by Rosetta Stein's unquenchable passion for ornamentation. She had painted four sets of breasts along the tub's side, coloring the nipples with a nail polish of whorehouse red. The setting made Caroline uncomfortable when she had to mount the throne.

You could tell a man by his library and a woman by her decoration, Caroline thought. She stood, urinating. The warm shower played on her back.

That was a sexist concept.

She must remember not to say that to David.

Sexist, but generally true.

The water made her feel delicious.

Damn.

She'd forgotten her silk robe. It was in the bedroom.

She dried herself quickly, and draped a blue towel so that it covered her from her breasts to her loins.

" 'Scuse me," she said to Joel. The damn robe was in the damn closet on the damn far side of the bedroom.

What the hell. She reached for the robe. It stuck on the hook of the hanger. She lifted the hanger from the closet and began delicately to work the fabric free of the hook. The blue towel loosened and fell off. She was naked. What the hell.

Joel's large dark eyes hurried from Caroline's sketch pad, to a window looking over an alley, to a wall; everywhere but where his stepmother stood with her breasts and pubic hair exposed.

"Joel," Callie said. "We should be comfortable with these things. Our bodies. We're going to be together for a long time."

"I know," Joel said. He looked at her eyes and blushed.

"It's not as if I were your girl friend," Callie said, but her cheeks felt hot and she realized that she was blushing herself.

Caroline was dressed when David burst into the apartment cheerful and whistling the regal final theme from Saint-Saëns's Fourth Piano Concerto.

"I had a good day with a minister of Christ," he said, "and, Joel, I've made a special Madison Square Garden date for us, and what did you people do with this almost spring afternoon?"

"Skated," Joel said. "Callie showed me some of her paintings from Deerfield County, but mostly we skated at the rink."

"I don't understand you," David said, with the onset of a smile. "When I was a kid, Jewish boys played basketball. The only people who ice skated were goys."

Joel looked up blankly. "What's a goy?" he said.

Callie laughed a high, delighted giggle and hugged her stepson to her breasts and announced, "Me."

IV

Irish bargeworkers hauled bluestone that would become the façade of the African Zion Methodist Episcopal Church. They hauled it down a 120-mile canal that had joined the Delaware and the Hudson rivers, the Reverend Jeremiah Tunney announced to David. "You can still see remnants of the canal upstate in Ulster County, near a village called High Falls. Stone walls with the grooves the bargemen's ropes etched into them. The Irish were persecuted immigrants who could make protests with their songs. They hated a barge owner named Hill."

The Reverend Tunney incanted:

"Between Hill and hell is only one letter.
Between Hill and hell, I doan know which is better.
If I run away from Hill, they say I'm gonna be in
*   hell,*
And my pretty Kitty's cryin' by the iron church
*   bell."*

Jeremiah Tunney was tall and very black, with hewn narrow features. "Do those sentiments sound familiar?" he said to David. "The bargeworkers were not much more than slaves. You can compare their songs to persecutors of the black people were these same Irish immigrants worked from sun to sun, pulling stone sleds down to the barges until their bodies broke, the way John Henry's body broke. And yet"—Tunney's long face opened in a hard grin—"among the very worst persecutors of the black people were these same Irish immigrants."

The African Zion Methodist Episcopal Church had

been famous for its bluestone façade years ago, when it was St. George's By-the-Meadows. Jeremiah Tunney's voice rang with the undertones of a kettle drum. "History is my hobby," Tunney said. "Did you know that the first black community in New York City was situated in the East River on an island overrun with barnyard animals? The people called it Goat Island, and the sanitary conditions were excrementous. More than half the babies born on Goat Island died there.

"Then black people had a little community on the west side of midtown. Hell's Inferno, right inside Hell's Kitchen. But the Irish harassed them, and there are cases of Irish policemen splitting the skulls of black children. I've seen documentation. The police reported, 'Nigger skulls crack open easier than cantaloupes.' "

"Do you have any coffee?" David said.

"Who was it who said 'History is a nightmare from which I am trying to awake'?"

"Stephen Dedalus said 'History is a nightmare from which I am trying to awake.' He said it in the first chapter of *Ulysses*. He said it a quarter of a century before Auschwitz."

"It's difficult for a black to relate to Auschwitz," Tunney said.

"I shouldn't think so," David said, magnanimously.

"Oh, yes it is," the minister said. "Nothing as terrible as Auschwitz has ever befallen the black people."

Tunney stood up. He was six foot three. His large, fine-featured head lolled on massive shoulders. Football, David thought. Defensive end. Face mask protecting the lean nose. "I'll fetch coffee," he said. "No, I won't *fetch* it—I'll *get* it." Jeremiah Tunney laughed, his baritone booming about the echoing stone study.

Theotis Blaine was to meet David in half an hour. Then David would pick up Joel and take the boys, Theotis and Joel, to Madison Square Garden, where the New York Rangers were playing hockey against the Montreal Canadiens. David had parked his gray Porsche outside the church. "Leave a car like that on the wrong street," Tunney said, returning with steamy mugs, "and cannibals take everything but the gas cap."

"And outside now?"

"Your Porsche is safer in front of my church than it would be on the grounds of the White House. Some of my young parishioners make sure of that. My choirboys, I call them. A private army. One or two actually can sing. They keep the rowdies out of the immediate neighborhood."

"It's a worn theme," David said, taking out his reporter's notebook, "contrasting black and Jewish misfortune, Auschwitz and Harlem."

"Worn?" Tunney said. "Because a book or two and a film have touched it. Because of certain parlor conversations downtown." Tunney gestured with uplifted palms. His hands were enormous and bony and supplicatory and throttling. The hands of Othello, David thought.

"I went to the University of Illinois," Tunney said, "in the state where my family lived. Years before, my family was Mississippi people. There was a dean at Illinois, also named Tunney, Scotch-Irish, and American for seventy-seven generations. He had a great-great-great-grandfather who'd come from Mississippi, and out of a curiosity that would delight the Freudians, the dean asked if any of my people had come from Mississippi too.

"I told him that he was using the wrong verb. My great-great-great-grandfather didn't *come* from Mississippi. He *escaped*."

In the spare study, two bridge tables covered with a tan cloth served as a desk. Out a window David saw drifters standing under a billboard advertising Phillipots' Mortuary.

DIGNIFIED BURIALS $150, UP. ALL FAITHS.
BODIES SHIPPED TO JAMAICA, HAITI, SAN
JUAN. ASK ABOUT PREPAID FAMILY PLAN

"You're here because someone named Priest *escaped* from Europe," the Reverend Tunney said.

"No one named Priest," David said. "After 1848, someone named Cohen left the Rhine valley. Cohens are supposed to be descended from the high priest Aaron. So this Herr Cohen, trying to Americanize his name, stuck us with a handle to please an archbishop."

"And Tunney," the minister said, "was the name of a sadist of a straw boss, famous for his shoulders. Big Bull Tunney could make a nigger cry quicker at the whipping post than anyone in the state. And hold a black gal stiller, while he had his way. So *my* name, it seems, and some of my physiognomy derive from a brutal rapist."

"But as a bonus you got the shoulders and the build."

"Physical strength enabled me to play end for the Illini. I never liked football. Organized bullying. But I used football as material for fusing an education. Now, through hockey, you're trying to fuse the lives of a street rowdy, who would cannibalize your car, and your own son, who discourses on evil in *Macbeth*."

"I like Theotis; I sympathize with him."

"Living downtown, you can afford to." Tunney got up and walked about. His black cassock swung open, like a physician's white examining gown. David saw the dull black handle of a gun.

"I ration my sympathies," Tunney said. "I want a Harlem that is orderly and free of rowdies, so that people from Mississippi and Illinois and the Rhine valley all can live here safely. I can't afford to extend my sympathy to rowdies. That's downtown liberal stuff."

"I've befriended a couple who come from Budapest. Imre and Esther Podgorny. They run a delicatessen called the I. and E. We need them here. They're honest people, a little frightened. They run an honest store.

"During the World War, Imre was put in a camp called Oranienburg, and in the last days of the war, he was required to march for seventy-two hours. *Iter facere*, the Romans would have said. A forced march." Jerry Tunney, the old Illini end, beamed at his own good sense. "Imre was sixteen and fairly strong, so he kept on his feet for all that time. Dutch guards assassinated those who fell. Afterwards Imre began to make a life in Hungary, but then the Russians came back and Imre despised the Russians for what the Red Army had done in 1945.

"Imre has *escaped* to America, where his honest store is threatened by rowdies like Theotis. My commitment, my Christian commitment, is to help the white working-man ahead of the black street rowdy."

"How can you help Imre Podgorny?" David said.

"I've gotten him a pistol permit," the Reverend Tunney said. "I've taught him to draw and fire in self-defense."

Theotis shuffled into the minister's study and stood in a stone archway, looking at his buff-and-blue sneakers.

"Remove your hat," the Reverend Tunney said.

The tam came off.

"Do you know anything about hockey, anything at all?" Tunney asked.

"Ice," Theotis said.

"It's a game," Tunney said, "like basketball or football, and a game means a discipline. You know what discipline is?"

"Yeah," Theotis said.

"Discipline means saying 'Yes, sir,' " Tunney said.

"Yes, sir," Theotis said.

The Reverend Tunney looked at David. "We folks

who live up here would appreciate, Mr. Priest, if you could point out how discipline rather than raw force determines who wins in hockey. We folks appreciate anybody showing our young people that discipline wins over rowdiness every time."

"You'll see that, Theotis," David said. "The Montreal team is favored. Montreal plays a disciplined game."

"Yes, sir," Theotis said to David.

Joel waited in front of the building at Riverside Drive and Seventy-ninth Street, accompanied by a doorman named Eddie, who wore a uniform of green and gold and spoke with a County Mayo brogue.

"Yes, sir." Eddie the doorman greeted David loudly through the Porsche window. "Fine night and a fine boy you have. Yes, sir."

No discipline in "Yes, sir" here. Servility. Like Zellbach's father, champion waiter from the Bronx. Theotis, in the front seat of the Porsche, must be laughing at Eddie, the Uncle-Tomming white.

David looked. Theotis had cocked his head.

"What he do?"

"Opens doors and helps ladies with their groceries."

"And for that," Theotis said, "they let him put on the uniform?"

"No," David said. "For that they *make* him put on the uniform."

Joel wore a navy-blue cardigan but no overcoat. Theotis started to clamber onto the back ledge of the sports car. "Stay," David said. "There's room for both of you up front. Joel, where's that new velour coat your mother says she bought you?"

"I don't want to dress too fancy for a hockey game, Dad."

Or too fancy, David thought, for a new companion

from the ghetto. He should not have imposed the velour comment on the boy. "Joel and Theotis, say hello."

"Hiya," Joel said. "I'll get in the middle of that seat on the right. We can share it. You take the window side. I'm used to watching out for the gearshift. Doesn't my dad have a neat car?"

"Yeah," Theotis said. "I like that noise when he takes off. Tha-rumm."

"Tha-rumm-rumm-rumm, when he really hits it," Joel said. "In the summer, Dad, would you show me how to do that?"

"In the summer." He turned the Porsche down Broadway. "Why don't you explain hockey to Theotis?" David said.

"All right," Joel said. "It's got a lot of rules. There're zones—the New York zone, the Montreal zone and the neutral zone—and a lot of stuff like that. When you play, the coaches want you to stay in certain positions. They call that discipline. Have you seen much hockey?"

"Nope."

"Well, mostly you can figure it out if you think of the ice as a couple of funnels. New York is trying to funnel everything into the Montreal goal. Montreal is trying to funnel everything into the New York goal. You can run a guy, belt him as hard as you can, as long as you don't take more than three skating strides before you hit him."

"So's you don't kill him?" Theotis said.

"You've got the idea," Joel said.

They were passing Lincoln Center. Bernstein was conducting Nielsen tonight. Symphony Number 4—the "Inextinguishable." Someone was reviving Pirandello's *Tonight We Improvise*. Levine, or was it Kubelik, would lead *Wozzeck* at the Met.

"What's them paintings," Theotis said, "behind that glass over there, to the other side of the fountain?"

"There're a lot of shows here," Joel said. "Music.

Stuff like that. The paintings are decorations to mak
the place look nice for the people who come for th
music."

The fountains erupted into arcs.

"Awright," Theotis said. "First time I ever seen
waterfall go upside down."

David walked behind the two boys into the lobby o
Madison Square Garden. Joel was bigger. Theoti
moved lightly. Joel's cardigan, from Saks, fit wel.
Theotis's electric-blue pullover, lifted from Forzan
Freight Forwarding, Inc., spoke more loudly.

White faces bobbed in the Garden corridors. Ol
Yalies come 'round to see the great Montreal wingman
Guy LaFleur. There was something glorious about th
way French Canadians played hockey, the Yalies tol
each other. They recited names: Joliat, Morenz, Vezina
Lalonde, pantheon players from the past. (Aurele Jo
liat's ancestry was Belgian; Howie Morenz was born t
immigrants from Germany.) Ahead, some hard-eye
businessmen, out of the New York University School o
Commerce, said they liked the price. They had the fee
the businessmen agreed. "Besides," one said, possibl
beyond Theotis's earshot, "it's a pleasure to bet o
athletes who are *white*."

David, Theotis and Joel sat in orange seats close t
the red line at the center of the ice. "How they freez
this stuff?" Theotis said.

"Electricity," Joel said.

"Ammonia," David said.

"Which?" Theotis said.

"We aren't sure," Joel said. "I guess we'll have t
ask an engineer."

"If we woke up in King Arthur's court," David sai
to Joel, "we wouldn't be able to show anybody any
thing."

"You know King Arthur?" Joel said to Theotis. "Did you study him in school?"

"There's the one in school and there's one in my park. Like my gang, we're the Crusaders. We follow Pharaoh Gallen. These other guys are the Knights. They follow Arthur. He likes to be called King Arthur. The Kingman. Man, the Kingman. But Pharaoh can take him."

Joel blinked, as he tried to catch up on the ghetto all at once.

According to the betting line, the New York Rangers would lose by at least two goals. "Montreal has been beating the Rangers for years," Joel told Theotis. "You like this place?"

Theotis sat low in his seat and looked around. "It's like a spaceship, man. I seen this show on the TV. Everybody's in the future, all sealed up in a spaceship, bigger than my house. That could be us. You know that? How do we know what's goan on outside?"

"That's what I like about it here," Joel said. "I watch the hockey players. I want to play the way they do. I don't care what's going on outside."

Haughty in blue and white and red, the Canadiens attacked. Guy LaFleur reigned up and down one wing. Serge Savard cruised behind him, a reserve battleship. When the teams changed lines, Joel pointed out Yvan Cournoyer of Montreal. "Watch him accelerate. He's like Dad's car."

"Tha-rumm, tha-rumm, tha-rumm," Theotis said. "Hey, man. How fast these guys?"

"Maybe twenty-five miles an hour," Joel said. "Maybe more."

The Rangers, who wore white, played a game of passionate intensity. They could not skate with Montreal, but they threw their bodies before LaFleur and Cournoyer, disrupting rhythmed charges.

Les Canadiens grouped at their end of the rink. Crossing, weaving, accelerating, they hurtled up the ice. They passed the puck from stick to skate to stick. Then they funneled toward the goal until a Ranger defender leaped into the dangerous Montreal wave. The Rangers' courage blunted the attack and agitated the crowd.

The early pattern persisted. The bookmakers had been wrong. The Rangers' desperate hockey meant that one goal would decide the game.

With three minutes and nine seconds remaining, a Canadien forward named Doug Risebrough stole the puck from a Ranger defenseman's stick. Risebrough broke clear of that defender and barreled over another. Lunging, straining, finally diving, he slammed a rising shot into the left corner of the Ranger net. Risebrough lay on the ice, panting. Cournoyer threw both fists into the air. The Garden crowd sat silent.

"The end?" Theotis asked. "Hey, that guy's tough. That guy with number eight."

"Risebrough," Joel said. "I don't know if it's the end. There's time. The Rangers can still score. Maybe."

A roar broke from the blue seats near the roof. It rolled and swelled. Risebrough suddenly was fighting two Rangers. Players pulled off their gloves and dropped their sticks. Another Ranger fought mustached Pierre Bouchard. Four fights had broken out at once. The creamy ice filled with sticks and gloves, litter of battle.

The players paired off. LaFleur held the jersey of Pat Hickey, who in turn held Guy LaFleur. Savard locked arms with Big John Davidson, the Ranger goalie. Risebrough punched his Ranger to the ice. Two other fights stopped quickly. Bouchard and a big Ranger defenseman fought evenly until the incessant punching exhausted them. They held each other, then, in the hugs of angry Grizzlies.

Theotis stood up, grinning, wide-eyed, laughing. "Awright," he said. "Awright. Fightin' on ice." The crowd about them cheered and stamped their feet.

Montreal dominated the closing minutes. The Canadiens won, by 1 to 0. "Hey, man," Theotis said to Joel, "about that fight."

"A good one."

"But how come they was taking off their gloves? How come they was putting down their sticks? Was that fight real?"

"Real?" Joel said. "Didn't you see Risebrough punching? Number eight. And Lambert. Sure it was real. A Ranger was bleeding, wasn't he? Real blood."

"Then why doan that Ranger pick up his stick and get the guy who cut him?"

"Because there're rules," Joel said. "Even when there's fighting, there are rules. You're trying to win the fight, not kill anybody."

"Some big guy come at me, some big Pierre, I have to kill him. Otherwise, maybe he'll kill me."

"You've got it wrong," Joel said. "There isn't any killing in hockey. They're just trying to win a game."

Theotis looked thoughtful. "Ain' so much discipline in hockey either. Ain' none of that there 'Yes, sir.' It's the force, man. Hockey's the force. I like it, 'cept for one thing."

"What's that?" Joel said.

"Ain' no spades playin'."

Joel blinked. "Spades?"

"You know.

Black.

Like me.

Niggers."

Joel paled. David put a hand on each boy's shoulder. He thought, A dialogue has begun.

V

Snow fell hard all night on Thursday, January 19. Friday morning broke bright and almost silent, and Caroline and David walked in Central Park, between the white knolls and the glassed-in people who lived on Central Park South, and the cold air snapped against their faces, and Caroline spoke excitedly of skiing with Joel down a Pennsylvania slope called Chestnut Hill. Later she brewed tea while David called Joel's mother.

"Ski?" Joyce said. "Tomorrow? He'll be killed."

"No," David said. "He's supple. *I'll* be killed."

"Is that what your new wife wants?"

The familiar tone rasped. Joyce's cheer. Urgent cheer. Insistent, forced, relentless cheer. The grating, unfamiliar tone sounded a morbid joke.

"Can we take Joel tomorrow or not?" David said.

"Oh, boy," Joyce said, her voice hardening. "You're really putting me in a corner. You know how much he wants to develop his skiing. If I say no, your new wife will tell him that he's missed a great weekend, and Joel will get angry at me. If I tell him yes, I have to undo plans."

"I can appreciate that."

"Can you? I was going to take him to hear a lecture by Leakey at the Museum of Natural History. But what chances does anthropology have against skiing?"

Joyce must be sitting alone. David reminded himself that when you lived as a single person, the smallest change of schedule could appear shattering. "Try to take things easy," David said.

"I am taking things easy," Joel said. "The snow has given me a day off from work. But oh, boy, what are you doing to me? Yes, you can have Joel tomorrow. What can I do? But please, from now on give me notice."

"We're all trying to do what's best for Joel," David said.

"Are we? Are you and your new wife? Or is there an ego thing, that makes it difficult for you two to treat me with respect, treat my plans with respect, treat my household with respect?"

"Tea's ready," Caroline called.

"I've got to go," David said into the telephone.

"Aah," Joyce answered.

David had not thought that after separation and divorce—when the abrasions of daily contact and arguing lawyers were removed—he and Joyce would have less patience with one another than before.

The new snow brightened Deerfield County, crispening the countryside, and red-stocking-capped children appeared on the hilltops, and other boys in darker colors tramped out toboggan runs. Caroline drove sixty miles an hour along a twisting blacktop. "Is she scaring you?" David asked Joel, who curled on the back ledge of the sports car.

"I want to go even faster to get to skiing."

"I'm not that eager myself," David said.

"Does skiing scare you?" Joel asked.

Caroline smiled, leaning into the glossy walnut steering wheel.

"Not exactly," David said, "but it goes against my antecedents. Skiing isn't a Jewish sport."

"What does Jewish have to do with it?" Joel said.

"You have to watch old movies," David said. "The Hollywood Nazis against the Decent People. The Hollywood Nazis ski beautifully. They're doing kick turns toward the Swiss border. They're chasing three Decent People, who are Jewish."

"Who *happen* to be Jewish," Caroline said.

"The Jews trample through fake snow, carrying rocket plans in an oilskin bag. It's a good thing they have a lead, because the Gestapo skis faster and faster.

A Jewish man says, 'Those plans are more than just plans. They are the future of civilization.' You hear a fusillade from Mauser rifles."

"If the Jewish people skied well in the old movies," Joel said, "there wouldn't have been any suspense."

"There isn't any suspense anyway," Caroline said. "The Jewish people made it." She beamed. "We're here."

"We?" David said.

"I'm becoming Jewish by osmosis," Caroline said.

They arrived at Hickory Ridge Farm at three-thirty-five and ten minutes later they reached the slope Caroline called Chestnut Hill. She wore a bright, clinging yellow ensemble, and with her first run David saw that she was a good skier, confident and graceful. Joel, who wore denim, almost kept up with his stepmother. Watching the two figures from the top of Chestnut Hill, David moved his skis back and forth.

The late sun threw orange light against a snow-bright hill. Far out, pines spread in a valley beyond a swift-water brook. Closer in, the two figures slid into an easy stop, Joel following and imitating Caroline.

Why intrude with his own run?

He could finish in the brook.

Why hadn't he told them he had never skied before?

Ahead lay Bern and Zurich. The Swiss border.

David heard the crackle of snow crust under his skis. Mauser rifles. The wind rose around his ears. Bend knees. It was easy, really. Toe in to control speed. The hell with kick turns. Leave them to Gestapo agents from Pacific Palisades. Don't toe in. Show speed. The wind laced David's cheeks and he threw a jubilant look at the white and orange hillside and bumped over mogul and wanted to laugh. He snowplowed to a stop three yards short of the brook.

"Do you enjoy it?" Callie shouted.

"It's not that difficult."

"The way you do it," Joel said.

"He's referring to your style," Caroline said. "You chuss. You'll have to learn to parallel. That *is* difficult on steeper slopes, among trees and other bodies."

"You went straight, like a long skid," Joel said. He and Callie looked at each other and giggled. David grinned at their teasing friendship.

"All right," he said. "How the hell do we get up?"

"Sideways," Caroline said. "Sidestep. That means a little sweat, but it tightens the thighs."

Joel moved out, sliding up the hill ahead of them. "David?" Snow crusted Caroline's shining face, which suddenly clouded.

"What's the matter?"

"Are those Jewish-Christian-Nazi comments necessary? I mean, what's the sense of making Nazi jokes in front of Joel?"

"Wickedness doesn't lie still," David said. "Auschwitz 1944 and Harlem today are pieces of the same wicked puzzle."

"But, David, we aren't there. In Auschwitz or in Harlem." She made a little pleading smile. "Look at this gorgeous afternoon. Can't we keep Deerfield County as a place where we simply enjoy ourselves, you and I and your son?"

"All right," David said. "I'm willing to try." He tumbled but kept his footing and he hugged her.

"Evan Waller's giving a party," Lottie Devon said, in the living room of her stone house above Roundout Creek on Hickory Ridge Farm.

"You'll like Evan," Caroline told David. "He's the teacher who got me through French at boarding school."

Joel looked surprised. "*You* had trouble with French?"

"Never mind about my marks," Caroline said. "Why

don't you tell your step-grandmother about *your* marks, and the rest of the things you do in school."

David busied himself at the fireplace kindling a pyramid of charred logs.

"Sure," Joel said. He rose and dropped onto an ocher cushion beside the gaunt bleak woman, Lottie.

"Don't drop so, young man. You shake the couch."

"Sorry," Joel said. "Well, I go to a terrific school in New York and we take poetry with Mrs. Talbot. You know. Longfellow and Thoreau. But I'm getting more interested in dramatics with Miss Searing. We're reading *Romeo and Juliet* and the other day the actor Richard Dreyfuss came to school and spoke at assembly."

"My older one, Patricia Beth, was great for shows," Lottie said, "but she moved away."

"We're working on two more assembly programs. We're doing *Macbeth* with a black and white cast. Then we're doing 'Music of the Sixties.' We write arrangements that sound like the Beatles. Songs like 'Yesterday.' We score them for flute and sitar."

"I don't think your step-grandmother knows what a sitar is," Caroline said.

"Or cares," Lottie said. "Who cares what a sitar is?"

Perhaps she feels laughed at, Caroline thought. Besides, intelligent children unsettle her. She doesn't know what to make of Joel; she never knew what to make of me.

Long ago Mother fell back on sayings.

"Just worry about today. There's time to worry about tomorrow tomorrow."

"Always behave like a duck. Look calm and unruffled above the surface, but paddle like the devil underneath."

"This family's a team and there's no I in that word 'team.'"

"Everybody dreams about becoming an artist. The sensible person learns a trade."

Caroline heard her own voice entreating, "But, Mother, I *want* to be an artist."

"The big *I* again? Trade's good. Trade's fair. The Jews are in trade and the Scots are in trade and neither one of them goes hungry. Right around here, in sight of Roundout Creek, there's Quakers that can buy from a Jew and sell to a Scot and make money. Teach yourself shorthand, Callie Devon."

"I want to be an artist, Mom. I want to be a painter."

That was twelve years ago. Now when Lottie didn't know what to make of someone, she simply went stony gruff.

"Do I get to go to this party?" Joel asked David.

"You get to go," Caroline answered.

"He'll be the only child there," Lottie said.

"This is a visitation," David said. "You spend as much time with me as you can stand."

"Besides, *I* want to show you off," Caroline said.

"Then tell him to bring his sitar." Lottie glowered at her daughter. Lottie's ugliness made Caroline gasp.

Evan Waller was short, with ruddy cheeks and slightly protruding teeth. "Thanks for asking us," David said.

"In *South Wind*," Waller said, "Norman Douglas points out that many a man who thinks to found a home discovers that he has opened a tavern for his friends." Waller smiled. "I know about your work, Mr. Priest. I'm glad to number you as a friend."

The room was small, with a stone fireplace and a wall behind the hearth rising at an acute angle. "Used to be an outside wall," Waller said, "but why they built it on that steep slope, God only knows. If he remembers, If he's alive."

"This is my son, Joel," Caroline said.

"I hope you're better at French than your stepmother was," Waller said.

"I'm worse."

"Oh, dear."

"Because I'm not taking French. I take Latin."

Waller gazed at Joel with amused indignation. The boy wore a blue blazer, a claret turtleneck and gray slacks. "I'll get you a special drink," Waller said. "An *agri-cola*."

"Farmer," Joel said.

"Academic joke," Waller said.

"I don't know what Agri-Cola tastes like," Lottie Devon said.

"Well," the Reverend Merrill Clymer said, loudly. "Have the newlyweds been traveling?"

"David's gone through with his big promise," Caroline said. "Not Paris, but Harlem."

"Meet my son, Joel," David said.

"How do?" the minister said. Then to David: "Are you comfortable moving about Harlem?"

"Lottie," horse-faced Becky Comfort called, across Joel's brushed brown hair. "A forty-acre tract has just been listed in Upper Waynesport. The interstate goes through in two years and the price is only two hundred thousand now. That's five an acre. It's sure to go to twelve."

"They have colored in Upper Waynesport," Lottie said.

"In town, darling," Becky said. "This is four miles outside. It's positively gig-proof."

"Harlem is bleak and miserable, Dr. Clymer," David said. "It isn't a comfortable place."

"But, Dad," Joel said. "The people who live up there. Like Theotis. Aren't *they* comfortable there?"

"For a while," David said. "Then they open their eyes. They see your claret turtleneck. They see my gray Porsche. They watch television and they get to want what they see. They want to climb out of the ghetto. Maybe they even want to speculate in land."

"What did the man mean when he said 'gig-proof'?"

"That has to do with drinking," Merrill Clymer said. "How much alcohol—proof—is in a certain cheap wine."

Becky Comfort smiled and clapped the minister on the shoulder.

Caroline glared. She said, "We don't use words like 'gig.'"

Clymer placed his hands on his wide hips. "You know we work with the Negro poor, Callie." He drummed his fingers on his thighs. "At any party you hear remarks in questionable taste. After Sammy Davis, Jr., converted to Judaism, his rabbi asked him for one favor. 'Please, Sammy,' the rabbi said. 'Don't move into my neighborhood.'"

Caroline heard a whooping sound. Lottie's big-boned body quivered. Chords of laughter broke across her lips.

"Please," Caroline said to Clymer. "There's a child here."

"My point is inoffensive," Clymer said. "That joke may be in questionable taste. You can find poor taste anywhere, even in this lean-to of a living room. But there is no prejudice here."

Caroline thrust her chin forward and said, "Bullshit."

"Please," Evan Waller said to Caroline. "Your stepson."

"And if he weren't here," Clymer said, "we still wouldn't want language like that."

"*Merde* is preferable," said stumpy Evan Waller, flailing toward irony.

"If any daughter of mine spoke foul language to a minister," Clymer said, "I'd take her upstairs, bend her across my knee and spank her."

They would go on, David knew, in this thoughtless, heartless manner, now that their xenophobia was roused. He had done that, he and his son, outsiders intruding, gray horses entering among palominos. If he and Joel came to such parties ten years from now, nothing would change. Except by then, some other xenophobic drinker, who had grown used to their specific shade of gray, would remark: "You two are different. You're all right. You're not like the others."

You Jews are almost goyim. You're only semi-Semites.

There was a matter to attend to.

David stepped between Clymer and Caroline. He slowly turned his back on the minister and said over one shoulder, "But you, Dr. Clymer, don't have a child or even a wife."

Nobody spoke. Caroline took a deep breath. David clenched his right fist.

The matter had been attended to.

David walked toward a coffin-shaped table, clutched a bottle of Grant's Scotch by the neck and poured himself four fingers of whiskey. "Joel."

The boy hurried to him.

"I have something to explain. Do you feel up to auditing a lecture?"

Joel smiled, glad for affectionate attention. "Do I have a choice?"

They found a corner of Evan Waller's living room, where a plush blue couch rested under stark lithographs.

PRES. A. LINCOLN PRESIDES OVER HIS CABINET
THOS. JEFFERSON AND OTHER FOUNDING FATHERS

In ten years, at a party here prints might hang of Eisenhower, looking statesmanlike, and even a philosophic Richard Nixon.

There was another matter to attend to.

"Divorce," David said, "is not so bad a deal."

Joel frowned and looked surprised.

"It's a kind of luxury," David said.

"A luxury for you, maybe," Joel said. "For me, it's just a hard situation."

"Not that hard, really, is it? Come on. Admit it. You have marvelous choices, Joel. New York, Midtown. New York, West Side. Pennsylvania."

"That's kind of it," Joel said.

"What's kind of it?"

"I always have to choose."

David blinked and drank his Scotch.

"I mean, I'm glad you asked me to come down here," Joel said, "but don't you think I wonder about Mom being alone in New York? Do you think just because I'm fourteen, I don't wonder about things like that? I feel sorry for Mom. I miss her now, but I want to be with you. I mean, you pull one way and Mom pulls another, and I'm in the middle. Is that what you think is not so bad a deal?"

David drank again. Attending to this matter would be vexing.

"Mom drinks and that bothers you," Joel said. "We come here and everybody drinks, and it's okay."

"Callie—"

"She's fun," Joel said, "and she didn't marry Mom and she didn't divorce Mom."

The party buzzed beyond them. Clymer was kissing Becky Comfort on the cheek.

"Every day," David said, "I go to Harlem, and sometimes I forget what I started looking for, but I know what I find. Children your age and children younger, fighting to stay alive.

"That reminds me of how matters were when the human race was arranging itself out of a million varieties of genes. Parents made a lot of children. They lost one to pneumonia. Bad respiratory system. They lost two to appendicitis. Weak guts. They lost another to a saber-tooth tiger. Luck of the wild. A smallpox epidemic came along and knocked out four. You made ten children and counted your family fortunate if two survived. That was good for the race, the fit surviving, but hard as hell on the parents. They loved the less fit children as intensely as they loved the warriors."

"I guess it was hard on the parents," Joel said, "but you know who it was hardest for, don't you? The kids who died."

"See how far ahead you are, Joel. Your survival is guaranteed."

"You don't know," Joel said. "Kids in school, my age, get drunk and mess with cocaine. You can die from that."

"We're back to choices," David said. "Young people like you have the chance to choose. You can make a bad choice, like mixing cocaine and whiskey. You can make a good choice, like deciding someday to write a play or to compose a symphony. You may end up unhappy, but you have the freedom to pick your route. The one thing worse than too many choices is no choices at all. That's how it is in Harlem. Theotis struggles, but he doesn't get to choose."

Across the room, Evan Waller was waving both hands as he told Lottie Devon a story.

"Poverty," David said, "makes people live scaled-down, primitive lives. There's no chance to be creative. I can show you blocks in Harlem where it's as if Beethoven and Shakespeare never lived."

Waller reached his punch line. Lottie clapped strong hands and whinnied with laughter.

"Life begins before conception," David said, "with what the parents have in mind. Family planning is a rotten phrase, but a life starts best after the parents decide they want to have a child, they can afford to have a child, and that there's hope the child will grow in a better world. But up in Harlem there isn't any hope. Things haven't gotten better for three generations. A man and a woman roll into bed, and nobody thinks about creating a child who can grow up to be President." David lifted the glass toward A. Lincoln and Thos. Jefferson. "The man and woman are thinking about something else. Do you know what?"

"Fucking," Joel said.

In all my father's lifetime and my own, David thought, I never dared say "fuck" in his presence.

"You *have* to go to Harlem," Joel said. "That's your work. I don't have to go there and I don't have to live there."

"Do you understand that makes you fortunate?"

"Mom says I should think of the children in Vietnam. You say I should think of the children in Harlem. I say I'd be better off if there hadn't been a divorce."

"Then there wouldn't be any Callie."

"Everything's pulling at me," Joel said.

"Maybe," David said, "you'd enjoy spending more time with Theotis."

"He's all right," Joel said.

"I'll set something else up," David said. "The three of us, or maybe Callie too. A big meeting—"

"Young man," Evan Waller said, interrupting with great heartiness. "Tell me about your curriculum in school. I'll bet you New York kids are way ahead of ours."

"I'm sorry," Callie said, "that everybody seems to have been ignoring you two."

"Nonsense," David said. "This party has given me and Joel the chance to have a private talk."

Callie hugged Joel toward her hip, with an intense, awkward clutch. "Damn."

David stood. "Damn what?" he said.

"Damn, what you must think of this place," Callie said. "On your first trip you had to listen to nonsense about Judaism. Tonight it was as if you and Joel were invisible."

David stepped between Joel and Callie and hugged

them both. Except for the presence of his wife and child, David thought, he felt less comfortable among the manicured farms and stone houses of Deerfield County, Pennsylvania, than he did in a mean, stinking Harlem apartment.

Callie lay on a firm, high single mattress, listening to David breathe in sleep. He had chatted with her only briefly, saying that anti-Semitism was fixed and constant as the Northern Star. He had felt weary. He put off thought by using someone else's words. Then he said something funny. He'd had this friend named Shelley Goldberg who became a gynecologist on Park Avenue. To accompany his new persona and his new surroundings, the doctor selected a new name. Shelley Goldberg became Sheldon Ormont, M.D.

Mountains of gold.

There was neither bad taste nor anti-Semitism in David's telling of the incident. It was a patronizing comment on pretentiousness. "I've gotten almost forty years of practice at reacting to Semitism and anti-Semitism," he had said lightly, and he kissed Callie and sipped a Scotch, and fell asleep by himself in the high matching single bed.

Anti-Semitism made Callie feel hurt, shock and, at length, terror. In becoming, sort of, a Jew by osmosis, she felt defined not by herself but by others.

She lay musing that she was becoming more like David. She was beginning to wonder in the ways he did. If there had been no anti-Semitism across three thousand years, Callie thought, would people survive as Jews?

She herself was not absorbed by what she knew of Jewish theology. She did not intend to study Jewish cooking. She would read a book of Jewish history.

Sometime.

But now, at night, alone, she thought of the wicked

skiers from the Gestapo. If they came, they would take David and Joel. She would defend her men. Although she was only a Jew by osmosis, sort of, the Gestapo would kill her, too.

Merrill Clymer, simply enough, was a bigot. The Comforts, the Meenans from Paoli and the Kinsolvings from Mother's Thursday bridge accepted bigotry. They were the good Germans of eastern Pennsylvania.

You didn't find many overt bigots, but neither did you find many ardent anti-bigots. Her uncle, Les Devon, was an oak-ribbed anti-bigot. Evan Waller was an anti-bigot, made of softer matter. Supported by Uncle Les, or Evan Waller, Caroline could deal with all the bigots except one.

Mother.

It was a sense Caroline had. You couldn't tell much behind Mother's opaque eyes. You had to imagine.

Mother studied at Hobart and finished at Cornell and people said she had been gifted in mathematics. But Mother concealed herself, and to understand Mother now, you had to make her up, the way you made up a figure when you painted without a model.

Mother looked soft-faced in an old photograph in which a few Maitland men still wore wing collars and spats. They must have told her, "You are a Maitland lady." Then they recited names in the line of Maitlands that ran back to East Anglia.

Mother married a Devon, but a *radical* Devon. A radical Devon without money. That could not have rested easily with the Maitland elders. At Mother's wedding forty years ago, Mother fought her background and her preordained future. Not Calvinist, Caroline thought, but predestined nonetheless. Maitland ladies lived brown, narrow lives.

Considering the background, Mother struck out bravely, but Daddy died. She lost her purpose and her direction. She almost lost her sense.

Cancer.

Widowed Lottie Devon had to give doctors command of her body. They violated the privacy of excretion.

Shitting.

They had to teach her a new way to move her bowels.

Colostomy.

Caroline admired Mother's strength, but in surviving, Mother had evolved into what she once had fought. A Maitland lady, living a brown, narrow life.

Gather those you love, Caroline thought. Hold David and Joel to your breasts.

Move on.

Otis Pond lay under Chestnut Hill, except it didn't really, so that even in her dream, Caroline was aware that she was dreaming. The seasons had got mixed and timothy blew on the ridge, with Queen Anne's lace and goldenrod. The pond below lay frozen, a gleam of ice. She was not afraid in her dream, although she wondered why the pond was empty of skaters, with the sun so bright. She wondered how her dream was going to turn out.

Warm summer sat on the hill and people had come with bridge chairs and tables and checkered tablecloths of red and white, and she knew them. Merrill Clymer. The Comforts. The Meenans from Paoli. The Kinsolvings from Mother's Thursday bridge. They did not seem to know her. They were talking to Lottie, who looked young and soft-faced, the way Lottie looked in the family picture someone had taken in 1937.

"Hello, Mother," Caroline said.

Lottie shook her head, laughing, but when she saw Callie she became serious. "Your father wanted a boy," Lottie said.

"I can't help what I am," Caroline said.

Her sister, Patricia Beth, stood near, wearing a white blouse and a jumper that reached below her knees.

Patricia Beth was dark-haired and olive-skinned and ish-faced. In Caroline's dream Sister looked older than Mother.

"She can help what she is," Patricia Beth said. "Look how she's dressed."

Caroline was wearing only a white halter and brief white shorts. There was nothing wrong with that, except her sister's stare made her feel like a whore. Then Mother stared the same way.

In the sunlight, the down on Callie's thighs looked white.

"Set the table for the Reverend Clymer," Sister ordered.

A black boy stood beside Caroline, and together they set paper plates and plastic utensils on the red and white checkered cloth. Callie talked quietly to the black boy, to free his eyes of fright. "It it hard being colored?" Caroline said.

"Never been anything else," the boy said in a gentle, musical tone. "Can't tell about the heat, if you always een dark meat."

"Please don't talk that way to me," Caroline said. "I'm not the same as the others. I'm going to be an rtist and I'm going to have colored friends."

"That's like you," Patricia Beth said. "Mother suffered so to have you. She lay on a bed and never cried out in pain but she gripped the posts that held the headboard, and twisted them so hard that they were all loose before they took her to the hospital. We all wanted a boy and when you were little you had a boy's ace with big ears and you never listened. You never listened to anybody. And you always tried to come to inner in your slip."

"Anybody would," Caroline said, "if they were prettier than their sister."

The colored boy was not colored any longer. He wore ray slacks and a blue blazer and he was Joel.

"Boy," the Reverend Merrill Clymer called, "bring me a bourbon."

"Don't call him 'boy,'" Caroline said. "They don't like to be called 'boy.'" She wanted to protect Joel from the meanness. She wanted to mother him and she wanted to rush off where no one would know about the bad thing that had happened to her at school, and where they would like her in white shorts for her straight legs and downy thighs, and where she could sit beside paintings she would make. Paintings that were beautiful. She would make paintings that were beautiful and strong, blues and oranges and chrome yellows, and everyone would admire the paintings. There was nobody to tell this to, with Daddy dead.

"Boy," shouted the Reverend Clymer. "Where's my drink?"

Caroline wanted to run with Joel toward Otis Pond and another season, but the way was blocked by the Comforts and the Meenans and the Kinsolvings, who looked suddenly large. They were talking and pretending not to see her, but, of course, they could, and she was sorry she had worn the silly white shorts that made her feel naked. She stood with her arm around Joel and called at Clymer, "He's not a servant."

"You're so uppity since you married the Jewish feller," Patricia Beth said. Patricia Beth with her dark hair and salmon nose had sometimes been mistaken for a Jew.

"The child," Caroline said.

"He's not your child."

"He is" Callie heard herself shouting. She remembered her father. Daddy was reciting:

> *About the house,*
> *Ladies don't shout.*

She still was dreaming. She saw her father in the Levi's and green and black plaid shirt that he had worn when he drove off to die, and there was David, finally, the suggestion of a smile starting under the mustache. She was pleased to see him and flooded with love at this expression, the beginning of the suggestion of a smile. He smiled so gently, but David's clothing was peculiar. Instead of a tailored suit with side vents, he wore Levi's and a green and black plaid shirt.

"Why are you wearing that outfit?" Caroline said.

His voice was deeper than her father's had been. "When in Rome, wear tailored togas."

"You're not Roman," Patricia Beth said. "You're Jewish."

Mother laughed and David's gentle expression was gone and they were closing in, Clymer and the Comforts and the Kinsolvings and the Meenans. David drew his lips against his teeth and clenched a fist.

"No," she said. "There are too many of them."

"I'm not afraid," he whispered.

"I'm not afraid either, except about your anger. Merrill Clymer is an anti-Semite, David, and you have a low threshold of homicide."

They fled down Chestnut Hill, the others clamoring but moving slowly, because there was no escape, except Otis Pond, now surging with whitecaps, snapping into froth before a wind.

Joel's hand slipped from hers and Caroline cried out and when she turned Joel was gone.

She would not cry now, although she had lost Joel, just as she was learning his delights. David ran far ahead and she called a warning because the waters looked angry, and he could not swim as well as she. But he dove and stroked toward reeds that rose stiff along the far bank. She would have to dive herself, although going into the water in her white shorts and halter would mean that everything would show. The Comforts and the Meenans and the Kinsolvings were very close behind her.

As Caroline swam in the turbulent pond, waves rocked her body and she was alarmed. She might get seasick. She forced herself to think of the paintings she would make, the blues and oranges and chrome yellows, as she made for the stiff green reeds where David had gone.

The water lay still about the green reeds. She pushed slowly among the grass, which was not quite thick enough to hide a body, thinking of the blues and oranges and yellows, and she saw without surprise a red stain, spreading very slowly in the shape of a Japanese fan.

Beyond, someone in Levi's and a green and black plaid shirt lay on his stomach. She swam up through the blood. She could not tell whether it was her father or David who lay bleeding.

Kneeling in the shallow water, she tried to turn the body so that she could see the face. But something had happened to the face The features were missing. Blood surged from what had been a face and Caroline could not tell whether it was her father or her husband who lay dead amid the stiff green reeds.

She woke calmly, relieved to be awake. She would guard the men she loved. David. Joel.

She climbed into the other bed and pressed her arms about David, to protect him, scarcely aware that she was screaming in terror.

VI

As soon as Theotis Blaine woke, in the bed without sheets beside the cratered wall, he curled away from the younger children who played on the mattress. Julie and Clyde Blaine were slapping each other's forearms and giggling. Theotis did not want his brothers and sisters to know what he had to do. He dressed quickly. He kissed his mother on the forehead as she slept. He felt in the special pouch of his slacks. "You goan to school," Barbara Blaine said, dreamily. "That's right. Go to school, Theotis. Good boy."

He was going to the I. & E. Delicatessen, where the Jew feller had turned him in to the cop for a penny, a fucking penny, when he was little and he couldn't fucking defend himself, no fucking way. He was going to take fifty dollars from the cash register at the I. & E. Or one hundred dollars. He had nothing in his pocket except change. Pharaoh Gallen said the Crusaders needed bread and Theotis would like to hand Pharaoh a twenty-dollar bill, and say, "Here. This is for the gang. This is from me."

Then he would go down near that Madison Square Garden again and buy something. One of those watches with numbers on the face. Digitals. Two of those watches. One for himself and one for Mother. She ought to have a watch.

"If you need a hand*out*," Pharaoh Gallen had said, "go into some store you know and put a hand *in*."

"But if I know *them*," Theotis said, "they'll know *me*."

"Take off your hat," Pharaoh said. "Anybody would know you with that hat. First you take off your hat. You know what they call panty hose?"

Theotis laughed. "I fucked this fox on the roof. She had on two pair. We had to take off two pair of her panty hose. Me and the fox."

"You just need one pair," Pharaoh said. "You cut off both legs. Then you pull the legs, both legs, over your face. You'll see them okay but no one can see it's you."

"My clothes."

"Wear common clothes. Levi's pants. A lot of people wear Levi's pants. Common pants don't give much away. Go into the store. Help yourself. Run around the corner. Pull the panty hose off your face. *Walk* away.

You just one more dude. One more dude with a hundred bucks."

"That's no big deal."

"Be careful," Pharaoh Gallen said. "Don't use no gun. You're pretty strong. Show them the ice pick. With a gun, somebody might get hurt."

"If I show them the pick and they don't do nothing, then what?"

"Then you scratch him. He'll do something. Holler. But if they don't do nothing, don't help yourself. Run around the corner. Pull the panty hose off your head. Walk away, just one more dude. One more dude without a hundred bucks."

"Yeah," Theotis said. "You makin' sense, there, Pharaoh."

Imre Podgorny, a bald-headed man who wore black-rimmed spectacles, was working by himself at the I. & E. Delicatessen on the morning of January 31. Esther had felt a lump, and he had felt a lump, in her left breast, near the armpit. She was being examined this morning in the tumor clinic at the medical center on 124th Street. They were not really afraid. It was a small lump and Dr. Feinstein said that eighty percent of small lumps were benign, and even if it wasn't benign, there still wasn't anything to be afraid of. Look at Shirley Temple Black. Look at Betty Ford. They had cancer, both of them, Dr. Feinstein said. Now they were fine.

Imre Podgorny was not afraid, but edgy. Ordinarily, when he and Esther opened the store, she began cooking chickens on a spit. He set out little trays of good things like cold noodles with crisp vegetables, or sweet-and-sour cucumber salad, or hot stuffed peppers.

Esther joked with some of the black women. She was better at joking than he. "Budapest soul food," Esther said. She and the customers laughed together.

Imre wished she were back from the examination

at the tumor clinic. Dr. Feinstein said you could often tell about small lumps right away just by touching them. They could be cysts.

Cysts responded to heat.

A lump could be neurodermatitis. If that's what it was, Dr. Feinstein would give Esther pills, to help her relax.

Imre was thick-bodied and powerful, but his skin was pale. He worked inside all day, and until nine o'clock, many nights.

White people, who didn't know, asked him fearfully about Harlem at night, but the evenings, when the people of the neighborhood were all around, actually felt safer than the days.

He saw three large cream-colored plastic bags stacked in the back of the store, in front of shelves of breakfast cereals and juices. He had forgotten to carry out the garbage bags last night.

Imre Podgorny puffed air and lifted his arching eyebrows. He must be more concerned about Esther than he admitted to himself, forgetting something like that, carrying out garbage.

Theotis saw a stocky man hauling a cream-colored garbage bag halfway up the aisle in the I. & E. Delicatessen. That was the one who turned him over to the police.

"Doan go no further," Theotis said.

"What?"

Theotis decided he had to speak loudly to be heard from under his mask of panty hose. "I said, doan go no further." Theotis held the ice pick in his right hand, near a hip.

The white man froze.

"No. Go behind the counter to where the cash register is," Theotis said, "and you're goan to do what I say."

The white man dropped the garbage bag.

"Hold it."

"All right. All right," the white man said, rolling his *r*'s.

"You're goan to open the register and then you're goan to lie down," Theotis said. "I'm goan to get out quick, and you won't get hurt, but you got to do what I say."

"Are you alone?"

"My buddy's outside," Theotis said. "I got this ice pick. My buddy's got the gun. Hurry up."

An apron hung from Imre Podgorny's waist. He did exactly as Theotis ordered. There was nobody outside the store, Imre Podgorny guessed. He walked behind the counter and punched the no-sale key in the old register so that the drawer opened.

Theotis moved closer, lifting the ice pick to show that he was serious.

The white man's right hand moved quickly, in a motion he had learned from the Reverend Jeremiah Tunney.

He drew his Colt Police Positive revolver and fired, in a single motion. He continued firing. The bullets tore away the left side of Theotis's head. The dead boy fell backward, his brain and blood and shards of skull running onto the cream-colored garbage bag.

It was not murder. Mr. Podgorny had been defending his property, his liberty, his life. But quite suddenly the big-bodied white man bent at the waist and put his head on the counter and became hysterical.

"It's nothing," the Reverend Jeremiah Tunney told David Priest. "The death of a rowdy. At least ten thousand rowdies roam Harlem. I'm more concerned about my good friend Esther Podgorny. It turns out she has metastasized cancer of the breast."

"Theotis wasn't just a rowdy," David said. "He had a certain promise. He could quote Wordsworth."

"I'm sorry," Tunney said. His eyes flickered like quartz, then glared. "I'm not hard-hearted, but neither can I afford to be soft-headed."

"I thought you might deliver a eulogy for Theotis," David said. " 'A Promise Broken.' "

"What I will do," Tunney said, "is stop across the street at Phillipots to see that he gets proper burial. All right?"

"It's got to be all right," David said. "It's the best offer Theotis has."

Probably it had been this way near the little cemetery in Mill River, Massachussetts, that David had visited with his first wife, Joyce, sixteen years before. Probably it had been this way in the families of Jonathan Caleb and Rebecca Bartlett and Josiah Bowen, whose epitaph said he was taken up by the Lord on February 7, 1803. The mother and father made many babies, and when one died, you didn't grieve long. The others wouldn't give you time to grieve. "Clyde, stop hitting your sister," demanded Barbara Blaine.

"I'm sorry about Theotis," David said.

"He liked you, Mr. Priest, and he liked that son of yours too. What's the name?"

"Joel."

"Theotis told me you and Joel was fine people. I been cryin'. He was a good boy. Wasn't no reason for him to rob, was there?"

"He was trying to grow up," David said.

"Crazy," Barbara Blaine said. "Crazy is what it is. Believing you got to rob a store to be growed up."

"Joel and I liked Theotis too."

"Julie," Barbara Blaine said, "if you hit Clyde first,

he's got a right to hit you back, and I ain't gonna stop him, Julie. How you like that?"

Objective correlative.

Eliot's phrase, dry as the bones of dead men in rat's alley.

The poet was commenting on expressions of emotion. Specifically *Hamlet*. Specifically, the poet argued, the facts in *Hamlet* did not warrant all the ranting. Specifically, the poet protested, the ranting was ratiocination.

"O, what a rogue and peasant slave am I!" The events of the drama, the poet said, did not support such rhetoric.

The wind felt suddenly raw. David was passing Patti's Place on bare, littered 114th Street, as he walked to the corner of Sydenham where the taxi driver Patrick Henahan had let him off in anger nine weeks earlier. If life were a play, then David was performing a drama counter to Eliot's *Hamlet*. A boy had died. A dream was trampled. There were no soliloquies, no eulogies, no epitaphs, nor even any worthy sounds of grief. There was only a death.

Near the Hospital for Joint Diseases and Medical Center, David found a taxicab. He was surprised to hear himself direct this driver, Miguel Fuentes, to 80 Riverside Drive.

Joyce blinked to see him. She looked wary, then glad. "You seem upset," she said. "Come in."

She mixed drinks. She was wrapped in a flowered beige tunic, belted at the middle. David sat on a black Barcelona chair, under the solid walnut shelves that bordered the fireplace. He allowed himself an upward glance, pausing at titles on each shelf. *The World of Fiction,* De Voto. *Bang the Drum Slowly,* Harris. *Letters from Robert Frost,* Untermeyer. *Pushkin,* A Biography by Henri Troyat. He had mechanically followed the advice of counsel, not to argue for custody of the books. He should have argued. No matter. The books were gone. "Joel worries me," David said to Joyce, who was sitting on the blue crushed-velvet couch.

"He's going through a time of adjustment. We all are."

"This boy in Harlem, Theotis, has run out of time. He's dead."

"Aah, so that's what's bothering you." Joyce's insights had been finely tuned. "I'm sorry. I know you felt close to Theotis."

"It makes me wonder about divorce."

"Oh?" Joyce set her teeth on edge.

"I look for a balance of things, a sense of order."

"That would be important to you now."

"We, you and I, care more about Joel's visitations—*visitations*—than people in Harlem care about Theotis's death."

"You want to write your book," Joyce said, "but you have only fragments under control. You feel threatened by the chaos of the unmade book. That's why you need order in the rest of your life."

David retreated. "Where's Joel?"

"Joel may have a girl friend. He was behaving mysteriously, and finally it turned out that he wanted to make a telephone call in complete privacy. He went to a friend's house. He wouldn't tell me what the phone call was about."

"It isn't the unmade book that's chaos," David said. "It's living."

"How did he die?"

"Holding up a store."

Joyce fixed David with a gaze of great gentleness. "Just a kid? Like Joel? A kid who had to prove he was grown up?"

"In the most assertive way he knew. Theotis made his point by dying. He was as grown up as he was ever going to be."

"Poor little kid." Joyce's eyes showed tears.

"Nobody else has taken the trouble to lament."

"We go back years," Joyce said. "We look at things the same way."

"I'm writing a good book," David said. "I thought that writing a good book would simplify my life."

"It complicates your life," Joyce said. "You're always having to remember what's real and what's writing, which people are the real people and which are pretend, which child is the real child, Joel or Theotis."

"They're both real, or they were."

"But only one is ours." Alarm turned Joyce's face grave. "Thank God he's alive."

"Do you know what I mean about balance, order, counterpoint?"

"The Harlem child is a sad pause," Joyce said. "His death is pitiful, and unfair. But you still have to go on helping Joel."

"It was kind of you to hear me out," David said, standing.

"Whatever the lawyers tell us," Joyce said, "you can always come here when you're in trouble."

He kissed her on a puffy cheek. As he did, David thought, But I can't always come over like this. We have to release each other and the past.

"I'm sorry about Theotis, really," Joyce said. Her eyes were still wet and David wondered if her tears were for the dead boy or the dead marriage.

He made himself stop wondering.

The famous epigram about mistresses sacrificed truth for wit.

A man can indeed serve two mistresses.

But he cannot serve two wives.

Caroline burst toward David as he opened the apartment door. "I have rather momentous news," she said.

David prolonged his ritual for Theotis. "Poor little

bastard," he said. "That's what Theotis was. And none so poor to do him reverence. Why am I using someone else's words?"

"I don't know what you're talking about," Caroline said, "but my momentous news is this: While you were out, Joel telephoned. He wants to change his place of residence. He says he wants to come and live with us."

PART THREE

Trials by Love

Your star lawyer wins litigations.
Your superstar doesn't let litigation begin.

SOLOMON (CLIPPER) ZELLBACH

CHAPTER ONE

The Cage of Law

I

Seated at the gray-veined marble table, David typed a sketch of the feisty, round-faced barmaid who worked at The Black Rooster, where Theotis Blaine had drunk beer with him nine weeks before. Her name was Florence Turnure and she once worked as a registered nurse in a ward for premature babies at G. W. Carver Memorial Hospital. Carver had neither enough incubators nor enough physicians; so many babies died that Florence Turnure became despondent. In her talks with David, she understated her importance as a nurse and overstated the possibilities for doing good behind her dark-stained plywood bar.

Florence talked over and over about an infantry private who came into The Black Rooster, shortly before he was to leave for Vietnam. The private did not want to go to Asia and felt so depressed that he talked about jumping off the highway bridge that spans Spuyten Duyvil, Spitting Devil, where the Harlem River and the Hudson River collide. He spoke of disappearing into the black currents. "Black man; black currents," he told Florence.

She took the soldier home and embraced him and made love to him and mothered him. She believed she had saved his life. She wanted David to understand that she could save lives as a barmaid as surely as she had saved some lives, but not enough, when she was a preemie nurse at G. W. Carver Hospital.

At the marble typing table, David's fancy wandered from Florence Turnure.

Joel telephoned. He says he wants to come and live with us.

David tried to remember what it was like to be fourteen years old. It had been twenty-five years before, David thought, that he was fourteen years old.

Fourteen.

Twenty-eight.

Forty-two.

Fifty-six.

Death.

At fourteen, he liked street football. He had been a good pass catcher, and he spent hours inventing patterns. Run to the manhole cover and cut left. Run to the manhole cover and cut right. Run to the manhole cover, fake a cut and keep going. See the ball against the sky. Keep your hands loose. As the football tumbles toward you, leap. The ball thumps against your fingers. Cradle it gently; draw it in. Was that fourteen? Leaping about manhole covers?

Fourteen was resisting French, the way Callie resisted French, and enjoying plane geometry and liking—even taking seriously—the Millay sonnet that begins: "Euclid alone has looked on Beauty bare."

Fourteen was hungering with more intensity than taste. It was trying to catch up in an instant on Cheops, Justinian, Charlemagne, Alexander Nevsky, and sort out, as if anyone could sort out, the relative contributions of Einstein, Marx, Freud, Camus and Hermann Goering.

It was still to be the child, excited by Thanksgiving turkey, and also to be a young adult, debating: Resolved that capital punishment should be abolished. It was wanting to be taken seriously by elders and learning how to think and finding, when you had thought well and expressed yourself clearly, that your parents heard only the utterings of a fourteen-year-old boy.

David was not sure how much had changed, but fourteen had been discovering, simultaneously and separately, girls and his own sexuality. It was having your first wet dream, without knowing the locker room story about your first wet dream. "Look, Ma," cries the boy in the story. "No hands!"

It was shaving once every ten days, and using sulfur cream to subdue acne. It was learning how a blue blazer complemented gray slacks and that it was possible, after much effort, to fashion a dark-red necktie into a dimpled Windsor knot. It was finding, after even greater effort, ways to chat with girls.

As you spoke, you hid the lust that flickered in you. Fourteen was balancing your secret ardor with the soft affection young women seemed to want. Try then to speak with soft affection, hoping that the blazer sat properly on your shoulders and that the Windsor knot held. Reconcile your lust and soft affection. Fourteen was fortunate, David thought, the guide would be his pretending, both you and she, that nobody was touching anything.

Fourteen was fright that manhood neared and it was—yes, it was—leaping about manhole covers and making a good catch and feeling the exultation of the body, your own gangly, hair-sprouting, erectile, virginal, unfinished, wet-dreaming body.

A fourteen-year-old boy needed a guide; if the boy was fortunate, David thought, the guide would be his father.

On the next afternoon, a Thursday, Joel sat with David at the writing table, which had become a place for serious things. Caroline withdrew to the bedroom, bearing the French novel of holocaust, *The Last of the Just*.

Joel wore a fitted maroon and blue plaid shirt. "Is your book going all right?" Joel said.

"Sure. Don't worry about it."

"But Callie says you haven't written much yet, so how can you know it's going all right?"

"You can tell a little from what you're going to be writing about. And I think I'll be writing about dramatic things."

"Theotis?"

David nodded. They sat separated by silence. David wished that they were in the growling Porsche. "Does his death shake you?"

"It shakes me, but it doesn't undermine me."

"Doesn't it make your own problems seem minor?"

"It doesn't have anything to do with my problems. I mean, now we can't have the meeting you wanted, but, Dad, he did try to rob a store."

"Do you know why?"

"You're going to talk about economics, but economics doesn't matter anymore."

You find in certain fourteen-year-olds a core of nascent diamond. You can denigrate their natures as self-involved, or romanticize them as existential, but fourteen is not a sentimental age. "Callie says you'd like to live with us," David said.

"I would, if you have the room."

"We'll have the room. I can't keep Callie in a bachelor pad much longer. We'll find another apartment, right away." David excused himself and made a Scotch. "Look, Joel," he said. "I have to tell you how much I want you living with us. It would complete my life. That's how much I want you."

"It would be fun. It would be more fun for me."

"Have you told your mother?"

"No. Or sort of. I've said sometimes that I wished

I was living with you and Callie. Mostly when I was mad. Then Mom gets mad herself and says, 'You may not!' "

"All right. I've said having you here would complete my life, but I don't want you to come just because it would be more fun. You'd still have to do homework and study French."

"Latin. I'm taking Latin."

"You'd be expected to make your bed and help with the dishes. What do you hate?"

"Vacuuming. Mom makes me vacuum my room."

"You'd have to vacuum here. What else do you hate?"

"Going to bed early."

"It'll be lights out at ten."

Joel looked grave, even alarmed. "I'm saying these things," David said, "because I want you to realize that it isn't all going to be ice skating and skiing. It isn't all going to be fun. I'm saying these things because I'm afraid to be too happy. Do you know what happens to people when they're too happy?"

"They cry."

David squeezed Joel's hand, and Joel squeezed back. "Why haven't you told your mother?" David said,

"I can't," Joel said.

"Are you afraid of her?"

"It's not that. She gets mad, but she likes me. She loves me. It would hurt her if I told her, and I don't want to hurt Mom."

Joyce will be hurt soon enough, David thought. But that perception extended beyond what you understood when you were a fourteen-year-old boy.

Clip Zellbach took David's call at ten o'clock on Friday morning, and suggested that they confer at four-thirty that afternoon. "I was supposed to leave early for

Killington, but this is more important. We were looking forward to skiing Vermont."

"I didn't know your wife skied," David said.

"What does my wife have to do with the trip to Killington? My wife is in Aruba. Remember to bring Caroline to my office."

Zellbach's new suite opened directly off elevators on the forty-eighth floor of a tan glass tower at Madison Avenue near Fifty-eighth Street. "Change partners and move," Zellbach said. "One of the ways of current law." Pale-blue grass cloth and a scattering of silhouettes covered the walls of the inner office. A burgundy carpet completed the décor. Zellbach had placed an English partners' desk diagonally in a corner that commanded a view toward Central Park. It was a clear late-winter day. Even from the height of forty-eight stories, the park showed a suggestion of spring.

"I wanted to mention your pending bill for looking over my contract," David said, sitting on a buff Queen Anne chair.

"Mention it?" Zellbach said. "Or pay it?"

"Mention it."

"You're not here to talk book contracts. You're here to talk about a child. You can see from the furnishing that I'm not starving."

"Very nice move, Clip," Caroline said, "and very nice furnishing. Mercifully free of Daumiers."

"My rate in this matter will be seventy-five dollars an hour, but since you're working on a book, David, I won't ask for an advance. Satisfactory?"

"Satisfactory," Caroline said.

"Now," Zellbach said, "I've been doing some research, and so has Ellis Warburg, a young associate. The courts do not agree on how to determine contested custody for a fourteen-year-old boy. I have citations in which the court accepted the wishes of the child; and citations in which they did not. I have cases where the

courts ignored both father and mother and institution-
alized the child."

"What about the specific wishes of the father?" David
said.

"Unfortunately," Zellbach said, "courts consistently
hold that the father's specific wishes are not important
in custody. Visits, yes. Custody, no. Courts pay attention
to the father as custodial parent only if the mother is
a prostitute, a psychotic or a late-stage alcoholic. Otherwise, with fourteen-year-olds, the courts hold that a
father's thoughts on custody aren't worth a damn."

Caroline's jaw jutted. "I never thought I'd suggest
this," she said. "We need a men's liberation movement."

"I'll lead it," David said. "I'll wear kilts." He sighed.
False gaiety was as brittle as November ice. "As matters
stand, Clip," he said, "what do things depend on?"

"What they always depend on in matrimonials.
Things depend on the whim of a judge."

"The feeling I like least," Caroline said, "is help-
lessness. I can't stand to feel the way I do now. Helpless."

Zellbach smiled and examined tiny rampant lions
gold-tooled into leather on the partners' desk. "We
aren't helpless. We just can't be headstrong. We have
to use tactics." He tapped a gold lion with a gold
and black Mont Blanc pen. The smile froze. He looked
uncomfortable. "Straight, or with Swiss chocolate coat-
ing?" Zellbach said.

"Straight," David said.

"Litigation is the bottom line. I particularly dislike
litigation centering about a child, but we have to be
prepared for Family Court. There's a lavish new family
courthouse down on Lafayette Street with free-form
sculpture in the lobby. The place is a sewer."

"I never covered courts much," David said.

"Family Court is full of wretched, impatient people.
You find deserted mothers and welfare cheaters and

desperate men and crying children. Family Court is crowded with crying kids.

"The good judges are overworked clearing the calendar. The bad judges take two-hour coffee breaks. All the judges hear misery, bickering, hate. They grow irritable and capricious. Sometimes, as in a case like this, their capriciousness shapes important lives."

Zellbach pressed his palms in front of his angular chin. "I've thought often that alimony and support should be fixed in one court, and that a child's well-being should be monitored somewhere else." He held his prayerful pose. "But where?"

"There ought to be a board of child psychiatrists," Caroline said.

"If there's anything worse than a society run by lawyers," Zellbach said, "it would be a society run by doctors."

"Aren't we going too fast?" David said. "The other side—Joyce—is no more anxious than we are to nail Joel to a witness stand."

"But our strategy must assume the worst, if it's worthy of being called strategy at all. Ellis Warburg and I have evolved a plan that demonstrates Joel wants to live with you."

"Assuming court," David said, "Joel can simply say what he wants on the stand."

"Testimony is one form of evidence," Zellbach said. "The weakest form, by the way. You can refute testimony. A document is better A demonstrable fact is better still. We're going to begin our case by creating a fact. Joel will present himself physically at your door and say, 'Take me in, Dad.' "

"We can just keep him after the next visitation," Caroline said.

"That's not the same thing," Zellbach said.

"You're preparing a scenario," David said.

"Exactly. I want to be able to tell a judge, 'You

Honor, these are all decent people.' I'd get nowhere attacking Joyce. 'Your Honor, these are all decent people, but this boy, who performs well in school and is becoming old enough to know his own mind, wants to live with his father. He wants that so badly that he stole away from his mother's home and presented himself at the father's door and said, 'Daddy, Daddy. Take me in.'

"And the father, busy as he is with his creative work, threw his arms around his son and said, 'Yes. Yes, I will. Yes. Yes.' "

"It's a soap opera," Caroline said.

"He's concluding with James Joyce," David said. *"Ulysses."*

"If I could get an electric organ into court, I would," Zellbach said. "We learned in law school that when the facts are on your side, argue the facts. When the law is on your side, argue the law. When you have neither the facts nor the law, make as much noise as possible.

"I'm trying to create a fact. If I have to, I'll make noise. Right now, just sell Joel my scenario."

Caroline began to cry. Zellbach tapped the Mont Blanc pen and considered his fingernails. They were buffed.

"Are you all right, Callie?" David said. "Clip, do you keep stuff in the office? Can we get her a vodka on the rocks?"

"I'm all right," Caroline said. She wept harder. "It's not me. I'm thinking about Joel. He's going to have to take the witness stand against his mother. And he loves his mother. The poor little kid."

It was good walking in the cold. The cold was real. His love for his son was being distorted into a scenario.

"Twenty brisk blocks, Callie?"

"A year ago," she said, "I was in Isla Verde and the

biggest problem was whether to drive to El Junque tomorrow or the day after."

"With whom?"

"A disaster called Hayes Morgan." Caroline wore her red coat against the cold.

"Did this Morgan fellow abuse you?" David said.

"How do you mean?"

"Oh, sexually, I suppose."

"Yes, he did," Caroline said. "I'd lie on the beach and feel the warm sand under me and the sun turned me on and the sand turned me on and the beach boys turned me on, and we'd go to our room in the Caribe Hilton. Then Hayes Morgan would contend with his impotence. He said it was difficult for him to make it with an attractive woman. But he was in therapy. Could I be patient? So I'd be turned on and Hayes Morgan stayed limp. I consider that sexual abuse."

On Thursday, David recounted Zellbach's proposal to Joel. The boy listened distantly. Interest glimmered in the large pale eyes. Then Joel exploded.

"Why do I have to do all that? That's ridiculous. Why do I have to pretend I've run away? Why do we have to worry about a court?"

"Because," David said, "in divorce, the courts take it on themselves to look after the welfare of a child."

"And *that's* ridiculous," Joel said. His deepening voice wavered from baritone to tenor. "Mom looks after me and you look after me and Callie looks after me. Why do we need a court?"

David met Joel's eyes. He had three answers. Six answers. He had none.

"Shit," Joel said. He looked at his father to see if the word was accepted.

"That's right," Caroline said. "Vent your anger naturally."

"Why can't we just go to Mom and tell her what we want?"

"We could, and then she'd tell us what she wanted," David said. "She'd disagree. She'd just say no. You'd stay with her. But you'd still want to live here, and we'd still want you to live here. So it turns out that we really may need the courts, doesn't it?"

Joel sat on the ivory couch with his knees apart and his strong forearms resting across his thighs. He looked at his hands and winced and nodded.

"Shit," Joel said again. With his head bent low and his body held immobile, he looked defeated.

David was typing an impression of Detective Liam Farrell late the next afternoon. Farrell was a general assignment detective, attached to the 135th Street precinct, who lived in a white neighborhood of tract houses in southern Westchester County. Farrell's work partner, Grouse Manders, was a black from East Elmhurst, Queens, and Farrell talked about how they relied on one another, when they had to search a tenement roof for "perpetrators." The Irish detective said he and the black, who would be denied a mortgage even at usurious rates by Farrell's local bank, were "closer than neighbors. In fact, except for our skin, we could be brothers."

The telephone rang. Joel sounded breathless. "Mom just went out for a minute. Dad?"

"What is it?"

"I told her I want to live with you."

"What? You told her? Why did you tell her that?"

"I wanted to tell the truth to my own mother."

"Wait a minute." David held the green notebook he had used when he was interviewing Detective Liam Farrell. He scaled the notebook toward the marble table. It scattered a stack of papers onto the rug. "I can't blame you, Joel," he said. "Sometimes you just want to forget the lawyers and the courts and say what's true."

"Mom got mad as hell." Joel still sounded breathless. "She called this fellow Mr. Cassidy, her lawyer.

"Mr. Cassidy got me on the phone and said that if I went more than three blocks from home without Mom's consent, he was going to have the police arrest me as a runaway."

"The police have other things to do. Besides, they don't work that quickly. Besides, Cassidy is a lying son of a bitch. Pack a toothbrush. Jump into a taxi. Come over right now."

"I can't. Mom took my money. She cleaned out my wallet."

"Get into a cab and tell them your father will pay."

"I don't want to go looking for a cab. Suppose I can't find one. I am *not* going more than three blocks from the house. I don't care what you say, Dad. I don't want to get arrested."

"All right. I'll meet you somewhere. I'll slip you a fast six dollars. Then you give one dollar to the doorman. He gets you the taxi. Then ride down here."

"Mom's gone to the supermarket. Then she's going to see Mr. Cassidy. I can meet you in the bagel store on Broadway. That's only two blocks from the house."

"Twenty minutes," David said. He telephoned Clip Zellbach, fighting through a new secretary by saying "a matter of utmost urgency." He felt ridiculous saying "utmost urgency." That was the way not-quite-real people spoke getting past Watson to see Holmes.

Zellbach said in flat tones that Joel should not come to his father's house today. "With what Cassidy knows that would work against the spontaneity of the scenario Ellis Warburg and I devised. Sometime next week would be better."

"Joel wants to come now," David said.

"I want to make sure," Zellbach said emotionlessly, "that when he comes over, he can stay."

"How many, mac?" said an extremely fat, perspiring man behind the counter of the Hot Broadway Bagelry.

"You want a bagel, Joel?" David said.

"No, thanks."

"None, thanks," David said to the fat, perspiring man.

"Then what did you come into the bagel store for, mac?"

"We're shills," David said. "We make it look as though people are lining up to buy your delicious bagels."

"Can I have the six dollars?" Joel said.

David handed him six dollars, and another ten dollars. "But you can't come over until next week."

"What?" Joel's face twisted. The left side of his mouth drooped in pain.

"You could use a bagel, kid," the counterman said. "A little food could cheer you up."

"If you came today, it would look too much as if I put you up to it."

Joel's face showed controlled, adult anger. David did not remember that look before.

Joel thrust out his jaw the way Caroline did. "I know, I know," Joel said. "It's because of some judge. Well, let's go down to the judge now and tell him what we want."

"It doesn't work that way. The courts have calendars. You have to wait your date. The judges are busy."

"I'm going to have a bad week with Mom," Joel said. "She's upset and she'll start drinking. Last time I disobeyed when she was drinking, she started kicking me in the shin. This Mr. Cassidy is threatening to arrest me. Mom will bring Grandma over and Grandma will start giving me a lecture. Why didn't I get bar-mitzvahed?

Mom will keep drinking. She hugs me sometimes when she drinks, and sometimes she kicks me in the shin."

"Go home quickly," David said. "Pack in a hurry. Come knock on our apartment door in half an hour."

"Great," Joel said. He sprang into a trot, fleeing the Hot Broadway Bagelry.

"You're better off divorced," the counterman said.

"Beg pardon?"

"I'm still with mine. All I hear is, the long hours I spend making bagels, she would have been better off marrying a doctor. I tell her, Esther, what doctor would have taken you?"

II

The docket of New York City Family Court, formerly the Court of Domestic Relations, was posted under a hanging sculpture: steel bent into the shape of a kidney, and later stippled. The court was housed in a shiny, slab-fronted lump of a building on Lafayette Street, below the Soho section, where artists were moving into loft buildings and driving out marginal businessmen.

"What's that?" Joel said, gesticulating at the kidney-shaped hanging sculpture.

"Renal failure," Caroline said.

In another circumstance, David would have laughed. On this bland March afternoon, as he awaited trial in Family Court, Part IV, David felt remote from humor.

The docket was a hexagon, shaped from porous lava, with four bulletin boards worked cleverly into the flowing form. Perhaps a Soho artist had outbid a businessman for lot space, with proceeds from the hexagonal lava docket. It was a docket still. David blinked to see himself listed as defendant.

He had been ordered to report to a courtroom on the ninth floor at 2:15 P.M. David stood in the family courthouse lobby. It was 1:58, according to a digital clock, white numbers on black plastic posted behind the metal sculpture. While judges and bailiffs went to lunch, all the courtrooms closed. Iron gates and armed guards barred the courts to lawyers, mothers, fathers, children. David stood with Caroline and Clip Zellbach and Joel.

He walked into the mild afternoon. An officer had parked a gray van marked "New York City Probation Department" ahead of a flat-bed truck that carried a whirling ride for children. A sign in red and blue and orange announced "Johnny's Lightning Whizzer." Both trucks, the probation van and Johnny's Lightning Whizzer, were closed and locked.

Zellbach wore a tailored camel's hair topcoat. Joel wore a velour coat, over his blazer and gray slacks. But David's suit was five years old, and Caroline's khaki raincoat lay open revealing a plain, high-collared white blouse and a blue denim skirt. It was important, Zellbach had said, that neither overdress for court. "David," he said, "you should appear somewhat poorer than the judge. Caroline, try to look like a cross between a rape victim and a virgin."

People clumped about them in the pale March sun. A stocky woman lawyer in platform shoes was taking a history. David did not eavesdrop, but the woman lawyer's voice was a tuba. "So you take drugs from time to time. A lot of girls do that."

The client shrank and hunched her shoulders and whispered.

"Of course you love your baby. Of course you want your baby back from the home. But we have to make sure you're ready to look after your baby. You may need rehabilitation."

The mother put a finger to her lips and began to cry.

A well-dressed couple bickered between attorneys. The man demanded the right to enter his former wife's home, so that he could help his son, Rolland, with homework in European history.

"You just want to get into the house," the woman said, "so you can slug me again."

"I never slugged you," the man said. "I shoved you. There's a big difference. Not that you didn't deserve to be slugged."

"We'll see what the judge decides," the woman said. She had a long, pretty face, marred by a downturned mouth. "And where the hell is last month's alimony, Professor?"

"Come inside," Zellbach said to Joel. "The court should be ready for us now."

Caroline and David each put a hand on Joel's shoulder, as if to protect him from the whimpering and the raging.

The courtroom opened off the east side of ninth-floor reception. Through slanted windows on the west side, you could see eighth-floor reception. Slanted windows showed on the eighth floor too. From an ideal angle, you could see all the way down to the iron-gated lobby. "Let me review Gabe Cassidy's motions," Zellbach said.

A digital clock, matching the lobby clock, was broken. Only three cases were scheduled that afternoon before Judge Victor Lombardo. Fewer than a dozen people sat waiting.

"This feels like a holding pen," David said. "They used to have holding pens in Chicago. They'd keep steers there before the slaughter. But the Chicago stockyards have been leveled. The only thing left is a yellow gateway."

"I want you to concentrate on the motions," Zellbach said.

Having to dress for effect, David thought, made

Family Court resemble amateur theater. His mind rebelled against taking court seriously.

Chicago stockyards.

All the courthouses in Chicago once burned down.

Zellbach was right. He would have to concentrate. They would all have to concentrate. "I'm concentrating, Clip," David said.

"Cassidy has filed three motions," Zellbach said. "First, he wants your child-support payments increased by two hundred fifty dollars monthly, on two grounds: Joel should have regular psychotherapy, and inflation."

"I've been divorced six months," David said. "A claim based on six months of inflation is absurd."

"I think so," Zellbach said, "but I don't matter. Judge Lombardo matters."

"What do you know about Lombardo?" David said.

"We'll get to that," Zellbach said. "Ellis Warburg reports that he's a woman's judge."

"Pro woman?"

"That's what Ellis reports."

"Joel," David said. "You don't want to go to a psychotherapist, do you?"

Joel looked at David and shrugged.

"Cassidy's second motion calls for reduced visitation," Zellbach said. "He charges that frequent visitations are disruptive to Joel's mental health, and further"—Zellbach scanned a legal form—" 'defendant attempts to destroy minor child's respect, esteem and love for his mother, the plaintiff, Joyce S. Priest, during visitations.' "

"I'm not even around," David said. "I'm in Harlem."

"A courtroom rule," Zellbach said, "is deny everything the other side says. This is an adversary proceeding. But be careful. Don't overdeny, as you just did. The correct courtroom answer is, first, that you are *always* around, as a good father should be. Second, you *bolster* Joel's love for his mother."

"But perjury," Caroline said.

"This isn't a homicide case," Zellbach said. "Family Court judges allow for overstatement. David, take your time in answering. That gives you a chance to think, if necessary, and gives me a chance to object, if necessary."

Another time a Chicago courthouse burned, David remembered, was in 1920, after the White Sox deliberately lost the 1919 World Series. All the records proving the fix burned too. Please. Forget baseball. Concentrate.

"Cassidy's final motion," Zellbach said, "seeks to have you cited for contempt. He alleges that you unlawfully failed to return Joel to his mother, in violation of an agreement dated September twenty-sixth. I'll deal with that myself."

"Could they send David to jail for contempt?" Caroline said. "That's happened to writers just for being left of center."

"Jail?" Joel said. "Dad in jail?"

"Cassidy is saber rattling," Zellbach said. "He's knocking shillelaghs together. Don't worry about jail. Don't worry about contempt. The only way you can get in trouble in there, David, is if you punch the honorable Victor Lombardo."

David tugged his mustache. He put a hand on Joel's forearm. "It's one of our family rules," he said. "Never hit a judge when court's in session."

"When you're the defendant," Caroline said.

David said to Zellbach, "What do we have going for our side?"

"One motion. To convey custody of Joel from his mother to you. One reason. The best interests of the child."

"We're outgunned," David said, "three motions to one."

"At a Columbia seminar last month, an appellate judge said that lawyers who created a blizzard of motions made him suspicious. He tended to trust the lawyer who made a single motion, simple and direct. Ellis Warburg attended the seminar. While there, he saw one Victor Lombardo."

"So you're following a hunch," David said.

"It's an educated guess," Zellbach said. "Highly educated. Four years of law school and twenty-six years of practice."

"What about the woman's judge business?" Caroline said.

"Thanks. I'd almost forgotten. We want to take our time with our answers in the courtroom, and we want to know something about the individual sitting as judge who'll be reacting to those answers.

"Victor Lombardo is Italian, of course. He was a Democratic clubhouse leader from Greenwich Village. He's conservative. He's a staunch Catholic. He opposes abortion and gay rights. He supports capital punishment. He'd say Alger Hiss was guilty and Caryl Chessman was guilty, but that reasonable doubt persists about the guilt of Richard Nixon.

"He could have landed higher in the judiciary—he may yet move up—but Judge Lombardo *chose* to serve in Family Court. He spoke of the family as a threatened unit. He said divorce was too easy and too many men deserted their responsibilities. In a capsule, Victor Lombardo believes in Mary as the symbol of the church, and mother as the symbol of the home."

"He'd vote against the Equal Rights Amendment," Caroline said.

"But women get better than equal rights in his court," David said.

"Exactly," Zellbach said.

Joyce appeared in ninth-floor reception, beside Gabe Cassidy. She wore a boxy brown suit.

"Mom looks mad," Joel said.

David patted Joel's arm. "She's upset. She'll feel

better. We'll all feel better in a few hours, Joel, when this idiocy is done."

"Idiocy?" Joel said. "Where I live is not idiocy, Dad."

"Counselor," Zellbach said. He and Cassidy exchanged bloodless smiles. Trial was at hand. Zellbach's eyes showed a hunter's excitement.

Within Family Court, Part IV, molded chairs were fixed in a wide semicircle below the bench and fifteen feet away from it. A clerk, a court reporter and a uniformed guard were positioned at the front of the plastic-paneled room. David had thought there would be spectators, and possibly someone from the *Daily News.* "Family Court is closed to outsiders," Zellbach whispered. "It's a sewer, but not a circus."

Judge Lombardo was signing papers. He had a huge, square head, under a thicket of black hair, which he brushed straight back. His jaw was square and he wore square-framed spectacles and his close-set gray eyes looked angry.

The lawyers stood and identified themselves. Joyce rose and swore to tell the whole truth. The clerk, a white-faced, thick-lipped man, asked David, "Do you solemnly swear to tell the truth, the whole truth and nothing but the truth?"

"I do," David said. He had meant to affirm. But the judge was Catholic. David wanted to win. Was anyplace on earth, he thought, as immediately corrupting as a court of justice?

"It's rare to find distinguished counsel in this little court," Judge Lombardo said.

Zellbach bounced to his feet with a deferential grin. "Thank you, Your Honor. I have an interesting case."

"I feel like taking on an interesting case," Judge Lombardo said.

"That sounds like trouble," Zellbach said.

"Perhaps for distinguished counsel," Judge Lombardo said. "Not for the court."

"Yes, sir," Zellbach said.

"Of course, you have a worthy adversary."

Thick-necked Gabe Cassidy bounced up. "We have a plain, straightforward case, Your Honor."

The majesty of the law, David thought: a politician with a big head, wearing a black robe, above a pair of bouncing lawyers. Wealthy lawyers. Vested lawyers. Custom-tailored, manicured, fobbed lawyers; lawyers of astounding affluence. But bouncing all the same. Like toys. Good toys. Astounding toys. Zellbach and Cassidy, attorneys from F. A. O. Schwarz.

Concentrate, David told himself. You are the defendant. You are not a commentator from the *New Left Press.*

"Let's see what this is about," Judge Lombardo said. His voice rang deeply but his accents were flat. A New York workingman's speech.

"I've filed motions," Cassidy said. His muscled neck bulged behind his pale-gray collar.

"I can read motions, counselor. I read motions all day. Sometimes I read motions at night. That's a requirement of my job. If you're colored, or Jewish, or a woman, it don't matter. To be a judge, you've got to be able to read motions."

Cassidy flushed. "Yes, sir."

"Why don't you come up to the bench, counselor, and the other counselor too, and bring your clients, if you can control them."

The lawyers and David and Joyce moved under the judge's impersonally angry expression. "This is off record," Judge Lombardo said. "Let the people tell me what's going on, not the lawyers."

"Go ahead, Joyce," David said. "I'll follow you."

"I determine the order you speak in," Judge Lombardo said to David. "Now. *You* begin."

"Yes, sir," David said.

He had to articulate someone else's scenario for a judge whose grammar was shaky. Keep the story line simple, David told himself. Screen treatment. Paramount pays $100,000 for some. This is worth more. Don't muse!

"My son, Joel, presented himself at my door and asked me and my wife to take him in. And we did. And he wants to stay with me and I want him to stay with me."

"Mrs. Priest?" Judge Lombardo said. "Tell me your side."

"He didn't run away," Joyce said. "They bribed my son away from me, with fake glamour and money and sex. I want Joel back, Your Honor. I've just taken a full-time job as a guidance counselor at Moro Memorial Junior High. It's hard work and it isn't glamorous, and I don't get paid much, but I contribute to young people. When I'm done working, I put everything into giving Joel a good home and proper values."

"Do you take him to the opera?" Judge Lombardo said.

"I can't afford—"

"Then let him listen to records. Puccini, instead of rock music."

"We have a nice album of *La Bohème*," Joyce said.

"I bought that album," David said.

"Gentlemen," Judge Lombardo said. "Mrs. Priest was awarded custody a short time ago. An old rule and a good rule goes like this: Unless the mother don't want custody, or is incompetent, the mother gets custody. And she keeps it. I'm inclined to dismiss."

"We have special circumstances, Your Honor," Zellbach said.

"You're an intelligent woman," Judge Lombardo said to Joyce. "Your former husband is an intelligent man,

You don't want to put a child on the stand. That's what a trial will mean."

Joel sat at a table fifteen feet away. His hands were clasped as if he sat in a schoolroom.

"Fine-looking boy," Judge Lombardo said. "And the woman with him?"

"My second wife," David said.

"She's very young," Judge Lombardo said. "They could be brother and sister, the boy and your second wife. Believe me, I know about this kind of case. I know about all kinds of cases. Nobody benefits from a trial, except the lawyers."

"I might be able to convince my client to drop her motions if her son was returned to her," Cassidy said, "and the threats against her custody stopped."

"Mr. Priest?" Lombardo said.

"We have facts to present," Zellbach said.

David nodded.

"Then we'll adjourn to chambers," Lombardo said. "Just counsel and plaintiff and defendant. Priest, tell your wife to take the boy out for a sarsaparilla. Court is no place for a boy."

The judge stood, a tall, powerful man, built like a linebacker. "I may have to knock heads together," he announced.

The judge's chamber was a square, cream-colored office, furnished with rectangular modern furniture, and one old plush coral sofa. Four awards hung on a wall, under Lombardo's diploma. He had graduated from St. John's Law School in Brooklyn. The judge shed his robe and walked behind a gray metal desk, with rolling, athlete's strides. "Gentlemen," he said to Zellbach and Cassidy. "You know better than to drag a nice boy into my courtroom, and if you tell me that you don't know better, you know what I'll tell you?" He put his hands on his hips. His suit was dark gray with a silvery metallic plaid. "I'll tell you to blow it out your ass.

"Pardon me, Mrs. Priest. Sometimes I have to speak plain English to reach fancy lawyers."

"I understand," Joyce said. She smiled warmly at Victor Lombardo. She looked suddenly younger. David recognized her tomboy grin.

Zellbach wet his lips. "Judge," he said, "I know this boy. I know this family. Mr. Priest isn't only a client, but a friend. I do not have him down here for a fee. In fact, if we lose, I'm not going to charge him anything."

"Did you know that?" Judge Lombardo asked.

"Not until now," David said. He had answered too quickly. He had not paused. Now Zellbach's offer could be interpreted as show.

"I myself don't want Joel subjected to the witness stand," Zellbach said, "but I believe, and Mr. Priest agrees, that one difficult day will win the child an easier decade."

"That's why we're here," David said.

Lombardo's eyes moved. The head was motionless. "Counselor," he said to Cassidy.

"This is such nonsense." Cassidy's lisp became assertive. "As you said in the courtroom, the child belongs with the mother. Particularly a boy who's just fourteen. We will demonstrate that the visitations have been disruptive, to a point where Joel needs psychiatric help. Fewer visits are a must."

"I ain't buying all that either," Lombardo said.

"The nature of our special circumstances—" Zellbach began. Lombardo raised a hand.

"Everybody thinks his case is special," the judge said. "They're not. Before this court, every case is the same. A docket number. Even when we get intelligent people like this. Both sides think God and His angels are with them. Nobody trusts the other guy. I make my ruling and everybody leaves court dissatisfied. I don't care. That means I've done a good day's work.

"Now, here. This can be settled in five minutes." Lombardo banged his right fist into his left palm. "Let's discount the psychiatry crap. Those monkeys do more harm than good. Next, forget the motion for increased support. Six months of inflation is beneath the notice of this court. Finally, I'll say here, or in open court, I'm dismissing the motion for contempt. This man isn't guilty of anything except loving his son."

Joyce shook her head and said faintly, "No."

"Cheer up, Mrs. Priest. That's only the part that dissatisfies you.

"Now, here, Mr. Priest! I'll tell *you* what I said in the courtroom. A child belongs with his mother. Give him back."

"He doesn't want me to give him back," David said.

"That part dissatisfies him," Lombardo said. "All right. Drop the motions. Return the kid. You both have my proposals.

"Don't confer.

"The lawyers will fill you full of crap.

"Accept what I tell you.

"Follow my proposals.

"Yes or no?"

Simultaneously, Joyce said "Yes" and David said "No."

Lombardo stood and put on his judicial robe. "Very well, Mr. Priest. We'll take up your case without prejudice." The judge's face furrowed with fury. "Let me give you a final piece of off-record advice, Mr. Priest. You have a pretty new wife. Make another baby. You're laying too much crap on the one boy."

"It wouldn't be the same," David said, but he found himself addressing Victor Lombardo's back, as the judge who was built like a linebacker left chambers, trailing the black toga of his Soho office.

The plastic paneling in the courtroom was finished in imitation oak. The judge's desk was molded from synthetic dark wood. Below the desk, the judge's supernumeraries worked at appointed stations. The thick-lipped, white-faced clerk sat to the judge's right. The court reporter, who always looked downward, sat to the left. The armed guard, sallow and vague-eyed, slouched beside the imitation-white-oak door. The builders had gone to the trouble of imitating scrollwork in the plastic paneling.

A plastic scroll, David thought. Artificial artifacts. *Please do not muse.*

"Call your witness, Mr. Cassidy."

"I call Mrs. Joyce Priest."

Joyce proceeded uncertainly toward the stand. She seemed to test the courtroom floor before settling a foot in every stride. She sat delicately, smoothing the brown skirt. Her mouth was turning down. David saw pain in her face and fright at her mouth, but then Joyce sat straight and tried to mask both, the pain and the fright. She was a square-faced, stocky woman of thirty-five, no longer immediately attractive, but abruptly dignified. Indeed, who she was and what she was doing embodied dignity. She was a mother fighting to raise her own son.

Looking at his former wife, David saw Judge Lombardo's madonna. For an instant he felt sorry that he had followed the battering roads to court. He sighed and looked at Joel. The boy gave him a cheering smile. David smiled back. He did not feel sorry anymore.

"Now, Mrs. Priest," Gabe Cassidy said, "are you comfortable?" Joyce nodded. The witness chair was below and to the left of Judge Lombardo, close to the stooped court reporter. During questioning, Cassidy had to stand among a semicircle of molded plastic chairs. Fifteen feet separated the lawyer from his witness. "I understand your custody of Joel has been disrupted by certain happenings. Is that right?"

Joyce nodded.

"Please answer audibly, Mrs. Priest," Judge Lombardo said. "That helps the court reporter, who keeps the transcript for us."

"Thank you," Joyce said. "My answer is yes."

"What were these happenings?" Cassidy said.

"Whenever my son returned from visits to his father, and Mr. Priest's new wife, he seemed agitated. Upset with his home. Upset with his life. Upset with me. Apparently he heard things at his father's little apartment—"

Zellbach bounced up. "Objection. Conclusionary."

"Sustained," Judge Lombardo said. "We have these rules, Mrs. Priest, and we have to follow them. You can only testify on what you have seen or done or heard yourself. You can't assume. You can't draw conclusions. These are good rules most of the time, so we have to stick to them all of the time."

"Let me save waste motions," Cassidy said. "I'm going to ask Mrs. Priest about certain remarks from the son, which may contain comments the boy heard from the father, or the second Mrs. Priest."

"If you do," Zellbach said, "they'll be objected to. Every time."

"Your Honor," Cassidy said, "we can spend a day niggling about minor points."

"Not in my court," Lombardo said.

"To expedite," Cassidy said, "let me stress, we want the boy's comments to his mother regarded simply as comments. We don't seek determinations as to accuracy. We only wish to demonstrate the existence of family disruption. We have to show the pain between mother and son."

Zellbach shook his head. "I have a duty. I have to object to hearsay."

"Why don't we listen to the witness?" Judge Lombardo said. "This ain't easy for her."

"If hearsay is permitted," Zellbach said, "I have no alternative but to register an exception, for a possible appeal."

"You have a choice," Lombardo said. "Your alternative is to trust me. But you didn't. All right. The exception is registered. Let's get going."

"Mrs. Priest," Cassidy said, "please tell the court the pattern of visitations as you perceive it."

"In the beginning, after the divorce, Joel was extremely concerned that his father didn't want him. He had a sense that he had failed as a son, that if he had been a better child, his father wouldn't have deserted us."

"And was that so?" Cassidy asked.

"Conclusion," David whispered to Zellbach.

Tears came to Joyce's eyes. "No. I don't question David's love for Joel. I never have. That was absolutely not so." Joyce shook her head and paused to compose herself.

"Sure it's conclusionary," Zellbach whispered to David, "but the judge knows the rules of evidence. He likes Joyce. An objection now could set him off against me again."

"But regardless of his feelings for his son," Cassidy said, "your former husband did walk out on you and Joel."

"It's complicated," Joyce said.

"But Mr. Priest demanded the divorce."

"No. He demanded that I divorce him."

"And not content with destroying the stability of your marriage and Joel's home, he's come here now to steal your son."

"Objection," Zellbach said.

"Sustained. Go on with your story, Mrs. Priest."

"Immediately after the divorce," Joyce said, "Joel was unsure of his father. I spent many nights listening to Joel and reassuring him. I explained one reason we had stayed together for so long—one reason I never pressed for divorce—was our mutual love for our child."

Judge Lombardo made a brief approving nod.

"Then within a few months of our divorce, Mr. Priest remarried. Joel began to complain that his father wasn't paying enough attention to him. On some visits, he said, his father simply wasn't there."

"Where did Joel say his father was?"

"In Harlem."

"Harlem?" Judge Lombardo said.

"Yes, sir," Joyce said. "After that, I noticed a distinct pattern. Joel would come back and talk about Caroline, Mr. Priest's second wife. Caroline was very pretty. Caroline had lovely clothes. Caroline had a wonderful figure."

"Are you suggesting," Cassidy said, "that in this new relationship, between a nubile son and a youthful stepmother, one element was *sexual?*"

"Objection," Zellbach shouted.

"She is attractive, Your Honor," Cassidy said. "She's sitting right over there."

Caroline pressed her knees together and curled her shoulders forward.

"I couldn't suggest sexuality in their relationship," Joyce said, "because that would be drawing a conclusion."

Judge Victor Lombardo smiled. "The witness," he said, "is learning the law."

"Understand the thrust of Cassidy's case," Zellbach whispered to David. "You are so-so. Joyce is fine. Caroline is the seductress."

"Why do we have to argue off Cassidy's premises?" David said.

"We don't. We'll rebut what it pays to rebut, and proceed with the case we planned."

"Now, Mrs. Priest," Cassidy said. The gray chalk-striped suit fit too tightly at his back. "Can you give the court examples of your son appearing upset?"

"He'd come back and be agitated."

"Be more specific, please," Judge Lombardo said.

"I'm sorry," Joyce said.

"Take your time," Judge Lombardo said.

"I can think of at least four occasions," Joyce said. "Once Joel and I had something planned at the Museum of Natural History. A day before, *one* day before, they talked him into a ski trip to Pennsylvania. When Joel came back, he appeared almost hostile. Then he wanted me to ski with him. I broke both ankles as a child, and I can't ski. Joel said that the second Mrs. Priest had said it was a crime, *a crime,* for a young boy to live with someone inactive."

"That's not only agitation, it's destructive," Cassidy said.

"Another time Joel came home and wanted to ice skate with me. I can't skate for the same reason. I'd just gotten back from school and I was wearing a smock. Joel said that Caroline told him there was no reason for me to go around like a fat old lady."

Judge Lombardo winced. David imagined Mrs. Victor Lombardo. He saw upper arms like flapping thighs.

"Then Joel said Caroline told him it was terrible that I dressed like a slob. I work with angry, dirty kids. I don't have the time, or the means, to visit boutiques. You don't wear designer clothes in Moro Memorial Junior High School."

"We understand," Gabe Cassidy said. "Is there, perhaps, another instance of disruption?"

"Yes."

"What was that?"

"Caroline Priest, the new wife, showed obscene paintings to my son. Obscene paintings she had made herself."

"And?"

"And then, in the little apartment, she paraded back and forth in front of Joel, completely naked. Prancing. With no clothes on. Naked."

"Like a bottomless dancer?" Cassidy said.

"Objection," Zellbach said.

"Exactly," Joyce said.

"Sustained," Lombardo said.

"I didn't." Caroline stood in her plain blouse and denim skirt. "That wasn't—"

Judge Lombardo said, "Resume your seat."

"The situation is obvious, Your Honor," Gabe Cassidy said. "The witness is a working woman, a devoted public servant and a loving mother. Now she is threatened. Her only child is being seduced away from her by the wiles and perhaps the body of a childless younger woman. The younger woman can devote herself to sirenlike lures, because she doesn't have to maintain a job."

"Do you wish to cross-examine?" Judge Lombardo said to Zellbach.

"No cross, thank you."

"Why no cross?" David said angrily.

"Do you want that story repeated?" Zellbach whispered.

"Pick it apart, Clip," Caroline ordered.

"Then I attack a woman alone." Zellbach shook his head. "No cross, Your Honor," he said.

"Call David Priest."

Walking to the stand, David nodded at Joyce. She stared without loathing, without fondness, without recognition.

"Mr. Priest," Zellbach said, "would you say what we've heard accurately describes the pattern of visitations?"

"I would not. The visitations took place at my house. My former wife wasn't even there."

"We understand that," Zellbach said. "There is no need to be argumentative. Just give us the pattern as you saw it."

"Surely." David cleared his throat. He must not muse. He must not be argumentative before the judge. "After the divorce, my new wife, Caroline, and I discussed ways of making Joel comfortable, giving him an apartment key, things like that. Meanwhile I had to work. There was this stiff alimony and support—"

"By the way," Judge Lombardo interrupted, "are you current on alimony and support?"

"I think so."

"Think or know?"

"There is no claim for back alimony and support," Zellbach said.

"I know what they're claiming," Judge Lombardo said. "I just want him to tell me if he's current."

"My wife does the checkbook," David said. "As far as I know, we are current."

"You let your wife sign alimony checks?" Judge Lombardo asked.

"And rent checks too," David said, flaring.

"We aren't trying to be argumentative, Your Honor," Zellbach said.

"If he wants to argue," Judge Lombardo said, "I'm a guy that can give him an argument he'll remember."

"Yes, sir," Zellbach said. "But he doesn't want to argue. You were mentioning your work, Mr. Priest."

"The book contract I signed called for hard research. I had to be out of the house a lot. I was going to Harlem, trying to understand the beat, or the beats, of ghetto life."

With no warning, Judge Lombardo smiled. "The court can wait for the plot," he said, "until the book is published."

"Right," David said. "I thought it was sensible to establish Joel's visits as regular things, even if I wasn't there. My wife, Caroline, was wonderful about that. She took Joel places and looked after him, and my boy and my bride became more than stepparent and child. They were friends."

"Did Joel complain to you about conditions in his mother's home?"

"Yes."

"Did he complain about his mother's behavior?"

"Yes."

"Specifically, Mr. Priest, what were his complaints?"

"I don't want to go into that specifically," David said. "His mother has rights of privacy."

"Either be specific," Judge Lombardo said, "or this line of questioning will be disallowed."

David touched his mustache. He stroked a cheek. He surveyed the room. Plastic paneling. His wife. His lawyer. Another lawyer. His former wife. The judge on high. "Disallow it, then," David said.

Zellbach grimaced. "I remind the witness that he *is* a witness, not a jurist."

"You can still go into specifics," Lombardo said.

"No," David said.

"Then tell the court," Zellbach said, "how your son came to reside in your own house."

"Objection," Cassidy said. "The child's legal residence remains with the mother."

"Get on with it," Judge Lombardo said to David.

"He presented himself at our door," David said. "He was distraught. He presented himself at the door and said, 'Dad, I want you to take me in. Dad, I want to live with you. Please don't send me away.'"

"Did you expect this, Mr. Priest?"

"No."

"So the suggestion that you or your wife sought to lead Joel away from his mother is inaccurate."

"More directly," David said, "it's a lie."

"That's more direct," Judge Lombardo said.

"I never thought of asking Joel to live with us," David said. "It was Joel's own idea."

"Thank you. Your witness, Mr. Cassidy."

The lisping, thick-necked lawyer stared at David. "How did the boy get to your apartment, Mr. Priest?"

"I'm not sure."

"Didn't you ask your son how he got to your apartment? Didn't he tell you?"

These questions had not been in Clip Zellbach's scenario. "He may have mentioned something about a taxi," David said.

"Did he? Yes or no?"

"Yes."

"How did he get the taxi fare?"

David looked to Zellbach for help. The lawyer was whispering with Joel.

"I don't see the relevance," David said.

"Answer the question," Judge Lombardo said.

"My client," Cassidy said, "buys her bagels at a store called the Hot Broadway Bagelry."

"I don't see the relevance of *that*," Judge Lombardo said.

"I met Joel in the bagel store," David said. "I gave him cab fare."

"On the day he presented himself to you?"

"On the day he presented himself to me."

Gabe Cassidy smiled toward the bench. "There's a bit of a plot here, Your Honor. Almost a conspiracy. They want to make it appear as though Joel took a spontaneous trip down to his father's house. Actually, the stepmother and the father planned that trip for Joel as carefully as Cook plans a tour of Europe.

"Your Honor, Mr. Priest has been liberal with the word 'lie.' He sits before us, as we approach the close of this sordid play, himself revealed as the liar."

Zellbach bounced up. "Redirect." He glanced at David without expression. His voice was cold as the command of a drill sergeant. "Is it correct to call you a liar, Mr. Priest?"

"It is not correct."

"Why not?"

"Mr. Cassidy asked if I *expected* to have my son come to my door. I didn't *expect* that. I *hoped* for it."

"Get beyond wordplay, Mr. Priest. Why didn't you ride downtown with Joel after he called you to meet him at the bagel store?"

"The absolute truth," David said, "is that I knew we might end up in court. I knew things could be distorted. I thought if I rode with Joel, Cassidy would try to make it look as though I'd kidnapped my own son."

"Thank you, Mr. Priest," Zellbach said.

"I got a clear picture," Judge Lombardo said.

Caroline stumbled with her first step toward the stand. Then she walked purposefully, but she sat with unusual heaviness and David noticed in surprise that her knees were slightly apart. From his seat fifteen feet from the witness stand, David saw the outsides of his wife's thighs.

"Mrs. Priest," Zellbach began.

"Why don't you call this one by her first name," Judge Lombardo said. "That way the transcript will be less confusing."

The lawyer winced and nodded. "Caroline, allegations have been made that you tried to lure Joel into living with you."

"That's not so. All I did was love him the best way I knew how."

"Did you call Joel's mother a fat old lady?"

"I said something quite different."

"What did you say?"

"That it was a shame for a woman as young as Joyce to go around *looking* like an old lady. I was trying to discuss beautiful things with him. We were skating. It was a lovely day. I was talking about beauty and a poem by Hart Crane."

"Were you making advances toward Joel?" Zellbach said.

"I've been brought up . . . Mr. Zellbach, I don't make advances."

"So Mr. Cassidy's slant—that you were trying to romance Joel, a fourteen-year-old-boy—is a distortion."

"I was concerned about him. I want to help him." A little smile appeared. "Yes. Romance is a gross distortion. A *sick* distortion."

"How often did Joel see you naked?" Zellbach said.

"I beg your pardon." The smile fled. Caroline blushed.

"Naked," Zellbach barked. "Nude. Without clothes."

"I don't know how many times."

"But he did see you naked at least once."

"At least several times."

"You had better explain that to the court."

"I come from a prim background," Caroline said. Judge Lombardo leaned forward to hear. "It was strict and religious, and some of the people tried to act as though they didn't have bodies at all."

"I don't imagine that worked."

"I believe people should be natural about such things as nudity."

"Natural," Zellbach said, "but not promiscuous."

"He's leading her," Cassidy said.

"Tell it in your own words, Caroline," Judge Lombardo said.

"Before we married, my husband and I discussed nudity around the house. I didn't want to put extra stress on Joel in any way, including sexually.

"I'd read about boys' sexual fantasies. But my husband said boys could fantasize more from what they didn't see than from what they saw. I remember coming out of a shower in front of Joel. I was wearing a towel. I reached for a robe. The towel dropped."

"So you were naked in front of the boy," Judge Lombardo said.

"My grandmother dressed in a closet," Caroline said. "I don't."

"I think we've had enough in this line," Lombardo said.

"Two questions," Gabe Cassidy said. "First, where did you read about the sexual fantasies of growing boys? In *Playboy?*"

"In a psych book at college," Caroline said.

"Did it occur to you to discuss this situation with a professional psychologist?"

"It did not," Caroline said. "After all, my husband had been a growing boy with sexual fantasies himself."

Caroline walked from the witness stand. Her expression was frightened and questioning. "Fine," David whispered. "Very fine."

"Thanks, Callie," Joel said.

"All right," Victor Lombardo said. "Why don't both counselors and Mr. Priest and Mrs. Priest, the former wife, approach the bench."

When they gathered beneath him, the judge said, "Does somebody intend to call the boy?"

"I have to," Zellbach said.

"Do you really?" Joyce said. "Do you really have to put my son on a witness stand?"

"He has a job to do," Judge Lombardo said, "and in this case the evidence is conflicting. But I'm not going to let it drag. I don't want the boy on the stand for more than ten minutes."

"How about cross-examination?" Cassidy said.

"Is your lawyer going to cross-examine my son?" David said to Joyce.

"This is my court," Judge Lombardo said. "I won't

have either side hurt the child. You take a few minutes, Mr. Zellbach, and then we'll see where we are. I can tell both attorneys this: Anybody who hurts the boy loses the case."

Joel jumped up as David returned from the bench. "You're going to have to testify," Zellbach said.

"I don't want to testify," Joel said.

"There are a few things you can clear up," Zellbach said. "Simply go up there and tell the truth. I'll help you. The judge wants to help you too."

"But what about Mr. Cassidy?" Joel said.

"We'll keep him in line," Zellbach said. "All you have to do is tell the exact truth."

"Nobody else has," Joel said.

"Nobody else has what?"

"Told the exact truth." Then, in a gesture of manliness or disdain, Joel drew back his shoulders and started toward the stand.

"This won't take long," Judge Lombardo said. "The most important person in this case is you. We're going to do what's best for *you.*"

"Yes," Joel said with a quick nod.

"Joel, where would you like to live?" Clip Zellbach said.

"With my father and with Callie," Joel said. "That is, Caroline."

"Just take it easy," Judge Lombardo said.

"Do you know why you want to live with your father and Caroline?" Zellbach said.

Joel tapped his palms against his thighs. "It's hard to put into words."

"Can you try to put it into words?"

"I just want to."

"What about seeing your mother?"

"I'll see Mom. I'll see her a lot. The visits would go the other way. It's just at Dad's it's more exciting and there's more to do."

"What do you think about the proceedings here today?"

Joel set his teeth. "Well, that stuff about Callie luring me by being naked—that stuff was terrible."

"Joel, whose idea was it for you to live with your father?"

"Mine. It was my idea."

"After everything you've heard today, do you still want to live with your father?"

"Yes."

"Speak up, please, Joel," Zellbach said.

"Yes. I do."

Gabe Cassidy looked toward Judge Lombardo. "A few questions?"

"But no rough stuff," Judge Lombardo said.

"Of course," Cassidy said. He addressed Joel in a conversational way. "You know, I wonder how much you've *really* thought about your mother. I mean, thought about her point of view. Joel, you're the most important person in your mother's life. You're important to others too, but do you know what will happen to Mom if you move out on her? Her home will be empty. She'll leave an empty house in the morning. She'll come back to an empty house at night. Your mother bore you, Joel. She carried you inside. She suffered through labor. In every way, she's been with you from the beginning. If you leave her now, she'll be completely alone."

"But we'll still see each other."

"Most of the time," Cassidy said, "your mother will be completely alone. Think about that, Joel. The court has time. Think about that and then tell me where you really want to live."

Joel's eyes hurried about the room. "With Dad," he said softly.

Clip Zellbach's right fist clenched in tension. "That's enough, counselor," Judge Lombardo said.

Lombardo leaned across the bench. "Joel, do you know the Bible story, where King Solomon has to choose?"

"Oh, sure," Joel said. "I've known that for a long time."

"I have a problem something like Solomon's," Judge Lombardo said. "Maybe you can solve it for me."

"Sure," Joel said. "I want to live with my father."

"But *I* have to rule," Judge Lombardo said. "Then you and I both have to live with my ruling." The judge sat back. "Joel, I want you to look at your mother. Are you two looking at each other? Now, Joel, if you can look your mother in the eye and tell the court and your mother that you want to live with your father, then that's the way I'll decide."

Joel turned toward Judge Lombardo in alarm.

"Look at your mother," the judge ordered.

Joel's eyes moved slowly from the judge, along a wall of plastic panels. They leaped to the pale court clerk and the bent reporter. Then Joel loked back toward the plastic wall.

Except for air hissing through invisible vents, the court was silent.

Joyce stared stoically.

Joel's eyes moved onward.

Then the gazes of the two, mother and son, joined and locked. Joyce's face softened. Joel's lower lip shook. Tears ran from Joyce's eyes. Joel winced in pain.

"Can you say it?" Judge Lombardo demanded. "Can you look at your mother and say that you want to live with your father?"

Joel's mouth twitched. Pain cut lines into the flesh about his eyes and the eyes themselves went puffy and wet. Agony distorted Joel's smooth face into something sorrowful and old.

Joel shrieked. "No! No. No." He ran from the witness

stand. His mother stood. They embraced, weeping. "It's all right," Joyce said. "It's all right, Joel. Stop crying."

Zellbach bounced up, calling, "Your Honor."

Judge Lombardo shook his head. "The case has found its own resolution. I have presided. I don't have to rule."

David shouted, "He stays with her?"

Judge Lombardo gestured toward the embracing mother and son. "You have your answer, Mr. Priest."

David stood. "Not fair," he shouted. "A fucking, lousy, horseshit, dago decision."

"But not all of your answer, Mr. Priest," Judge Lombardo said calmly. "This outburst suggests instability. You're too worked up over this whole matter. You need time to cool. Your visitations are suspended for six months."

"Exception," Zellbach said.

"Help me, Joel!" David screamed. "Help me."

The weeping boy did not respond.

"Perez versus Perez is next," the white-faced court clerk said to Judge Lombardo.

David lay face down on the brass bed and Caroline worked her fingers into his trapezius. "I've been finked," David said.

"Relax and enjoy your rub."

"What kind of a way is this to resolve lives?" David said. "Lawyers preparing scenarios. Judges like Mussolini."

"What did you tell Judge Lombardo?" Caroline said. "A fucking, lousy, horseshit, dago way." She drew her nails across his shoulder blades. "How does that feel?"

David punched the mattress. "Why couldn't Joel stand up? Why didn't he do what he said he would do? Damn it. In the scenario we finally played, Joel was Absalom."

David rolled over and Caroline kneaded his arms.

"Oh, my goodness," she said. "A gray hair. You have a gray hair on your chest." She reached and straightened the curl of gray. "You know Joel did everything he was able to do. It became too much for him, and it became too much for you. Neither of you could stand that courtroom anymore."

"The genius of modern justice," David said. He sat up. "A loving father and a loving son, sentenced to parallel terms of solitary confinement."

CHAPTER TWO

More Weathered Dunes

Full summer and warm rain embraced Pokanoket Island, where David and Caroline had rented a shingled beach house. They stood on a gray wooden terrace, feeling the rain, which fell on Caroline's white blouse, touching her breasts. The nipples showed large and dark.

"I don't want to go to Trudy Schuman's party," David said.

"Hermitize," Caroline said. "Is there such a word?"

"Verb," David said. "Transitive."

"I feel I'm being hermitized."

"You have your painting," David said. Each morning Caroline drove to Lantern Cove and made bright water-colors of the harbor.

"It's almost enough, but not quite." The breakers sounded gentle through the rain.

"I guess my work affects me differently," David said. At the end of June, he had finished treading Harlem. He packed a suitcase full of notepads, roughed-out scenes, reference books, and the poetry of Langston Hughes and Countee Cullen. Then he wedged the valise, three boxes of writing paper and his typewriter along-side Caroline's luggage in the Porsche. "With the beach and my work and you, I don't need parties."

"Just this one," Caroline said. "I want to see what's happened to everybody from last year."

"Nothing's happened to everybody," David said.

She continued to ask with her expression.

"You'll see tonight," David said, conceding. He would leave his labors and his wedge of beach.

At the doorway of a high yellow house on a knoll of stubby oak trees, Dr. Gertrude Beckmesser Schuman descended with the weight of *Mitteleuropa.* "So you are settled." She offered Caroline a small nod. "She is such a piquant child. How did you catch him, my dear?"

Caroline let her head roll back. "Why, with piquant charm, my dear."

"So," Trudy said. "Very good. You know almost everybody, Caroline. I want to borrow your husband."

Jeremy Johnson, the talk show host, said, "Hi. Say, I got a terrific deal on an unabridged dictionary. Eleven hundred pages for two ninety-eight. The only thing is, it isn't alphabetized." Jeremy grinned and blinked and turned away.

"Nothing happens to everybody," David said to Caroline.

"Come, David." Trudy thrust a hand against his elbow and walked him toward the kitchen. "Please help me get more ice. Is it going well, the marriage?"

David emptied a bronze-colored ice tray into a pewter bucket.

"You're so different," Trudy said. "I mean, you are an intellectual and almost a poet, and Caroline is— what can I say—a water skier."

"Let's get back to the others," David said.

"Do you know that Joyce is on the island?" Trudy walked in front of David and stood so that her breasts were pressed against him. "Joyce is drinking vodka afternoons again. She calls me. It would be all right now for you to see the boy."

David's throat caught. "Joel," he said.

"Joel is beautiful," Trudy said, "and tanned. Hi manners are lovely."

David put the ice bucket on a porcelain table. "Why would Joyce suddenly let me see Joel?"

"He's already been meeting with your wife."

"When?"

"Mornings. Sometimes they swim together. That's not good, David, for him to see his stepmother but not his father." Trudy wore a patterned peasant blouse.

"I write mornings."

"Joyce said they swim near New Eden Beach, with all those naked bodies next to them. Besides that, she says your wife wears a bikini that's so brief, it's just like nakedness."

"My wife used to wear brief bikinis. She has fuller ones now. She's four and a half months pregnant."

Trudy touched his arm. "Congratulations, David, but I know from Joyce you have some problems of your own. Some morning when your wife and the boy go swimming, come over so we can talk. Or I can pick you up."

"I'll take in the ice bucket," David said.

Rick Sensabaugh was drunk in Trudy Schuman's living room. He lurched toward David and said, "That Mennonite broad you married has a great ass."

"She's Congregationalist," David said.

"To me," Sensabaugh said, "there's only Catholics and Jews. Everything else is Mennonite—right, Davey?" He blinked. He realized that he was drunk.

Caroline and Clip Zellbach chatted before a stucco fireplace. "Where have you been?" Caroline said.

"In the kitchen," David said. "I was getting professional advice I didn't ask for."

"Marital counseling?"

"That was part of the sermon."

"When the vixen preaches," Zellbach said, "look to your geese." His shirtsleeves were rolled carefully to midbicep. "Anyway, *I've* been staked out by Trudy. Her husband's away, he's always away, and my wife's been under the weather and I can count couples. Trudy's the odd woman. I'm the odd man."

"You may be flattering yourself," David said. "Rick Sensabaugh seems to be free."

"Trudy and a smashed Sensabaugh?" Caroline said. "Don't be ludicrous."

"Rick goes either with the tall, vapid one in the peach blouse, or the brunette in the corner who has a librarian's face," Zellbach said.

"The tall one looks uncomfortable," Caroline said.

"She's not used to the blouse," Zellbach said. "Rick found her in a topless bar."

Sensabaugh lurched toward them, his blue eyes focused on the mantel. "Where did you discover the new girl?" Caroline said.

"Which one?" Sensabaugh said. "Do you mean bullet tongue? You know why I call her bullet tongue, don't you?"

"Clip, I need you," Trudy Schuman said. "But only in the kitchen for now."

"Say," Jeremy Johnson said. "If Richard Nixon were captain of the *Titanic,* you know what he would have told the passengers? 'Don't be alarmed. We're stopping for ice.' "

"Let's get out of here, Callie," David said.

"Explain bullet tongue," Caroline said in the bedroom of the rented beach house.

"I'd rather not."

"Please."

"In two words, oral-anal."

"Ugh," Caroline said. "Do people do that?"

"Not me," David said. He was drinking a beer. "Why haven't you told me that you were seeing Joel?"

"Oh?" Her face colored. "You know."

"I mean, he is my kid."

"I was driving to Lantern Cove and I passed him